Following
the Harvest

Also by Fred Harris

FICTION

Coyote Revenge
Easy Pickin's

NONFICTION

Alarms and Hopes
Now Is the Time
The New Populism
Social Science and Public Policy
Potomac Fever
America's Legislative Processes: Congress and the States, with
    Paul L. Hain
America's Democracy: The Ideal and the Reality
Estudios sobre los Estados Unidos y su relación bilateral con México,
    with David Cooper
Readings on the Body Politic
Understanding American Government, with Randy Roberts and
    Margaret S. Elliston
Quiet Riots: Race and Poverty in the United States, with
    Roger W. Wilkins
America's Government, with Gary Wasserman
Los obstáculos para el desarrollo
*Deadlock or Decision: The U.S. Senate and the Rise of National Poli-
    tics*
In Defense of Congress
*Locked in the Poorhouse: Cities, Race, and Poverty in the United
    States,* with Lynn A. Curtis

Following
the Harvest

A Novel

Fred Harris

UNIVERSITY OF OKLAHOMA PRESS : NORMAN

This book is published with the generous assistance of the Wallace C. Thompson Endowment Fund, University of Oklahoma Foundation.

Library of Congress Cataloging-in-Publication Data

Harris, Fred R., 1930–
    Following the harvest : a novel / Fred Harris.
       p.   cm.
    ISBN 0-8061-3636-7 (alk. paper)
       1. Migrant agricultural laborers—Fiction. 2. World War, 1939–1945—
    Oklahoma—Fiction. 3. Great Plains—Fiction. 4. Harvesting—Fiction.
    5. Young men—Fiction. 6. Oklahoma—Fiction. I. Title.

    PS3558.A64455F65 2004
    813'.54—dc22

                                                      2004041287

The paper in this book meets the guidelines for permanence and durability of the Committee on Production Guidelines for Book Longevity of the Council on Library Resources, Inc. ∞

2 3 4 5 6 7 8 9 10

This is for Kathryn Harris Tijerina, Byron Harris,
and Laura Harris, Oklahomans by birth,
and Amanda Elliston and Amos Elliston, by something like osmosis.

Following
the Harvest

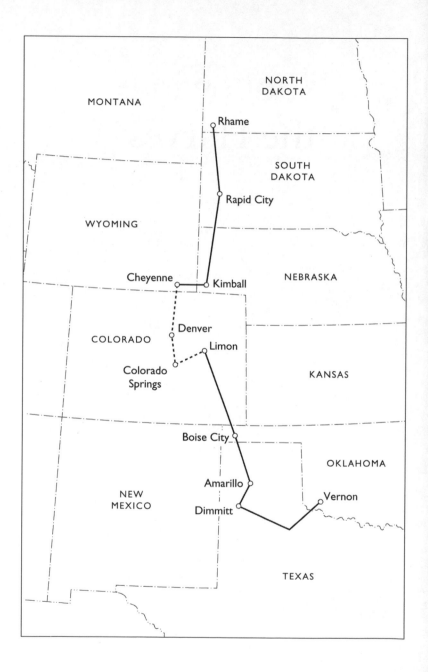

Chapter One

"Reckon this boy of yourn can manage that big machine?" Old Man Taylor asked my dad. Taylor sounded skeptical about me—maybe had a right to be. He folded Dad's hundred-dollar check with rough, big-knuckled fingers and stuffed the check into the bib watch pocket of his scruffy striped overalls. The overalls looked like they might not have seen a washtub and rub-board since dust bowl days.

The three of us were out by Taylor's saggy barn and slack-wire cow lot, standing right next to a squat, faded blue Fordson tractor that looked like it belonged in a farm implement museum. I was glad to see that it did have rubber tires, though, instead of outdated metal lugwheels. Dad'd just bought the old machine. Big sloppy drops of afternoon rain began to fall from a darkening late-May Oklahoma sky, splattering indigo blotches on the tractor's hood and fenders.

I answered Old Man Taylor before my dad could. That near-summer of 1943, I was going on sixteen years old, but I felt grown—had for some time preferred the company of adults and worked in the fields with them as equals. I was pretty sure of myself. "Drove my first car when I was twelve," I said.

"Willie damned sure did," my dad said to Taylor. Then, without smiling, he tacked on something that I thought was completely unnecessary. "Wrecked it," he said.

Dad was right about that.

Something over three years earlier, still not thirteen years old, I did wreck my uncle Don's rusted Model A Ford Roadster on my first attempt at solo driving. Ran the car squarely into an iron post when I tried to stop and suddenly found out that the car didn't have any brakes. Uncle Don had sent me walking the two miles into town to pick up the old car at Tobe Jordan's blacksmith shop, where a hole in the Ford's radiator was being soldered. I was to drive the car back out to the bottomland field where we were baling alfalfa hay, Uncle Don told me.

I usually worked summers back then for Grandpa Haley and two of Dad's younger brothers, my uncles Clif and Wayne. But that week in 1940, I'd hired on temporarily in the crew of a third brother of Dad's, my uncle Don, whose regular buckrake driver was in jail for stealing a wagonload of hay. I agreed to fill in, though I never liked to work for Uncle Don. He was slow pay, for one thing, and he'd hire a kid when he could get by with it, instead of a grown man, because he could pay a kid less.

That particular afternoon, it apparently never occurred to Uncle Don to ask me, before he sent me into town, whether I could actually *operate* his old Model A Ford. Of course, I was too excited at the prospect of getting to drive it to let on that I myself had any doubts. And Uncle Don never thought to advise me about how you stopped a vehicle that had no working brakes.

"Willie drives all right, now," my dad said to Old Man Taylor.

I'd ridden out to the Taylor place with Dad in our black Chevrolet truck, a '41 model, bought new two years earlier just a few months before Pearl Harbor. Dad wanted me to bring the old Fordson tractor back to town for him. He often gave me grown-up jobs. So did Grandpa Haley, when he was still alive. Uncles Clif and Wayne, too, before they'd joined up in the U.S. Army and, after basic training, been shipped off to fight the Nazis. From the summer when I was five I'd worked in the fields, haybaling, with Grandpa and the two uncles. I'd started out riding a horse, around and around to a horse-powered baler, for a dime a day and later graduated to driving a two-horse buckrake. Farmers that we baled for in our home county, Cash County, called us the "Haybaling Haleys." We thought we were the best there was.

Old Man Taylor spoke up again. "Your boy's leg may be a mite short to reach the clutch of that tractor good," he said, just about to wear out what I thought was already an irritating subject.

I was small for my age, no question. Took after my dad in that way. He farmed some and raised cattle for a living and looked a lot like James Cagney, some people said. Not, though, the laughing, dancing, singing James Cagney of the picture show *Yankee Doodle Dandy*, which I'd seen fairly recently. More like the gritty little truck driver-turned-prize-fighter James Cagney in *City for Conquest* of a couple of years earlier.

Dad was mostly serious and all business. Didn't talk much, either. Didn't hand out much praise. But his friends were more loyal to him than kinfolks. And for good cause. He'd do anything for you. Myself, I was never totally comfortable working for him, though, because, being his son, I got griped at more than other hired hands—or at least that was the way it felt to me. But my dad was given to occasional generous acts without explanation, just like the night before our trip to Old Man Taylor's for the tractor. Dad'd shown up at home with a pump-action .22-caliber squirrel rifle that he knew I wanted. The only thing he said when he handed it to me was that he'd traded a neighbor Comanche Indian guy a pocketwatch for it.

Dad worked harder than anybody you ever knew. He'd always made us a living, even during the depression, without having to take a public works job with the WPA. Mama worked, too. We raised a lot of our food. We weren't well-off, not even close, but we'd never gone hungry, and we'd never had to go on relief or sign up for free food commodities. Not that there was anything wrong with that.

Neither my dad nor I was very tall, but by the end of my sophomore year, which I'd just completed at Vernon High School, I'd sprung up to Dad's same size. I knew he hated it that I'd grown to where I could wear most of his clothes—the Acme cowboy boots, the Stetson hat, the white dress shirt with the mother-of-pearl buttons, and the iron-creased Levi's. But that didn't keep me from sometimes asking to borrow his stuff when I was going downtown, as I always did on a Saturday night, to Joe Lammer's Confectionary. That's where we hung out in Vernon—Joe Lammer's. I thought I looked pretty good in Dad's clothes.

But while Dad and I were about equal in size, people always pointed out that we didn't otherwise look anywhere near alike. His lean face and muscled forearms were permanently sunburned red, but he had the palest Scots-Irish body skin you ever saw, a shock to see when some of us now and then stripped off at the end of a hot workday and took a swim in the cold water of East Cash Creek. Dad's eyes were a hard gray, and his sandy hair was so fine that it took a good dose of brilliantine to keep it from flying every which way when he didn't have his cowboy hat on. Myself, people said I took after my mother's side of the family in my looks. I had brown eyes, dark and wiry hair, and the kind of complexion that stayed tanned up by the Oklahoma sun.

In Old Man Taylor's yard, Dad dragged on a Camel cigarette and blew the smoke out his nose. He dropped the butt and pressed it into the red dirt with his boot heel. Turning to me, then, he motioned with his head toward the old Fordson tractor.

"Climb on that sucker, Willie, and let's get a move on," he said. He glanced up at the dark sky. "You liable to get as drenched as Noah's neighbors before you make it back to town."

Trying not to look as eager as Lum on his first date, as Grandpa Haley might have put it, I walked smartly around to the back of the Fordson and, with my right hand on a fender for balance, stepped up on the old machine, then settled myself onto a worn-metal seat that was shaped like the palm of a giant hand. I adjusted the gas lever on the steering column, just under the big steering wheel, putting the lever in the middle of the gauge. I rattled the gearshift back and forth to make sure that it was in neutral, noting with relief that the gear positions were diagrammed for me in the metal at the gearshift base. Wouldn't have to ask anybody. First gear was top left, I saw, reverse to the far left and down.

To get a quick feel for things, I extended my left foot forward and down, to the clutch pedal. It was a worn-slick, shiny steel rod. The tractor seat felt slightly too far back for me. I scooted a little forward on it, so I could get my foot more securely on the clutch pedal and press it all the way down.

"Have to choke her when she's cold," Old Man Taylor told me.

Conscious that his and my dad's eyes were on me, I reached forward with my right hand and pulled the choke out about halfway from the dash. I turned the key on. I took my left foot from the clutch and pushed it down on the starter pedal. The big motor grumbled two or three times, belched white smoke from a rusted upright exhaust, then raged to life, almost like a brand-new one. I pushed the choke in, then eased back on the throttle. The rain was getting heavier.

Dad's orders to me were always too detailed, like he didn't think I could figure out anything for myself. "Don't go back to town the way we come, Willie," he now said, over the noise of the Fordson's engine, which, though in a loping idle, was still running pretty loud. "That hardpan road gets too slickery when it's wet. Go up north, yonder, a quarter of a mile to Lincoln Valley School, then turn west three miles on the gravel school bus road till you get to that red hill, you know, then turn straight on south the two and a half miles to town."

"I know," I said. I did. I was pretty familiar with the country roads around there. I'd gone to the first grade at Lincoln Valley, before my folks moved into town.

But I would have had to admit, if forced to, that my dad had some cause for making sure I could find my way home. If I daydreamed or didn't pay attention when I rode somewhere with him—to a farmer's, say, to buy some cattle—it might not always stick in my memory just exactly how we'd gotten there. So once, for example, when he sent me with his truck to haul back a load of hay from the same farmer's place where he and I'd lately been, I turned at the wrong corner and got myself lost. Later, finally back home after taking nearly all afternoon at a two-hour job, I explained to Dad what'd happened. His response was "By God, if I've ever been someplace, I can damn sure go there again!"

Maybe *he* could.

"Come to Jim Gruber's, Willie," my dad said, as I got ready to back the Fordson tractor around. "His yard. We putting new wheel bearings on my combine, and some other things."

Gruber, a near giant of a blond-headed, German-looking guy, was Dad's number one friend and the man he was partnering up with for the wheat harvest. Big Jim, as some people called him, was a local farm equipment dealer and had already followed the wheat harvest the year before as a custom combiner, all the way up to Rhame, North Dakota. Side by side, Dad and Jim Gruber looked like Mutt and Jeff. But they had the same size hearts—that was the way people who knew them put it. Do anything for you. And they were closer than twins. Big Jim lived across the alley, north, from us in Vernon, and he and Dad spent a big part of their time together, in both work and what might have been called play.

It was only the night before that Dad'd told me that he wanted me to drive back the Fordson tractor he was buying from Old Man Taylor. Better still, he'd announced at the supper table—to Mama, my older sister, Janie Marie, my younger twin sisters, Millie and Mollie, Grandma Haley, and me—that he'd borrowed nine hundred dollars at the bank and bought a 1938-model Gleaner-Baldwin pull-type grain combine, powered by a Model A motor. He'd bought the machine from a guy in town who'd had a stroke.

Then Dad said that he and I were going to follow the wheat harvest that summer with Jim Gruber as combiners for hire. Not Grandma, of course. And not Mama and the girls. They would all stay home. Mama would have to keep on working at her regular job as a bookkeeper at Stewart Drygoods, where she drew down thirty-two dollars a week.

Wheat ripened sequentially—earlier in Oklahoma, at the south end of the Great Plains, and later the higher the elevation or the farther north you went. We'd start out combining around Vernon the last of May, Dad said, and wind up by the end of summer in the little town of Rhame in the southwest corner of North Dakota, where Jim Gruber had finished up the year before.

History was my favorite subject in school—favorite reading subject, too. Particularly western history—cowboys and Indians. And I imagined that following the wheat harvest would be a lot like going on one of the old-time cattle drives, something I was disappointed to have been born much too late for.

In fact, our 1943 wheat-combining trek north would follow pretty closely the path of what was called the old Western Trail or the Texas Trail, up from West Texas, north through western Oklahoma, farther north through western Nebraska, and eventually to and through western North Dakota. Drives like that moved scrawny longhorns from the sparse ranges of Texas to what were then mostly untouched northern grasslands.

Another old cattle trail, the Chisholm Trail, had also passed through Oklahoma, and not fifteen miles east of where my folks and I lived in Vernon. You could still see traces on the

9

ground over there where that trail'd snaked its way up from Texas, then pointed on north through the grassy plains, all the way across Oklahoma to the railhead at Abilene, Kansas. From that point, one historian I'd read said, the trail'd later cut west to join up with the Western Trail, then continued on north.

I'd read a lot of pulp Westerns in addition to western history books. Of course, I'd seen a lot of cowboy picture shows, too. And I could sometimes daydream myself right into the spurred boots and weathered chaps of an old-time trail-driving cowhand. Part of a razzing, hard-riding gang of saddle-studs, signed on to prod north a herd of restless longhorn cattle.

I imagined having to skirt the herd around a bad grass fire. Or working to head off a wild stampede. Having to teach a bully a lesson he deserved, over behind the chuck wagon. Or winning a week's wages in a tense poker game. Falling hard for a teary-voiced saloon singer. Or speaking a prayer before burying a dead comrade, out on the windy prairie.

It seemed to me that I could have been a tough little horse wrangler, say, in Chisholm's own outfit. Or maybe a lonesome night rider for Old Man Goodnight, the guy who brought the first cattle to the Texas Panhandle. I would have whistled a cowboy tune, like "Little Joe, the Wrangler," while circling a bedded-down herd, beneath a jillion stars.

My closest friend in Vernon was a skinny redheaded guy named Junior Randall, who lived on a farm east of town and was a year ahead of me in school. He could do several things that I wished I could do. He could play the guitar. He could at night hold a flashlight in one hand, a .22-caliber rifle in the other, and with one shot cut a twig off a tree limb twenty yards away. And he could roll a cigarette with one hand, when he wanted to, though, like me, he wasn't much of a smoker. Junior and I rode horses together, hunted and fished, and were both Future Farmers of America boys, members of a state championship chicken-judging team.

Chicken judging? That was the question my dad'd kind of sarcastically asked me when I told him what Junior and I were doing in the FFA. Dad thought we ought to focus on something serious, like fattening out a steer or a hog. Certainly not wasting our time on judging chickens in competition, for God's sake! But chickens happened to be a special interest of our FFA teacher. So chicken judging it was for Junior and me, and we got pretty good at it.

The year before, the summer of 1942, when I'd stayed home and worked in the family haybaling crew, Junior'd got to go on the wheat harvest with a neighbor guy, reaching up as far north as southwestern Nebraska. And it was Junior's report about that summer which particularly strengthened my idea that following the harvest would be a lot like going on a cattle drive. Junior and I both had a kind of homesickness for the "old days." He was a big reader, like me. He didn't go out at all for sports, and I was too little to be a star at competitive physical activity, though I tried. Junior said that following the wheat harvest north was something like what he called an "odyssey on the Great Plains" and a "moveable adventure." But you had to head up the trail on a tractor, instead of astraddle some rank little cow pony.

With Dad and Old Man Taylor watching, I put the Fordson in reverse and backed around a little, then shifted to first gear and got the tractor lumbering toward the road. The archaic powerhouse machine growled hoarsely under me and felt like, if you log-chained it to Vernon's four-story brick school building, it'd drag the whole thing right off its foundation and on into the next county. But, talk about slow! A herd of terrapins could have outrun us.

I rumbled through Taylor's front gate finally, turned the old tractor north, then went to shift into third gear while rolling.

Couldn't be done.

To my major disappointment, I found that the Fordson's clutch served also as the foot brake. Push down the clutch, dead stop. No shifting gears on the fly. And no road gear, either. When I did later get the tractor running down the road in third gear—though "running" wasn't exactly the right word—we sure didn't kick up any mud from the spin of the big back tires. Somebody'd built the Fordson for pull, not for quick.

I still liked driving it, though, even with the slow pace—and despite the rain, which had started coming down pretty hard. I commenced to sing a few verses of "Little Joe, the wrangler, he'll wrangle never more . . . ." The sad words of the song got lost in the whining roar of the faded blue tractor's big motor.

But I decided pretty quickly that when I got to town, I wouldn't, after all, detour a block out of my way and go east on Ohio Street before turning back south toward Big Jim Gruber's. I'd earlier thought I might do that, in the hope that Rebecca Milton would come out on her front porch to see me drive by. Now, I wasn't as proud of what I was driving as I'd thought I'd be. And besides, Becca, who was the popular doctor's daughter and cheerleader blonde I'd been sweet on since the third grade, had lately started going with that year's Vernon High School quarterback, a guy named Bert Wriston, who'd just graduated. And she'd told my best friend, Junior, that she was attracted to old Bert because of what she called his "maturity."

I was a little afraid that my driving the Fordson tractor by Becca's house and waving at her might not strike her as especially mature. It came to my mind how something *less* than mature I must have looked the first time I'd tried a drive-by-and-wave routine, back when I was twelve. That was in Uncle Don's old open-air, no-top Model A Ford Roadster.

I hiked into Vernon to Tobe Jordan's blacksmith shop to pick up the rattletrap car Uncle Don used as his kind of carryall. Jordan made me wait a few minutes while he finished with a cow yoke he was working on. That was Tobe Jordan's specialty, making iron cow yokes that farmers bought to keep straying cattle from getting out through barbed-wire fences. With his son, Sammy, standing by, Jordan pulled a couple of red-hot metal rods from a coke-fired forge, then hammer-banged them on an anvil and deftly bent them around each other until he soon had another yoke in finished shape, which he pitched in the dirt to cool.

Finally he turned to me. Tobe Jordan was my Sunday school teacher at the First Baptist Church. He wore thick round glasses and always looked at you like he was accusing you of something. But he didn't raise any question about my driving Uncle Don's car away. He only asked about payment.

"You bring the dollar and a quarter?"

I was embarrassed. "Uncle Don said tell you, Mr. Jordan, soon's he gets paid for the haybaling job he's on, he'll come in and settle up with you," I said.

Tobe Jordan stared at me for a moment. "Radiator's soldered," he said, simply. "The key's in the car." Then he turned back to his cow yokes.

I motioned for Sammy to come with me, and we walked to the back fence where Uncle Don's old Model A Ford was parked headfirst into a corner. Sammy was in high school. I was in the sixth grade.

"You ain't lying, Willie, about being able to drive?" he asked, eyeing me skeptically.

"Sammy, all I need is for you to back the car around straight," I said. My main problem was that I didn't know where the reverse gear was. But I didn't want to tell Sammy that.

He got in without saying anything further, started the motor, and backed the car up. He then pulled it forward into the gravel driveway, pointed north toward the concrete east-west Comanche highway in front of the blacksmith shop. He stepped out, leaving the motor running. I crawled in under the wheel and slammed the tinny door shut.

"Be seeing you, Sammy," I said, trying to sound as casual as Oklahoma's Wiley Post looked in an old newspaper photograph that was snapped just before he took off on his record-setting round-the-world flight in the *Winnie Mae*.

Forward in first gear, I steered the beat-up old car down the drive to the highway, then looked left. No other vehicle was coming. I turned right onto the narrow pavement, in the direction of the town of Comanche. Extending the toe of my left high-top tennis shoe as far as I could, I was able to shift into second, then finally into high. The Model A Ford began to percolate.

Shitting in tall cotton! That's what Grandpa Haley would have said. Life was good.

I began to look for someone along the highway to wave to. But at first, nobody was around. Then, as I neared Morgan's Conoco station, a mile east of town on the north side of the highway, I saw fat, balding Arch Morgan himself, out front sweeping up around the glass-globed gas pumps.

He immediately stopped what he was doing, turned to holler something back into the store, and then took a step closer to the highway, wide-eyed, to watch my approach. Morgan later told me that he'd yelled to his wife, "Ethel! Car coming without no driver in it!"

Whizzing east on the cement strip of a highway at thirty miles an hour, I quickly came abreast of the Conoco station and Arch Morgan. Steering with my right, I took my left hand from the wheel and proudly waved at him and hollered, though I knew he probably couldn't hear me, "How you doing, Mr. Morgan?"

At the last minute, Arch Morgan saw my head barely sticking out above the side door, recognized me, and waved back. There was an astonished, but what I took for admiring, look on his face.

A great moment for me. The high point of the whole trip.

Which wasn't even diminished much by the way it wound up, when I later jolted the car into a teeth-banging stop, head-on against an iron pipe. The Model A Ford's front bumper bent into a bow, and the just-patched radiator busted again and started hissing steam like a train engine.

On the old Fordson tractor, after I'd turned south at the red hill, I plodded along on the gravel road, through low rolling pastures and flatter fields in cultivation. A mile short of Vernon, I came to the timber-floored one-way bridge over snaking and wooded East Cash Creek. When I went to stop to let a car come past me, I had some trouble trying to keep my foot from slipping off the tractor's wet clutch pedal. But I made it all right, then started on again.

The overhanging clouds were beginning to lighten up. By the time I reached the edge of my little fifteen-hundred-population hometown, built on a rise above the frequently flooding creek, the rain had slackened off to a drizzle. I crossed the east-west Comanche highway and continued south on blacktopped Church Street. I turned east on Indiana, our street, and two blocks later rolled just past our white frame house to the football field corner. I turned left toward the alley behind our house, cut left again into the alley, then immediately right into Big Jim Gruber's spreading dirt yard. The rain had made it into a slick mudfield.

The used but still shiny, galvanized metal Gleaner-Baldwin grain combine that Dad'd bought was parked there, facing me. In front, toward me, was its hitch and small, swiveling fifth wheel, as it was called, though it was really a third wheel, ahead of the two big wheels on each side of the combine, farther back. The combine's twelve-foot header, with its sickle, augur, and rotating reel, had been temporarily taken off and dragged aside on its own special little trailer, and behind where the header would have been, the combine's righthand-side, fat-tired wheel had been removed, its bare axle propped up on a block of unsplit stove wood. Dad's black Chevrolet truck with grain sideboards was parked on the far side of the combine, between the combine and the back porch of Big Jim Gruber's tan stucco house.

I drove the Fordson tractor farther into the yard. Dad, Jim Gruber, round-faced and hulky in gray coveralls, and Jim's hired hand—everybody called him "Little Jim"—were hovering on the porch, out of the misting rain. Little Jim *was* little, made even smaller looking by the big farmer-style straw hat he wore and the fact that he couldn't straighten all the way up. He was humpbacked. That's why he wasn't off in the war. His eyes, I'd always thought, were as hard as Humphrey Bogart's in *High Sierra*, and he was as dark as a gypsy. Some people thought he was a Mexican, but I personally knew that "Swyden"—that was his last name—wasn't a Mexican name. He lived by himself in an unpainted two-room shack, west across the tracks, in what people called Snuff Ridge.

Dad, Jim Gruber, and Little Jim stepped down into the muddy yard at my approach. Dad was in front. He motioned for me to pull up and park toward the propped-up combine axle. I cut the two widely spaced front wheels of the Fordson in that direction. When I got to where he wanted me, Dad nodded for me to stop, then drew a hand across his throat, a signal for me to cut off the engine. I got my left foot on the clutch, pushed down, and brought the ponderous machine to a halt.

Then, suddenly, my foot slipped off the wet clutch pedal! The heavy Fordson grunted and did the nearest thing it could to a hippo-like leap forward. I rapidly got my foot on the clutch again, but only for a moment. My foot slipped off once more, sending the big tractor into another lurch ahead until its radiator was almost touching the combine axle that rested on the block of wood. I saw a look of horror flash onto Dad's face. He and Jim Gruber and Little Jim all hollered at me at once.

"Kill it!"

"Hold her!"

"Shut her down!"

My foot was on the slippery clutch again. Stop. Then, unbelievably, another slip! Another lurch—this time tapping the combine axle, knocking it off the block and right down into the mud. The combine crashed sideways at a crazy angle.

Everybody was yelling at me. I quickly depressed the tractor clutch again—and held it this time. Thank the Lord! Full stop. Switched off the key, killing the motor. I sat there shaking for a second or two with everybody looking at me.

"Clutch's too slick in this rain," Big Jim said. I knew he said this to make me feel better. He was a good guy.

Then he and Dad and Little Jim turned their attention to Dad's combine.

I felt relieved when Little Jim said, "Ain't no harm done." He pointed to the bare axle, stabbed into the mud. "We can just jack her up again."

"God almighty damn!" Dad said. Then, talking to the other two, not me, he said, "I was fixing to run and move my truck before Willie knocked the combine over and hit *it*!"

Rattled, I blurted out the first retort that came to mind—not an apt one. "Well, I'm not as dumb as I look!" I said.

"Your looks are sure deceiving, then," Dad said.

Little Jim snickered. Big Jim laughed.

I didn't see anything funny.

And I vowed to myself that on the harvest trail north toward Rhame, Little Joe the Wrangler would show them all a thing or two.

Chapter Two

It was one o'clock the next morning—the middle of the night—when more trailriders-to-be, the Mississippi cousins, showed up. We'd been expecting one, but we got two. I was sound asleep in the lower bunk bed in the bedroom that Dad'd built for me on the back side of his and Mama's room. What woke me up was Dad hollering "Who's there?" I heard him get out of bed, pull on his Levi's, and head to the front door, where a loud knocking was coming from.

I jumped up, too, hustled through my folks' bedroom in my shorts, dashed down the short, narrow hall past the bathroom, then cut left into the living room. The cousins, it turned out, had driven straight through from Decatur, Mississippi, east of Jackson, and they looked it—rumpled, unshaven.

Troy Deering, the one we'd expected, was first in. As he came through the front door that Dad held open, I could see that he was gangly and skinny, long armed and wide shouldered. His wavy yellowish hair was combed straight back, and I noticed that he was trying to grow a pencil-line moustache, but it was so light-colored that you could barely see it on his upper lip.

He introduced himself to my dad, in case Dad didn't recognize him at first. "I'm Ida Deering's boy, Troy," he said in a southern ribbon cane syrup accent, then added, sort of proudly, "but they call me 'Spider'—my arms, I guess. Played basketball in high school." Great Aunt Ida, one of Grandpa Haley's two sisters, had earlier written Dad about her boy finding work out in Oklahoma.

Cousin Troy—Spider—dropped his bag to the floor, a scarred, paste board suitcase with a man's leather belt cinched around it to keep it closed. He shook hands with Dad, then turned to introduce the other cousin, Emmett Torley, who'd come in right behind him and pulled the front door to.

"I don't know if you remember Emmett, here—Aunt Pearl's boy," Spider said to Dad. "Home from the merchant marine—looking for work, too. Emmett's got his own car and I talked him into carrying me out here to Oklahoma." My great aunt Pearl, the younger of Grandpa Haley's sisters, was looked on as kind of a black sheep. She ran a beer joint in Decatur.

Cousin Emmett Torley set down a blue duffle bag from his shoulder. He was darker, stockier, and more muscular than Spider Deering. His black hair was parted in the middle. Like Spider, he seemed to be in his early twenties. I wondered why the two of them weren't in the war.

Emmett said hello to my dad, and they shook hands. "Sorry to come in on y'all like this, Mr. Haley, this time of night," Emmett said. His slow molasses way of Mississippi talking matched Spider's.

"Drop the 'mister'—Bob's good enough," Dad said. "You boys are just as welcome as Joseph coming home to his pa."

Emmett Torley went on. "My old '37 Plymouth like to fell apart on us, back there in Monroe, Louisiana," he said. "Thought we'd get here sooner, but we had to stop and get the old thing fixed."

Dad nodded toward me. "This here's my boy," he said to the cousins.

I shook hands with them. I remembered Spider from a trip we'd made to Mississippi when I was eleven, but not Emmett. He'd been off on a fishing trip at the time, or something.

Spider leaned over and punched me on my left arm. "This here's little Willie, then," he said.

"Will," I said.

"Will it is," Spider said. "You older now, but you ain't growed much." He turned, then, to my dad. "Bob," he said, "got a spare smoke on you? Run plumb out a few miles back."

Dad reached over and picked up his tan pack of Camels and a Ronson lighter from the wooden fireplace mantle that hung over a fake-logs gas stove, then handed both to Spider without looking at him. I knew my dad thought bumming cigarettes was a sorry habit, though it was becoming a more common one around Vernon, what with cigarettes in such short supply because of the war. Dad didn't say anything about Spider's bumming off of him, though.

"Much obliged, Bob," Spider said, then lit up and greedily inhaled the first smoke. He handed the lighter and Camel package back to Dad, and Dad set them on the mantle.

Mama came in, wrapping a pink chenille robe around herself, over her rayon gown of the same color. Big metal curlers in her dark hair. To me, she looked like England's Greer Garson in *Mrs. Miniver*, heading for an air raid shelter, but composed and ready for whatever. Mama *was* solid like Mrs. Miniver—solidly built, solidly reliable, and unshakeable. I don't know how many women had sent for Mama in the middle of the night, wanting her to help as a midwife with a problem birth. She was the kind of person you liked to have around when things got tough. "I wait to go to pieces until after the emergency's over," she liked to say. Nearly a school bus load of Cash County babies had been named Irene, after her.

Now, seeming totally unflustered at being awakened in the middle of the night, she wiped sleep from her eyes, then shook hands with both the cousins and inquired about their folks. Afterward, she asked, "Heat you boys up some leftovers?"

Spider looked like he was about to say yes, but Emmett spoke up first. "No ma'am, thank you," Emmett said. "We ate us some hamburgers back there in Monroe. Raft of tater chips since then. Could use a cold drink of water, though, won't trouble you too much."

"That's two of us," Spider said.

The cousins followed Mama into the kitchen, with me right behind. They quickly emptied the glasses that Mama filled from the sink faucet, then all four of us came back into the living room, where Dad was still waiting. Mama got some sheets and a pillow and fixed the living room divan for Emmett. She said Spider could sleep in one of my bunk beds.

"Hitch you boys up in the harness, first thing tomorrow," Dad told the cousins.

I was already awake the next morning when, a little after sunup, my dad knocked on my bedroom door to rouse me and Spider. "Daylight in the swamps, boys!" he said in his chain gang boss's voice.

I'd been lying there on the top bunk—Spider'd taken the bottom one—listening to Grandma Haley banging pots around in the kitchen and whistling church hymns. She alternated between her two favorites, "The Old Rugged Cross" and "I Come to the Garden Alone." Grandma's unbreakable habit was to get up at four o'clock every morning, and she couldn't stand it if other people in the house were still in bed at daylight.

A little over a year before, Dad'd redone our garage, in back—plumbed and insulated it—for Grandma and Grandpa Haley after they'd moved off the farm and into town. Then Dad'd had to redo the little place all over again a few months later after Grandpa had set it and himself on fire one afternoon when nobody was around. Grandma was away making a little secret cash on the side to supplement the skimpy checks she and Grandpa got from their old-age pensions. She cleaned Old Lady Stauber's house and washed and ironed clothes for her for two bits an hour. That day, Grandpa had come in from the domino parlor—maybe, Mama later said, a little too tooted up on Pabst Blue Ribbon beer to remember to snuff out his hand-rolled Bull Durham cigarette before he lay down on the divan to take a nap. The fire chief reported that it was actually the thick smoke from the divan catching on fire that really killed Grandpa and his little feist dog. It was a sad day.

Dad was back at my bedroom door again. "Hadn't wanted to work, boys, you oughtn't to have hired out!" he barked at me and Spider.

"We're getting up," I yelled back. We were.

Not too much rush on the one bathroom in the house. Mama and Dad'd already used it, and Grandma had her own. It was Saturday morning, so the twins didn't have to get up for Daily Vacation Bible School. Mama had let them sleep. Millie and Mollie and my tiny, dark-haired older sister, Janie Marie, whom I dearly loved, shared the front bedroom. It was furnished with both a double bed and a daybed. Janie Marie, prettier than Judy Garland in *The Wizard of Oz*, but no bigger, had just graduated from Vernon High School and had already landed a job as an operator with the local telephone company. Her plan was to work a year, save up a little money, then enroll at Cameron College in Lawton. She wanted to be a teacher.

Janie Marie was just leaving the bathroom when Spider and I came down the hall to line up to be next. I introduced them.

"Hey, cousin," Spider said to Janie Marie, pushing back a loose strand of wavy yellowish hair that had fallen down over his forehead, "what a hot number you turned out to be." Then he bent, gathered her into his long arms, and hugged her real tight against his bony chest, even though she was in her blue satin bathrobe and he was just wearing a cotton undershirt above his khakis.

Janie Marie didn't seem to like the hug too much. At least I hoped she didn't. She blushed and pulled away. Then, mumbling a quick hello to Spider, she turned and went right on to her and the twins' bedroom.

I let Spider have the bathroom first and headed to the living room to wait there for my turn.

Emmett had apparently gotten up before any of us, except Grandma. He was already shaved and dressed in a pair of blue denim bell-bottoms, plain black low-cut shoes, and a clean white T-shirt that contrasted with his dark complexion. His muscled biceps bulged at the end of the short sleeves. His dark hair, still wet, was parted in the middle and combed back neatly on each side. Sitting in the living room rocker, he was reading from what I could see was Janie Marie's high school Oklahoma history book. On the end of the wine-colored divan behind him, the bedsheets he'd slept in were neatly folded and stacked with his pillow.

"Short night for you, I guess," I said.

Emmett closed the history book and looked up. "Will, this E. E. Dale guy—whoever he is—writes a mighty fine history, especially about cowboys and Indians."

"He lived it himself," I said. "Professor up at OU now, but he grew up and cowboyed in old Greer County, west of here, before Oklahoma became a state. Knows all about the old cattle trails . . . Indian history, too. Last fall he came and talked at our high school assembly."

"Me, I always wanted to be a cowboy," Emmett said. "Ride the range like Tom Mix."

"Same here," I said.

"Always wanted to meet me some Indians, too," he said.

"That's easy around Vernon."

"We got a raft of Choctaw Indians back home in Mississippi," Emmett said. "Treated pert near like the colored, but they're off by theirselves on a reservation. You don't get to know 'em."

"Different, here," I said.

"Any coloreds in Vernon?" Emmett asked.

"Not a one," I said. "Back before I was born, it was against the law for them to live here in town. Quite a few in Wardell, though, south of here."

"I've had colored guys on my ships," Emmett said. "They worked in the mess, acourse. But I found 'em same's anybody else, once you got to know 'em."

"That's what I figured, too," I said.

"Whole lot of Indians around here, though, right?"

"Lots," I said. "This area was an Indian reservation—Comanche tribe, this part. Government broke the land up into quarter sections—hundred and sixty acres—and, after each Comanche got an allotment, the rest of the land was opened for white settlement. So here in Cash County, the Comanches live scattered all around us, right in amongst us. Go to the public schools with us."

"You know some Indians, then, do you, Will?"

"You bet," I said.

"They mix right in with whites?"

23

"Sure," I said. I paused a moment to think about that, then went on. "Well, you hardly ever see white kids and Indian kids going on dates together, and I don't know of any of them marrying each other."

"Ever have a Comanche girlfriend, yourself?"

"No, but I wouldn't mind it–right girl," I said.

"Me neither," Emmett said.

Our family and the two visiting cousins sat ourselves down at the rectangular, oak dining room table—all except Grandma Haley, still in the kitchen, and Millie and Mollie, still in bed. Dad was, as usual, at the head of the table, his back to the arched, stained pine double doorway between the dining room and the living room. Breakfast was mostly already laid out—fried home-cured ham and sausage, a bowl of white gravy, a big platter of fried eggs, over easy, a dish of home-churned butter, fig preserves, and ribbon cane syrup.

A lot of families in Vernon had a hard time getting butter, it'd become so scarce since the start of the war. They had to make do with oleomargarine, which looked just like lard until you colored it by mixing it up with a yellow powder that came in the package. But, ourselves, we kept a Jersey cow out back and made our own butter. And though meat and eggs were strictly rationed because of the war, that was no real problem for us, either. We generally butchered a calf and a hog every year. We raised fryers, and we had about a dozen laying hens. We grew our own vegetables, too, for eating fresh and for canning. We'd done that long before the government had taken to calling plots like ours "victory gardens." We even canned our own lard when we killed a hog.

At Calloway's Grocery, Mama usually tore out and used only the sugar and coffee stamps from our family's small leather-backed ration books that the government issued to us. She traded our meat and egg stamps to other women for their coffee, sugar, and cheese stamps, though the government said that trading rationing stamps wasn't patriotic and you weren't sup-posed to do it. But Mama *was* strictly patriotic about saving leftover cooking grease, like the government asked you to, turning it in for use in the war effort—for making bombs, or something.

That morning when we sat down at the breakfast table, the coffee'd already been poured—for everybody except me. Even Janie Marie got a cup, since she was more or less officially grown. I, of course, going on sixteen, wasn't considered full grown yet. So instead of coffee, I got my usual sweet milk, cold from the pitcher in our Frigidaire.

Grandma Haley came from the kitchen with a heaping plate of her hot biscuits. She made biscuits the way I liked them. She used eggs and a lot of lard, and not much baking powder. So the biscuits were a little yellow and greasy, pretty flat, not fluffy. Just right for me. You could split a couple up and pour bacon-grease-and-flour gravy over them. You could butter and eat two more with preserves or syrup.

Grandma Haley, her thin gray hair severely combed back and held in a tight bun, her pale and well-wrinkled skin as white as flour, set down the big plate of her steaming biscuits. She took the seat at the opposite end of the table from Dad, her back to the kitchen door. "Bow your heads," she ordered us, and began at once to pray. Grandma talked to God like he was one of her kinfolks—and always for a good while, like God was just back from a long trip and needed to get caught up.

Toward the end of her prayer that morning, Grandma said, "And, Lord, we ask that you be with the visiting kinfolks thou has seen fit to send into our midst, that they may be a blessing to all them they come in contact with." She finished just when I thought she might never, with the standard closing: "Now, Lord, bless this food to the nourishment of our bodies and us to thy service. For it is in Jesus' name we pray. Amen."

Everybody said, "Amen." The food was passed around, and all of us but Grandma Haley commenced eating. Instead, she fixed her sharp gray eyes on the two cousins, who were sitting together on the long side of the table to her left. "You boys Christians, I hope?" she asked.

Spider was nearest Grandma. Next came Emmett, then me. Emmett may have nodded yes to Grandma's question. I wasn't sure. But Spider spoke right up. "We are, ma'am, and only live each day to serve the Lord," he said. He looked across the table and winked with his left eye at Janie Marie, where Grandma wouldn't see. Janie Marie grinned a little, then ducked her head.

"That's right good, son," Grandma said to Spider. She was what people called a "hard-shell" Baptist. Never missed a Sunday service at the First Baptist Church, nor a Wednesday night prayer meeting there, either. "Wait on the Lord in prayer, boys," she now instructed Spider and Emmett, "read your Bible, don't work on the Sabbath, go to church regular, and God will surely prosper you."

"Yes, ma'am," Spider said.

Grandma Haley's focus then narrowed to Emmett alone. "And you, son," she said, "your mammy still running that old beer parlor, down there in Decatur, like she was?"

"Yes ma'am, afraid she is," Emmett said. "Only way she could figure to make a living for her and us kids, after my dad drownded."

"Well, I wish she'd get into something decent," Grandma said.

"Thank you, ma'am," Emmett said.

My dad hardly ever said a word at the table, but he spoke up now to change the subject. He'd surely been raised in the church, but, as far as I knew, he'd never been much for religion. Mama wasn't overly religious herself, though she'd always made us kids go to Sunday school. "What's kept you boys out of the service?" Dad asked the cousins. "Myself, I ain't as old as Methuselah yet, but I'm past the prime draft age. Plus I got a family."

"I *was* in the army, Bob—enlisted," Spider said to Dad. "After boot camp, they sent me to the tank corps, over yonder in Kentucky. Made corporal." He looked proudly across the table at Janie Marie to make sure she was paying attention. "Then," he went on, "before they could send me to North Africa to help beat the tar out of old Rommel, Mama made the army let me out because I was her only boy."

My own mother asked a question. "You can do that?" Mama was thinking about me, I imagined, should the war last long enough for me to get into it and should it really be true, which I myself sort of doubted, that a mother actually had a right to get an only son out of the service.

"Sure can, ma'am," Spider said. "And you're looking at living proof of it." Then he turned back toward Dad. "I swear I didn't want to leave that tank corps, Bob," he said. "But there weren't no other choice, seem like. Had to pack up my gear and light on out home to Mississippi."

Dad paused between bites. "Spider," he said.

"Yessir?"

Dad wasn't much for remembering people's names. And those he remembered, he often twisted out of shape, like maybe he didn't hear them clearly. For instance, he called an older friend of mine, whose name was Glendel, "Grendel." In Cousin Troy's case, Dad probably found it easier to remember "Spider," I figured, than Troy's real name. And a minute or so later, that breakfast, Dad would also start us all calling the other cousin, Emmett Torley, "Sailor."

"I can use both you Mississippi boys in the wheat harvest, working for me and my partner, Jim Gruber," Dad said. "Knowing tanks like you do, Spider, probably help you on a tractor and combine."

"That's for sure," Spider said quickly, though I figured he didn't yet have the least idea of what combine work would be like. "Emmett, here," Spider said, nodding to his left, "he was in the merchant marine, like I said last night. Seven round-trips around the world, ain't that right, Emmett?"

Emmett hardly looked up from his plate. "About that, I reckon," he said.

"Until his ship caught a torpedo, and he got hisself hurt," Spider said.

"Wadn't hurt *too* bad," Emmett said. "Throwed to the deck, and one of my knees got busted up. But the limp's near 'bout gone now."

"Went into the merchant marine did you, Sailor, instead of the service?" Dad asked him, coining Emmett's new name.

"Yes sir, that's exactly what I done," Emmett said. "Always had me a broke eardrum. Don't bother my hearing none, but the army and navy, neither one, would take me. Tried two semesters at Decatur Junior College, there, then took off for New Orleans. Pretty soon, got my seaman's ticket and sailed off to see the world—*and* help out in the war. That's about it, until my ship got itself hit."

"How *you* feel, Sailor, about following the wheat harvest?" Dad asked Emmett. "We going might neart all the way up to Canada. Snow be flying by the time we get done in North Dakota, last part of August. Pay each of y'all seven dollars a day, days we work."

"Mr. Haley, you looking at a guy that knows about as much about the wheat harvest as he knows about fixing women's hair," Emmett—now Sailor—said, "but I'm a quick learner, and I work hard. I'll make you a hand."

Spider spoke up. "Both of us," he said.

"Stick with me, boys," Dad said, "and like old Moses, I'll lead y'all to the promised land." Then he became his more quiet self again.

After breakfast, my dad took Spider, Sailor, and me across the alley to Jim Gruber's backyard to work on the combine Dad'd bought. Walking over there behind Sailor, I noticed how he limped, favoring his left leg. The merchant marine knee injury, I figured.

At Big Jim's, Dad introduced the cousins to Little Jim Swyden, already waiting there for us in his blue overalls and farmer straw hat. Jim Gruber had gone downtown to open up his Gleaner-Baldwin dealership place.

"Now, you boys, Little Jim's gonna be like old Pharaoh—put y'all to work," my dad said to me and the cousins. "Whatever he tells you, it's *me* talking." Then dad himself went ahead and gave us our orders, and, as usual, in too much detail. "One of y'all help pull the combine's motor off and haul it in Jim Gruber's pick-up down to Ty Dirksen's shop to get the valves ground. Other ones put new bearings on that combine axle, then stick that big wheel back on it. Combine needs new cylinder bars and new concave bars. Little Jim'll show y'all how to take out the old ones and put in the new ones. All the belts on the combine gotta be replaced, too. Put a new sickle in the header. Parts are on the porch, yonder, carried yesterday from Jim Gruber's. Get everything else done, roll the header back around here and bolt 'er in place, ready to go."

Dad looked to Little Jim. "Think you can keep these here boys busy?" Dad asked him. "Gotta go do some chousing around, myself. See if Jack Cofer's wheat's about ready to cut. Line up more cutting for after that."

Little Jim hitched himself up as straight as he could with his left-shoulder humpback. "Ain't gonna let 'em rest, Bob," he said, grinning. "Drive 'em like slaves."

Dad walked back across to our house and his grain truck.

Little Jim put Spider to helping him, scraping off the greasy crud that had accumulated on the combine's side-mounted Model A motor, loosening, then taking off, the big drive belt from its back pulley, and, finally, unbolting the motor from the combine frame. Close by, he put me and Sailor to replacing the combine's cylinder bars and concave bars. Sailor and I raised the heavy cylinder and began to unbolt the concave bars, worn smooth beneath it.

"Exactly how's this wheat combine actually work, boss?" Sailor Torley asked Little Jim as we all went about our tasks.

"Ever seen an old-time thrasher in action?" Little Jim asked.

"Naw," Sailor said. "Ain't hardly a full truckload of wheat raised back home in Mississippi."

Myself, I *had* watched threshing machines, when I was littler. And I pretty well knew, too, how a combine worked. But as the four of us went about our repair work, I paid attention to Little Jim's explanation anyway.

"Old time thrashing was a two-step deal," Little Jim said. "First, the wheat still not plumb ripe on the stalk, you went in the field with a McCormick-Deering binder that was pulled by a team of horses. Binder cut the wheat and tied the headed stalks in bundles." He paused. "Least that's what the binder was supposed to do, when the damned thing was running

29

right. But, God almighty, it was hell on wheels to keep one of them sonsabitchin' binders baler-wired together and working! But when it did work and you got the binding over with, you had to gather up and shock the bundles into, like, little Indian tipis, scattered all over the field."

"And the idea of that?" Sailor asked.

"So the wheat heads'd cure and dry out by the time the thrashing machine got to your place," Little Jim said. "Course, you hoped like hell it didn't come a rain first. One year I was working for an old farmer out west of town, here, and it come a flood damned near ever other day that May, after we already shocked the wheat. Toad drownders, ever one of them rains. Duck stranglers. Grain up and sprouted in the shock. Whole crop was plumb ruined. The old man went broke, and I had to go looking for other work."

"But what if the crop *ain't* ruined like that?" Sailor asked.

"Well, then the thrashing crew showed up," Little Jim said. "They pulled the thrashing machine into your field with a big tractor, or, old days, a steam engine. Parked the thrasher where they wanted it—middle of the field, maybe. Unhooked the tractor or steam engine and turned it around and run the thrasher off of a long belt from the tractor's side-pulley. Bundle wagons pulled by teams of horses and mules rolled out all over the field and brung in high loads of grain bundles to the thrashing machine. Wagon drivers throwed the bundles up to the thrasher man with their pitchforks, and he fed the bundles into the machine. Down inside the thrashing machine, iron bars on a spinning cylinder ground against the concave bars underneath, and that knocked out—thrashed, you could say—the kernels from the grain heads. Wheat kernels fell through a shaking sieve, then a augur carried 'em to a spout where they got sacked up or poured out, loose, into wagons with grain sideboards. Leftover straw and chaff got carried to the back end of the thrasher on a moving raddle, then was blowed out for a strawstack."

"And with a combine, nowadays, what's different?" Sailor Torley asked.

"Well, you skip the binding step, main thing," Little Jim said. "Cutting and thrashing is all run together—how come they call it a 'combine.' You let the wheat get ripe in the field, on the stalk. Combine rolls along and cuts it and thrashes it, all the same time.

"Bob Haley's Gleaner-Baldwin here, it's a pull type, acourse—ain't many self-propelled ones," Little Jim went on as the rest of us continued our work. "Tractor, like that old Fordson there, drags the combine 'round and 'round a field, cutting in tighter and tighter circles. Back of the tractor, sticking out to the left from the front of the combine, that's where we're gonna bolt back on that twelve-foot header, yonder. The header reel turns like a riverboat wheel, but up front. Reel bats catch the headed wheat tops, drive 'em backards against the sawing sickle. Heads fall into the header trough, and the big augur carries 'em sideways into the combine's guts for thrashing."

Sailor found an odd way to make Little Jim's explanation graphic. "Fordson tractor's like a big old toad, then, sounds like," Sailor said. "Crawls ahead, dragging the Gleaner-Baldwin behind it like a big old one-clawed crab that keeps stuffing its mouth with wheat as it goes along."

"Huh?" Spider said, raising his head from unbolting the Model A motor from the combine frame.

"Weird way to put it, sailor man," Little Jim said, "but you got it 'bout right."

Spider Deering didn't work two whole hours that morning before he asked if he could use cousin Sailor Torley's '37 Plymouth—the "Green Lizard," Sailor called it—to go buy himself some cigarettes.

Spider was gone a good while. Sailor and I had to do the heavy lifting by ourselves when it came time to load the combine's motor onto Jim Gruber's gray GMC pick-up. Little Jim backed the pick-up against the side of the combine and stood by as Sailor and I got ready to move the greasy engine.

Sailor took one front corner of the motor, under the radiator, me the other, so we could lift, then scoot, it.

But at first, it seemed like I couldn't get a good hand hold. "I can't pick my side up," I said to Sailor, though I was trying hard.

31

"*Cain't?*" Sailor said. The word nearly exploded out of his mouth. "Don't ever say 'cain't,' Will. I despise to hear that word worse'n dogs farting."

He *would* hear the word again, though, during the next days we worked together. And each time I said "can't," I was immediately sorry because it always got the same quick reaction out of Sailor. And he'd usually add: "Man *says* 'cain't,' Will, he *does* 'cain't'; *says* 'can,' he *does* 'can.'" I soon found out that that was Sailor's basic philosophy about work. In time, he would break me of the "cain't" habit, but it was to take him a while.

That particular morning, Sailor Torley showed me where to put my hands under my corner of the combine's Model A motor, how to bend my knees and get my feet directly under the weight. And it turned out that, after all, I *could* lift my side. He and I picked up the heavy motor and slid it, got behind it and lifted and scooted it again, then let it down into the bed of the pick-up. The motor's weight bent the pick-up's springs almost level.

I was impressed by Sailor's bulging muscles. His thick arms made mine look like broom handles, I thought. "How'd you get so built up?" I asked him, after Little Jim drove off with the motor toward Ty Dirksen's shop, and as he and I went back to replacing the cylinder and concave bars.

Sailor gave me what I thought was an odd answer. "Charles Atlas," he said.

Charles Atlas? That was the former Mr. America who advertised on the back page of pulp Westerns and comic books—funny books, we called them—claiming "If you'll give me fifteen minutes a day, I'll make a man out of you." The ad featured a cartoon strip that began in its first frames with a "ninety-seven- pound weakling" getting beach sand kicked in his eyes by a muscular bully, while a pretty girl in a bathing suit looked on. The cartoon wound up in its final frames showing a transformed, newly muscular, *ex*-weakling, after he'd sent off for the Charles Atlas course, shoving the mean guy out of the way and taking his place with the now admiring girl.

"You're kidding," I said to Sailor. I'd always figured Charles Atlas's claims were on about the same level as the other regular funny book ads I'd seen. Like the one that touted a little ventriloquist thing you could send off for and put in your mouth to "amaze your friends by throwing your voice." Or the one that advertised a set of secret eyeglasses you could order that would allow you, they said, to see through girls' dresses.

"Nawsir, Will, old Charles Atlas knows what he's talking about," Sailor said. "Borrowed the course myself from a shipmate that ordered it. Charles Atlas named his method 'dynamic tension,' but it's really what some people call 'isometrics.'"

"Yeah, what's that?" I asked, still a little skeptical.

"It's making one muscle work against another one," Sailor said. "Builds up both of 'em. You can do it anywhere—real tight place, even. I can show you how, Will, if you want to."

"Good deal," I said. I thought I wouldn't mind having a muscular chest, arms, and shoulders like Sailor Torley's. Might even impress Rebecca Milton, for one thing. That was something I almost ached to do.

Little Jim was long since back from dropping off the combine motor at Ty Dirksen's and we'd already had time to put the tire and wheel, with the new bearings, back on the Gleaner-Baldwin's bare axle when Spider finally drove up in Sailor's old car. The bony yellow-haired cousin sauntered over, his eyes hidden behind dark aviator sunglasses, and casually apologized for being gone so long. Said he'd had a hard time finding a store that wasn't already out of cigarettes.

"Forced to buy these here Raleighs, and Raleighs are worse'n smoking grapevines!" he said. He held up the brown cigarette package. It'd been doubled under the left sleeve of his white T-shirt, just above a lean bicep that I noticed for the first time was tattooed with a red spider in the middle of a blue web.

Little Jim, his eyes now as dark as his walnut-brown face, fixed Spider Deering with a cold stare. "Next time you take off like that, son, maybe you oughta just keep on going," he said.

"But not in my car," Sailor said.

Spider ignored Sailor. He didn't return Little Jim's gaze, either. Instead, he looked off and sort of caressed his thin blond moustache with the thumb and finger of his right hand. Then to Little Jim, he said. "You ain't the boss of me, Humpy."

"Right now, I'm the *straw* boss of this chickenshit outfit," Little Jim said. "You working for me, the same as for Bob Haley and Jim Gruber. You don't like it, son, might better go on now and hit the road."

At that, Spider turned belligerently to face Little Jim. I watched in disbelief and alarm as the lanky cousin doubled his fists and took a menacing step toward the dark little humpbacked bantamweight. "You the one that might hit the road, Little Darkie—hit it flat of your damn humpback," Spider said.

This cousin's trouble!

In a flash, Little Jim's small right hand was in and out of his overalls' side pocket. He suddenly held a big red-handled pocketknife. Another quick motion and he'd flipped open the knife's large and dangerous-looking blade. Spider Deering froze, practically in midstep.

"Keep on coming, Blondie," Little Jim said, his voice low and scary, his eyelids slits, the pupils like black dots. "I'll cut you a new asshole."

But Sailor quickly put a stop to things. He was in between the two men in one long step and shoved Spider backwards with both hands.

"We ain't come to Oklahoma, Troy, to pick no fight," Sailor said. "We come to find work, and we found it. Don't screw things up."

You could hear us all breathing. We stood where we were for a minute. Then Spider unclinched his fists and dropped his hands.

Little Jim relaxed, too. He took a plug of Days Work chewing tobacco from the bib pocket of his overalls, cut off a chunk with the big knife, and stuck the chunk inside his jaw. Then, after putting the plug of tobacco back where he got it, he carefully closed the knife and slipped it into his right front pocket. When he finally spoke, it was as if nothing at all out of the way had happened. His voice was smoothed out. "Y'all all three give me a hand, now," Little Jim said to us. "Let's roll that header around here and bolt it back on the front of the combine, like Bob Haley wants us to."

Sailor, Spider, and I moved toward the header. Sailor picked up the tongue of the rubber-tired trailer that the header rested on. He guided. Spider and I pushed from the back. We soon had the header in place. Little Jim showed us how, and we reattached it, then got its drive belts and drive chains back around their pulleys and sprockets, and tightened them up.

The sun was by then straight overhead, and we knocked off for the noon dinner that Grandma Haley had fixed. As the four of us walked silently across the alley to the house, I was thinking to myself that following the harvest road north might not turn out to be as many laughs as, say, Bing Crosby and Bob Hope's *Road to Morocco*.

Spider and I were walking a little behind Sailor and Little Jim. "I can't stand for people to order me around, tell me what to do," Spider said to me, low enough so that the others didn't hear. "Never could, never will."

Must have been a little strange for you, being in the army.

Chapter Three

We didn't finish work on Dad's Gleaner-Baldwin combine that late-May Saturday afternoon until just before dark. But when we finally did quit for the day, the combine was ready for the field. We'd bolted the repaired Model A motor back onto the combine frame and hooked up its heavy drive belt. We'd finished by changing the oil in the Fordson tractor and greasing up both it and the Gleaner-Baldwin, a job I quickly picked up a distaste for, using grease guns packed from a big can of the slickiest and stickiest black Marfak grease that was ever made.

Time, then, to take a weekly bath and scrub my hands like crazy after washing them in gasoline to get most of the grease off. Time to dress up in good clean clothes, and, after supper, get ready to head down to Joe Lammer's Confectionary, the same as every Saturday night.

I was the last one of our bunch at home to get into the bathroom. And when I came out, I started through the hall to the front room to rejoin Sailor Torley. I'd left him there, reading. He'd bathed earlier and put on clean clothes, though he'd told me that he wasn't going to go with us to town. "Gonna just hang around the fort here, Will, and read," he'd said. It seemed like the merchant marine had gotten him used to a solitary way of living.

I came even with the open door to the front bedroom that Mollie and Millie and Janie Marie shared. The twins were outside, catching lightning bugs. Janie Marie was sitting at a vanity dresser, fixing her face. Spider was standing right beside her, his back toward me. The two of them were talking in low voices. I slowed, then stopped a minute, wanting to know what they were saying.

"But you oughtn't to have come down there this morning," I heard Janie Marie say.

"Had to see where you worked, didn't I, Little Bit?" Spider said. "And buy you a sody pop on your break."

That's where he'd been so long—Janie Marie's telephone office. I didn't like it.

"And me and you gonna jitterbug tonight, ain't we?" Spider said.

"I told you I'm going steady," Janie Marie said.

"Yeah, but the boy's not here—off in the Navy," Spider said.

"I'm wearing his class ring," Janie Marie said, turning. She held up her right hand to show the big ring. She'd put tape on it to keep it on her finger. Janie Marie saw me. "Oh, hi Will," she said.

Spider glanced at me too as he took a comb from his pocket and ran it through his wavy yellow hair. "Willie, I ain't asked her to take off no ring," he said. He turned back toward my sister. "And 'sides all that, hon," he said, "we just cousins." He paused a second before continuing. "But maybe *kissin'* cousins."

Janie Marie joined in Spider's laugh. I started to walk on, wishing she hadn't.

Later, Grandma Haley and Janie Marie set the table and put supper out. But none of us sat down right away. We all waited for Dad and Mama, who weren't home yet. Spider'd seen Uncle Wayne's guitar in my room. He asked me to go get the instrument, and when I brought it to him, he enveloped it like a daddy longlegs to tune it, his wavy blond hair falling down over his forehead. Then he struck up a surprisingly expert picking and singing of Jimmie Rodgers's hobo song, "Waiting for a Train." Spider was a charmer, and I noticed that Janie Marie seemed like she was impressed. I was, myself.

When Spider started his song, Sailor got up and stepped over to his blue duffel bag at the end of the divan and brought out a French harp. Sitting back down, he began to harmonize his instrument's wailing chords with those of Spider's guitar and at one point even made the French harp mimic almost exactly the sad sound of a freight train's whistle. When the hobo song was finished, Spider led the way, and the cousins launched into "San Antonio Rose," the popular Bob Wills tune. The two of them were good enough, to my way of thinking, to make it on the Grand Ole Opry.

The music session ended, though, when Mama finally drove up out front and came in. Her dark hair was a little frazzled, and she looked worried. She put her purse down on an end table and unbuttoned the jacket of her blue suit. "Will, have you seen your daddy today?" she asked me.

Uh-oh.

"No ma'am, not since he left us over at Big Jim Gruber's this morning," I said.

"Where'd he say he was going?" she asked.

"Had some chousing around to do," I said.

"I *bet* he did," Mama said.

She stepped at once through the arched doorway into the dining room and sat down at the little combination seat and telephone stand that was in the righthand corner there. The stand was something I'd bought her on her last birthday. I'd hitchhiked the eleven miles down to Wardell, to B&O Cash Store, where you could sell anything from pecans to fresh eggs and buy anything from bathing suits to tenpenny nails. I'd bought the dark little cherry wood stand with its purple velvet seat for seven and a half dollars, using my own money, then hitchhiked back to Vernon with it, catching a ride with a guy in a cattle truck.

Mama grabbed up the phone that rested on the top of the stand on a white doily crocheted by Grandma Haley. She said to the operator, "Central, get me Viola Wamsley." When her friend Viola came on, Mama said, "Viola, you want to go with me out to that five-mile honky-tonk?" She listened a moment. "Yeah, tonight." Listened again. "Yeah, that's where he is, I expect." Listened. "Can't? Okay. Thanks, though, Viola. I'll just have to figure something else out."

Mama came back into the living room. She paced a little. Then, ignoring everybody else, she said to me and Janie Marie, "Your daddy and Jim Gruber're, sure as the world, out at that beer joint at the five-mile corner. Not in one of his usual hangouts around town here. I've looked. He's got that old sorry gal out at the five-mile corner, doesn't think I know about her."

"Now, caution, Irene," Grandma Haley said to Mama. Grandma'd come from the kitchen to stand under the dining room archway, wiping her hands on her apron. "Body oughtn't to talk like that in front of these here kids and our kinfolks. Son's probably just out looking for wheat to cut."

"Not all he's looking for," Mama said.

"Well, anyway," Grandma Haley said, "y'all all come on in and eat."

We went into the dining room and scraped our chairs out and sat down in silence. Grandma Haley said the prayer, then we started to pass the food around.

After a while, Mama spoke up. "Emmett," she said to Sailor, "I want you to go with me out to that old beer joint after supper, if you will, see if we can find Bob before he gets in too bad a shape. I don't like to go into that place by myself."

I was glad she hadn't asked me and Janie Marie to go with her this time, as she sometimes did. My sister and I dearly loved them both, but neither one of us ever wanted to get mixed up in Dad and Mama's fights. We faulted Dad for drinking too much and for running around, but we faulted Mama some, too, for carrying on so much about it and for always being so suspicious of Dad, so eaten up with jealousy. Janie Marie'd once said to me, "They've been married twenty years, and she knows Daddy's not going to change. She ought to just either go ahead and leave him or get reconciled to the way he is." But when Janie Marie'd said something like that to Mama, too, Mama'd answered her: "Life's like making a quilt, hon. You've got to follow the pattern the Lord gives you, no matter how difficult it is." There was a lot of shame in Vernon to getting a divorce, too. And besides, I thought, Mama loved my dad, in spite of everything. I did, too, of course, but I was embarrassed about Dad's drinking, and I envied other kids who, the way I imagined it, all had happy, upstanding folks.

Dad sometimes made it home from his carousing before Mama was back from looking for him, but he wasn't always in the best condition when he got home. One night like that, he came in while Janie Marie and I were still up, working on our school lessons in the living room. His face was skinned, his clothes dirty, and he wasn't even close to sober.

"Oh my goodness, Daddy!" Janie Marie had said when he slouched in the front door. "Sit down here and let me help you." She put him in the rocking chair and ran and got a wet washrag and some peroxide and started to fix him up. "What happened to you?" she asked as she worked on his face.

Dad's eyes weren't totally focused. His words were a little slurred. "I was coming back to town in my pick-up," he said slowly, "and just the other side of the East Cash Creek bridge, got sleepy. So I pulled off on the shoulder. Slope's pretty steep right there. Next thing I knowed, the damned pick-up'd rolled. I come to later, upside down, near 'bout at the bottom of that ditch, plumb in the dark, like old Jonah in the belly of the whale. It taken me a while to figure how to get the door open and climb out."

"How'd you make it home?" I asked him.

"Rocked the pick-up a little on that slope, then pushed it real hard, and it rolled on over, pretty as you please, and landed right on its wheels," Dad said. "Backed it up out of there and come on."

He laughed, was quiet a minute or so, then his eyes watered up. He started getting a kind of catch in his voice. I'm certain that, sober, Dad never let anybody see him cry, but drinking too much, he sure would. At least he would Janie Marie and me.

"I love you kids," he said and wiped his eyes with the back of a hand.

40

"We love you, too, Daddy," Janie Marie said. Tears filled her own eyes. "But why do you drink so much?"

"I *feel* better when I'm drinking," he said—the most honest answer I ever heard.

I wondered what kind of devils chased Dad, what woke him up in the middle of the night and made him reach for a cigarette in the dark, why he felt so bad a lot of the time when he was sober.

Then, that particular night for some reason, he took a notion to confess to me and Janie Marie about an earlier drunken episode of his. "You remember that time they telephoned you, Willie," he said to me, "to come down to the Vernon hospital when I broke my foot and your mama wasn't back yet from hunting me?"

I said I did.

I found him, that night, sitting in the x-ray room, drunk as old Cooter Brown.

The nurse spoke to me as soon as I came in. "His heel's crushed, and we need to cut his boot off so we can get an x-ray," she said.

"Ain't gonna let 'em ruin my good boot, Willie," Dad said. He wouldn't look at me.

"They've got to take it off to x-ray your foot," I said.

"That's why I wanted you to come," he said to me. "So you could *pull* my boot off."

"Can you stand it?"

"I can stand it, if you can stand to pull it off," he said.

He lifted his leg. I got a good hold at the back of the heel of the cowboy boot. He gritted his teeth, and sweat popped out on his forehead as I began to pull, steadily and hard. Not a moan from Dad. The boot gradually came loose—and off.

The x-ray showed that his heel was crushed upward from the bottom.

"How in the world did you do this, Mr. Haley?" Dr. Marion asked him.

"Wild old cow stepped on me," Dad said.

41

I thought that that was not a believable explanation. Neither did Mama when I got Dad home after they fixed his heel up, put a pin in it, and set it in a plaster cast. But he stuck with that story.

Sitting in the living room rocking chair that later time, while Janie Marie cleaned up his skinned face, Dad decided to tell me and her the truth about the crushed heel incident.

"I was up in that old gal's bedroom, up over that five-mile corner beer joint," he said, still talking in a kind of drunk voice. "Heard her old man stomping up them stairs, like old Cain after Abel. I grabbed on my Levi's and jerked on my boots. Jumped out the window. And that's how my heel got hurt."

Certainly a more believable explanation, but one that Janie Marie and I would just as soon not have heard.

"Why do you do stuff like that, Dad?" I asked. "Don't you love Mama?"

"Sure, I love her," he said. "I'm just a sorry guy, I guess. Old Devil's got too strong a hold on me."

With that, Dad closed his eyes and quickly dozed off to sleep in the rocking chair. Janie Marie and I went off to our beds, leaving him for Mama to find.

Now, after speaking to Sailor at the supper table about him going with her to find Dad this time, Mama turned to me. "You go on to town and have fun tonight, Willie," she said. "But I'm warning you that you've got your work cut out for you this summer, trying to keep your daddy sober and not wrecked in a bar ditch somewhere. He's going to be your responsibility."

Her saying that nearly gave me the chills, made me worry about what I might be letting myself in for, going on the wheat harvest with Dad—and without Mama. But I shook off the feeling, glad that I was free that night, at least, to head on to Joe Lammer's Confectionary right after supper.

"That's what you want, Miz Haley, I'll go with you," Sailor said to Mama.

There was no way I could have pictured the town of Vernon back then without seeing Joe Lammer's Confectionary right in the middle of it. If home was the one place you wanted to return to when you were away from it, as someone put it, then Joe Lammer's was home to me. Hard to be away from it on a Saturday night, as I had been a time or two, off on an FFA trip. What's going on down at Joe Lammer's? Who's there tonight? That was all you could think about. And not being there made you feel as lonesome as an orphan.

After supper, Janie Marie, Spider, and I took off afoot for downtown. Janie Marie was as cute as could be in a middie blouse and pleated navy skirt, her well-brushed dark hair hanging loose and down to her shoulders. You could see from how pretty she was and from her sunny personality why she'd been so popular in high school. Spider was dressed up in khaki gabardine slacks—part of his old army dress uniform, I figured—brown penny loafers with taps on the heels, and a tucked-in white T-shirt with a pack of cigarettes, as usual, doubled into the left sleeve above his spider tattoo. I'd borrowed the outfit I was wearing from Dad, since he wasn't home to object—well-shined boots, white dress shirt, pressed Levi's.

Janie Marie and Spider, close together, sauntered a little way behind me on the cement sidewalk, talking low. I found their hanging back annoying.

We walked two blocks east of our place on Indiana Street, to Church Street. Just about every third house we passed carried in a front window the little red, white, and blue cloth banner with a white star that indicated a boy from the family was away in the war. One house, the Moore's, had a gold star in the window. Their son, Tommy Moore, had just lately been killed in North Africa. It was sad. His sister was in my same grade at school. I took a lot of pride in the fact that my two uncles were off in the war, but I worried a lot that they might get hurt, or worse.

We crossed Church Street and turned north on an old sidewalk that was badly tilted and cracked by tree roots. Still walking in front, I turned for a minute to point out to Spider with a touch of civic pride a certain sidewalk bench we passed. The bench carried a faded sign advertising the dental practice of a long-dead Dr. Heflin that everybody said was the father of the famous movie star Van Heflin, who was supposed to have been born right there in Vernon. We Vernonites took advantage of anything we could to make our hometown seem a little less ordinary.

Three blocks north, Janie Marie, Spider, and I crossed Nevada Street. The gray brick First Baptist Church—first and *only* Baptist church in Vernon—sat on the northeast corner of the intersection. We veered the other way, left, across the graveled schoolyard block, skirting around the north side of the four-story, buff brick Vernon school building, and came at last to Broadway—we called it Main Street—then continued north along it two more blocks to the middle of Vernon's four-block business section.

Main Street: schoolhouse on the south, courthouse on the north, and in between, one- and two-story red brick dry goods, furniture, and grocery stores, a five-and-dime, two barber shops, a corner bank, a bakery, a beauty shop, a dress shop, a couple of drugstores, a hardware dealer, three car dealers, two picture shows (only one open all the time), and three beer joints.

Vernon was the county seat of Cash County, Oklahoma, built on a low hill on a ten-mile stretch between heavily wooded East Cash and West Cash Creeks, but much closer to East Cash. "Fifteen hundred friendly souls," the chamber of commerce said of Vernon. Proud home of the Fighting Blue Devils. Turkey Capital of Southwest Oklahoma. Gateway to Red River.

Familiar brightly colored war effort posters were, of course, on display in nearly every downtown plate glass window that the three of us passed. One with an evil-looking caricature of Hitler trumpeted the words "Waste helps the enemy! Conserve material." In Vernon we were practically religious about scrap drives—paper, aluminum, iron, and copper.

Several business window posters pushed war bonds. One of these showed two menacing black hands—one hand with a Nazi swastika on it, the other with a Japanese rising sun— both grabbing for an angelic mother and her baby. The poster read "Keep these hands off! Buy war bonds." In school we bought savings stamps that, if you ever accumulated enough of them, you could turn in for a war bond.

Another window poster showed a struggling shipwrecked American sailor about to sink beneath rough ocean waves. The poster carried the big-lettered words "Someone talked!" In Vernon, Oklahoma, we certainly believed, as we were told, that "Loose lips sink ships!"—though we weren't clear about just what information any of us had that we were supposed to keep from the enemy.

We served as air raid wardens and junior wardens and committed to memory the silhouettes of enemy airplanes, such as the German Stuka and the Japanese Zero, should these threatening warcraft have ever shown up in the night sky over Vernon. We'd even been taught how, if suddenly face-to-face on Vernon's streets with an unknown Asian man, we could quickly tell whether he was from China, one of our ally nations, or was an enemy Japanese and, therefore, maybe a dangerous spy or saboteur. Look at his feet! we were told. A lot of space between the big toe and the one next to it was a dead give-away, they said, that the person was a longtime wearer of Japanese sandals. Was I the only one who wondered how you were supposed to get a suspicious Asian visitor to take off his shoes and socks?

Joe Lammer's Confectionary was on the east side of Main Street in the middle of the bank block. And it was, as usual, jammed full that Saturday night. Standing room only in the front lobby, between the soda fountain on one side and the magazine racks with a stern hand-lettered sign—"This is not a public library!"—on the other. Crowded booths in back with names and initials carved into the heavy wooden tables. Glenn Miller records blaring louder than the crowd noise from the flashing Wurlitzer jukebox in a corner of the dark, bathroom-sized dance floor.

As an alternative to Joe Lammer's, though nobody said why an alternative was needed, the Vernon Rotary Club had a year earlier moved a small frame house onto a westside vacant lot at the foot of Vernon's water tower, blocks from downtown, and fixed it up as a "Teen Canteen" to provide wholesome fun for the town's kids, they said. But the Teen Canteen never caught on. It seemed artificial. Couldn't compete with Joe Lammer's, the real thing.

Janie Marie and Spider meshed into the lobby swarm at Joe Lammer's, then sifted through everyone toward the dance floor in the far back. I saw my best friend across the lobby— thin, freckle-faced, and redheaded Junior Randall. We nodded to each other.

But first I had to get some cash. I turned right, just inside the glass front door, and stepped over to the cigar and cigarette case at the near end of the soda fountain counter. Doughy Joe Lammer, about fifty, his remaining sparse hair dyed a too obvious, inky black, finished making a couple of malts and handed them across the counter to Walt Mason, a little man, thin as a fence post, who always looked embarrassed. Mason was, as usual, taking orders from the booths. Some people in Vernon said there was more than just a business relationship between Lammer and Mason, but I wasn't sure what that meant. At least not until Junior Randall explained it to me some.

I finally caught Joe Lammer's eye. He moved down the counter toward me, wiping his hands on the soiled white apron tied around his waist.

"Yeah, Haley?" he said.

"Cash a check for two dollars?" I asked.

He frowned. "Is it any good?"

"Good as your mother's virtue," I said.

"Better be better," Joe Lammer said. He didn't smile.

I'd had a checking account at the First State Bank of Vernon since I was in the sixth grade, from money I saved from summertime haybaling work and school year jobs shining shoes, sweeping out stores, and as a paper boy. Right then I also had four springing heifers pasturing with my dad's, and he'd let me put in twenty acres of wheat, as my own, on a quarter section of wheat land that he rented on the shares from a local guy, Bill Wishard—one-third to Wishard, two-thirds to us.

Joe Lammer waited with an impatient look on his face while I hurriedly filled out a blank check that I took from my shirt pocket. He handed me two dollars from the cash register, then drifted back down the counter to resume his soda fountain work.

I moved along with him on the outside of the counter. Junior Randall came over. He and I'd known each other since the summer I was in the fifth grade, when my uncles Clif and Wayne had tried to get me and Junior in a fistfight.

That day, the Haybaling Haleys were baling millet for Junior's dad on his dryland farm east of Vernon. Junior'd come out to the field during the afternoon when our crew was getting ready to move the baler to a new location.

"See this redheaded boy, here, Willie?" Uncle Clif said to me at one point, motioning with a thumb toward Junior. Lean and wiry, sandy-haired Uncle Clif was my favorite, five years older than me and like a brother. "He said you had shit on your neck. You gonna take that, Willie?" Uncle Clif said this loud enough so that Junior could hear him.

Then, standing a little closer to Junior, but still where I could hear, my other uncle, Uncle Wayne, two years older than Clif and a little taller and heavier, and also like a brother to me, said to Junior, "Willie, here, wants to whup your ass, Red, and he thinks you're yellow."

Why would my uncles have tried to start a fight like that? Bored, maybe? Teasing? Toughen me up? Wanted to teach me to fight better, the way Uncle Wayne taught me to swim by once pitching me into a flooded East Cash Creek, almost out of its banks? Both uncles boxed occasional prizefights at the local Wollam Theater and up at nearby Lawton, and they'd started to train me to spar with them, using their scratched-up pair of faded red boxing gloves.

Whatever my uncles' plan was that day for getting Junior and me in a fistfight, it didn't work. Neither Junior nor I fell for it, and in fact, before Junior left that afternoon to go to the house, he and I actually began to get acquainted a little and to like each other. The next fall Junior started riding the bus into Vernon to school, and before long, we became each other's best friend, almost constantly together. One school joker called us the Bobbsey Twins.

I ordered a cherry Coke for Junior Randall and for me, a "four hundred"—a small Coke-glass of chocolate milk with ice.

"Going to the wheat harvest myself, it turns out," I told Junior. "Dad bought a twelve-foot Gleaner-Baldwin."

"Martin's just got a little Massey seven-footer combine," Junior said. Martin was the neighbor guy Junior went to the harvest with. "Called the 'Massey Clipper.' About big enough to clip hair. Either that or shell pecans."

"How far y'all going *this* summer?" I asked.

"Imagine to about Kimball, Nebraska—same as last year," Junior said. "You and your dad?"

"Says all the way up to Rhame, North Dakota. Says snow'll be flying before we wind up."

"Be good if you and I could run into one another, up the way somewhere," Junior said.

"See if we could get into some trouble," I said.

Joe Lammer set our drinks on the counter, and we paid him.

"Your girlfriend's back there in a booth with Yvonne Morton," Junior said, motioning in that direction with a jerk of his head, his red hair cut in a burr.

"Becca?"

"How many girlfriends you got?" Junior said.

"If Becca was, that'd add up to one," I said.

"She and Yvonne are by themselves," Junior said. "Boyfriends not here yet, looks like. Wanna go back and keep 'em company until the boyfriends show up?"

We twisted our way through the lobby crowd, saying "hi!" and "hey!" here and there and punching a few guys on the arms. Becca's booth was in the far back, almost to the small, dimly lit dance floor, which she was facing, her back to us. Yvonne sat across from her and greeted us as we came up. Becca turned to look at Junior and me.

48

"Join y'all for a minute?" I asked the girl I'd been crazy about since we were in grade school, even though I'd always worried that she, maybe, felt a little above me, since her dad was a doctor.

"Sure," Becca said, blue eyes friendly, her glowing face unpainted except for a little lipstick. She scooted over for me, afterwards straightening her flared red skirt with both hands as I sat down next to her. She was wearing a white embroidered peasant blouse. Her blond hair was pulled back and tied with a red ribbon.

Yvonne moved over to let Junior in on that side of the table. Those two began their own conversation. Junior and Yvonne weren't interested in each other, except as friends. But they actually sort of looked alike. Both redheaded.

"Will, who's that older guy with your sister, the terrific dancer?" Becca asked. I was close enough to her in the tight booth that the fragrance of her familiar Evening in Paris perfume, heavy as the sweet aroma of a gardenia corsage, overcame the smell of cigarette smoke that hung so thick in the room.

"Cousin from Mississippi, going on the wheat harvest with us this summer," I said.

"You're going to follow the wheat harvest yourself?" Becca asked.

"All the way up to Rhame, North Dakota," I said. "Driving a tractor. Maybe I'll mail you some postcards from the hot spots along the way. What are you going to do this summer, Becca?"

"Nothing as interesting," she said. "Leaving tomorrow noon, right after church, for close to three weeks at the Methodist camp, over at Turner Falls. After that, home here to Vernon, working at Paris Dress Shop." Becca changed the subject back to her first comment, then, as she glanced toward the little dance floor. "Your cousin and Janie Marie sure don't dance together like kinfolks," she said, watching them swing around to the music.

"Girls like the mature type, I heard," I said. I tried for a kind of joking tone, but I still must have sounded a little sarcastic.

Becca knew what I meant, and she knew that I wasn't really joking. "Now, Will, don't be jealous of Bert," she said. "You know I like you."

"Like a brother," I said.

"More than that, Will," Becca said. "Good cow! You and I've known each other since the third grade."

"A lot longer than you've known old Bert," I said.

"Will, he's leaving Monday for San Diego to go into the navy," Becca said. She paused a moment, then went on. "There's just something *about* Bert—I don't know. He reminds me of Robert Taylor. That darkness along his jaw, even when he's shaved close."

"So, it's five o'clock shadow that makes you swoon?" I said. "Hell's bells, any man's got that!"

I said this, though it wasn't fully true, at least not in my case. My own scraggly moustache and beard were so scanty, yet, that when I shaved with my Gillette safety razor, I could generally get by with hot tap water only, not even having to use the Burma-Shave I'd received for my birthday.

Out of nowhere, Becca said, "You wanna dance?"

On the jukebox, "Chattanooga Choo Choo" had ended, and another Glenn Miller song had started, this one "Tuxedo Junction." Everybody knew that Glenn Miller had broken up his band and gone into the army for the duration, but his records were more popular than ever.

"What?" I couldn't believe I'd heard Becca right.

"Well, *do* you . . . wanna dance?" Her lips were crimped into a teasing grin.

"Does a muskrat wanna ramble?" I said. Clever.

In fact, I wasn't much for dancing. I wished that the tune on the jukebox was a slow one. But I wasn't about to pass up the chance to put my arms around that girl, even if only off and on while jitterbugging.

I quickly slipped out of the booth and momentarily stood in the aisle as Becca came out, too. She led the way, and we headed back toward the dance floor.

Janie Marie and Spider shared the small space with two other couples and were going at it like they were in a dance contest. Spider yelled at me above the music and between whirls, "Way to go, Willie boy!"

I took Becca's hand, put my arm around her waist, and she and I started. I was as nervous as a calf about to be dehorned.

But I soon began to get into the beat of the music, and Becca was so good that she made my part easier.

Close, then away. Twirl her as smoothly as I could. Come together in a tight clasp, then, quick, dance out again, stepping in time to the fast rhythm, me in my dad's black cowboy boots, Becca in saddle oxfords and white bobby socks. Magic.

When that song ended, she and I laughed, a little out of breath. We applauded lightly as we stood close together, then held hands. Things got better. Spider fed another nickel into the jukebox, and as the black vinyl record inside the colorful glass bubble dropped onto the turntable and began to spin, he looked over at me and said, "This one's for you, son."

It was a wonderfully romantic slow dance—Bing Crosby singing, "I Don't Want to Walk Without You." I gathered Becca into my arms.

The dreamy rhythm of the music got to me. The sad and loving words. Bing Crosby's mellow voice. The unbearably sweet smell of Evening in Paris. Becca pressed against me, her head on my shoulder.

She saw Bert Wriston before I did, and she started to pull away from me even before Bert was fully on the dance floor. He suddenly grabbed her arm and yanked her toward him.

Then, squaring up to me, he said, "Twerp, what you doing, dancing with my girl?" His black eyes were hot behind rimless glasses.

Everybody on the dance floor stopped still, except for Spider. He quickly moved over to us. "What's with *you?*" he said to Bert Wriston.

Bert glanced at Spider, then back at me. "This your bodyguard or something?" Bert said to me.

Becca, Janie Marie, and everybody else on the dance floor seemed like they were frozen in place and holding their breaths. People from the booths began to crowd the entranceway to the little dance floor to watch us.

"Willie don't need no bodyguard," Spider said to Bert. "He can whup your ass with one hand tied behind his back."

Thanks a lot, cousin!

Bert glared at me. "That right, what this guy says, twerp?" Bert was half a head taller than me and outweighed me by at least thirty pounds.

I spoke up. "That's right."

What else could I have said? Becca was standing right there.

Bert snatched off his glasses and handed them to Becca. "Let's go to the alley," he said to me.

"Oh, my God! Oh, my God!" Becca said. She seemed near tears.

"Don't do it, Will," Janie Marie said, her eyes wide with fear for me.

But there was no other way. Bert and I started off the dance floor toward Joe Lammer's front door. Guys scrambled ahead of us. People parted to let us through. Bert was in front of me. Spider was, too.

Junior jumped up from the booth when I stomped by and fell into step beside me. "You're not fighting old Bert Wriston, are you?" he asked in a low voice, so nobody could hear him.

I answered the same way, out of the corner of my mouth. "No choice," I said, tromping ahead as if I could hardly wait for the brawl to get started.

"Take your time, Will," Junior said quietly.

He knew the routine, like everybody else. You didn't fight in Joe Lammer's. That'd get you permanently kicked out, maybe arrested. You and your opponent stormed out the front door, followed by a bunch of eager onlookers, all male, stalked north two doors past the Broadway Theater, turned right at the alley, then marched all the way to the back of the building to the bare gravel under the streetlight there. That's the spot where all the downtown fistfights took place. At least until Vernon's city night watchman, old Tiny Mallory, who was twice as large as his nickname and always lurking around somewhere, could hurry to the scene and break things up.

What Junior Randall meant about my slowing down on the way out of Joe Lammer's was that I should waste all the time I could, so that Tiny Mallory could get wind of things and make it to the back alley soon enough to stop the fight before it got started. Honor saved. Nobody hurt.

As we surged out Joe Lammer's front door, Junior grabbed me by the arm as if to hold me back, dissuade me from the fight. I pushed on, though moving maybe a little more slowly. Bert Wriston and the knot of guys around him were yards ahead. They disappeared around the corner of the Broadway Theater.

Junior and I and the others with us, bringing up the rear, soon turned the corner, too. Junior let go my arm. Down the alley we tramped, together.

Bert Wriston waited for me under the streetlight. I stepped up toward him and took a stance, hands on hips. The spectators made a circle around us.

Still no Tiny Mallory.

"Come on," Bert said to me, raising his fists.

"You think you're pretty tough, don't you?" I said.

"Show you *how* tough," he said, mad. "Put 'em up!"

"You can't keep a guy from dancing with a girl," I said.

"We'll see about that."

"It's her decision," I said.

"You gonna talk or fight?" Bert said, put out. "You don't get your dukes up, I'm gonna slug you anyway."

"Okay," I said. "You've got this coming." I made fists and brought them up in front of my face. Time to shit or get off the pot, as Grandpa Haley would have said.

A shrill police whistle!

Then, "Stop that! What's going on here?" Tiny Mallory had arrived, breathing hard from the rush. "Get on out of here, y'all—all of you!" he shouted in a hoarse voice.

"Now, which ones of y'all is fighting?"

Bert Wriston and I moved quickly to melt in among the onlookers. That was the way the system worked. Nobody would have thought, of course, of pointing us out to Tiny Mallory so he could arrest us for disturbing the peace.

The whole bunch of us began to straggle back toward the street, Junior and I holding back a little to let Bert Wriston get quite a bit ahead.

"You shoulda busted right into that asshole, Willie," Spider said to me. "You hadn't pretty quick, I woulda done it my ownself."

"Will'd cleaned old Bert's plow if the night watchman hadn't of shown up when he did," Junior said.

Reaching the street, Junior and I pulled aside to let Spider and everybody else go on.

"Would you have tied into old Bert, Will, if Tiny Mallory hadn't finally got there?" Junior asked me.

"You bet," I said.

I thought I would have, too. But no question I was relieved that it hadn't come to that. Glad I hadn't been beaten up or made to look too bad.

"My old Ford pick-up's over yonder, Will, front of Stewart Drygoods," Junior said. "Let's me and you drive down to the foot of the hill and buy us a couple of quarts of Falstaff from Speedy Sprague. He'll sell to me if nobody else's around."

It was 3.2 beer, of course, the highest alcoholic content that could legally be sold in prohibition Oklahoma. But drink enough of it, as Grandpa Haley would have put it, and it'd still knock you on your coon dog.

"Good idea," I said.

Chapter Four

Old Man Cofer's grain was ripe, and his field had dried up after the rain. We began cutting on his place the last Monday in May. As adventures go, the 1943 wheat harvest started out for me as a pretty hot and dusty one. I wasn't too crazy about the dirty work of helping gas and grease up the machines early each morning while we waited in the field for the dew to dry out. But that was part of the job.

I couldn't have said I loved cutting wheat on the downwind leg of a field, either. That was when the plague of combine dust and chaff blew forward and settled like an ugly cloud all over and around me on the tractor, making it hard for me to take a clean breath and chafing my neck inside my shirt collar worse than the seven-year itch.

Still, I *was* crazy about the idea of being a solid and needed member of our custom combining team. And it was most of all the idea of a moveable adventure, following the wheat harvest north like a cowboy on the old Western Trail, that I was looking forward to. Cutting wheat near home was the first stage of that trek, like the roundup before the cattle drive.

Together, my dad, stern as usual, and Jim Gruber, big and good-natured as always, explained the wheat harvest work to the first-time members of our crew. They also warned us about the dangers of fires in dry wheat fields. They said that anybody who smoked should make damned sure that their cigarettes were completely out before they threw them down. And they told us to keep a careful watch on truck and car exhausts that, running through tall wheat stubble, could set a field on fire.

Dad and Jim Gruber lined out what each of our jobs would be. Mine came as no surprise. I was to drive the Fordson tractor, of course, pulling my dad's combine. Little Jim Swyden was assigned to run that combine, and despite the fact that he was short and, unfortunately, humpbacked, he proved to be a master at the job.

I soon found that I liked working with Little Jim. He was mostly good natured. He whistled all the time—hillbilly songs. He was patient with me as I learned my job better. I didn't even hold it against the little brown man that he had a paregoric habit. I figured he needed the stuff for pain in his back or something. Several times a day, he'd pretty openly take a swig from the small dark bottle that he carried in the hip pocket of his blue overalls. I knew what paregoric was; mothers gave it to their babies when they were teething. Little Jim kept a stash of extra bottles of the stuff in the glove compartment of Big Jim's GMC pick-up and in the toolbox of our Gleaner-Baldwin combine.

I mentioned the paregoric thing to my dad one night, asked him about it. Dad said paregoric had something like morphine in it. He told me that he'd once said to Little Jim, "Why don't you just drink good bourbon whiskey? Be better for you." But Little Jim had answered, Dad said, that the paregoric kept him kind of "evened out" and feeling all right, and that he knew how to manage it. And it was true that you never saw Little Jim either over the edge or nodding off. "Each to his own," Dad said. And that's pretty much the way I felt about it, too. I didn't think of Little Jim as a "dope fiend," but more as a guy who was kind of doctoring himself.

Standing on the high front platform of our Gleaner-Baldwin, up a small ladder, Little Jim, sunup to sundown, wrestled a big metal wheel that was like a ship pilot's wheel. It faced the combine's header and was the way you raised and lowered the header and its slicing sickle according to the height of the grain you were cutting. Especially in rough or hilly fields, Little Jim had to be alert to keep the sickle skimming along high enough off the ground so that it wouldn't stab into the dirt, but low enough to stay under the wheat heads.

As a combine man, Little Jim was the commander, the captain, of his and my two-person wheat-cutting team. He used hand signs, since voice commands couldn't be heard over the tractor and combine noise. As I regularly shot glances back at him from time to time from the Fordson tractor, he twirled his forefinger in the air to signal me to speed up in thin wheat, so we could cover more ground faster. He slowly moved his palm-down hand back and forth to signal me to slow the tractor, when the wheat was thick and threatened to overload the combine and choke it down. A hand sliced across his throat meant that he wanted me to stop, when our combine's fifty-five-bushel bin, on top, was full of wheat. He could then let down the spout and unload the grain into a truck that pulled up alongside.

It was the combine man's job, too, to make adjustments to the Gleaner-Baldwin's inside cylinder and shaking sieves now and then with the combine stopped, so that when we were cutting, the fewest possible wheat kernels would get carried out the back of the machine with the chaff and straw and be lost in the stubble on the ground. Once or twice a day, he got down off the moving combine while it was running and walked behind the straw spreader to search on the ground for any sign of wasted wheat. Afterwards, he readjusted the combine if necessary.

For the other Gleaner-Baldwin, Big Jim Gruber's, Sailor was picked as the combine man. Spider was assigned the job of driving the red Farmall tractor that pulled it. Spider didn't think much of this arrangement. He didn't like Sailor being his boss, even though the two of them got paid the same wage of seven dollars a day when we worked.

"Emmett wouldn't even've been here, I hadn't asked him to come with me," Spider said resentfully to me that first day when we were alone, gassing up our tractors. Dad and Jim Gruber qualified for work-related "C" gasoline rationing windshield stickers and stamps. They bought fuel in bulk quantities and stored it in two fifty-five-gallon barrels with a rotary pump, loaded in the back of Big Jim's GMC pick-up. "Now I'm sup-posed to let Emmett order me around, tell me what to do?" the skinny cousin said, rubbing his thin blond moustache with thumb and finger. "Bull hockey!"

Spider'd taken pains to avoid anything else happening like his first-day confrontation with Little Jim. But he certainly wouldn't have wanted to switch tractors and work in my place under Little Jim. Still, he clearly hated being commanded by Sailor. The fact was, though, that my dad'd apparently seen more in Sailor right away than he'd seen in Spider, that he placed more confidence in Sailor's judgment. And this was the cause of a souring feeling that Spider began to develop toward the Mississippi cousin who'd driven him to Oklahoma.

Spider hadn't helped himself in my dad's estimation by the way he'd roaded Big Jim Gruber's combine on our first day. When he and I crawled on our tractors and pulled our Gleaner-Baldwins from Vernon out to Jack Cofer's place, three miles west and two south of town, Spider'd driven too fast for safety. The fairly new Farmall had a fourth, road gear on it, which, of course, my old Fordson didn't, and Spider soon way outran me once we were through Vernon to the Comanche highway. He stood up out of his tractor's seat, John Deere cap turned around backwards, aviator glasses masking his eyes, and took off like a scalded dog at maybe fifteen miles an hour. Dad'd seen this. He'd also seen, as I had, too, before Spider got out of my sight that morning, an instance when Spider, in pulling over for an oncoming car without slowing, swerved danger-ously to the right toward the bar ditch before he was finally able to straighten up again and speed on.

Spider made it to Old Man Cofer's field that first day with-out crashing—and a good while ahead of me, with my terrapin pace. Still, my dad and Jim Gruber waited for me to start the cutting. Turned out they trusted me more than Spider to open the new field, and that's the way it was to be all the rest of the summer. Commencing a new field, I made the first round clockwise, my tractor and our combine running in the wheat, the header pointed toward the field's outside fence, cutting a swath right up against it. You had to have a good eye and steady hands to clip the last possible stalk of wheat along the fence without disastrously snagging the end of the header on the wires or posts. It made me feel good to get to be the field opener.

And I thought I did a good job at it, too. But I stopped the tractor after the first round at Jack Cofer's so Little Jim could get down and adjust the combine's sieve. And my dad, walking past the tractor toward the back of the Gleaner-Baldwin, said to me as he passed, "Willie, you damned near hit the corner post on that first turn." It seemed to me that my dad would have sooner given me a raise in pay than a compliment.

In a new field like Cofer's, Spider and Sailor always made the second round, counterclockwise. The wheels of their tractor and combine ran not in the wheat, but in the stubble that I'd left, their combine's header pointed away from the fence and out into the grain. I would turn around and follow them, and the two tractor-combine teams would cut away, round and counter-clockwise round. The uncut square of wheat would slowly dwindle down until it finally disappeared altogether, leaving only stubble from fence to fence. That gave you a feeling that you'd accomplished something. Then we would move on to another field, which gave us a brief break from the monotonous routine of combining.

At first, our six-man custom combining crew was short-handed. We needed another two-hundred-bushel grain truck and a driver, and they weren't that easy to find with the war on. Able-bodied men were away in the service, and factories were turning out very little new farm equipment and no new civilian trucks. In our combine bunch, my dad drove his own grain truck, of course, the black '41 Chevy, and Jim Gruber drove his, a blue, '40 Ford. But in pretty good wheat—say, twenty-five bushels to the acre, which was about what Old Man Cofer's wheat was making—two trucks couldn't keep up with two twelve-foot combines like ours. This was especially true when there were long lines of trucks waiting to unload at the grain elevator, delaying them getting back to the field.

You never wanted the combines to have to stop cutting and wait for a truck so they could empty their full bins. You lost money that way. Jim Gruber liked to say, "Let's roll, boys!

Even if one of them combines breaks down, crawl on the biggest piece and keep on cutting!" And farmers didn't like it if you temporarily had to dump their wheat on the ground to be scooped up later.

Dad found our third truck and driver on the day he hauled the first load of the Cofer wheat to the Farmers Co-op Elevator, which sat alongside the highway at the northwest edge of Vernon. And he got us a harvest cook, to boot. Forty-something wrestler-looking Burford Wynn—Dad dropped the *r* and called him "Buford," and soon, so did we—and Bonnie, Buford's young wife, with bleached blonde hair and Betty Boop lips. They were from Meade, Kansas, and had arrived in Vernon only a couple of nights earlier, we learned, parking their little homemade plywood house trailer in the grain elevator's graveled lot. The two of them were sitting there in Buford's orange '39 Dodge truck, hoping for work, when my dad saw them and the hand-lettered sign in their truck windshield that read "Wheat Hauling Wanted."

The deal that Dad made with the Kansas pair was that Buford and Bonnie would go with us all the way north. Buford would get the same half-cent a bushel for hauling wheat to the grain elevator that my dad and Jim Gruber got, and, after we left Vernon Bonnie would cook dinner and supper every day for our whole crew—we'd make our own breakfasts—and get paid four dollars a day, plus grocery expenses.

I was pretty happy when I found out that Dad'd hired a cook. He wasn't the kind to worry much about eating, especially the noon meal. Often in the past when he and I were working together—dehorning, branding, and cutting calves, say—and the sun got straight up overhead, I'd have to remind him that it was time to eat dinner. And still, it might be another hour before he'd get around to finally driving into town to Calloway's Grocery. And even then, he was liable to come back with only a loaf of sliced light bread, two or three small cans of Vienna sausage—he called it "Vy-eena" sausage—and a chunk of yellow cheese that we'd have to cut up with his pocketknife. I was glad that, with Bonnie Wynn, we'd be able to count on having real, and on time, wheat harvest dinners and suppers.

60

Besides, the young woman seemed to me like a sweet and nice person. Pretty, too, and kind of full up front in the cotton print dresses she wore. Bonnie's appearance was probably the reason Mama didn't think much of our new cook as a person.

I loved Mama to pieces, but she had her human failings like everybody else. Her overboard jealousy about my dad was one of those faults. Another, I thought, was how critical she always was of what she called "fast" young women, especially any girl who, as Mama put it, "got herself in trouble"—that is, got pregnant without being married. As if the girl did this by herself without any help! Of course, Mama wasn't alone in these mean sentiments. All the women in Vernon were equally critical.

Two years earlier, the local banker's unmarried daughter was ruined and had to leave town when she got pregnant. And not long afterwards, when it was gossiped that another Vernon girl, also single, had gone off to Oklahoma City to have an abortion, that girl was seen by Vernon women, including Mama, as having committed *two* unforgivable sins. She was also promptly more or less run out of town. Any time Mama and the other women heard about a local girl having a baby in less than a year after getting married, they immediately started counting backwards nine months on their fingers, suspicious that the child had been conceived before the wedding ceremony.

In the two and a half weeks that we were cutting wheat around Vernon, Mama never had anything to do with Bonnie Wynn, though you couldn't have said that she was outright hateful to her. Just ignored her. The real problem, I was sure, was that Mama was afraid the young woman would prove to be a temptation for Dad while we were away on the harvest. But what Mama actually said to me and my dad, soon after she met Bonnie for the first time, was "That girl's no better than she should be!" To Mama, that was about as bad a thing as you could say.

But most of our combine bunch didn't actually see much of Bonnie, ourselves, until after we'd left Vernon. She camped all day in the little house trailer, still parked in the Vernon

61

grain elevator's lot. And she sometimes went to sit in the truck with Buford after bringing him his meals there while he waited in the long line of trucks at the elevator to get his wheat unloaded.

She later told me that each time Buford finally weighed up and drove inside the elevator, then got out to wait for his receipt, wearing the flattop khaki chauffeur hat with the shiny black visor that he seemed pretty proud of, she herself would stay in the truck cab. She liked it, she said, when the elevator lifted the front end of the truck, with her in it, high in the air so that the wheat could run out the open tailgate and down into the pit from where it would be augured up into the tall metal granary. "It's kinda like getting to go on a free ride at the carnival," Bonnie said in that flat Kansas accent of hers. I decided that, when they were first going together, she must have been a pretty cheap date for Buford. It didn't take a whole lot to keep her entertained.

"No atheists in a foxhole" was a popular American saying after the start of World War II. I figured that the same sentiment probably applied to wheat farmers, too. I especially thought this after I put in my own first wheat crop. So much could go wrong—stuff like the weather that you had no control over. Most wheat farmers around Vernon and throughout the Great Plains—that wide, north-south trough, stretching from Canada down to Texas and bounded on the west by the Rocky Mountains and on the east by the woodlands—had turned, years before, almost totally to hard red winter wheat instead of spring wheat. The seed first came from Turkey or Russia, or some place like that, and it adapted well to the climate of the Great Plains. In southwest Oklahoma, you plowed—with a rowed-disc "one-way" or a deep plow-shared "moldboard"—and harrowed your ground by late August, then drilled your wheat in by early September. If moisture was plentiful—and no doubt a special lot of prayers went up for rain at that time of year—you got an ample stand of rowed, deep green wheat shoots before winter came on. With a good enough stand, you might have some fall wheat pasture for your own cattle or to rent out to some other cattle owner.

When spring warmed up the ground, the wheat shoots would sprout higher, looking like green bristles on a brush. The wheat "stooled," as farmers put it, spread out, and began to grow upward until the field was covered like a thick green blanket. That was the hope, at least, and it meant good spring pasture. Cattle cropping the wheat down didn't hurt it—maybe even helped it. You took your cattle off, though, when the spring rains began—and you prayed the rains *would* begin. Of course, if the spring rains didn't come when they were supposed to, your wheat might turn out to be yellowish-green, thin, and stunted short, sometimes winding up not even worth cutting.

You needed plenty of moisture, again, after the wheat headed out, but was still in what people called the "milk" stage, the grains soft and not yet hardened in their husks. You hoped, maybe prayed, that not too much wild cheat grass would come up with the wheat. Cheat seeds mixing in with the harvested wheat kernels could lower the test, and the price, when you hauled the wheat off to sell it at the grain elevator. You hoped that your wheat in the field didn't get infected with rust. That could ruin the whole crop altogether. You also prayed that, about the time the wheat was getting ripe, there wouldn't come a thunderstorm with driving rain and winds that would flatten the wheat stalks so low that the combine's reel bats and sickle couldn't pick up the heads for harvesting, or that a bad hailstorm wouldn't hammer the wheat irretrievably into the mud.

During that last-of-May and early-June 1943 wheat harvest in Cash County, Oklahoma, there were only two rains in the areas where we ourselves were cutting. No hailstorms and no tornados. Other places in the county did have some of those troubles, or all of them. Like the bottomland fields north of Vernon, near the south side of East Cash Creek. Some farmers there saw their rich forty-bushel wheat totally ruined by flooding rains, high winds, and heavy hail. We ourselves, cutting wheat farther south in the county, were luckier. The two times it did rain on us, it didn't come a gully washer, as people put it, and we were able to get back to our cutting by noon on the next day.

Southwest Oklahoma *was* tornado country, no question about that. So was the whole Great Plains area. But no tornados—my dad called them "cyclones"—hit anywhere close to us while we were cutting around Vernon that summer. Two funnels did touch down in another part of the county during that time, one causing no damage, the other tragically killing an elderly Comanche Indian farm woman, Old Lady Lucy, and throwing her grandson and my high school classmate, Tony Timbo, across a road, miraculously unhurt. But my family and I were ourselves never really threatened, although my dad insisted that we all spend an hour or so on two different stormy nights in our concrete storm cellar, built into the ground right behind our house, as was typical in Vernon.

Dad and Jim Gruber and our bunch had a good Oklahoma wheat harvest run that year. Couldn't have been much better. I saved a little money from my wages. I made some money, too, on my own wheat. After we finished cutting Old Man Cofer's wheat and before moving on to another farmer, we pulled two miles farther south and cut out mine and Dad's crops. My twenty acres yielded close to twenty bushels to the acre. Not bad. Our landlord, Bill Wishard, got his third. My part I decided to go ahead and sell at $1.50 a bushel, which I thought was a good price, rather than store it as some farmers were doing, hoping the price would go up. From my Farmers Co-op Elevator check, I paid Dad and Big Jim the customary two dollars and a quarter an acre for cutting and the half-cent a bushel for hauling. Figuring in my earlier expenses for seed and for plowing and sowing, that netted me a little over three hundred dollars from my wheat operation. I salted the money away in my checking account at the First State Bank.

It was the start of my college fund. I'd already decided that I wanted to be a lawyer, an ambition that my friend Junior had tried to talk me out of. He wanted us to go into cattle raising together and a little farming after we both got out of high school—and, of course, after we got out of the service, if the war lasted that long. But I thought there surely must be a better and more interesting life waiting out there for me than that. I wanted to amount to something. I wanted to help people. I wanted to go places and see things.

I'd met a lawyer in Vernon, and I looked up to him. Dad knew the man, Tom Hough, and had had some business with him. Hough was always dressed in a suit and tie, he'd twice been elected state representative from our county, and he seemed like a substantial citizen to me. He'd fought for the Comanche Indian tribe and its members, who lived in Cash County. Helped them get some land back that had been wrongfully taken. Helped them get more money for land that they couldn't get back. I thought it wouldn't be bad to be like Tom Hough.

I'd once embarrassed Dad about the man, though. We'd run into Hough on Vernon's Main Street, right in front of his law office. He and Dad talked for a minute. Then, as we were about to break up and go on our separate ways, I said something to him that I intended to be complimentary. To my mind, Tom Hough, with his "fiddler's haircut," as people called it, hair chopped off square in back, was pretty old. He was probably about fifty.

"Mr. Hough, I don't know how you keep looking so young," I said to the lawyer. "You don't have a gray hair in your head!"

He seemed a little startled before he quickly thanked me and then turned and walked on. Dad could hardly wait until we were out of the man's hearing before he said to me, "Jesus Christ, Willie, everybody in Vernon knows that Tom Hough dyes his hair!"

Well, *I* didn't.

Dad always prided himself on never letting liquor interfere with his "tending to business," as he put it. That was a matter of honor with him. And he didn't have much use for anybody who drank so much on the job and got in such bad shape that it affected the way he did his job. But even off work that summer, Dad didn't go on any more bad drunks while we were cutting around Vernon. He and Mama got along tolerably well with each other.

My darling sister, Janie Marie, and the lean, yellow-haired cousin, Spider Deering, saw too much of each other. At least, that's what I thought. Spider also got to where he wasn't speaking to Sailor Torley. Or if Spider did answer some question from Sailor, it was only in a hateful or smart-alecky way.

Sailor got me going on the Charles Atlas system of "dynamic tension." I could work my muscles against each other even while driving the Fordson tractor. And when we had a little extra time to kill after gassing and greasing up in the field each day and before the dew dried out, Sailor also got me to join him in some calisthenics, like I'd done in football practice. Sometimes we jogged together around the wheat field in our heavy work shoes. Sailor'd first tightly wrap a homemade bandage, a long strip of cloth, around his hurt left knee, on the outside of his blue bellbottoms. With all our workouts, I imagined that I could feel my body beginning to build up some. I thought that I was even growing a little. And because of Sailor, I began to get a lot better about not using the word "can't"—about not thinking "can't."

One afternoon, when a rain shower sent us home early from the field and we were not too tired out from work, I was able to take Sailor with me to meet some local Indians. He'd been wanting to do that. Kent Coffee, a Comanche Indian and a high school classmate of mine, had earlier invited me to come out that Wednesday evening to his folks' house, south of Vernon on East Cash Creek, for a birthday party for a cousin of his, a girl named Marcy Redelk. She'd lately moved in with the Coffees. When I told Sailor that the party would probably be a kind of powwow with Comanche Indian singing and dancing, he was especially interested in going.

He and I bathed and put on clean clothes, including new cowboy boots and straw cowboy hats, blocked bulldogger style, that we'd both lately bought with some of our first wages.

Then, about dark, Sailor and I drove off in his old Plymouth, the Green Lizard, Sailor at the wheel, east to the edge of town and then two miles south. The rain had cooled things off some. Kent Coffee's folks' barbed-wire gate was open. Sailor and I turned east through it, toward the creek. We drove two hundred yards down a rutted pasture road, passing among scattered low mesquites on the way.

The Coffee home was a government-built one-story frame house, painted green, with two big junipers in front of its west-facing porch. As we got near it, we heard through our open car windows the rhythmic booming of a big drum in back of the house and high-pitched Comanche voices in the distance, singing as a group in time to the beat. It was pretty thrilling.

"Man, Will!" Sailor said as he pulled in and parked among a dozen or so other cars at the side of the house. "We amongst the Comanches now!"

My classmate Ken, a brown welterweight with a boxer's lean, hard body, saw us when we got out of the Green Lizard and came to meet us. I introduced Sailor to him. The three of us walked together toward the party.

At the back of the house, two older Comanche women stood behind a food table, and a couple of others tended a small mound of glowing coals with a big black coffee pot sitting on them. The older women wore long, traditional-looking cotton dresses with butterfly sleeves, their hair in braids. A bonfire blazed under some giant native pecan trees a little way toward the creek. Close to the fire, a round dance was in progress. Two tight concentric circles of about thirty men and women, their arms linked, shuffled in time to the left, orbiting a big drum that five seated Indian men in big hats and long braids were vigorously flogging with padded drumsticks. The voices of the drummers and the dancers were joined together in piercing chant-singing. Sailor caught my eye, and I could tell that he was getting worked up by the spectacle and the exotic rhythm and beat. I felt the same way.

The song and dance abruptly ended, exactly on one last simultaneous set of drum blows. The air went still for a moment. Then, talking and laughing, the dancers began to disperse temporarily, some of them to scattered kitchen chairs set up on the ground, others to the hot coffee. Marcy Redelk and Kent's considerably older sister, Zona, came over to be introduced. Sailor and I shook hands with the two of them.

"Still a little to eat, y'all," Marcy said to us, smiling warmly. Tall and intriguing, she had tan skin and long dark hair, plaited in two red-ribbon-wrapped braids. Her eyes were a discordant green. She had a fringed black shawl around her shoulders and, under a long gray skirt, wore black stockings and beaded, long-fringed Comanche moccasins. She took in Sailor's and my new cowboy boots and straw hats and said, "Now that you guys are here, we'll make this a *cowboy* and Indian party."

Zona Coffee, pretty as Marcy Redelk, though not as tall and a little darker and plumper, led the way as we all turned toward the food table. The two women and Kent waited while Sailor and I loaded our plates with mortar-pounded dried beef the Comanches called *taw-aw*, red beans, and a boiled beef and potato stew. We all found chairs and sat, Marcy and I slightly apart, as it turned out, from the other three. Sailor and I started eating. He was hunched to the side, toward Kent and Zona, and was more animated in talking to them than I'd ever seen him. You could tell he was in hog heaven, as people said, and I thought he soon appeared to be especially intent on Zona, too.

I leaned toward Marcy. Between bites I said, "Sorry I didn't bring you a birthday present."

Marcy laughed. "Silly, at an Indian party, with us *nuhmenuh*, us Comanches, you *get* something, not give it," she said. "We're not like you *taivos*, you white people."

"How come you've got green eyes?" I asked her. It was kind of a rude question.

She didn't seem to take offense. "Part white myself," she said. "My dad was an Irish guy, long time out of the family picture now. He couldn't take too much of us Indians, I guess. My Comanche mother works for the Indian Agency, up at Anadarko. That's where I've been living, too, until mother up and married a local Kiowa guy and then shipped me back here to live with Uncle Fred and Aunt Julia."

"Going to go to school next September, where?" I asked.

"With you, here at Vernon—and I'm in your same grade," she said. "Kent tells me you were the tenth grade class president." She stuck out her hand teasingly. "Glad to know you, Mr. President." We shook hands for the second time.

"Kent didn't tell me much about you, but I'm glad me and my cousin came out here," I said.

Sudden loud blows to the big drum interrupted us. "Come on," Marcy said to me. We got up like everybody else and moved toward Marcy's uncle, Fred Coffee, who stood next to the drummers with a couple of open cardboard boxes at his feet. He was wearing a blue ribbon shirt, buttoned tightly over a big stomach. Long graying braids hung down from inside his unblocked white hat. His brown face was completely hairless. I knew that older Comanche men plucked out their naturally sparse whiskers, even their eyelashes and eyebrows. Fred Coffee began to speak in Comanche. Marcy quietly translated for me and Sailor, who was right next to me.

"My uncle says it makes him feel good that his sister's daughter has come back home, and he and his wife are going to honor her—meaning me—with a 'giveaway,'" Marcy said.

Coffee motioned his wife, Julia, and Marcy over to his side. Then he began to call out, one by one, the names of several people in the crowd. When a person came forward, Coffee reached down into one of the cardboard boxes at his feet, brought out a blanket or a shawl, depending on whether the person was a man or a woman, and handed the gift to his wife and niece to present. Each time, Marcy and her aunt unfolded the blanket or shawl and wrapped it around the shoulders of the recipient, finishing with a hug or a handshake. And this caused the drummers to hit the big drum with several unsynchronized blows—a kind of applause, I took it.

The giveaway ceremony ended, and Marcy's uncle began to speak to the crowd in Comanche again.

"He says he wants everyone to join in a 'forty-nine' now. It's what's called a war-journey song," Marcy translated. "My uncle composed this one just for me."

Fred Coffee asked Marcy to join him, then turned toward the drum. She grabbed my hand. "Come on, y'all," she said.

I went along with her. Zona, Sailor, and Kent followed right behind us. The rest of the crowd moved in, too.

Marcy linked herself up with her uncle's right arm and my left. With others, we made a close circle around the drum, facing inward. A second circle formed around us, pressed in tight. The drummers began a pounding beat.

Marcy's uncle started a Comanche song in a high-pitched voice, and, simultaneously with the first sound out of his mouth, stepped off to his left. Marcy and I and all the rest in our circle followed in unison, keeping time to the drumbeat. The outer ring of dancers behind us stepped off, too. We all moved perfectly together. When Coffee finished his song's introductory phrase and began its repetition, the drummers and all the Comanche men and women dancers suddenly raised their voices, too, to join in with him. They seemed already to know the strange song by heart.

Dark settled around us. The bright flames of the bonfire nearer the house illuminated our faces and the tall trees beyond us. The two close rings of dancers swayed slightly back after each leftward step, then shuffled left again, arm in arm, pulsing as if one big living thing. The thirty-some voices rang out together. The echoing drumbeats were like our own heartbeats. I soon felt almost like I was in a trance.

That particular song—Marcy's song—and that dance ended, but a different one started at once, and after that, another. Somewhere in the middle of each song and dance, there always came a sort of goose bumps point when the drummers raised their waving sticks above their heads, not hitting the drum, while the singing continued on, with only the swish-swish and low stamp-stamp of the many feet to mark the beat. Then the heavy drumming would begin again, as the song rushed on to a cold-chills final note.

A couple of the war-journey songs had some Comanche words in them, and these Marcy translated into my left ear as we danced. "See those white buffalo bones over there," one song's words went. "Soon you and I are going to be like that. So don't think anything of it if I get a little familiar, because, onc of these days, you and I are going to be like that." She laughed a little between the translated sentences.

The drum finally went silent. The dancing and the gathering were over. The crowd began to break up. Marcy, Kent, and Zona took me and Sailor to shake hands with Fred and Julia Coffee and, afterwards, walked us to the Green Lizard.

"I liked that song about the white buffalo bones," I said to Marcy before getting into the car.

She leaned in quickly and gave me a little kiss on the cheek. "See you in school, I guess," she said.

"Maybe sooner," I said.

Later, heading home, Sailor looked over at me and said, "You didn't get the sweet ass did you, Will?"

"What about yourself?" I said.

"Something for me to write home to Mississippi about, son," Sailor said. "'Gone out west and almost got captured by the Comanches!'"

Our custom combine crew cut wheat in Cash County every day for two and a half weeks, including two Sundays. And each Sunday we worked, Grandma Haley, as we all expected, let Dad know of her disapproval as soon as she saw we were getting ready to go to the field.

"You oughtn't to work on the Lord's Day, son," she told Dad both times.

Dad's response was always the same. "The ox is in the ditch, Ma," he said.

But even though I knew in advance when we were planning to work on a Sunday, I went down to Joe Lammer's the night before anyway. On the first Saturday night, which was ahead of Marcy Redelk's birthday party, I hooked up with my friend, Junior as usual. Rebecca Milton wasn't around, of course. She was still off at the Turner Falls church camp. I missed her, hated not to see her. Becca's "mature" boyfriend, old Bert Wriston, wasn't around, either. I was glad of that. He'd left for San Diego and the navy. A lot of other people were out of town, too, for one reason or another. Joe Lammer's was a little slow.

With Don Milford, another high school friend, Junior and I drove in Junior's old '35 Ford pick-up down to Speedy Sprague's store at the foot of the hill. Don and I sat outside, and Junior, after waiting until no other customer was around, went in and bought us three big quart bottles of 3.2 Falstaff beer—"Fall Stiff," Junior called it. We pulled into an alley, up the hill a ways, and chugalugged the beer and shot the bull for a while. Finally Junior had an idea for something else to do. His mother and daddy were over in Chickasha, visiting kinfolks.

"Let's go out to my place and rope calves, you guys," Junior said.

"In the dark?" I asked.

"Not off of horses," Junior said. "Off my pick-up, here, with the headlights on. One guy drives, other two sit on the front fenders with a leg under the headlight and snag them little boogers. What do you say?"

"You ever done that before?" I asked.

"Naw," Junior said, "but if we try it tonight, next time we can say we're *experienced* pick-up ropers."

"Okay," I said.

Sounded to me like something to do, all right. Don thought so, too. We took off for Junior's place, east of town. There we first stopped at the barn and grabbed up a couple of lariat ropes, then drove on down the road toward his dad's hilly pasture.

"You ever think about whether it hurts the calves, roping them?" I asked Junior.

"Naw, Will, they like it," Junior said.

"Like it?"

"Sure, breaks the monotony for 'em, keeps 'em from getting bored to death," Junior said.

We stopped at the wire gate into the pasture. Don and I jumped out and opened it. Junior drove through, then got out of the pick-up with his rope. I closed the gate.

Back in the headlight beams with the other two, I said, "I'm no good at roping, myself."

All three of us had entered the FFA rodeo in Vernon the preceding spring. My events were bull riding and saddle broncs. I hadn't done worth a damn with the bulls, which were all pretty rank, but I'd placed second in the bronc riding.

"You drive then, Will," Junior said. He'd won first prize in calf roping at the FFA rodeo. Don had roped, too, but hadn't placed.

Each of those two tied an end of his lariat to the pick-up's front bumper, then got on a fender and, to keep his seat, wedged a leg under one of the headlights, which on that '35 Ford were like eyeballs on stems. I went around and scooted in on the driver's side. Off we rolled, then, until our pick-up lights found the cattle, bedded down in a corner of the pasture. As we got closer, the herd jumped up scared and began to scatter in a run.

Managing the fast little pick-up like it was a nimble cutting horse, I picked out a roan stocker calf on Junior's side, and we careened after it through the rolling short grass. The calf cut left, I cut left. He cut right, I cut right. I mashed the foot-feed to the floor, and we closed on him. Junior swung his loop and dropped it right around the calf's neck on the first throw. The calf was caught, but for a moment didn't know it. I hit the pick-up's brakes. The vehicle skidded to a sudden stop, like a cutting horse sitting down on his back legs, tightening the rope and jerking the calf to a flipping halt in the grass. Junior was off the fender before the calf totally hit the ground. He ran along the rope. The calf struggled back up to his feet. Junior quickly flanked him down and kneeled on him, grabbed a front leg, then went through the pantomime of tying up three feet with a pigging string that he playlike took from between his teeth. At the end, he stood and threw his hands up in the air to stop a make-believe rodeo timer. Don and I whistled and clapped.

Junior let the calf go, and it trotted away, seemingly fine. I took off and soon found another, this one Don's. His loop missed the first time. I stopped the pick-up. Don dragged his rope back and began to re-coil it as Junior yelled out the rodeo announcer's familiar words from his front fender seat: "Don

Milford's time is '*no* time.' All he gets is your applause, folks."
Junior and I applauded.

Don had good luck with his next calf. Junior, too, with his.
We stayed at it for an hour or more before we finally wore out
and quit, then Junior drove me and Don back to town. I didn't
slip into the back door of my room and crawl into the top
bunk bed until after midnight. But when I did, I found it odd
that the lower bunk bed was empty. Spider was still out. I
hoped it wasn't with my sister Janie Marie.

The next morning it was hard for me to get up when my
dad banged on my door before daylight. Hard for Spider, too,
who'd come in after I was asleep. After a quick breakfast,
Sailor and I, as usual, rode to the field in the back of Dad's
truck. Spider, as always, jumped into the cab with my dad. In
back, I curled up in a corner of the truckbed and grabbed a
little more sleep. Working that day, Little Jim several times
had to throw a handful of wheat at me to wake me up, when
I dozed off on the Fordson tractor and let the combine's
header drift too far into the wheat or too far out of it. I didn't
know how Spider got along.

The next Saturday night, a week later—this was after
Marcy Redelk's party—Sailor drove out to Marcy's uncle's
house in the Green Lizard to pick up Zona Coffee, and the
two of them, on a date he'd arranged by telephone, went
together up to Lawton to go dancing at an illegal nightclub
there. I walked down to Joe Lammer's, as always. So did Janie
Marie and Spider. Junior was at Joe Lammer's, of course.
Marcy Redelk was, too. She and her cousin, Kent, were in a
front booth. I got Junior to follow along, and we scooted in
with them.

Marcy seemed as glad to see me as I was to see her. Junior's
and my friend, Don Milford, soon joined the four of us in the
booth. But I must have pissed Junior off, paying so much
attention to Marcy and not to him. He and Don got up after
a little while, Junior saying that they were going to go down
to the foot of the hill. The two of them left, but not before
Junior muttered to Don, loud enough for me to hear, "Sweet
ass'll ruin a guy sooner'n rabies."

I didn't think I had the sweet ass, unless it was for Rebecca Milton. But what was the harm in spending some time with Marcy Redelk?

She and I and Kent wound up going to that night's movie at the Broadway Theater. It was a Ginger Rogers and Fred Astaire picture with a lot of dancing that I didn't much care for. But it was something to do—and it allowed me to sit next to Marcy. I bought the popcorn.

When the picture show was over, I suggested that we stay around for the midnight "preview," as it was called in Vernon, even though it wasn't a preshowing of anything. Kent didn't much want to, but Marcy coaxed him, and he gave in. He was her ride. We bought new tickets and went back in when they opened the doors of the Broadway Theater again.

The midnight preview, as nearly always, was a scary movie. This time—*The Mummy's Tomb*. Marcy and I sat fairly close together, and, toward the end, I ventured to put my arm around her shoulders. Afterwards, out on the street, she gave me a peck on the cheek when I put her in Kent's car.

I walked home alone. And a time or two on the way, I even got the feeling that I could hear the mummy himself, dragging his bad leg back behind me somewhere on the dark sidewalk. But I would have died before admitting that to anybody, admitting that I was ever scared of the dark. I wasn't as open about this as my uncle Wayne would have been. He always said, "I'm not afraid of the dark; I'm afraid of what might be *in* the dark."

Getting up the next morning wasn't any easier than it had been the Sunday before. Not for me and not for Spider Deering, who'd again stayed out late—this time, I learned for sure, with Janie Marie. Again for me, staying awake on the tractor that day, especially during the hot afternoon, was a hard chore.

We finished cutting wheat in Cash County on a mid-June Thursday afternoon. We could have left town the next morning, but my dad was superstitious about moving on Friday. "Never move or start anything on a Friday," he always said. I never understood why. "Bad luck," was the only reason he ever gave. Grandma Haley felt the same way about Fridays that my dad did. Her reason was that that was the day of the week that Jesus was crucified. Not much of an explanation for the superstition, I thought.

We pulled our combines into Vernon and parked them on the vacant lot just east of our house. That gave us all day Friday to get loaded up and ready to go. We took the headers off of each of the two combines and loaded them onto their own little rubber-tired trailers. First Dad, then Jim Gruber, backed their trucks down into the ditch at the side of the vacant lot. We removed the truck sideboards and tailgates, laid down a couple of bridge timber planks, then drove the tractors up onto the truckbeds and securely boomer-chained them down. Afterwards, we slid the sideboards, tailgates, and planks in under the tractors, between the wheels. Finally, we hooked a combine, with the front fifth wheel lifted off the ground and made rigid, behind each truck, then a header trailer behind each combine.

I got more and more excited as the loading process continued—excited about finally being about to hit the harvest trail.

We put a lot of bedding, suitcases, and personal things in cardboard boxes, securely covered with a tarp, in the back of the gray GMC pick-up, behind the gas barrels, oil and grease cans and buckets, spare parts, and water can. Sailor and I stowed our own stuff in the trunk of his green '37 Plymouth. I threw my .22 rifle in there, too. My dad told me to. He was taking his and said we might shoot some rabbits, or even pheasants, up the way north somewhere.

About dark, Buford and Bonnie came. Buford pulled their truck and house trailer onto the vacant lot, next to the other vehicles, so we'd all be ready to take off the first thing Saturday morning.

The plan was that we'd actually start our northward harvest trek that year by first heading *west*. We could have, instead, trailed directly up north toward Enid, near the Oklahoma-Kansas border, and after that, moved on into Kansas. Junior and the neighbor guy he worked for were going to do that, the same as they'd done the summer before. But Dad and Jim Gruber'd learned that the wheat around Enid was going to be late getting ready. So rather than sitting idle in Vernon, waiting for the Enid wheat to ripen, Dad and Big Jim'd decided to head out west to the Texas plains first, "up on the Caprocks," as they put it, to the town of Dimmitt, south of Amarillo. Jim Gruber had cut maize around there the preceding fall. On the telephone with the Gleaner-Baldwin dealer in Dimmitt, Big Jim'd found out that the Dimmitt wheat crop looked pretty good and was just about ready for combining. He'd also found out that custom combiners were scarce out there.

Junior came by my folks' house that Friday night to say good-bye to me. I reported to him that, after Dimmitt, our bunch would probably cut a little around Boise City in the Oklahoma panhandle before going on up to Limon in eastern Colorado. That was what Dad had told me. Junior and I thought it would be great for the two of us to meet up, around Limon, if he could manage to get off work and come over there from Kansas. So we made that plan before we split up.

Early Saturday morning, my whole family walked over to the vacant lot to see us off. All except the twins, Mollie and Millie, who were still in bed. But we'd said good-bye to them the night before. Mama and Dad didn't hug. Things were still a little strained between them. She just patted him on the shoulder and said, "Mind your p's and q's, now, Bob." Then she hugged me.

Janie Marie hugged me, too. And she was crying. But I knew that that wasn't the first time she'd cried that morning. Earlier, going around to the back of the house to get a T-shirt of mine that Mama'd hung out to dry on the clothesline there, I'd unexpectedly surprised tiny Janie Marie and gangly Spider Deering in an intimate huddle. They'd quickly moved apart, and she'd tried to turn away so I wouldn't see her tears. I just said "hi" to them, grabbed my T-shirt, and left. But before I turned the corner of the house, I glanced back and saw that they were close together again. Janie Marie was crying and talking to Spider in a low voice.

The whole thing worried me and made me feel bad for a while, but then renewed excitement about finally taking off on the harvest soon perked me up.

At the edge of the vacant lot, the final words to our bunch that Saturday morning were Grandma Haley's. "I'll be praying for the Lord to keep y'all all in his care and bring you back home safe," she said.

A prayer that couldn't hurt.

Chapter Five

"Off like a herd of turtles!" Sailor Torley said. We all went and climbed aboard our various vehicles and cranked up.

Big Jim Gruber would ride point in his blue '40 Ford truck that carried the red Farmall tractor on its back and dragged behind it his Gleaner-Baldwin combine and, behind that, the header trailer. He'd earlier said good-bye to his wife, Earnestine, before he'd left their house, across the alley. Big Jim had no children, even though he'd been married twice. Earnestine was his second wife. I knew that much. I knew he'd been married before, but for some reason nobody wanted to talk about that or about what'd happened to his first wife. The whole business was kind of off limits.

Dad went second in line in his black '41 Chevy, with the faded blue Fordson squatting in the truckbed, the combine and header trailer snaking out to the rear. Spider rode in the truck cab with Dad.

Little Jim Swyden, in Big Jim's gray GMC pick-up, was slow getting underway after taking time to be sure that his tarp in back was well tied down. So Sailor and I, in Sailor's car—the Green Lizard, which he'd promised to let me drive, some—pulled in to follow right after Dad. Then came Little Jim in the pick-up. Finally, Buford and Bonnie brought up the rear—riding in the drag, as they said in the old cattle drives—in the orange '39 Dodge truck, pulling their little homemade house trailer, our version of a cattle drive chuck wagon.

The long caravan eased north, down to the foot of the hill, to the highway. We turned west, toward Frederick, and were strung out for nearly a mile on the narrow concrete strip of State Highway 5 by the time we passed the Vernon cemetery on the outskirts of town.

With the war on, the government had lowered the maximum highway speed limit to thirty-five miles an hour, and Jim Gruber, setting the pace for us and looking like he was pulling a short train, had no trouble staying within that thirty-five-mile limit. Our other drivers matched their speed to his. Still, it wasn't long before we crossed over West Cash Creek and left Cash County, not expecting to see it again for close to three months.

The sky was clear except for some fluffy-topped, flat-bottomed white clouds on the far western horizon. We ginned along through familiar rolling grasslands, with mesquites in the draws and low places, fields of cut-out wheat stubble not yet plowed under, and furrowed ground newly planted to cotton for late fall and winter picking.

After not quite an hour of travel, just past the little off-the-highway town of Grandfield, Sailor suddenly veered from the concrete strip and braked to a stop on the gravel shoulder in front of an Oklahoma historical marker. He motioned out the window for Little Jim, then Buford and Bonnie, to go on ahead, and the two vehicles whizzed past us.

In 1905, Theodore Roosevelt, the marker read, had come there to what was then the lush grass prairie of the "Big Pasture"—a part of the Comanche Indian reservation in that area before it was broken up—to hunt wolves with Comanche chief Quanah Parker.

"I think Teddy Roosevelt shot about anything that moved," I said, as Sailor pulled back onto the highway.

"Maybe including Cubans," he said.

I told Sailor about something I'd read. "Folks that put that wolf hunt together brought up a Negro cowboy from Texas who could jump off his running horse and catch wolves by hand. Teddy Roosevelt was amazed. He said, 'Bully!'"

"What was the colored guy's name?" Sailor asked.

"Can't recall."

"Only the big boys get remembered," Sailor said.

He pushed the Green Lizard above the speed limit. We caught up with the strung out parade of vehicles, passed Buford's truck, then Little Jim in his pick-up, and soon got back into our starting lineup place, just behind my dad.

Frederick was a cotton and wheat town that I was familiar with. But, when we got to its outskirts, I still unfolded and studied the Oklahoma-Texas map that Sailor'd picked up at a Texaco station in Vernon.

"We turn south, here, on U.S. 183," I said. "If we went straight on, we'd come to the old Western Trail, not too far ahead, that they drove cattle up from Texas on. But we'll cross that trail anyway, I guess, farther south on it, after we're over Red River and we turn back west in Texas."

Painted on Frederick's silvery water tower was the name of the town, then the words "Home of the Bombers." I already knew that. Vernon played Frederick in football—and mostly lost. The town's wide, red brick Main Street was the highway we wanted. Following Big Jim and Dad, Sailor turned south on it. We passed the three-story limestone county courthouse and were soon out of town, headed southwest toward the river boundary between Oklahoma and Texas. Cultivated fields of ankle-high cotton lined the highway.

We cruised through tiny Davidson, and the land got sandier. On our left, a dozen big catfish heads had been hung along a barbed-wire fence. The fish would have run thirty to thirty-five pounds each, when alive and whole. Caught in Red River, I figured.

"Bragging?" Sailor asked. "That why they hung them fish heads out like that, you reckon, Will?"

"Dead *coyotes* they hang on the fences around home to warn live ones off," I said.

"Maybe same kind of message here, then, Will," Sailor said.

"How you mean?"

"Says, 'Big old catfishes, let that be a damned lesson to y'all. Come flopping up *this* highway, gonna lose *y'all's* heads, too.'"

On a long and narrow two-lane bridge, we crossed the shallow and meandering Red River, with low willows and salt cedars on its wide sandbars. The river wasn't as red as its name, of course, not Crayola red. Sort of brownish red. Probably should have been called the Rusty River.

Ahead of the Green Lizard on the tight bridge, we could see that the rolling left big tire of Dad's wide combine extended all the way over to the highway's center line, so that, to pass him, oncoming cars had to pull over to their far right, the same as Dad had to hub it as close as he could to the bridge bannister on his side. A close squeeze with little room for a mistake.

Not far after we crossed the Red, we soon rolled to a stop at the north edge of Oklaunion. Our first Texas town wasn't much more than a wide place in the road, as the saying went. It was where U.S. 183 intersected U.S. 287, which came up from Wichita Falls, to the southwest, and headed northwest toward the town of Childress and, much farther on, Amarillo. Leading our wheeling column, Jim Gruber, after halting briefly, turned right at the intersection onto the Childress highway. Then, almost immediately after that, he pulled his truck, combine, and header trailer off on the grassy highway shoulder, leaving enough room for the rest of us to do the same and stop behind him.

We all got out to see if everything was roading all right—all of us except Bonnie. She stayed in Buford's truck, reading a *True Romance* magazine, as I later saw when Spider and I walked back that way and spoke to her, me through the driver's side window, Spider through Bonnie's. She was fixed up nice and looked as pretty as when we left Vernon—round cheeks freshly rouged, bee-stung lips newly reddened, and bleached blonde hair still brushed back neatly away from her sweet baby face. Whatever the kind of perfume she wore, it sent out what seemed to me like tantalizing signals in every direction.

"What you readin', Miss Bonnie?" Spider asked her. She quietly held the magazine up for him to see. Spider lingered on after I turned to rejoin the others, leaning his long arms on Bonnie's open window.

We checked the boomers and chains that held the tractors down tight in the truckbeds, and we looked to make sure all the hitches were secure. Everything was in good shape, except that, when our bunch huddled at last beside the GMC pick-up Little Jim was driving, burly Buford Wynn spoke up in his high-pitched voice, which always made it sound to me like he was whining. He said that his old Dodge truck was "using oil" and smoking too much. Taking off his black-visored chauffeur cap and wiping the sweat from his forehead, he said he thought we ought to stop again after about an hour, so that he could check his gauge and add oil from the extra cans he carried, if it turned out he needed to.

Everybody scattered back to the separate vehicles then, ready to take off northwest on U.S. 287 in the direction of Childress, Texas.

"Drive if you want to, Will," Sailor said when he and I got to the Green Lizard.

I did want to. I slipped in on the driver's side and started the engine, then pulled onto the highway behind Dad. I soon found out why Sailor had fixed a knob to the car's steering wheel. There was about a full turn of play, slack, in the wheel. The car pulled to the left, too. So you had to hold the red plastic knob to the right, against the leftward pull. Then, whenever you wanted to turn left, you had to use the knob to quickly wind the wheel to the left, past the slack, before you could press into a turn in that direction. But I soon got the hang of how to do it. Using the knob, I could drive with one hand and stick my left elbow out the window. Both front windows down gave us a good breeze. The sky was clouding up.

I was worried about something other than driving the Green Lizard. "Not even noon, and Dad's already hitting the bottle," I said to Sailor after we were up the road a ways. "I could smell it on his breath. Narrow bridges could get dangerous for him."

Sailor didn't turn to look at me. He was busy with exercising his forearm muscles, using "dynamic tension"—locking his hands and straining against them. He said, "Don't worry about it, Will. I imagine this ain't the first time your dad's drove while drinking." He paused, then went on. "You ever been in Texas before?"

"We lived out here when I was real little," I said. "Whole family came out here again for cotton picking, too, the winter

I was six." Then I went back to the earlier subject. "About Dad driving and drinking," I said, "it's a good thing Spider's riding in the truck with him. Spider might have to take over if Dad gets in too bad a shape."

"Don't count on that, Will," Sailor said. "Old Spider's drinking, too—*with* your dad. I know him well enough to tell. Fact, Spider may be further along than Bob is."

"Lord help us!"

Neither of us said anything more for a while, but then I got around to a question that'd been on my mind. "Sailor, ask you something about Spider?"

"Go on ahead."

"You think he really got out of the army because his mother requested it?"

"Will, the Good Book says, 'Sufficient unto the day is the evil thereof.'"

"What's that mean?"

"Never look for trouble," Sailor said. "Just go on about your own business."

"I guess," I said.

Sailor finished his forearm exercise. He spoke up again. "Spider really ain't too bad a guy, though, Will—basically good-hearted, usually fun to be around," he said. "Just all his life, he's been a mama's boy. That's his main problem. He never knowed for sure how you supposed to act, after you get grown."

"I don't like my sister, Janie Marie, being so taken with him," I said.

"Spider's got a way with the girls, that's a fact," Sailor said.

"He caught Janie Marie at a bad time," I said. "She's been real lonesome, her boyfriend being off in the navy and all."

"Will, no need still worrying about Spider and Janie Marie," Sailor said. "They gonna be miles apart, now—Spider here with us, your sister, back yonder at home."

"I hope it's not true that absence makes the heart grow fonder," I said.

"Won't on Spider's side, you can bet on it," Sailor said.

The sky became grayer and more overcast the farther northwest we rolled on the Childress highway. The land was mostly flat. You could see for ten or twelve miles. The railroad ran alongside us on the right, and paralleling us five or six miles still farther to the right were the breaks along Red River. Close in on both sides of the highway there were big fields of cultivated land. Some with cut-out wheat stubble. Some with ripe wheat that looked like twenty-five bushels to the acre, not yet harvested. Some with green row-cropped maize, ankle to calf high, planted in April, I knew, to be harvested in late fall, after the frost.

We crossed the old Western Trail, just as I'd expected. Next to the highway there was nothing of it left to see. You'd have missed it altogether, except for a Texas historical marker. Farther north, the marker said, was Doan's Crossing at the Prairie Dog Town Fork of Red River. There, you could still make out traces of where the great herds of longhorns, in drive after drive, forded Red River in the old days, then were pressed on north through the western side of what became Oklahoma and on up past my home state's panhandle.

Rain began to hit us as we roaded through the two-block main street of the little town of Chillicothe and headed on northwest. The railroad crossed over to our left. Several miles on, we began to notice, off to the south, four little rocky peaks in a row. The one on the northwest, the largest of the four, was sort of a mound, the next one toward the southeast, a nipple, the third one, a smaller pointed peak, the fourth, smaller still.

"Landmarks, those would have been, Sailor, when Comanche war parties rode through here to raid down near San Antonio," I said to him, motioning with my head toward the four peaks.

"How you know that kind of stuff, Will—Comanche raiders coming through here?" he said.

"History book, plus Kent Coffee's grandpa, when he was a young man, was actually one of the raiders. Kent told me about it once," I said.

"Zona's grandpa was in them kind of war parties?" Sailor asked.

"Right," I said. "He was Marcy's grandpa, too."

Nearer, to the left and right of the narrow concrete highway, were more great wheat fields, some already cut, some still not. A combine and tractor stood idle in one big field of ripe wheat, work obviously stopped by the rain, which was coming down pretty hard. Sailor and I rolled up the front windows of the Green Lizard, but the windshield quickly fogged up, and it got too hot inside for us. So we cracked the windows some. We began to get a little wet from the rain that blew in, but we didn't care. It felt good.

Toward the south, with the four little peaks now three or four miles behind us, the land got hillier and rockier. We came to the town of Quanah, about the size of Vernon, back home. A sign at the edge of town read: "Quanah, City of Legends." No mention of what the legends were. I pulled off and let the rest of our caravan go on by. Then I cut south across the highway to look at an old railroad depot and a Texas historical marker over there.

The depot had been moved northwest to Quanah, the marker said, from the town of Medicine Mound, after that old town burned. The town'd been named after the natural Medicine Mound, which I took to be the largest of the four peaks we'd seen back down the road, and was "where Quanah Parker and his Comanches prayed and rolled in the gypsum dust for healing." Before reservation days, Quanah Parker and other Comanches came by here on the way to raid and steal horses? Sure. Prayed at Medicine Mound? Likely. Rubbed gypsum dust on their arms and legs for healing? Maybe. Rolled in the dust? That didn't sound right to me. It would be good to ask Marcy about this, I thought.

A snow cone stand on skids stood right next to the old depot. Sailor got out and stepped over there in the rain, favoring his left leg a little, to buy us a couple of cones—mine with grape syrup poured over it, his with strawberry. Inside the Green Lizard, it was hot with the windows almost up. Outside, the thermometer was rising toward ninety degrees, probably, before the day was over. The sweet snow cone felt cool to my insides, going down, as I pulled the car back onto the highway.

We caught up with our bunch on the other side of the town of Quanah, obviously named after the Comanche chief. I cut over into our regular slot in the parade. A highway sign said that Childress was thirty miles farther on northwest. The country became rougher. Lots of prairie, thick with mesquites, rockier land. Lots of native trees in the draws, maybe oak. To the south of us, the country was especially wild and rough—surely more of what had been Comanche country in the old days.

For a long stretch, then, we saw a number of scattered uncut wheat fields. After that, lots of grassland again. Here and there, dotted off in the hilly distance, were isolated farmhouses with surrounding clumps of ragged trees and tall windmills that stuck up like midget, bad imitation Eiffel Towers. Then there were more breaks. More rolling hills. Patches of red, sorry-looking soil where the vegetation was worn away.

Childress, when we got to it, was a good-sized place, maybe three times as big as Vernon. Two- and three-story buildings in several blocks of businesses. One five-story hotel. A wide north-south main street of red brick, and several blocks of other brick side streets in all four directions.

"Must have been an old-time booming cow town," I said to Sailor, as we passed a cotton gin and a grain elevator, then left the city limits on the other side of town.

"Grown, Will, you gonna raise cattle for a living, yourself, like your dad?" Sailor asked.

"My best friend, Junior Randall—you met him—that's what he wants me to do," I said. "And I might would, if it was still like the old days. But I aim to be a lawyer instead."

"Make your living out of *people's* hides, not cows' hides," Sailor said.

My response was quick. "You think, like Grandma Haley, that being a lawyer's not an honest way to make a living?"

"Naw, Will, just kidding," Sailor said. "Long as there's laws, gotta be lawyers, I reckon, just like, long as there's beer, gotta be beer joints. And probably ain't no more sorry lawyers than there are sorry preachers."

We saw more fields of uncut ripe wheat and drove by other fields of ankle-high maize, sprouted in reddish dirt. There was quite a lot of contour-farmed and terraced land under cultivation. Small green cotton plants, growing in rows. It all looked to me like pretty marginal farming around there, though.

Along the roadside, we passed a series of five little Burma-Shave signs—red with white lettering and each sign about a hundred feet apart—of the kind that my sister, Janie Marie, and I had always loved to read aloud, ever since we were little kids.

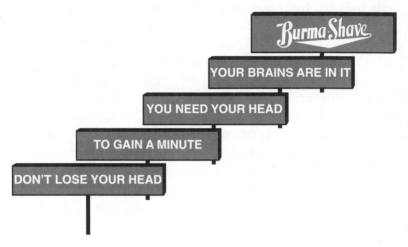

At the town of Estelline, Jim Gruber, ahead of Dad, turned west off of U.S. 287 and onto State Highway 86, pointed toward Turkey, Texas. It was past noon. Time to stop and eat dinner, gas up the vehicles, and check the oil in Buford's truck. Big Jim led our procession off the highway and into a nice WPA-built rest stop with a shelter belt of black locust and elm trees behind it. The rain had slackened to a light mist.

Little Jim pulled his pick-up, with the gas barrels in back, alongside each of the trucks, in turn. Sailor and I gassed the trucks up. I unscrewed the caps and held the nozzle in the tanks, Sailor turned the rotary pump. Little Jim made a note in a small tablet he carried about the estimated number of gallons that went into Buford's truck, turning on the truck's ignition to look at the gas gauge before we filled the tank. Buford regularly paid Dad and Jim Gruber back for the fuel he got from them.

Bonnie, with Spider helping, spread a doubled bedsheet on the concrete table under a rest stop awning, then brought out the fried chicken and a big bowl of potato salad that Grandma Haley had made us for the road. There were some fresh tomatoes from our home garden, too. We ate from tin pie pans with mismatched forks, and we drank pre-sugared iced tea from tin coffee cups. The ice came from a ten-pound block in the small icebox in Buford and Bonnie's little house trailer. Spider chipped it with an ice pick.

It seemed to me that Spider and Dad had slacked off some on their drinking. Neither one was in too bad a shape, though the sweat around my dad's eyes gave away the fact that he wasn't totally sober. So did his being a little more talkative than usual.

He spoke up between bites. "We used to live a little ways north of here, out in the sandhills close to Lakeview. Hard place to make a living," Dad said. "Willie was real little."

"I remember our house," I said.

"You couldn't," my dad said. "You was only two."

"I do, though," I said. "I can see it right now, me playing in the dirt, on the north side. The house faced west, was yellow."

"You remember that?" Dad said. "What about getting your elbow almost burned off?"

"Don't remember that, except what y'all've told me." I held up my left arm to show the bad scar on the elbow to the crew members across the concrete table.

"Let me see," Bonnie said. I turned to my right and showed her. "Poor thing!" she said. "How'd it happen?"

I related the story the way Mama'd always told it to me. "It was wintertime. Dad'd taken up some ashes and red-hot coals from the stove in the dining room, leaving them there in a washtub while he started making a new fire. Mama was ironing clothes. A neighbor girl and I were playing cars, pulling matchboxes with strings tied to them. She kept teasing me by stepping on my matchbox to jerk me down. And finally, one time, I fell with my back directly on the hot coals in the washtub. Mama said I put my left elbow into the coals to raise my back up. Burned the elbow flesh off by the time she got to me, so the bone was sticking out. Country doctor put some kind of grease on it, said the elbow'd never fully heal and always be stiff. He was wrong. The skin did finally grow back, and I was as good as new. But Mama said, by then, I'd been in bed so long that I had to learn how to walk all over again."

Sailor paused between bites of chicken to put in a comment. "Will, you can tell these Texas gals that Indians back in Oklahoma tried to burn you at the stake," he said.

"And I can tell kids that elbow grease really works," I said.

It wasn't long before Big Jim stood up, rising to his full six feet, and said, "Let's roll 'em, boys, if we gonna hit Dimmitt before dark."

The rest of us got up right away, too. We folded the bedsheet and put the pie pans and tin cups in a pasteboard box, which Bonnie and Buford carried back to their house trailer, the chuck wagon, for later washing. We were off again, straight west. Big Jim was still riding point, leading the van, as they called it in the old cattle drives, Bonnie and Buford still in the drag.

Along the blacktopped State 86, the country was pretty ragged. Evergreen shrubs here and there showed that the elevation of the land was rising. There were some terraced red dirt fields with cotton just coming up. Mostly rough country, though, and getting rougher. More hilly. Red ravines with white gypsum outcroppings. Some scattered wheat fields and cultivated plots. Miles and miles of harsh country, grass and mesquites. Scattered windblown elm and locust shelter belts, built by the government to keep the dust bowl from happening again.

"Turkey, Texas—Home of Bob Wills." That was what the sign at the edge of the little town—about nine hundred people— said. I'd read a newspaper story that reported that Bob Wills and His Texas Playboys, who'd long since moved their base to Tulsa and were famous for the "western swing" that Bob Wills more or less invented, were making more money than any other wartime band. Strange that Wills came from this small Texas burg, I thought. I started humming "Faded Love," one of Bob Wills's most popular tunes.

A Texas historical marker that I pulled the Green Lizard off for us to read said that the town of Turkey got its name from the fact that at the time it was settled, a huge flock of wild turkeys permanently roosted nearby.

"Turkey politicians probably feather their own nest," I said.

Sailor went me one better. "Town harvest song: 'Turkey in the Straw,' I bet," he said.

I couldn't quit. "Wonder if they call their basketball team the 'Turkeys'? Coach gives a halftime pep talk, says, 'You boys are a bunch of real Turkeys!'"

But Sailor got the last word. "Turkey team cheer," he said, "'Strut and gobble, strut and gobble; dribble that ball, and don't dare bobble!'"

State 86, through the middle of Turkey's several stores, was a thin concrete slab. The cross streets were gravel. Picking up speed, I drove out of town, hurrying to catch up and resume my place in line. Ahead of me on the narrow blacktopped road, a turkey vulture, no lie—a vulture from Turkey, Texas, it occurred to me—flapped into the air from a dead skunk that it was feeding on. "Quitaque—10 miles," a highway sign said.

The country was a little flatter than before Turkey, the soil sandier and browner. Off fifteen miles toward the western horizon, you could see the sharp mesa rise of the Caprocks, up maybe as much as two thousand feet above the land that we were coming from.

Quitaque, "Gateway to the Caprocks," was about the same size as Turkey. The oddly spelled name was almost certainly from a Comanche Indian word, I figured. Sailor and I stopped at a mom-and-pop store, around the corner south on a gravel street off State 86, the town's main drag. The little store was next door to an old railroad hotel, with a concrete cyclone cellar on the south side of it. We got us some peanuts and a couple of Cokes to carry away, paying two cents deposit each for the green bottles.

"How do you pronounce the name of this town?" I asked the snaggletoothed boy, about my age, at the cash register.

"Kitty-quay," he said, not looking at me as he made change.

"Where's the name come from?" I asked.

"Some kind of Indian word," the boy said. "Tribe, I ain't sure."

"Know what it means, Quitaque?" I asked.

"I forget," he said. He turned away and picked up the funny book that he'd been reading when Sailor and I came in.

Back in the lineup, we drove through two miles of rough, deserty looking country with scattered yucca plants, but with terraced farmland here and there, too. Then we hit the breaks and began to climb up—and up and up—the Caprocks. The steep rise in elevation made your ears pop. When we were almost to the top, first Buford, then, right behind us, Little Jim, began flashing their headlights off and on—our agreed signal to stop. I passed the signal on ahead to my dad, and he soon did the same, to flag Big Jim Gruber. Big Jim stopped on the highway shoulder as soon as he was up on top, where there was fine level farmland and grassland as far as the eye could see. And the eye could see pretty far, more than fifteen miles under an overcast sky.

A hundred yards back down the steep highway, Buford's orange Dodge had overheated and vapor locked. Little Jim put his pick-up in reverse, then slowly coasted backwards to the stalled truck. The rest of us walked. I helped Sailor lift the five-gallon milk can of drinking water out of the pick-up. It was the only water we had. Buford took a rag that Bonnie brought from the house trailer for him and carefully unscrewed his Dodge's radiator cap. He jumped back as steam roared two or three feet into the air.

"Mustn't put water in without you start 'er first," Jim Gruber said. "Bust the head."

"She won't start, though," Buford said in his whiny voice. "Vapor locked."

"It will in a minute," Big Jim said. "Air's a little cooler up here on the Caprocks."

"How much have we risen, you reckon?" I asked.

"I know Dimmitt's more'n twenty-five hundred feet higher'n Vernon—about thirty-eight hundred feet, Dimmitt is," Big Jim said. "We just climbed a big part of that, getting up to where we are now, on top of the Caprocks."

"First time I come this way was in a Model T Ford," my dad said. "Halfway up the Caprocks, we had to turn the car around and *back* up to the top, in reverse."

"Them old Model Ts had a lot more power in reverse than they did in forward gear," Big Jim said. He turned to Buford. "Get in and try 'er now," he said, motioning toward the truck cab.

Buford did, and the motor caught and started after turning over a few times. Buford stayed in the truck with Bonnie, keeping it running. Sailor picked up the five-gallon milk can like it was empty, his straining biceps big at the end of his T-shirt sleeves, and began to slowly pour water into the radiator. More steam shot up at first, then stopped. Sailor poured until the radiator was full and began to run over. Dad screwed the cap back on. Sailor put the can in Little Jim's pick-up.

We were soon strung out on the highway again, headed toward Silverton. A sign said it was ten miles away. On our left was a huge round lake as big as four football fields, not a tree in sight.

"Lord, look at all that water—lots of good fishing, swimming, too!" I said. "Hope it's that way around Dimmitt."

Good flat land everywhere. Big fields of ripe wheat. Other fields of ankle-high row-cropped maize.

"Silverton: Live the Dream!" the sign at the edge of the small town, about half Vernon's size, said. "Silverton Owls" was painted on the water tower. Grain elevators. Cotton gins. Briscoe County courthouse. A marker said the county was named after a Texan who'd fought at the Battle of San Jacinto, where the Mexican General Santa Ana was defeated. On the other side of town, a highway sign announced "Tulia—28 miles"

We're getting there, boys! I knew from the map that Tulia was the last town of any size before Dimmitt.

Rich farmland—flat as a flitter, Mama would have said. Ankle-high cotton. Twenty-five-bushel wheat. Some pastureland.

Close to Tulia, I pulled over and stopped at another Texas historical marker, letting Little Jim and Buford go on by. Two miles north of here, after defeating the Comanche Indians in Palo Duro Canyon, the marker read, General Mackenzie rounded up and shot all their horses, nearly fifteen hundred head.

"How come he done a shitty thing like that?" Sailor said.

"Put the Comanches out of commission; they couldn't steal their horses back," I said.

"Son of a bitch!"

That was the way I felt, too. "Mackenzie burned their tipis, too," I said. "Dead of winter, with just the clothes on their back, the whole band—men, women, and children—got force-marched on foot by the army all the way to Fort Sill, Oklahoma, north of Vernon."

The town of Tulia, three times the size of Vernon, and county seat of Swisher County, was laid out around a courthouse square, the same as the other Texas towns we'd seen. Blacktop and gravel streets. "Tulia Hornets." Several blocks of businesses. Gray metal cotton gins. Grain elevators of a type I'd never seen before—tightly clustered white concrete cylinders, maybe seven or eight stories high.

I figured that Tulia was named after Tule Creek, West Tule Creek, and Middle Tule Creek, all nearby. Should have called the town "Tulias," plural. A downtown monument said "Agriculture, law and order, and Christian principles have sustained Swisher County."

"That and runnin' off the Indians," Sailor said.

The rain stopped. On the west edge of Tulia, a highway sign said "Dimmitt—31 miles."

Vast, featureless landscape, with the same fifteen-mile visibility in every direction. Great wheat country. Spreading grasslands with scattered yucca plants topped by ivory flowers on two-foot stalks. Shelter belt tree rows. Here and there in the distance, farmhouses with windmills and knots of trees. We zipped past the tiny town of Nazareth.

Then, for the next several miles, I felt like I was holding my breath in dread as I watched my dad off and on begin to drift out of his highway lane. The liquor, I figured, might be making him doze off in the heat of the late afternoon. Several times he veered left across the yellow middle stripe, only to get back just in time to miss oncoming cars. Twice he ran the right wheels of his truck and combine off on the gravel shoulder on his side of the road, then finally pulled back straight again. We came to a narrow bridge. I was almost afraid to watch, but Dad apparently got things under control at the last minute and drove across the bridge with no trouble. And, maybe then scared awake, he showed no more difficulty in staying in his lane after that, as we rolled on toward Dimmitt.

We crossed into Castro County and passed between two more treeless lakes. Each one was as big as two football fields.

Before long, we saw what at first looked like city skyscrapers, maybe five miles away on the clearing western horizon below a still-clouded afternoon sun. I began to smile. For another couple of miles, I thought Dimmitt was going to turn out to be a good-sized town, maybe as big as Oklahoma City, even. But my smile faded when I realized that what I'd taken for skyscrapers were actually just grain elevators of the white, seven-story clustered concrete cylinder type. There were two big elevators like that and two more of corrugated metal. And Dimmitt, after all, when we got all the way to it, turned out to be no bigger than Vernon, if that. I was glad to see, though, that there were a couple of big lakes nearby.

In town, we drove along the north side of the usual one-block public square. The Castro County courthouse was built of smooth white limestone—three stories in the middle, two on the sides. Across the street from it in each direction was a city block of businesses—mostly one-story red brick stores, although there was an impressive three-story building of tan brick, too.

Jim Gruber braked to a stop at the northwest corner of the courthouse, where our east-west State 86 intersected with the north-south U.S. 385. To the right, toward the north, there was a lumberyard and maybe three blocks of scattered businesses. Big Jim turned left, south, on U.S. 385, which ran along the west side of the courthouse toward Littlefield. We passed a picture show—the Carlisle Theater—in the middle of that block. The marquee read "Robert Taylor in *Billy the Kid*."

Rebecca Milton's "mature" idol with the five o'clock shadow!

Jim Gruber led us to the southeast edge of Dimmitt, which didn't take long. He pulled off the highway, then west, across from a big white grain elevator of ninety-foot concrete cylinders. "Dimmitt Wheat Growers" was painted in black on the front of the tall clustered tubes. Big Jim drove into a vacant grassy area, just to the south of a Texaco filling station. The rest of us followed, of course, and sort of circled the wagons. A strong breeze was blowing from the south as we got out of our various vehicles. Low in the west, the pale blue Texas sky was clear. A big red sun paused above the horizon.

I tagged along with Jim Gruber and my dad, who seemed to be walking all right despite his drinking, to the Texaco station next door. They made a deal with the owner. We could use the station's toilets for a couple of days and get water from their hydrant. In exchange, we'd buy our gas at the station at the posted price of thirty-two cents a gallon, which seemed pretty high.

"Where's a good place for supper around here?" Big Jim asked the Texaco guy. We'd have to eat our first supper and breakfast in a Dimmitt café, until Bonnie could buy groceries.

"What kind of food you like?" the man asked.

How many kinds were there in Dimmitt?

Big Jim thought a moment. "Mexican, I guess," he said.

"Only choice, then, is El Rancho—across the street east of the courthouse."

We unhitched the trucks, took turns washing our hands and faces at the gas station, then divided up and drove to the café.

I'd thought Jim Gruber's choice of a Mexican restaurant was a good one because I figured it was hard to mess up that kind of food. Not impossible, though, as I soon found out. About the only thing really Mexican about El Rancho was its name. Not a Mexican person in sight. Not the cashier, not the cook, no waitresses, and no customers. Nobody in the place looked like they were even kin to a Mexican. The enchiladas and tacos I ordered were filled with a really greasy, gristly hamburger meat. The sauce was so bland that even an Englishman wouldn't have it found too spicy. A blanket of gooey, melted yellow Velveeta cheese was spread over everything on the plate. To conceal the crime, I thought.

Trying to be cheerful about Dimmitt, anyway, I mentioned at supper that I was glad to see so many big lakes close to town. But it turned out that the lakes were fakey, too.

"Them flat lakes ain't even knee deep, most places, Willie," my dad said. "And they dry up pretty quick."

"Shoot fire!" I said. That was as close as I ever came to cussing when I was around my dad.

"Saved my hide once, though, one of them flat lakes," Dad said. "Year before you was born, Willie; Janie Marie was a baby. Me and your mama come out close to here, down at Muleshoe, Texas. Sharecropped on the halves for Old Man Cope. Bad drouth year, turned out. I went plumb broke. Owed a lot for seed and living costs. We was about out of groceries. As bad off as old Job in the Bible. But I sure'n hell wadn't about to run out on my debts. I got to thinking about the big, dry, flat lake on the place. I went out and dug down in it a little ways and found lots of moisture still. So I broke that sucker out that late April—everybody thought I was as crazy as a peach orchard boar—and planted the whole thing to maize. Never rained again, but the maize come up good and then headed out good from the moisture already in the ground. Made myself a crop that fall. Cleared enough to settle up my debts and go on home to Oklahoma."

We finished eating. Back at the vacant lot next to the Texaco station, we rolled up in our separate quilts, spread here and there in the short grass next to the vehicles—except for Buford and Bonnie, of course, who slept in their house trailer.

A freight train went clacketing south out of town, the steam engine chuffing away and soon sounding its high, lonesome whistle in the increasing distance as it picked up speed.

All at once, the realization hit me that it was Saturday night back home in Vernon, too. Junior Randall would be down at Joe Lammer's. I wondered if Rebecca Milton had returned that day from church camp. Wondered if she was at Joe Lammer's, who she was sitting with, maybe dancing with.

I rolled over, then, and got as comfortable as I could on the hard ground. But I was homesick, my first night up on the Caprocks, out on the harvest trail.

Chapter Six

The next morning, I went and did a really unmature thing. My long-armed, yellow-haired cousin, Spider Deering, talked me into it.

Across a barbed-wire fence just west of where we were temporarily camped in Dimmitt, beside the Texaco filling station, was a pasture of short grass, pockmarked everywhere with the little dirt mounds and holes of a sprawling prairie dog town. After our wheat harvest bunch'd all had breakfast—at a different downtown café, this time, the Rosemont—Spider got fixed on the idea of me and him capturing us some young prairie dog pups.

"We could keep one for a pet for ourselves, Willie, and I bet we could peddle some more of 'em around town, here. Maybe get a dollar apiece," he said. "Wouldn't that be good?"

I *was* attracted to the idea of having my own little prairie dog pup to raise, maybe to take home to Janie Marie.

Spider and I surveyed the tan-haired mama and daddy rodents across the fence. Each stood straight up beside one of maybe thirty or so of their scattered holes, squeaking now and then and looking back at us. Dad and Big Jim were gone off to line up some wheat to cut, Little Jim was filling our gasoline barrels at the Texaco station, and Sailor was shaving in the filling-station men's room.

The prairie dogs looked totally tame, almost like they might *volunteer* to be pets. But any time we made a slight move toward them, they instantly shot back down into their tunnels and disappeared.

"This time of year, bound to be babies in every hole," Spider said.

"Yeah, but how're we going to get them out?" I asked.

"Flood 'em out," Spider said.

I don't know why, but Spider's suggested method for the prairie dog capture sounded at the time just as reasonable to me as the whole idea of the capture itself. Without Buford and Bonnie knowing the reason that we wanted a washtub, we borrowed one from them before they took off for the grocery store with a packet of our ration books that Mama'd handed over to Bonnie before we left home. Bonnie also let me and Spider have an empty flour sack.

He and I filled the tub at the Texaco station water hydrant. One of us on each side, we carried the sloshing tub to the fence, carefully slid it underneath the bottom wire, then crawled through the fence ourselves. We picked out the nearest prairie dog den for the flooding operation. Spider handed me the flour sack and got ready, by himself, to tip the tub over into the hole.

"You hold the flour sack open, Willie," Spider said. "I'll dump the water in, all at once. When them little devils start coming out to keep from drownding, I'll grab up the babies and pitch 'em in the sack."

Spider poured the water in. All of it went down the chute in a rush, like it was headed straight to China. Not even a pause for a gurgle. We waited. No sign of any prairie dog, big or small, except that, farther away from us, curious neighbor prairie dogs ventured cautiously out of other dens to see what was going on.

After a moment of reflection, caressing his blond pencil-line moustache with a thumb and finger, Spider said, "Gonna need a second tubful, Willie."

Back we went to the Texaco station. Back, then, through the fence with the full tub to our chosen prairie dog hole. Down the tunnel went the water. Same result—*no* result. Back to the filling station. Back to the hole.

Back and back.

Sailor returned from shaving, and between our trips I told him what Spider and I were up to. Sailor didn't say anything, just sat down in the shade of Buford and Bonnie's house trailer to read a little book that he'd brought from Vernon about the Comanche Indians, every now and then looking up to watch Spider and me with an expression of increasing disbelief. And I was growing a little skeptical myself, even before Buford, after he and Bonnie got back, came over to the fence and said what he did.

The water from our seventh or eighth tubful rapidly disappeared down the same hole we'd been trying so hard, without success, to flood. Spider and I were worn out from all our water carrying.

"Boys, prairie dog tunnels are all connected together," Buford said to us in his high voice. "You couldn't possibly drown them out, unless you used a fire hose hooked up directly to the water tower."

I knew he was right. Spider did, too. We came back through the fence, tired and disheartened. I felt a little silly.

"Much obliged for the use of your washtub and flour sack," I said to Buford. "I'll take them to Bonnie."

Bonnie'd learned from Sailor what Spider and I were trying to do. "Too darn bad, Will," she said when I gave her the tub and sack. "I was hoping for one of those little prairie puppies, myself."

Dad and Jim Gruber weren't back yet. "I'm going to walk to town and buy some postcards and stamps," I said to Sailor.

"Get in the Lizard, and I'll go with you," he said, standing up and closing his book. "Maybe we'll drive around a little and see the Dimmitt sights while we're at it."

Downtown, we parked in front of the Rexall Drug, across the street north of the courthouse. In a front window of the store was a war poster that showed a spurred Nazi boot smashing a church steeple: "We're Fighting to Prevent This!"

But Sailor stopped me before we got to the door of the drugstore. He guided me to the right, toward a little hole-in-the-wall store called Hartford Radio Repair, closed on Sunday. In its window, behind a hand-lettered "For Sale" sign, were four used radios—three wooden cabinet table models and a portable. It was the portable, a little Admiral "Bantam" camera-style model with a leather handle and leatherette covering, that'd caught Sailor's eye. I'd never seen a portable radio, except in the movies.

"Be good to have us a radio to listen to, wouldn't it, Will?" Sailor said. "Wonder what the guy wants for it?" There were no price tags on any of the radios in the window.

"Battery'd probably run down right in the middle of a song," I said.

Sailor said we'd come back in a few days when the store was open.

He and I turned and went on into the Rexall Drug. Inside, on a rack near the cash register, were two kinds of tourist post-cards, both in black and white. One was a photograph of the local courthouse. A paragraph on the back of it said that the 1891 selection of Dimmitt as the Castro County seat caused a gunfight between a retired local Texas Ranger and a resident of a rival town, that the first courthouse building was struck by lightning and burned in 1906, and that the second one was razed to make way for the present structure, built by the Public Works Administration in 1939. Too much information. Not enough room left on that card to write a good message.

The other tourist postcard was a photograph of the two-story brick Dimmitt High School, with the wing on the right labeled "Auditorium," the wing on the left, "Gymnasium," and, behind the gymnasium, a large, fenced swimming pool. The back of this card read "Dimmitt High School, home of the Bobcats." I showed these cards to Sailor, then bought six of them.

Afterwards, Sailor drove over and let me out in front of the post office. I ran in and bought six one-cent stamps. We toured around town a little, then, in the Green Lizard. Sailor was surprised to see a big, blooming magnolia tree in the front yard of a house on a residential street a block west of downtown.

"Real common—magnolias—back home in Mississippi," he said, as he pointed the tree out to me. "But 'bout as lost out here on the plains of West Texas as me."

Three blocks or so farther west of the house with the magnolia, the street dead-ended at the sprawling tan brick Dimmitt High School building, the one shown in the postcard. It faced east and was nearly a block long.

"Behold, the home of the Bobcats," Sailor said, with a sweep of his hand.

He turned left and drove south by the gymnasium part of the school, cut west alongside the fenced swimming pool, and stopped for a moment. A bored-looking boy sat under a lifeguard umbrella at the far end of the pool. But Sailor's and my eyes were drawn more to a few girls, nearer us, who were already at the pool, even though it wasn't quite Sunday noon yet. They looked pretty attractive in their one-piece bathing suits, lolling around on the towels they'd spread on a strip of grass.

"Bob*kitties*, I reckon," Sailor said. "Evidently not too eat up with religion, either."

He turned the car around, and we went back downtown. We bought us some hamburgers, then headed to our temporary camp on the south side.

Dad and Big Jim soon came back, successful. They'd made a wheat-cutting deal with a rich little baldheaded guy, a Mr. Duggert. He owned the bank in Dimmitt but farmed several hundred acres of wheat southwest of town. The manager of a local grain elevator'd told Dad and Big Jim about Duggert and some other farmers, too, who were all looking to find a custom combiner. So Dad and Big Jim'd driven to Duggert's house—a "mansion," Big Jim called it—and waited for Duggert to come back from church.

Our whole bunch moved out to Mr. Duggert's land that afternoon. We set up camp at a vacant and rundown old rock house that occupied a small corner square on one of Duggert's large, and ripe, wheat fields, everything unfenced. Next to the house was a working windmill and a round metal stock tank, pumped full of water.

Buford parked his and Bonnie's house trailer on the west side of the farmhouse, near the windmill and water tank and next to a raggedy elm shelter belt. In a patch of sunflowers and still-green tumbleweeds, north of the house toward the caliche road, we unhooked the Gleaner-Baldwins from their trucks, pulled the header trailers around, and reattached the headers in their places at the front of the combines. Then we backed the trucks into a bar ditch and drove the Farmall and Fordson tractors off the truckbeds, brought them around, and hitched the combines to them. We were ready to start cutting as soon as the dew dried out, early the next morning.

All of us, except Buford and Bonnie, unloaded our bedding, suitcases, and other personal stuff and picked out our individual sleeping places here and there on the sagging pine floor of the rock house. The inside walls of the old place were badly water damaged. Most of the wallpaper had partially peeled, then rolled up like ancient scrolls. Big Jim and Dad chose the western of the two front rooms for themselves. Little Jim, Spider, Sailor, and I took the other room. We put Dad's fold-up coal-oil camp stove, a blue porcelain coffee pot, a bucket of water, and a wash basin for shaving, together with Dad's mirror, on the counter next to a cracked window in what had once been the kitchen. There was a rickety old table pushed against the opposite wall of the room, and we arranged Big Jim's four folding canvas camp stools around it. We wouldn't all be able to sit down for breakfast at the same time.

A little after we got situated, exploring through the house, I found two weathered paperback books that'd been left on a shelf in a front closet. One was *You and Your Baby*, put out by the Extension Division of the U.S. Department of Agriculture. The other was *How to Win Friends and Influence People* by Dale Carnegie.

The books set me to wondering what'd ever happened to the people who'd built that rock house, the people who'd dug the windmill water well, who'd planted the still thriving lilac bushes in front, and who'd tried to make a home out of the place. *Did their baby grow up all right? How had the mother and daddy weathered the depression and the dust bowl? When the family moved off the farm, did they find success?* For some reason, I'd always identified with people who'd had a hard time of it, and was curious to know their story.

That evening, for our first harvest trail supper, Bonnie served us some sliced cured ham and some canned green beans and canned sweet corn that she'd warmed up. When the food was ready, she put it and a big jar of iced tea out on a card table beside the trailer. We all washed up at the stock tank by the windmill. Buford lit both of our two coal-oil lanterns. We filled our tin pie plates and tin cups, then sat around on the cleared ground to eat.

Afterwards, while Bonnie was washing the dishes and putting things away, Spider went in the house and got my uncle's guitar. I'd said that he could bring it with us from home. He began to pick out and sing an Ernest Tubb song, my favorite, "Walking the Floor over You." I talked Sailor into joining in with his French harp. He got it and did when Spider started the second song. It was Roy Acuff's "Great Speckled Bird."

The air grew cool as the night got darker. The sky was clear. There were plenty of stars. Off somewhere, a coyote pack—it sounded like three or four of them—set up a wailing chorus of their own.

Out on the lone prairie! It kind of gave me goose bumps.

Later, in the old rock house, it seemed like everyone but me went sound asleep almost as soon as they hit their quilts, which we'd each rolled out in our own spaces on the creaky and, here and there, busted wooden floor. In the other front room, Big Jim and Dad started a kind of singsong duet of high and low snoring. But that wasn't what kept me awake. My trouble was that you could hear too many scattered rattling noises in the walls and floor of the old house. I told myself that a lot of this worrisome low racket was probably made by mice, rats, or beetles. But some of it sounded to me suspiciously like the noise that a rattlesnake makes. I knew the sound well because we'd just that afternoon run onto a rattler while we were chopping weeds with wheat scoops to make a path to the front door of the rock house. Spider'd sliced the snake's head off with a scoop.

On my back, I lay there on the floor as still as I could, listening intently. Then, suddenly, I became conscious of a place alongside the calf of my left leg that seemed to be growing warmer and warmer. Old cowboys, I'd read, said that a hazard of being out on the range was that sometimes on a coolish night rattlesnakes would crawl into your bedding for warmth. Some cowboys laid a lariat rope in a loop on the ground around their bedding area, claiming that a rattlesnake wouldn't cross one. We didn't have a lariat rope with us.

Is a rattlesnake right now in bed with me or not?

I wasn't going to wait around to find out. And I decided that, when I moved, it had to be fast. I took a deep breath. Then, in almost one rapid motion, I jumped up, grabbed and shook out my quilt, and, with it under an arm, headed toward the door, not worrying about keeping the noise down.

"Will, what'n hell you doin'?" Little Jim said, rousing up a little. There were other muffled grumblings from my bunkmates.

But by that time, I was outside, barefooted and in my shorts. I figured I'd get up the next morning before Bonnie did and go back and get my clothes. Stepping high, I raced to my dad's truck and clambered up into the back of it. I hadn't heard any telltale thump of a snake hitting the floor when I'd shaken out my quilt. But snake or not, I made a quick and firm resolution that the truckbed was going to be my private sleeping place for the whole week and a half that we would be cutting wheat around Dimmitt. I decided not to worry about the rest of our bunch, still sleeping in the rock house. It would be every man for himself.

Next morning—Monday morning—when we were all up before daylight and washing up for breakfast out at the horse tank, Big Jim was the only one who said anything about snakes. And I figured that he actually said what he did so I wouldn't be embarrassed about having run out of the house the night before.

"I'm like Willie myself," Big Jim said. "Heard them damn rattlers all night long!"

Jim Gruber's saying that didn't keep my dad from making fun of both of us, though. "Jim, I've had 'snakes in my boots' a time or two," Dad said. That's what he called seeing things on a bad drunk. "But I think you and Willie've got snakes in the *head*."

Bonnie handed out supplies of eggs, bacon, bread, jelly, and coffee to us from the house trailer. We carried them back to the rock house's kitchen. Standing over the coal-oil camp stove in his undershirt, his sandy hair not yet slicked down and his red face bristling with unshaved reddish brown whiskers, Dad fixed and dished up breakfast for our bunch. When I poured myself some coffee in a tin cup, the same as everyone else, he glared at me for a moment, but didn't say anything.

After breakfast, Sailor, Spider, Little Jim, and I greased and gassed up the machines and, not long after the sun was up, pulled the combines over to the big field next to the house to start cutting. The field was level, the wheat, good. Thirty bushels to the acre, or something like that. With no fence around the place, it was easy for me to open the field and start the cutting. I only had to skirt the combine header around a wide, rowed-disc "one-way" plow. It was parked in the near corner, ready for a farmhand to use to turn the stubble under once the wheat was cut.

Mr. Duggert actively managed the bank he owned in Dimmitt, as we learned, but he still came out to the field a little before noon on the first day we started cutting for him, and he came back every single day after that, mostly to inspect our work. He drove a big blue four-door Packard, a 1941 "One Twenty" model with a silvery winged ornament on the hood. He always parked the low-slung car right out in the middle of the tall wheat stubble, which reached up several inches above the bottom of the car's doors.

Dressed in a suit, tie, and nice straw hat, he got out and watched us carefully. Twice or more on each visit to the field, he walked a short way behind each operating combine, bent over, spectacled eyes on the ground, checking to be sure we weren't throwing out too much wheat with the straw and chaff. When he thought we were, he signaled the offending Gleaner-Baldwin to stop and ordered Sailor or Little Jim to get off and make the indicated adjustments to the machine. And every day without exception, when we were stopped to dump our wheat or were eating dinner, Mr. Duggert warned us all about throwing down live cigarettes and setting the wheat or stubble on fire. He never mentioned the danger from vehicle exhausts.

My dad let Buford haul Mr. Duggert's first load of wheat to the Dimmitt elevator. I asked Buford to mail a postcard for me while he was in town. The card was one of those with a photograph of the local high school. I'd written out the message, addressed the postcard, and stuck on the stamp the preceding evening, just before supper.

Sunday, June 20, 1943

Dear Becca,

Dammit, we're in Dimmitt! Was hoping it'd be a bigger town. But there's a lot of wheat to cut, so we won't be spending much time in town, anyway. Guy we're cutting for says more rattlesnakes in this Texas county than chickens, but says they won't bother you if you don't bother them. Ha Ha. Hope you're back. Write me at Boise City, Oklahoma, where we go next—General Delivery. Missing you and Vernon.

Will

Nearly every morning before the wheat cutting started, Sailor and I did our calisthenics. We sometimes also jogged around the wheat field, after he'd wrapped his hurt knee. During the day, driving the tractor and when we were stopped to unload the combine bin, I regularly practiced Charles Atlas's "dynamic tension" as Sailor'd taught me, pitting my muscles against each other to build them up.

Bonnie Wynn, being from Kansas, had had no experience with southern cooking. For our first couple of Duggert-camp dinners and suppers, she served us a lot of dull hamburger-meat dishes, like spaghetti and meat sauce, or meat loaf. Once she even cooked us a totally meatless meal, with macaroni and cheese as the main dish. But Dad soon showed Bonnie how to fry up some floured meat—steak or chicken—and then how to make flour gravy afterwards in the grease. She caught on fast. She also learned to pour in a little leftover bacon grease from breakfast when she cooked canned spinach, say, or boiled canned green beans until they were as mushy and soft as we liked them.

Bonnie brought our noon dinner to the field each day in Sailor's Green Lizard. She said it took her a while to get totally comfortable using the knob on the wheel to overcome the slack in the old car's steering. At the field, she always spread a quilt for both seating and serving in whatever shade there was next to the old car and laid out the food and iced tea for us. Dad and Big Jim never wanted to stop the combines to let all our bunch eat at the same time. The two of them temporarily took over tractor and combine jobs, one by one, so that the rest of us could get off and eat in shifts.

Surprisingly, it turned out that Bonnie had grown up on a farm in Kansas and that she herself knew how to drive a tractor. She loved doing it, too. On our second day cutting for Duggert, Bonnie volunteered to fill in as a tractor driver while crew members were eating dinner, and my dad let her. I was amazed that she could manage both the old Fordson and the Farmall equally well, though she looked a little odd on the seat of either one of them in her clean and well-ironed slacks and blouse and a woman's wide-brimmed straw hat, her face and hair, as usual, all fixed up like she was going to church.

On one of our early evenings at the rock house camp, after everybody'd eaten supper and scattered, Sailor and I stayed at the card table alone. I picked up the little Comanche Indian book he'd been reading before he started playing his French harp. I thumbed through the book for a minute, and that made me think of Marcy Redelk. I decided that maybe I should write her. So I got out one of my Dimmitt High School postcards, addressed it to her, in care of her uncle, put a stamp on it, and wrote out a brief message to her. Then, while I was at it, I wrote postcards to Mama and Janie Marie, too. The next morning, I gave all the cards to Big Jim to mail when he went into town with the day's first load of wheat.

June 25, 1943

Dear Marcy,

    We're out here on the plains of West Texas where the Comanches used to roam. Thinking about the "white buffalo bones" of the 49 song, but haven't seen any. Is the name of the town of Quitaque, Texas, Comanche? Hope you're having a good time this summer. Write me at General Delivery, Boise City, Oklahoma. We're going there before too long.

Your friend, Will Haley

June 25, 1943

Dear Mama,

    Dad's found us lots of wheat here to cut. We're working hard. Dad's been tending to business real well. Don't worry. I'm looking after things. Tell Grandma hi and hug the twins for me. Don't work too hard.

Your son, Willie

June 25, 1943

Dear Janie Marie,

    I almost caught a baby prairie dog to bring home to you as a pet, but couldn't do it after all. When we leave Dimmitt, Texas, we're going to Boise City, Oklahoma, next, then Limon, Colorado, and after that, Kimball, Nebraska. Like being on an old cattle drive, trailing north through the country. Everybody's fine. Spider's trying hard to find him a girlfriend.

Love, Will

    As the wheat harvest got into full swing in more parts of the country, railroad boxcars for transporting wheat to the flour mills got scarcer and scarcer. Too many were tied up carrying war stuff. So grain elevators sometimes had to dump a lot of wheat on the ground temporarily and cover it the best they could with tarps. Unloading truck lines got longer, too, especially in the late afternoons and evenings. Truckers were frequently at the grain elevator as late as ten o'clock at night before they could get rid of their wheat and come on back. That's the way it was in Dimmitt, too, nearly all the time we were cutting around there.

But the weather was mostly good. We were blessed with a tornado-free stay, even though, of course, it was tornado season. Still, one afternoon, it did come a little rain at pretty near the same time that we would have quit work anyway. We knew we'd probably be able to sleep a little later than usual the next morning while the wheat dried out, so Sailor and I decided that we ought to go into town and take in a picture show. Over supper, Sailor asked Spider if he wanted to go, and he said he did, although things were still testy between the two of them. Buford was not back from town, apparently stuck in a line at the elevator. Jim Gruber, Dad, and Little Jim didn't think much of the picture show idea and said they weren't interested.

After eating supper, Sailor and I went out by the water tank to help Bonnie wash up the dishes. "Why don't you come go with us to a movie, Bonnie?" I said to her. "You've been working too hard. Need to take off and have a little fun."

She looked up from the pie pan she was drying, clearly interested. "What's showing?" she asked.

"No idea," I said. "That make any difference to you?"

"I don't know if Burford would like for me to go," Bonnie said.

"We could stop, first, at the elevator, so you could take him something to eat," Sailor said.

Bonnie thought about it a minute. "Well, okay," she said. "But let me clean up and put together a little sack of food."

We drove into Dimmitt in the Green Lizard. Bonnie sat in front with Sailor, looking really cleaned up and nice and smelling even better. Spider and I were in the backseat. At the tall white

Dimmitt Wheat Growers elevator on the south side of town, we found Buford in his orange Dodge truck, way back in line. Sailor, Spider, and I all gave Buford a wave, but stayed in the car, while Bonnie took the food sack and went over and climbed up into the truck cab with her husband.

It wasn't long before it appeared that Bonnie and Buford were getting into some kind of an argument.

"Uh-oh," Sailor said.

We could hear something of Buford's angry high-pitched voice all the way out to the car. Once, he alarmingly raised a hand as if he might hit Bonnie. Then she was out of the truck and back to the Green Lizard.

"Guess he just wants me to sit around the house trailer, knitting or something," she said, as she got into the car and slammed the passenger door.

"Wanna get back to camp?" Sailor asked her.

"Heck with him!" Bonnie said. "Let's go on to the movie, like we planned."

I was glad she said that.

"Heck with Buford!" Spider said. He reached a long right arm forward and gently patted Bonnie on the shoulder. I thought I noticed her flinch away slightly, a little toward the window.

Sailor cranked up the Green Lizard, and we took off toward downtown. We circled around the courthouse to the right, then came back and found a vacant parking place almost in front of the Carlisle Theater. Sailor angled into it. The movie that was showing was *Casablanca*, with Humphrey Bogart and Ingrid Bergman. I'd already seen it, but that didn't matter. After hot, boring, and dusty days of wheat cutting and early-to-bed nights in the back of a truck, I was hungry for almost any kind of entertainment.

Spider paid for himself and Bonnie, too. She let him. He slid two quarters to the woman in the glass-front booth and took two tickets back from her. Sailor and I stepped up separately and paid. In the lobby, Bonnie did protest a little when Spider said he'd buy her some popcorn, but Spider insisted. So Sailor and I gave him our dimes, too—told him to get us each a bag while he was at it. Bonnie left us for the restroom, and Sailor and I went on into the theater. He chose an aisle seat about midway down. I took the one next to him.

Spider came inside before Bonnie did. Handing over our popcorn and carrying his own and Bonnie's, he edged in and took a seat down the row, leaving a vacant place between him and me. But when Bonnie joined us, she said to me, "Would you move over one, Will?"

I did. That put Bonnie between Sailor and me, Spider on my right. He passed a sack of popcorn across me to Bonnie, looking, I thought, a little put out, not to be sitting by her.

"Thank you," she said, without glancing toward Spider. I was glad to see that his charm wasn't working on Bonnie.

I was glad, too, to be sitting next to Bonnie myself. I hoped, at first, that maybe she was kind of interested in me. But because of the way she soon leaned ever so slightly more toward Sailor than she did toward me and the way she talked a little more to him, too, before the picture show started, I decided that if she was interested in me, I wasn't her *main* interest right then. Not that she was flirting with Sailor. She was too sweet and innocent to think of two-timing her husband, I figured. And Sailor certainly wasn't the type to encourage that, either.

The theater darkened. There was a Three Stooges comedy first. Not too funny with the mean guy, as usual, always hitting the dumbest one. Then came a Pathé newsreel: Charlie Chaplin struck with a paternity suit. Race riots in Detroit, President Franklin D. Roosevelt sending in federal troops. Calumet Stables retires the great thoroughbred Whirlaway. U.S. forces land on an island in the Solomons, north of Guadalcanal.

The war news made me worry about my two uncles, Uncle Clif and Uncle Wayne. I'd heard on the radio before we left home that the United States was reportedly getting ready for a big invasion of the island of Sicily, and I knew that my uncles were near there, as the map showed, somewhere in North Africa.

Casablanca came on. My favorite scene was when, toward the end, Humphrey Bogart made his sad and patriotic little speech to Ingrid at the airport and said, "We'll always have Paris." Even though he was still crazy about Ingrid, he was noble enough to help her and her husband make their getaway on the airplane and shot a German major to protect them. I loved that picture show and, as the lights came back on at the end, I thought to myself that I wouldn't mind seeing it a third time.

Later in the car, headed back to camp, Spider Deering said, "Humphrey Bogart shoulda held on to Ingrid Bergman. She wanted to stay. He oughtn't to have let her go off with her old dull husband."

"Woman's choice, triangle like that," Sailor said.

"She's got to do her duty," Bonnie said.

Buford's truck was already parked at the rock house camp when we got back there. Everyone but me scattered right away to their separate beds, and after Bonnie went into the house trailer, I heard low quarrelsome words coming from inside it for a while. Feeling a little grimy in the heat and humidity of the night, I went and washed my face and hands in the horse tank. Then I came back and climbed up to get into the back of my dad's truck.

But all of a sudden, as I came over the tailgate and started to step down into the truck bed, a flashlight's harsh beam was switched on and pointed squarely in my face.

It scared me. "Great heavenly shit!" I said. I threw up my hands against the glare.

The light clicked off. And, despite the fact that I was still a little blinded, I quickly saw that it was Big Jim Gruber who held the flashlight. A brooding hulk in the dark, he sat in his shorts and undershirt on a quilt of his own, a few feet to the right of my quilt.

"Just me, Willie," he said.

I smelled his liquor before I saw him lift the pint bottle up and take a swig out of it. "What's up, Big Jim?" I asked, moving toward my bed.

"Hearing too much of them rattlesnakes, like you," he said. "Thought I'd change to a new location, too."

"Welcome to the Ritz," I said.

I stripped to my shorts, sat down, and rolled into my quilt.

But I was wide awake. After a couple of minutes, I quit trying to go right to sleep and raised up on an elbow. "Borrow your flashlight, Big Jim?" I asked. "Think I'll read a little."

He handed it to me, and I switched the beam on. I reached over to my Levi's and got the Dale Carnegie paperback, *How to Win Friends and Influence People*, that I'd been carrying in my hip pocket. I turned to the page, a fourth way through, that I'd earlier dog-eared down. I held the flashlight close to the page so that the circle of light was not much bigger than the book itself. I started to read from the second chapter, "The Big Secret of Dealing with People."

But I didn't get very far.

Jim Gruber wanted to talk. "Seen your book, yesterday, Willie," he said. "When I was not much older'n you, success was what I was after, too."

"Right," I said. It was pretty clear that the big man was going to keep on talking. Not much chance of my reading. I sat up and laid the flashlight, still switched on, in my lap.

"Success don't always come as neat as you might think it will," Big Jim said. "You liable to learn that yourself."

"Probably will."

Jim Gruber's long body seemed about as big around as a barrel. No waist. But he was hard all over, it looked like. His blondish hair was thinning. He took up a gold watch with a short chain from the floor next to him, glanced quickly at it, then put it back down. He picked up a crumpled pack of Chesterfields.

"Smoke?" he asked. Big Jim wouldn't have done that if he hadn't been drinking.

"Don't use 'em," I said.

"Good boy."

He fished out a cigarette for himself, dropped the package, then took up a kitchen match from a little stack of them, scratched it into flame on the floor, and lit up. He sucked in the smoke, held it a moment, then exhaled heavily. Cigarette dangling from the side of his mouth, he lifted up a half-pint bottle of Echo Springs whiskey. He unscrewed the cap and proffered the bottle to me, squinching his eyes against the smoke that curled up from the cigarette.

114

"Slug of this?" Big Jim asked.

"Too early for me," I said.

"Hell, Willie, it's *nighttime!*" he said.

"Well, all right then," I said. Taking a drink of whiskey was the very last thing I wanted to do.

"Help yourself," he said.

I took the bottle and swallowed a very small gulp. It made me shiver like I had malaria. About the worst stuff I'd ever tasted.

Big Jim took the half-pint back and, after pulling the cigarette from his lips and laying it and the bottle cap on the floor between us, said, "Now, hold the gun on me and make me take a drink!"

I assumed that that was part of some old joke. He gave a low laugh, then drank. He put the lid back on the bottle, set it down between us, and picked up his burning Chesterfield.

"At Cameron College, Willie, I was a rassler, you maybe heard," he said. "Had a chance, some, to be around guys with money—big rasslin' fans, supporters of the program. Made up my mind, back then, that I was gonna be worth a lot of money myself, a big success, by the time I was twenty-one. That was my goal."

"Good career plan," I said.

"Got out of college in 1918, the year before the First World War ended," Big Jim went on. "Only got drafted to go overseas at the tail end of the war, and, then, not in the trenches, thank the good Lord! Come back home and took a job teaching country school in the big kids' room out there at Pecan Grove, south of Vernon—sixth, seventh, and eighth grades—for forty-five dollars a month and a little house. Less'n I was making in college—with my rasslin' scholarship and waiting tables in the dining room—before I graduated. Still, I reckon I'd be teaching school yet, 'cept I liked to take a drink now and then."

"That's news," I said.

"Drove over one night to Cookietown, where there was a guy that sold bootleg whiskey, second floor over his grocery," Big Jim said. "I started up the stairs, and there was two big guys beating hell out of a little guy. Well, I took up the little guy's part, and we run them other two off.

"Him and me, then, went on up and bought ourselves some hootch. And after we come back down, we was having a drink together out by our cars, and he asked me what I was doing for a living. I said, 'Teaching school.' He says, 'How much they paying you?' I says, 'Forty-five dollars.' Well, sir, he told me then that he was working for Kelly Oil, blocking up leases over by Randlett, down close to Red River. Said there was gonna be a big strike, which later turned out to be right, as you maybe know. Man said he didn't get no salary but was taking a percentage override cut out of any oil produced. Said, 'Why don't you give up teachin' school and come block up leases with me?' Said he could get me the same override deal as him.

"Well, sir, I quit school in the middle of the term and went to driving out the section lines over in that part of the county, talking farmers into signing oil leases with Kelly. And acourse, it wasn't long after that 'til all them gushers commenced to blowing in.

"I turned twenty-one early the next year, Willie, and by then I *was*, by God, right well off, like I'd always planned on being. By then, too, I'd married my high school sweetheart, Annabelle Blackstock—you know her kinfolks. Pretty as a picture. Absolute love of my life. I had everything, Willie, complete success. At least, that's what I thought.

"But Annabelle and me liked to party. And one night, both of us drinking, we was coming back from a dance down at Wardell. Heading out of town, west, on the gravel highway toward the Essaquahnadale corner. I was driving fast. Annabelle said she needed to pee. She opened her door and got out, me going maybe forty miles an hour. God almighty!

"That was the end of ever thing for me, Willie, all my dreams of success. My sweet Annabelle died right there by the side of the road, me holding her head in my lap."

Big Jim Gruber stopped for a minute, leaned to his left, and ground out his cigarette on the floor over there.

After a little while, straightening up, he went on. "I wasn't worth a good God damn to nobody after that. More or less went to pieces. But I finally got myself back together after a couple of years, started over."

I felt like I ought to say something. "Well, life's what happens after you make your plans," I said.

"Where'd you hear that?" Big Jim said, his head snapping up so he could look directly at me.

"I read it."

"It's the damned truth," he said. "Better remember it!" He sat, downcast once more, for a while. Then finally he raised his head and looked at me again. "But maybe what I just told you about Annabelle and me ain't the whole story," he said. "What would you think of that?"

"Is it. . .the whole story?"

"The trouble is, Willie, I don't know," he said. "I was dead drunk. I know there's people—her own daddy, for one—who thinks me and Annabelle got in a fight, and I *pushed* her out of the car while it was running." He sat still for a moment. "And what I have to live with is that I don't actually know."

I couldn't think of any further comment to make. Finally, I said, "Let's go to sleep, Big Jim, and you'll feel better in the morning."

"Okay," he said. "But I doubt it."

I switched off the flashlight and lay down. Not long after that, he lay down, too. He seemed to go right to sleep. I stayed awake for a time.

I felt sorry for the man. And his story set me to thinking, some. Was he trying to say that it's no good having any ambition or even trying for success? If so, I couldn't buy it. I knew that, in my own case, I was going to grab for the brass ring when it came around, no matter what might come with it.

But the more I thought about Big Jim's story, the more I figured that he probably hadn't been trying to make any point at all with me. Maybe, drinking, he just felt the need to confess to somebody, even me–confessing his doubts and possible terrible sin.

Too bad I'm not a priest and can't give him some kind of absolution.

Then I was too sleepy to think about it any more.

Three nights later, after everybody else'd gone to bed, Sailor Torley and I stayed up by ourselves again for a while.

In a circle of lantern light, we sat outside around the card table on camp stools. He softly played his French harp, and I read from *How to Win Friends and Influence People*. Then I was surprised when Bonnie suddenly came quietly out of the house trailer and joined us. She had on yellow flowered pajamas. Her blonde hair was tied up in a bandanna. In the lantern light, she was just as pretty as ever, though her big eyes and baby cheeks were without make-up, and her soft lips were plain, too.

"You guys doing?" she asked as she took a seat with us at the card table.

"Me, if my leg keeps healing good, I'm thinking about getting back to sea as soon's this wheat harvest's over," Sailor said. "Will here's studying up on how to get hisself elected president of the United States."

"You want to be president, Will?" Bonnie asked.

I put down the paperback. "Might be a better job than cutting wheat for a living," I said.

"Hire me as White House cook, once you get in there?" Bonnie asked.

"Yeah, I would, and raise your pay to *five* dollars a week," I said. "Plus room and board, of course."

"It's a deal," Bonnie said.

The three of us sat still for a little while. I went back to *How to Win Friends and Influence People*. Sailor began to play a low but lively "Pretty Redwing"on his French harp. Bonnie started to sing the words of the song in a quiet and surprisingly sweet voice: "Oh, the moon shines tonight on pretty Redwing. . . ."

When the song was over, Sailor slapped the French harp against his pant leg, then dropped it into the pocket of his gray work shirt.

He turned to me. "Will, you think you might really wanna go into politics one of these days?"

"Possibly could," I said.

"That book any help?"

"What I've read so far, old Dale Carnegie's advice'd really work," I said. I opened the book to its table of contents. "I mean, he's got stuff here on 'Fundamental Techniques in Handling

People,' and 'Six Ways to Make People Like You,' and 'How to Win People to Your Way of Thinking.'"

"People already like you, Will," Bonnie said. "I know I do."

Sailor looked at Bonnie Wynn and said, "But the question is, Miss Bonnie, Could Will ever win you over to his way of thinking?"

Bonnie answered with a question. "What *is* his way of thinking?"

Sailor turned back to me then. "Yeah, Will, what *is* your way of thinking?" he asked.

"*My* way of thinking is that it's time to go to bed," I said. I stood up and put the paperback in my hip pocket. Then, after hesitating a moment, I said, "But, Sailor, let me ask you something. You think it's really right—ethical, I mean—for a guy to use Dale Carnegie's techniques to try to manipulate people, make them to do what *you* want them to do?"

"Lord God, Will!" Sailor said. "Worrying about stuff like that, you got no business going into politics."

"That what you think?" I asked.

"Naw, Will. Just kidding," he said, changing his tone. "Truth is, if you're the people's champion, they gonna want you as skilled as the guys you going up against. And I know you only gonna try to influence people, anyway, to do what's for their own good. So I say learn how to do it the best you can, Will."

Time to go to bed. "Good night, y'all," I said. "Tomorrow's another day."

"Hard to tell 'em apart." Sailor said.

I went and climbed up to my truckbed quilt. Big Jim was already wrapped up in his, but he wasn't asleep.

"Calling it a night, Willie?" he asked. He sat up, reached and got a cigarette out of the Chesterfield package near him, and lit up.

I pulled off my Levi's and crawled into my quilt in my shorts. But as I lay down, I was conscious that Jim Gruber was still awake, smoking. And I began to think about what he'd told me earlier about how his first wife got killed. I rolled over to face toward him and raised up on an elbow.

"Big Jim," I said, "you know what you told me about the death of your first wife?"

"Yeah," he said. "Why?" I could tell that he wasn't too interested in talking about all that again.

"I've been thinking a lot about it," I said.

"Have?"

"I think you've been too hard on yourself for too long," I said.

"How's that, Willie?"

What am I, some kind of psychiatrist?

But I went on. "You either didn't push her out of the car at all, and she jumped out on her own," I said, "or, if you did push her, since you can't even remember it, you must have been so drunk at the time that you can't keep on forever blaming yourself for what happened. You didn't know what you were doing. Ever confess about the whole thing to your priest?"

"Never have."

"You should," I said. "I'm not a Catholic, but maybe you ought to bring all this up in confession—your doubts about what happened and the part you might've played in it. You've got a right to forgiveness, Big Jim, after all these years—and a right to forgive yourself."

He didn't say anything for a while. He snuffed out his cigarette and lay back down. Then, finally, he spoke. "You got a good heart, Willie."

Outside, Sailor and Bonnie, I could tell, were still sitting together in the lantern glow at the card table. I heard Bonnie laugh at something Sailor said in a low voice. Then I turned back over and went to sleep.

One afternoon toward the last part of that week, Little Jim and I were stopped in the field to dump our wheat into Buford's truck, when Mr. Duggert, as usual, drove up in his big blue Packard sedan and stopped near us in the tall stubble. Dad and Jim Gruber were at the elevator in Dimmitt. Spider and Sailor's combine was some distance off, coming around the short side of the field toward Little Jim and me.

Mr. Duggert got out of his Packard to walk to where Little Jim and I were unloading, but for some reason, he left the car motor idling. That was a bad mistake. The Packard's exhaust somehow suddenly sparked a fire in the wheat stubble behind the car! And it didn't take more than a couple of minutes before the flames were high and spreading, practically surrounding the big blue automobile.

I was the first one to see the fire, when it was still small and mostly smoke. But by the time I could yell and direct the attention of Mr. Duggert and the others to the danger, the Packard was already in jeopardy. And with a stiff wind blowing, though away from our combine, a real wheat field catastrophe was rapidly becoming a frightening prospect.

I didn't even think at first. I just jumped off my tractor and, passing by Mr. Duggert, made a run for his car. Next to it, kicking dirt right and left to make myself a path in the flames, I jerked open the driver's side door and leaped in. I slammed the gearshift into reverse, gunned the motor, and backed out of the flames at ten or fifteen miles an hour, through the stubble and out of the field, onto the adjoining dirt road.

Leaping from the Packard, then, I raced back into the field. The fire had grown to at least half an acre in size, and it was expanding rapidly. White smoke swirled upward from it, three or four stories high. Our combines and tractors, Buford's truck, Mr. Duggert's rich uncut wheat—all were in serious danger of being burned up in the spreading flames.

All of a sudden, I thought of the one-way plow back in the corner of the field nearest the rock house. My first plan was to unhitch the Fordson tractor from our combine and go to get the plow so I could make a wide swath in the dirt around the fire. But I quickly realized that the Fordson would be too slow, that I needed the faster Farmall tractor that Spider was driving. On a hard run, then, past mine and Little Jim's Gleaner-Baldwin, I hollered at Little Jim, Buford, and Mr. Duggert to get themselves to the road in Buford's truck. I dashed on toward the approaching other combine.

"Stop and get off!" I yelled at Spider as I got close to him and the Farmall. He brought his tractor to a halt and jumped down, complying without objection. Beside him on the ground, I hollered, "Help me unhitch this thing from the combine!" He bent and did that. "You get to the road, away from the fire!" I shouted to him and he took off running like a turpentined cat. I climbed into his place on the seat of the now unhooked Farmall.

Sailor was down from the combine, beside the tractor. "Get on here with me!" I said to him. He stepped up onto the hitch behind me and grabbed ahold of the seat. I slammed the Farmall into road gear, and we took off so fast that Sailor had to hang on with both hands to keep from falling off. We raced to the one-way plow parked in the corner of the field. I turned and backed up to it. Sailor got off and swiftly hooked the wide plow to the tractor, then retook his place, standing on the tractor hitch. I put the Farmall in gear and we bounded back toward the fire, dragging the plow behind, the discs off the ground, not engaged. A patch of three or four acres of stubble was burning by then, and the fire was rapidly growing outward in every direction, ever closer to Mr. Duggert's uncut wheat and our own Gleaner-Baldwins and the Fordson tractor.

Sailor unlatched the one-way plow's long handle and shoved it backwards when I told him to, to drop the large discs into the dirt. I had to shift the tractor down to second gear because of the sudden heavy load, with the discs engaged, but we were still able to plow pretty fast. I twice half-mooned the fire on the side toward the uncut wheat and our machines, then I began to circle it. On the downwind side of the fire, Sailor and I had to tie bandannas over our noses and mouths to filter out the heavy smoke and keep from choking.

It took a while, but I eventually plowed a wide enough swath around the flames to be sure that the fire was fully contained and couldn't spread any more. I drove the tractor and plow back toward the road then, and Sailor and I got off and stood with Mr. Duggert and the others and watched until the stubble fire burned itself out, inside its plowed dirt collar.

"Son," Mr. Duggert said to me, when it was clear that all danger was passed, "I owe you a lot, and I won't forget it." After that, having had all the excitement he could stand for the day, the banker left for town, without his usual inspection of the cutting job we were doing.

Little Jim and Sailor—and Big Jim Gruber, too, when he got back to the field—praised me a lot for what I'd done, which I appreciated.

But not my dad. He didn't return from the elevator until our quitting time. And when he heard about the fire and my actions, he only griped that I should have first gotten the two combines and the Fordson out of the field, to safety, before I drove the Farmall over and hitched it up to the one-way plow.

Can't win for losing.

Chapter Seven

We got a late start on the morning that our harvest caravan was to leave Dimmitt, pointed toward Amarillo. After finishing all of Mr. Duggert's wheat, we'd cut the smaller acreages of two of his neighbors, too, winding up everything on the afternoon of Tuesday, the twenty-ninth. We packed up, loaded up, and hitched up, ready to roll. But Dad and Big Jim always required farmers to pay them in cash. They didn't want to wait for checks to clear, and they needed cash to pay the rest of us off, too. So they made arrangements to meet Mr. Duggert and the other two farmers at Mr. Duggert's bank in Dimmitt, as soon as the bank opened on that Wednesday morning, the last day of June.

Out at the rock house camp, we all got up early anyway—earlier than we needed to. The sky was clear, but the usual wind was blowing pretty hard out on the "windswept plains," as the pulp western stories always put it. It was moving day, and, as always, my dad began to get into the bottle that morning, almost from the time he was out of his quilt.

When the two of us were by ourselves for a moment, at the horse tank, I got up my nerve and tried to venture a word of caution. "Don't you think, maybe, Dad, that you ought to go a little lighter on the whiskey, this early?"

"Mind your own business, Willie," he said.

Dad's drinking *was* my business. At least that's what Mama'd told me before we left home. But I couldn't think of anything else I could do about it after he cut me off so harshly.

Bonnie made breakfast for us, which was a new departure. And she would keep on cooking breakfast as well as the other two meals as long as we were on the harvest trail together. Dad, it turned out, upped her daily pay by a dollar. When breakfast was over and the dishes were done, there was still time to kill. Sailor and I did some calisthenics. Then he wrapped his bad leg and we jogged a mile or so down the road and back. A little before ten o'clock, our harvest parade finally hit the trail, away from the rock house and back to U.S. 385, then north.

We snaked through Dimmitt past the courthouse. A couple of blocks farther north, as soon as there was room enough along the highway, we parked our caravan—trucks, pick-up, combines and headers, and house trailer—in an extra long line on the shoulder, strung out more than usual. We were careful not to block the entrances to the lumberyard and other businesses along there. I was driving Sailor's Green Lizard, with him in the passenger seat. I pulled off the highway behind my dad.

Dad and Jim Gruber got out of their trucks and walked back toward the bank, opposite the northwest corner of the courthouse. The rest of us stayed put for a while. Then Sailor took a notion for me and him to go back to town, too, so that he could buy the portable battery radio we'd seen in the radio repair shop on our first day in Dimmitt.

We got out of the Lizard and headed south, walking along the edge of the highway. He and I were both dressed in our best traveling clothes—cowboy boots, bulldogger straw hats, clean white T-shirts, and Levi's. On the opposite side of the highway, for traffic coming into Dimmitt from the north, there was a painted chamber of commerce sign that read "Welcome to Dimmitt. Getting better as we grow bigger!"

"Ain't gonna happen," Sailor said, more or less to himself.

As he and I passed Little Jim's pick-up and approached Buford's Dodge, Bonnie, pretty in a blue cotton dress, got out of the truck on the passenger side and came around to meet us. We stopped for her by the truck's left fender.

"Where you guys going?" she asked.

Sailor told her.

"I'll walk with you, maybe buy me a magazine," Bonnie said.

Buford stuck his big head with the tan chauffeur cap on it out of his driver's side window. "Now Bonnie," he said, the usual whine in his voice, "you've got no business going off. We want to be ready the minute the bosses get back."

"Too hot, sitting in that truck," she said back to him. It *was* getting hot. The midmorning Texas sun was beaming down hard from a cloudless, pastel blue sky.

Buford frowned but didn't say anything further as the three of us walked by him, and on toward Dimmitt's downtown.

At Hartford Radio Repair, next door to the Rexall Drug we saw that the Admiral "Bantam" portable radio was still in the window and for sale. We went inside. Hartford, the owner, turned out to be a moustached old man with one leg shorter than the other. He limped forward from his repair bench and asked us what we wanted. Sailor said he'd like to see the portable radio in the window. The old man went and got it, then handed it to Sailor.

"This thing work all right?" Sailor asked.

"Made in '41 and good, now, as it was new," old Hartford said. "I put two new tubes in it. Battery's a new one, too."

Sailor opened the small front door of the radio and turned the volume up by twisting the bottom knob, then tuned to the Dimmitt station with the top knob. The opening words of a popular soap opera, "Our Gal Sunday," came on, almost as clear as if it was being broadcast from right there in the shop: "The story that asks the question, Can this girl from a little mining town in the West find happiness with England's richest and most handsome lord, Lord Henry Breathrup?'" I was amazed that the little radio's reception was so good. Old Hartford said that there was a coiled antenna wire inside the back of the set.

"You ever see the movie *Shadow of the Thin Man*?" he asked. "Couple of years ago. Nick Charles goes into an apartment to investigate, and the landlady there is carrying one of these very radios, listening to her favorite program."

I'd seen that movie, but I only vaguely remembered anything about the woman with the portable radio.

"What do you want for it?" Sailor asked old Hartford.

"The guy that brought it in—it needed tubes and a battery—never came back for it," the owner said. "That was nearly a year ago."

"What if he comes back after you sell it?" Bonnie asked.

"He won't be back," the old man said. "They sent him to the pen for a bunch of burglaries."

"Maybe this portable's stolen," I said.

"Nobody's ever claimed it," old Hartford said. "By now, they're not going to."

Sailor asked again what the man wanted for the small portable. He said that for nineteen dollars, he'd throw in two extra batteries along with the radio. Sailor took out his billfold and paid.

After that we went into the Rexall Drug so Bonnie could buy herself a movie magazine.

Later, back at the vehicles, we all gathered around Dad and Big Jim, and they doled out our pay to each of us. Then, acting like it pained him to do so, my dad counted out and handed me an extra three fives and a ten, twenty five dollars.

"What's this?" I asked him.

"Duggert sent you a reward for putting out that wheat field fire," Dad said, then turned away to go to his truck.

The rest of us went to our own vehicles, too. We fired up and headed north on U.S. 385. A highway sign said "Hereford—20 miles."

We drove through acres and acres of the same kind of excellent flat farmland that we'd just come from around Dimmitt. There were big cut-out wheat fields, some already being plowed under. Flocks of birds here and there descended into still unplowed stubble to glean leftover kernels. A lot of the birds were grackles, black and long-tailed, but thin, like crows on a diet. And we saw scattered fields of long green rows of nearly knee-high maize.

We passed a roadside series of small red Burma-Shave signs with white lettering:

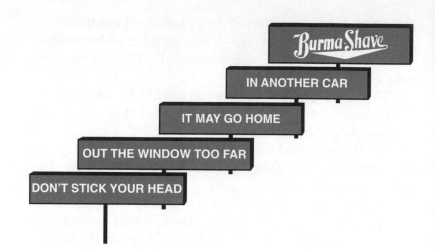

Burma Shave

IN ANOTHER CAR

IT MAY GO HOME

OUT THE WINDOW TOO FAR

DON'T STICK YOUR HEAD

Crossing into Deaf Smith county, we saw a government bill-board indicating directions to the nearby Hereford Military and Reception Center, identified as a U.S. prisoner of war camp for Italian soldiers captured in North Africa.

"We oughta stop, Will, and see if we can get a pizza," Sailor said.

"Or see if any of them saw my uncles over there," I said.

Several flat lakes. More large fields of wheat stubble. Smooth green pastures in the draws. Elm shelter belts.

Just outside the town of Hereford, three times as big as Dimmitt and also in the heart of rich farm country, a chamber of commerce sign said "Welcome to the home of the Hostile Herd and the Lady Whitefaces."

Neither Sailor nor I wanted to touch that. "Already funny enough," he said.

We crossed over a creek at the south edge of Hereford, passed under a railroad trestle, and stopped, then turned right on U.S. 60, a narrow concrete strip. It took us northeast along the south side of Hereford's main business district. To our right was the Santa Fe railroad track and, next to it, two big white concrete grain elevators and a Santa Fe railroad depot.

"Wind blowing like a son of a bitch!" Sailor said.

I remembered an old cowboy saying I'd read about that kind of country and wintertime wind. "Nothing between here and the North Pole but a barbed-wire fence," I said.

"And I ain't hardly even seen a *fence*," Sailor said.

We headed toward the town of Canyon. A highway sign said "Amarillo—47 miles." Same level country. Treeless, except for planted elms around an occasional farmhouse or scattered here and there on the highway shoulder. Our wheat harvest parade passed into Randall County, whizzed on by the little town of Umbarger, with a freight train holding there on a siding, and finally came to the northwest edge of Canyon, a solid cattle and college town about the size of Hereford.

After halting at a highway intersection, Big Jim turned and led us onto U.S. 87, north. A sign said "Amarillo—15 miles." We drove maybe a mile or so before Big Jim pulled off the highway at a shady cottonwood draw. Noontime. A stop for a quick bite of the dinner that Bonnie'd fixed in advance and to gas up the vehicles.

But I was more interested in seeing Palo Duro Canyon, east of the town of Canyon, than I was in eating. So was Sailor. Palo Duro Canyon was the place where General Mackenzie and Kit Carson surprised and defeated the last free band of the Comanche Indians, then drove them onto an Oklahoma reservation. I told Dad that Sailor and I wanted to make a quick run out to the canyon and that we'd catch up with the rest of them later, as fast as we could.

"Do that if y'all want to, Willie," he said, "but you ain't gotta hurry. We cain't make it to Boise City today. Too late a start this morning out of Dimmitt. Look for us somewhere at the side of the highway right in Amarillo. We'll spend the night there."

I was glad about that for a couple of reasons. My dad was still drinking, of course. I was scared to death that he might get into a bad highway accident if we roaded too long. And besides, I knew that Amarillo was a pretty big town—a small city, they said—and I was hoping that we might have time to look around a little there, see the sights some.

"We'll find you," I said.

"May just find our trucks and machinery is all, Willie, depending on when you get there," Dad said. "Me and Jim Gruber gonna buy the ticket for anybody that wants to go to the rodeo. Amarillo's got one of the best." My dad was crazy about rodeos.

Back in the Green Lizard, I turned it around and drove me and Sailor south toward the business section of the town of Canyon.

"We catch back up with your dad in time, I wouldn't mind seeing *me* a rodeo," Sailor said.

"Myself, I've been to enough of them," I said. "Only rodeo that'd interest me now would be Frontier Days at Cheyenne. They call that one 'the Daddy of 'Em All.'"

Downtown in Canyon, I followed a sign's directions and turned due east toward Palo Duro Canyon. The gravel road made me think of some old clichés: not "crooked as a dog's hind leg," for sure, but "straight as a string" or "straight as an arrow." A Texas historical marker said that this was the route Charles Goodnight used when he brought the first cattle into the Texas Panhandle in 1877.

We passed through ten miles of featureless plains—flat, but sort of rough. Then, suddenly, abruptly, we came onto Palo Duro Canyon, an unforgettably beautiful, deep, long, and massive gash in the sandstone and limestone Texas prairie. It was decorated around its rim with a growth of yucca, junipers, and mesquite. Below, the Prairie Dog Town Fork of Red River that'd carved the canyon in the first place still snaked along its southeasterly course and was lined with hackberries, oaks, willows, chinaberries, and cottonwoods. No wonder the Comanches thought that they would be safe and hidden down there. No wonder that, once the Indians had been forced out by soldiers, Goodnight, as the historical marker said, set up the headquarters of his million-acre ranch in the bottom of the canyon and ran a hundred thousand head of cattle there and close by, having a hard time finding them all at roundup time.

As we gazed into the deep canyon, impressed, Sailor delivered himself of one of his commentaries. "Willie," he said, "the Lord musta done his last practicing up on making canyons right here—and got pretty good at it—before he went for the championship blue ribbon at the Grand Canyon."

Later, back on U.S. 87, north out of Canyon, I pushed the Green Lizard past the speed limit, and we ginned along through level tableland, pretty much following the Goodnight Trail. I remembered reading in a history book that old cowboys said there were "about as many cattle trails north as there were ranchers." This was one of them. We steered toward Amarillo, the Texas Panhandle point where everything was said to have come together in the old days and later on, where major railroads and highways crossed, and where I knew that there was one of the biggest stockyards and cattle auctions in Texas.

I was a little concerned about whether we'd have trouble finding our combine crew in a town of Amarillo's size, but I needn't have worried. U.S. 87, joining with U.S. 287, became Amarillo's Buchanan Street, running straight north through the city's east side. I eased along this thoroughfare, impressed by the city's big downtown section, with a twenty-story, ivory-colored limestone Santa Fe railroad building off to our left. I stopped on red at traffic lights, which were something new for me, and eventually crossed the famous east-west U.S. 66, which was Amarillo's red brick Sixth Street. To the west was the county courthouse and local library.

As we came toward Second Street, Sailor and I at the same time suddenly spotted our vehicles and combines. On our right, they were rowed up on a vacant lot at the southeast corner of the intersection. And the whole crew was still there. Hallelujah! Reunited.

Dressed up, we all crossed Buchanan and walked west on Second Street. The sidewalk radiated heat like a cheap cookstove. After a couple of blocks in that direction, then south a block or two, we found the Cattlemen's Café. We pulled two tables together, sat down, and ordered. A big red and black poster on one wall advertised the Amarillo rodeo. It started at 7:30. Buford and Bonnie said they wanted to go with Dad and Jim Gruber. So did Sailor. I said I wasn't very interested. Little Jim offered to stay with the vehicles and look after them.

Down at one end of the tables, where Spider Deering and I were sitting, Spider turned to me. "Why don't me and you find us something more fun, Willie?" he said.

"Like what?" I asked.

"I don't know," Spider said. "Maybe shoot a little pool—or something better."

"Something better" sounded to me like it might be more interesting than a rodeo. Or even shooting pool.

"Can Little Jim go with us?" I asked this in a low voice, so Little Jim wouldn't hear me, in case Spider said no.

But Spider didn't object. He shrugged his bony shoulders. "Bring him along if you want to," he said, though he didn't seem overly pleased at the prospect.

After supper, the bunch going to the rodeo grabbed a couple of taxicabs on the street and were off to the fairgrounds. Spider suggested that he and I and Little Jim scout around downtown until we found some place we liked. A block and a half away from the Cattlemen's, we saw a corner beer joint and pool hall that looked pretty good. There were two army MPs out front, surveying everybody as they entered the place. Amarillo was a military town, and quite a few soldiers were on the streets.

Spider made a rapid about-face. "Come on," he said to me and Little Jim out of the side of his mouth.

We quickly turned and followed him back the way we'd come.

"What's the matter?" I asked Spider when Little Jim and I'd caught up with him.

"Cain't stand them shitty MPs," he said. "Never could."

We turned south at the next corner, then east after a block, and soon found another beer parlor and pool hall—the Pastime. High pressed tin ceiling. Bar in the front, five pool tables in the back. Lots of men, some of them soldiers. Lots of smoke. Bitter smell of beer fumes in the air. Crack of pool balls. Laughing and chatter.

We waited a few minutes for an available pool table, ordering three bottles of Lone Star beer in the meantime. The chunky middle-aged waitress showed not the slightest interest in whether or not I was of age. I tipped her a dime. Big spender.

We played a game of rotation. It turned out that Little Jim, short as he was, was the next thing to a shark. And even I was better than Spider. He complained that his cue stick wasn't totally straight and alibied a lot about being out of practice. He always chalked up and eyeballed his shot nearly forever before taking his turn. He kept warning Little Jim to keep one foot on the floor when it was Little Jim's time to shoot. And after Spider lost our first round—Little Jim won—he wanted another chance. We shot a second game. Spider and I lost to Little Jim again.

We racked our cue sticks. "Time for the main event," Spider said.

"Which is?" I asked.

"Cathouse," he said.

Little Jim laughed. "Imagined that was your plan, Spider guy," he said.

"You can go back to the trucks, you want to," Spider said to the small man.

"Naw, he's going with us," I said. Then I paused for a second or two. "What's a cathouse?" I asked, although I figured I already knew the answer.

Little Jim answered me. "Whorehouse," he said.

That's what I'd guessed. "You know where one is?" I asked Spider.

"Cabbies know, army town like this," Spider said. "They get a cut from the cathouse for bringing us."

Out on the street, we stopped a taxicab, and the three of us got in, Spider in the front seat with the driver.

"Carry us to the red-light district, Pop," Spider told the man.

"You bet!" the graying heavyset cabbie said. "Take you to the best house over there."

Spider turned and looked at me and Little Jim in the backseat. "What'd I tell you?" he said, a man of the world.

I was really nervous. *What am I getting into?* But there'd never been a chance for me to say yes or no. One minute we were in the pool hall. The next minute we were in a taxicab, heading toward the red-light district.

Still looking back at me, maybe noticing my worry, Spider said, "I reckon this is the first time for you, Willie."

I didn't say anything.

133

Somewhere on the east side of Amarillo, in a rundown residential area, the cabdriver pulled up in front of a sprawling one-story frame house, its white paint badly flaking off.

"Here we are, boys," he said. "I'll go in with you to make sure you're treated right."

The cabdriver wanted $1.20 from us. Spider walked ahead up the sidewalk toward the house, leaving me and Little Jim to split the fare.

Then the four of us bunched up on the concrete stoop in front. The cabdriver reached around Spider and pushed a doorbell. Right away, the door opened. A grossly overweight woman in a flowered Mother Hubbard, tied at the waist, let us into a kind of living room crowded with four faded and worn couches of mismatched upholstery greens and blues. A big framed beer advertisement print of "Custer's Last Stand" hung on the back wall. Angled into a far corner was a little liquor bar, covered in padded fake leather. An old black guy, oddly freckle-faced, stood behind the bar.

The fat woman spoke first to the taxicab driver, not bothering to remove the smoking cigarette that dangled from a corner of her heavily lipsticked mouth. "How ya doing, Al?" she asked him. She peeled off two dollars from a roll that she took from her dress pocket and handed the bills to the driver. She turned and yelled to the black bartender, "Scottie, give Al, here, a drink before he has to go back to work." The cabdriver started toward the bar.

The fat madam, focusing her attention back on us, said, "Welcome, gents. Hang your hats, them that's got 'em, and I'll fix you boys right up." Little Jim hung his big farmer straw hat and I, my bulldogger straw, on the hat rack. Spider was bareheaded. The woman surveyed us—a gangly yellow-haired guy with a pencil-line moustache who looked like he ought to be in the army, a dark little humpbacked man in blue overalls, nervously shifting back and forth on tiny feet, and a teenage kid in Levi's and boots who looked like he'd rather be in school, or anywhere else. "Early yet," she said to us. "Prettiest ones of my girls all available right now. You pay the girl in the room in advance. Who's first?"

Spider said he was. I was glad it wasn't me. He followed the fat woman through an open door, then disappeared, left, down a hall.

I was anxiously trying to think whether there was some way I could get out of this mess. "You go next, Little Jim," I said. "I'll be last."

But just then, the fat woman came back. She reached out and took my hand. "Come with me, honey," she said. "You look like you're plenty ready."

I followed—right, then down the hall. She stopped at a door that had the number four poorly painted on it in black. She knocked. "Come in," a woman's voice said.

The madam turned the knob and opened the door. Inside, a redheaded woman of about thirty, maybe, stood up from where she'd been sitting on a sloppily made bed with a ratty wood-veneered headboard.

"Show this boy a good time, Alice," the fat woman said, then left, closing the door behind her.

Alice gathered an untied blue chenille robe around her a little tighter, came forward, and took my hand. She was wearing too much make-up, but it didn't hide the wrinkles around her mouth or the corner of her eyes that stayed sad, even though she was smiling. "My, you're shaking," she said. "Don't worry, sweetie, we're going to have us some fun. What's your name?"

"Buddy Hart," I said, instantly making up a fake name, though I wasn't sure why.

"Well, here's the deal, Buddy," she said. "I don't kiss. I don't take my top off. French is $5.00. Straight, $7.50. Around the world, $10.00. What'll it be, sweetie?"

I hesitated, as much because I didn't want to take the final step as because I wasn't completely sure about the meaning of the three choices she'd rattled off so fast.

Maybe noting my indecision, she said, "Well that's okay. You can tell me in a minute, when you pay me. But, first, we've got to take care of a little business. So whip it out, Buddy."

"Do what?" I said.

"Whip it out, sweetie," she said. "What the army calls 'short-arm inspection.'"

When I didn't move, she reached down and started, herself, to unbutton my Levi's.

"I'll do it," I said.

I did, then pulled it out.

With cold hands, she took hold of my modest equipment and looked it over like a nurse. Sexual desire did not well up in me during this embarrassing examination. Far from it. The desire meter fell to zero. Would it ever rise again in these distasteful circumstances? I wondered.

Alice must have sensed what I was thinking. "Don't worry, Buddy," she said. "You'll be okay before I get through with you. But now we've got to have a little 'washy washy.' Stand right where you are."

I stood. She took a couple of steps toward a bureau, picked up a gray porcelain dishpan with soapy water in it, and came back and handed me the pan to hold in the proper position in front of me. Her robe fell open, revealing that she was wearing only a pink brassiere and that she had the beginning of a little potbelly. She began to wash me in the cold water. My sexual desire gauge fell *below* zero.

Alice handed me a soiled towel to dry off with, then went to return the washpan to the bureau. I was thinking to myself that if she had earlier offered me a fourth choice, sleeping with rattlesnakes, say, that was the option I would have taken no matter what the price.

Then a merciful thing happened—a distraction. Out in the hallway, a big argument suddenly exploded a door or two down from the room where Alice and I were. She and I froze to listen. I rapidly buttoned my Levi's back up, a little damp in front.

A woman said in a loud and angry voice, "I'll be goddamned if I'm going to go with some little Meskin freak!"

I recognized the fat madam's voice, next. She spoke in a quieter, soothing tone. "Now, Lana," she said, "don't get picky, darling."

"Pick my nose, you bitch!" the first woman yelled.

I bolted from Alice's room, slamming the door behind me and, outside in the hall, almost ran into Little Jim, the madam, and the woman named Lana, bunched together. Lana was tall with badly bleached hair, older than Alice, and red-faced with anger.

"Just a minute," I said to her.

"Who the hell are you?" Lana said.

"I'm this guy's friend," I said, nodding toward Little Jim. "He's okay, and he's not a Mexican, if that makes any difference. And let me offer you a good proposition." I stuck a hand into my right pocket.

Little Jim reached out and stopped my hand, obviously guessing what I was about to do. "That's all right, Will," he said. "I was scared this'd happen. I'll just wait for you and Spider in the front room."

"Naw, hold on, Little Jim," I said. He stepped back. I faced Lana and took out a ten-dollar bill. "What about this?" I said to her. "What if I add my money to his, and you give him the works? Wouldn't that be all right?"

The fat madam joined in. "Yeah, Lana, wouldn't that be all right?" she asked. "And you see, darling, he's not a Meskin at all."

"A freak, though," Lana said, not ready to give up.

"Just a crippled guy," I said. "But he's still a guy." I offered the ten-dollar bill again.

She looked at it with near longing. "Well . . . " she said.

"Go ahead, Lana," the madam said. "Do your good deed for the day and make an extra ten bucks, too."

"Well, okay," Lana said. She took the money.

I stood aside. She and Little Jim went into her room and shut the door.

Behind me and the fat madam, Alice stuck her head out of her own door. "Waiting on you, Buddy," she said.

The madam and I turned toward her. I was trying to think of something to say, what to do.

The fat madam must have seen the look of distaste on my face. She saved me. "Alice, I'll send you somebody else," she said. Then she took my hand. "Come on back to the bar, sweetie, and I'll buy you a drink."

I followed her to the living room. I got a free beer, had a little chat with the madam, who told me to call her "Ma," and watched a couple of men enter and be taken back to a room. I was standing up, more than ready to leave, when first Spider, then Little Jim, returned.

"Willie, you a pretty fast operator," Spider said to me when he came back to the front room and found me already there. "Get your money's worth?"

"Doesn't take me long to have a good time," I said.

Little Jim joined us, a smile on his face. "Much obliged, Will," he said. "Pay you back."

"No need," I said.

"Pay you back for what?" Spider asked, looking from Little Jim to me.

Neither of us said anything. Little Jim and I got our hats and put them on, then all three of us sat down on one of the greenish couches. We waited, occupied with our own thoughts, until the taxicab that the fat madam called for us drove up out front and honked.

A hard rain was falling by the time we got to our Second Street camp. The rodeo bunch wasn't back yet. Little Jim made himself a bed in the GMC pick-up cab. Spider and I hurriedly got out our quilts and unrolled them in the dry grass underneath each side of my dad's truckbed, in front of the back tires.

I was out of the rain. But as soon as I lay down, mosquitoes descended on me in swarms, like grackles after grain. Covering up with my quilt against them, I burned up in the heat. Uncovered, I was their pincushion. I alternated between the two no-good choices. It began to lightning bad, followed by great cracks, then roars, of thunder. I moved as far under the truckbed as I could, to keep dry.

I was wide awake, but not as much because of the mosquitoes or the lightning and thunder as because of the terrible worries that swirled around in my head. My mother's brother, my uncle Sidney, was in the mental hospital at Fort Supply, Oklahoma, his brain eaten up by syphilis. The whole family'd driven up there once to visit him. Took him some shaving stuff, three Baby Ruth candy bars, and a package of Juicy Fruit gum.

While we all sat on a bench in the yard that day, Uncle Sidney wouldn't talk but unwrapped and ate all three candy bars in a hurry, one right after the other, then peeled and put all five sticks of the gum in his mouth at once.

Under the truck in Amarillo, rain pouring down outside, I felt like I had avoided outright disaster by not following through with the prostitute. But I wondered if you could catch VD from wash water that somebody'd already used. And how would you know?

The rest of our harvest bunch returned. Dad and Jim Gruber made their own separate beds in the cabs of each of their trucks. Sailor quickly got his quilt roll from the Green Lizard, where we'd earlier stored both of ours, came back, and made himself a bed for the night under the back end of my dad's truck, behind the wheels.

"How was it, Sailor—the rodeo?" I asked him in a low voice, after he was stretched out good.

"First one of them things I seen," he said. "Better'n a carnival, not quite as good as a circus. Rain cut it short. What'd you guys do?"

"Shot a little pool," I said. "Nothing exciting."

Chapter Eight

Next morning, we had a scanty breakfast and some coffee that Bonnie'd quickly fixed for us. We ate and drank, standing or squatting in front of the house trailer door. We couldn't sit down because the ground in the vacant lot was too wet from the night before. Afterwards, we packed and "pulled up stakes," as the old cowboys said, ready to hightail it north out of Amarillo for Boise City, Oklahoma.

Our caravan, with me driving the Green Lizard, circled back out of the vacant lot and onto Buchanan Street—U.S. 87 and U.S. 287 combined. We turned right, went under a four-track set of railroad trestles, and hit the trail toward the next town of any size, Dumas, Texas.

We first passed through rough and hilly, rolling grassland with a lot of mesquite and yucca and some cactus. Badly blown elms and cottonwoods in low places. Great Indian and buffalo country in the old days, it was easy to see. Now it was all big ranches. Visibility was twelve or more miles under a pale blue sky with scattered puffy white clouds. Warm wind blew in our open car windows. It was going to be a hot day.

As I drove, Sailor opened the front of his Admiral portable radio and began to fiddle with the dial knob. He finally found a Dumas station and an Ernest Tubb song, followed later by more good hillbilly music. We went down into a wide and grassy valley. At the bottom of it, we crossed over the Canadian River, which wound its narrow way along a sandy, cottonwood-lined draw, northwest to southeast toward the faraway Arkansas River.

Then we began to climb back out of the low place, passing a highway sign that said "Dumas—29 miles."

A couple of Texas historical markers stopped us. Sailor and I did the usual and cut out of the parade to read the signs. Twelve thousand years ago, Indians lived along the Canadian River in stone and adobe villages. East-west through here, the old Spanish Road once passed from Santa Fe to East Texas, then later on, to San Antonio. Coronado came by here in 1541, Canadian traders in 1741, Josiah Gregg in 1839, California gold seekers in 1849. Cattle used to be driven on the Potter-Bacon Trail that came up from Texas, skirted around Goodnight's ranch, passed along here, then continued on north through eastern Colorado toward Cheyenne. This was a busy corner!

I started the Lizard, and we drove on, coming up all the way out of the river valley. We passed a couple groves of what looked like chinaberry trees in whitish blossom, then wheeled on through sandy and hilly prairie. Low green brush and yucca. Some mesquite. Windmills here and there in the distance. No trees. Hardly any fences.

We entered Moore County. Gently rolling green grassland. Scattered cattle, a few horses. Some roadside elm and juniper. Yucca in the stretching acres of pastureland. Still no wild trees.

Resuming our place in the caravan, Sailor and I soon spied the town of Dumas up on a rise to the north, maybe ten or twelve miles away. A couple of tall white concrete elevators and a big silver water tower marked its skyline on the horizon.

Over the sound of Sailor's small radio, I sang a bit of a funny song my dad'd often tried in his thin voice: "I'm a ding dong daddy from Dumas. You oughta see me strut my stuff!"

When we came to it, the town was pretty good-sized, a wheat and cattle center maybe three times as big as Vernon. Dumas was always rich in natural resources, a Texas historical marker said—known to early Indians for its flint deposits and for the dolomite that they quarried in slabs to build houses that they then plastered. Another marker said that, for a long time after cattle were introduced, there were no fences in all this vast area. But the loose stock grew in numbers and often drifted to the south until there were too many of them, too scattered, for ranchers to round up and sort out. So the ranchers got together and cooperatively built and maintained for years a barbed-wire south boundary fence. Stretching for two hundred miles, it ran all the way from the east side of the Texas Panhandle, past Dumas, and then on west until it was thirty miles into New Mexico.

Our wheat harvest caravan rolled through Dumas, passing by the Moore County courthouse on a typical Texas square. On the north side of town, a sign out front of a busy shop said "We fix flats." The highways split. U.S. 87 veered west toward Dalhart, but we took U.S. 287, a well-maintained gravel road that headed on north toward Stratford. A twenty-acre prairie dog town spread out on our right. A highway sign about there said: "Boise City—68 miles."

From Dumas on, we began to pass through good flat farmland of light brown soil. Huge fields of wheat stubble. Several fields not yet cut out—good twenty-five-bushel wheat. Some long green rows of ankle-high maize. We sped by the little town of Cactus on our right. Didn't amount to much. We entered Sherman County.

A roadside series of the small white-on-red Burma-Shave signs read:

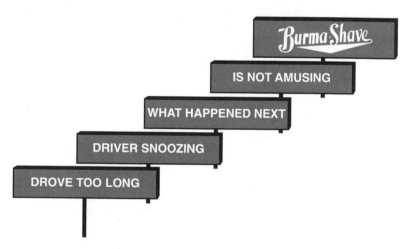

More extensive fields of wheat stubble and some wheat fields still uncut. No wonder, I thought, that people have called the

Great Plains "the granary of the world." We saw, scattered at long distances from each other, several farmhouses and windmills with elms and evergreens around them. Shelter belts near the highway. Spreading grasslands. We trailed down an incline, curved around to the left, then came up again into the little two-elevator town of Stratford, about the size of Vernon. A chamber of commerce sign at the edge of town said "Stratford—Home of God, Grass, and Grit."

"Too bad that ain't *grits*," Sailor said, ever the Mississippian.

The county courthouse and Stratford square were about three blocks east of us as we whizzed by on blacktopped U.S. 287. On the water tower: "Stratford Elks." Rundown tourist cabins on the right at the north edge of town. Coming toward a Texaco filling station and a truckers' café on the same side of the highway, we saw a sign that said: "Last Chance to Stop in Texas."

"Guess we gonna pass up that chance," Sailor said.

But we didn't forego it after all. Just on the other side of the café and station, Big Jim Gruber pulled off on the highway shoulder and stopped. The rest of us did the same. We pumped our own barrel gas into all the vehicles, then walked back in a bunch to eat dinner.

"Maybe we'll get some grits now," Sailor said to me on the way.

No such luck. But he and I did eat two juicy hamburgers. The others ate equally well, as we all sat around two pulled-together tables in the greasy spoon. We were about finished when Bonnie said to Sailor, "How's your little radio working?"

Sailor paused between bites. "Getting a little staticky, further away we get from Dumas," he said. "Reception'll be better, closer we come to Boise City." He pronounced the name of the Oklahoma Panhandle town as "boyzy city."

"It's 'boyce,'" Big Jim said.

"No radio in *our* truck," Bonnie said to Sailor. "Boring. What if I rode in your car for a while and listened to some of your good music?"

Without looking up, Sailor said, "What's your husband think about that?"

Buford shrugged, then spoke to Bonnie, not Sailor. "Suit yourself," he said. "Makes no difference to me."

I figured it did make some difference to Buford but that he was embarrassed to say so in the presence of all the rest of us. I felt a little sorry for him.

We paid up and headed back to our vehicles. Thinking that Sailor would want to drive his own car now, and deciding that maybe I ought to get out of the way, I said to Little Jim, "You mind me riding with you?"

"More'n welcome," he said.

Sailor overheard and offered a small protest. "You don't have to do that, Will," he said.

"I want to," I said.

I got into the pick-up with Little Jim. He sat way forward on the seat, adjusting a pillow behind him so he could reach the pedals. Just ahead of the pick-up, Bonnie scooted in on the passenger side of the Green Lizard as Sailor climbed in under the wheel. Before Little Jim started our motor, I heard Bonnie switch on Sailor's portable radio and search around on the dial until she apparently found a station she liked. We trailed on north then. A sign said "Boise City—37 miles."

High tableland farms all the way to the horizon in every direction. We crossed into Oklahoma. Back in my home state, but in the far northwest corner of it, nearly four hundred miles from Vernon.

Another sign said "Boise City—22 miles."

The country turned a little more rolling for a while. Lighter soil. Wheat not quite as good as we'd seen. Some vast acres of rough prairie dotted with yucca and gray sagebrush. Scattered windmills. Swirling high dust devils in the distance. Down in a draw, we crossed a sandy bottom that a highway sign labeled as "Beaver River." Little water, no beavers. Way off to the left, we could see cottonwoods in an elbow. No other trees anywhere, except clustered around the few and far between farmhouses.

Beside me, Little Jim pulled a small brown paregoric bottle from his hip pocket, unscrewed the cap, and took a slug. Before putting the cap back on, he offered it in my direction. "You want any of this, Will?" he asked.

"No thanks," I said. "How'd *you* get hooked on it?"

"Ain't," he said. He screwed the lid on and stuck the bottle back in his pocket, then gave his full attention to the road.

"When'd you start *using* it, then?" I asked.

"Long time ago," Little Jim said. We drove on for several miles in silence. Then he motioned with his chin toward the Green Lizard in front of us and said, "Must be nice being able to get girls, like Sailor can. No luck myself, built the way I am."

"You always had your handicap, from the time you were a kid?"

Little Jim answered a different question. "No girl—no *nice* girl—ever paid no attention to me."

"You grow up around Vernon?" I asked.

"Wouldn't say I grew *up* any place," he said, and laughed a little.

"You know what I mean."

"Over at Ardmore," Little Jim said. "I never knowed my real folks. They left me on a Methodist preacher's front porch, a little humpbacked baby nobody wanted. The preacher, Brother Roberts, hunted around and found my mama and daddy. They wouldn't take me back. They wasn't much more than transients, and they already had four other kids to raise, none of them afflicted, like me. Brother Roberts told me years later that my folks was Syrians, or something like that. Name of Swyden. He got me into a Chickasaw Methodist orphans home over in Durant. Home maybe thought I was Chickasaw Indian myself, brown as I was. When I growed to where I could, orphans home put me to work in the barn and the fields. And they give me a little schooling.

"I got throwed off a horse when I was about twelve. Hurt my back worse'n ever," Little Jim went on. "Missus commenced to give me paregoric for my pain. That helped me. Then, after while, she tried to cut me off. That was bad. I got good at breaking into the little clinic room and stealing the stuff. Lots of beatings for that—and other things. Orphans home finally kicked me out. First, though, they carried me over to Ardmore to Brother Roberts, the Methodist preacher, but he'd retired on account of old age. Wouldn't have me. Orphans home just dumped me out on the street then. I had to find odd jobs of work on my own."

"How'd you finally wind up in Vernon?"

"Thumbed it. Heard there was jobs over there in the oil fields," Little Jim said. "But nobody'd hire a humpbacked guy. Worked for this farmer and that, through the years, managed to make me a living. Couple a years ago, I got this steady job working for Mr. Jim Gruber, prince of a guy. Closest thing I got to family."

"I'm sorry about the life you've had," I said. I meant it.

"Everbody's got some kind of handicap, Will," Little Jim said. "Main thing's how you learn to make out the best you can anyhow. I ain't never asked nobody for nothing. Ain't never let nobody push me around, neither."

I thought a minute, then said, "I admire your being able to take care of yourself, Little Jim."

"Thank you kindly, Will."

"But you ought to get over being mad," I said.

"Who you think I'm mad at?" he asked, glancing over at me.

"The preacher, the orphan's home—maybe the world, maybe God," I said.

"You'd be mad, too, you was me," he said.

"You're right," I said. "I would be. But being mad eats at you yourself. It hurts you yourself, not the ones you're mad at. And it doesn't change the past any."

"You might be right about all that, Will," Little Jim said.

"Think about it some," I said. "You're probably a better man in a way, tougher, Little Jim, for having had to go through so much like you have. Think about it, and you might even wind up thanking the preacher, the orphans home, the world—even God."

"I'll study about it, Will," the little brown man said, his eyes on the road. He was quiet for a moment, like he was already thinking on the subject, then he added, "Really will study about it."

The farmland we were passing through began to get a little better, with wheat fields left and right. Harvest was already underway, and about a third of the fields were already cut out. But there was plenty left for us, too, it looked like. The skyline of Boise City that we could see ahead when we were still a few miles from it was dominated by two tall white concrete grain elevators and two shorter metal ones in between. A highway sign read "Boise City FFA Welcomes You." Our caravan stopped at a junction, then wheeled west. Another sign in that direction read "Boise City is a Garden Club city." We crossed over a railroad viaduct, good farmland and scattered shelter belts on each side. A third sign said "Boise City—4164' elevation." Three thousand feet higher than Vernon.

Straight ahead west, downtown, the red-brown brick Cimarron County courthouse squatted on a little island right in the middle of the highway. On each of the courthouse's four sides, sets of double doors, framed by tall limestone pillars, faced east, north, west, and south, each looking directly down a different street or highway. The center of town in every sense, the courthouse was surrounded in each direction by a block, or block and a half, of one-story stores and businesses.

Our custom combine parade turned north at the courthouse and, in less than a quarter of a mile, came to the sprawling county fairgrounds at the edge of town, on our right. Scattered whitewashed buildings with corrugated metal roofs and plenty of grassy space for us to park. We pulled off and made camp. Buford and Bonnie unhitched their house trailer by some elm trees, next to a water hydrant. The rest of us unloaded our bedding and personal stuff. The door of a nearby tin-roofed shed was not locked. We made places for ourselves inside the shed on the dirt floor.

Just like everywhere else, Boise City proved to be short of custom combiners. The county people were glad we'd come, and they told us that we were welcome to camp at the fairgrounds as long as we wanted to. Right off the reel, Dad and Big Jim found us some wheat cutting. We started work, northeast of town, on the afternoon of the day after we got to Boise City.

But before Dad and Big Jim came back to the fairgrounds from lining up our cutting that first morning, I drove the Green Lizard to the drugstore, then to the post office. I bought two kinds of picture postcards at the Panhandle Drug. One reprinted an early-day map that showed how the old Santa Fe Trail from St. Louis had run right near what was now Boise City, heading southwest. The other postcard was a reproduction of an old painting of a lot of buffaloes, spread out on the plains. A paragraph on the back of this card explained that the center of the range for the southern of two original gigantic buffalo herds of the Great Plains, before they were all slaughtered and went practically extinct, was located a little way north of Boise City.

At the post office, I bought some more one-cent stamps for postcards, then asked at the window for general delivery mail in the name of everybody in our crew. Spider and I were the only ones who had anything. He got a letter from my sweet older sister, Janie Marie. I recognized her handwriting and the peach-colored envelope. It was from a box of stationery I'd bought her as a gift when she graduated from high school. I was curious about what Janie Marie had written Spider, but I was never to find out. Back at camp, when I later gave Spider Janie Marie's letter, he didn't open it right then. He just stuck it in his hip pocket and walked off by himself with it.

Me, I received two penny postcards in the mail. But to my great disappointment, I saw at once that neither one was from Rebecca Milton. She hadn't written me. My mother and Marcy Redelk were the only ones who had. Marcy's card was full of information:

June 29, 1943

Dear Will,
     My uncle Fred laughed hard and said the name Quitaque sure enough is Comanche. Comes from a funny Comanche story and means—I hate to say it—"man shitting." Well, you asked me! My cousin Kent says you should

148

run for high school student president when school starts. Are you going to? I'll vote for you! I found a summer job at the library. Have fun in the harvest, but not too much. Ha Ha.

Your friend,
Marcy Redelk

Mama's postcard message was for me to be careful and take care of myself, and she added that I should remember that it was my duty to look after my dad to see that he didn't drink too much, especially when he was driving. How did she think I could do that? I wondered.

I had time to kill that morning, so I went to the high desk in the post office while I was still there and, dipping their scratchy pen in a full inkwell, wrote a postcard—the one with the buffalo herd on it—right back to Marcy Redelk.

Friday, July 2, 1943

Dear Marcy,

Got your postcard. Glad to know what Quitaque means. No lie? Tomorrow night's Saturday night. Wish I was going to be at Joe Lammer's. Maybe I'd see you there, and we'd go to the preview afterwards. Lonesome here on the harvest trail. Tell Kent I might run for student president if I could get more than his and your two votes. We'll be working on the Fourth of July, so light a firecracker for me. Here only a few days. Write me back at General Delivery, Limon, Colorado.

Your friend,
Will

I was a little put out that Becca hadn't written me back, but I decided to try her again anyway. I used a Santa Fe Trail postcard.

Friday, July 2, 1943

Dear Becca,

Your arm broken? I haven't heard from you. I'm back in Oklahoma, in Boise City, but a long way from home. How was the Turner Falls camp? How is your job at the dress shop? See any of our old friends at Joe Lammer's? Tell everybody hello for me. We won't be here long, so write me back at General Delivery, Limon, Colorado. That's where we go next.

Your third grade pal,
Will

P.S. Please write me.

The wheat around Boise City was good except that in a number of the fields, especially in the low places, thick stands of rank wild sunflowers had grown up with the grain. Too much rain at just the wrong time was the cause, maybe. Driving the tractor, you had to be extra careful not to go too fast, make the Gleaner take on too many green sunflower stalks too fast. That could choke the combine down, killing the motor. I only did that once, but once was enough. Little Jim and I had to stop and pull out the smelly, sticky-wet, and tightly wadded up stalks that were wedged under and wrapped around the cylinder. To do that, we reached in from the header in front and down from the top of the cylinder housing after pulling the cover off. It was a hot and nasty job. And just one time doing it was enough to teach me my lesson. After that, I was careful to slow down when we were in a lot of sunflowers mixed in with the wheat and I heard the combine start to groan too loudly. Little Jim and I never choked our machine again.

It was different for Spider and Sailor. They choked down two or three times a day during the first two days we were cutting. Back at the fairgrounds camp after the first day at work, Sailor and I walked downtown, after we'd eaten, to have a Coca-Cola at the Cimarron Café. It was across the street west of the court-house. I felt good that night, striding along toward the café with Sailor, confident. I was getting more tanned and in better shape, tough muscled, from all Sailor's and my exercising.

A kind of thin, but good-looking and cheerful, twenty-something dark-haired waitress named Marguerite—it was on the tag fixed to her white apron—set down our drinks in front of us at the counter, then walked away to do something else. Between sips, Sailor said, "I've been putting it off, Will, all the time since we left Vernon, but I guess I'm gonna have to frail old Spider's knob. No way around it."

"What's the matter now?" I asked him.

"Spider ain't never liked me giving him signals—to speed up, or slow down, or whatever," Sailor said. "Don't wanna take orders from nobody, that boy. Ever time we hit a bunch of them sunflowers, he won't even look back when I'm trying to get him to slow down. Just ignores me and goes on, too fast. Old combine chokes plumb down, he finally stops. Then he just sits there on his tractor and whistles while I have to clean out the sunflowers by myself so we can get going again."

"You want me to have my dad say something to Spider?" I asked.

"Naw, Will, it's my problem, and I'll just have to handle it my own way," Sailor said.

And handle it, he did.

Late on the second day of cutting near Boise City, Little Jim and I stopped for a regular dumping of our full wheat bin into Buford's truck. That's when I noticed that on the high, far side of the field from us, where I knew there weren't any sunflowers, Sailor and Spider were stopped, too. Even standing up off my tractor seat, I still couldn't see very well what the two of them were doing. Sailor was down from his combine on the ground right next to Spider, who was at first still seated on the red Farmall tractor. Then Spider dismounted, and he and Sailor walked together to the far side of the combine and out of my sight.

Buford also noticed that the other Gleaner-Baldwin was stopped. He was up in the back of his truck, scooping the wheat

151

that poured out of our combine spout, to spread the grain more evenly around in his truckbed. He stopped shoveling and said to Little Jim, motioning with his left hand toward Sailor's combine across the field, "You think they've broken down? Should I drive over there and see, after I get you unloaded?"

Little Jim was still on the bridge of our combine. Under his farmer straw hat, he shaded his eyes more with his hand and gazed for a minute over in the direction of Sailor's machine. "Cain't make out what's wrong with 'em," he said.

I turned and looked up toward Little Jim and Buford. "Not certain what it is," I said, "but I don't think they're broken down."

Sure enough, by the time our combine bin was emptied of wheat and we were ready to get going, all three of us saw that, across the field, the other Gleaner had suddenly resumed its regular movement through the grain, cutting wheat.

That night after supper, Sailor and I walked down to the Cimarron Café again for a Coca-Cola. On the way, I asked him, "What happened with you and Spider out there this afternoon?"

"Had to finally have it out," Sailor said. He didn't sound mad, but actually kind of down. "When he kept on not paying attention to me, went too fast in the damned sunflowers and almost choked the combine down again for the third time today, I waited until we got to the far side of the field, then I said to myself, 'Okay, Spider, past time to straighten you out.'

"He wouldn't look back at me, acourse, so I could signal him to stop," Sailor went on. "Combine going, I climbed down the ladder to the ground, trotted forward and jumped on the back of his tractor. Liked to scared the shit out of him when I hollered in his ear, 'Shut this son of a bitch down!' I stepped back on the ground, and I said, 'Get off of there, Spider, and I'm gonna whup your ass.' He said, 'I'm not getting down, 'cause you'll just hit me.' I said, 'If you don't get off, I'm gonna hit you, anyway, while you're sitting there.' He got down from the tractor then, and we went to the side of the combine. I said, 'This ain't gonna take long, Spider.' And it didn't. I knocked him down, blooded his nose. He commenced to cry, for God's sake! Made me feel sorry for him. I said, 'You ready to say calf rope, then, and start minding me like you're sup-posed to?' He said he was. 'Well,' I said, 'wipe your damned nose and get up. Crawl on that tractor, and let's forget about this and turn over a new leaf.'"

After that, Sailor didn't seem to have any more trouble with Spider not taking orders. And Spider began to act sort of generally subdued in his dealings with the rest of us in the combine crew.

My dad did have to warn Spider about something else, but it was in a nice way. If Spider stopped his Farmall tractor on a little incline, then started up too fast with a jerk, or if he shifted into a lower gear on a hill and let the clutch out too fast, the front end of his tractor sometimes reared up a little, the small, close-set front wheels actually rising off the ground slightly. Dad noticed this happening a time or two, then talked to Spider about it at supper that evening.

"You gotta watch out," my dad said to Spider. "You could flip your whole tractor over backwards, right on top of you, if you start too fast and make the front end jerk up. I knew a guy at home that did that once. Squushed himself to death. So be careful, Spider."

"I'll watch out, Bob," Spider said.

Dad went on. "And Jim Gruber tells me the field's are even hillier up in North Dakota," he said. "More dangerous up there than here."

Spider took my dad's advice okay, said he would watch out more on the inclines. He did, too. Me, I didn't have to worry about my own heavy Fordson's wide-set front wheels ever coming off the ground, steep hills or not. That would have taken dynamite.

The second night Sailor and I went to the Cimarron Café in Boise City, the twenty-something waitress, Marguerite, was very friendly to us. She was thin but nice-looking, and her blue eyes had a kind of teasing spark in them. The main supper hour had already passed when Sailor and I got to the café. Not many customers were still there. He and I ordered our

Coca-Colas, then sat and talked. Marguerite wiped off the length of the counter to our right, then refilled the several glass sugar canisters on the counter, finishing up with the one right in front of us.

She stood there for a moment, then said, "You guys new around here?"

"Harvest trash," I said.

"They warn girls about guys that follow the harvest," she said. "Breeze in, breeze out."

"We're a pretty wild and dangerous bunch," I said, "a menace to Christian womanhood."

"Yeah, you both look it," she said.

Sailor was quiet during this exchange. I glanced over at him and saw that he had a little grin on his face. I knew it was because he was amused at my attempts to flirt with the waitress. Once, while we were still cutting around Dimmitt, he'd grinned the same way when I took so seriously the unasked-for advice Spider Deering gave me about how to pick up girls.

"See, Willie, you gotta have a good line," Spider said. The three of us—Spider, Sailor, and I—were eating dinner in the field at noon one day, sitting by ourselves in the shade of my dad's truck. "You can't pick up girls without you have a good pick-up line ready."

"Like what, for instance?" I asked.

"Well, you take me," Spider said. "I meet a girl—say, in a café, or a bus station, or any place like that—I always start with something like this: 'Hi, my name's Roger Spence.' See, don't ever use your real name. 'Hi, my name's Roger Spence. They call me Spider. I was in the army tank corps. Got a nail stuck in my foot, one time. Got this thumb mashed. How would you like to go to bed with me, honey?'"

Up to that last part, I was practically taking notes on what Spider was saying.

"Oh, crap!" I said when he got to the punch line and started laughing.

154

Spider had a final word for me. "Willie, you'd be surprised how often that works," he said.

I sized up Marguerite, the Cimarron Café waitress. She was a little taller than me, I figured, but that hadn't kept Mickey Rooney and Ava Gardner apart. "What's a good-looking girl like you doing in a hot and windy place like Boise City?" I asked her. Smooth.

Now *she* was amused. "You can surely come up with a better line than that," she said.

"That's what he's been told," Sailor said, his first words in the conversation with Marguerite.

I pressed on. "You live here in town?" I asked her. "You don't sound like you're from Oklahoma."

"Moved here from Garden City, Kansas," she said.

"What's *it* famous for?" I asked.

"For one thing, smarty," she said, "Garden City's got the largest outdoor swimming pool in the world."

"That really true?" I asked.

"Well, our chamber of commerce does add some qualifiers," Marguerite said. "It's the largest outdoor *free concrete municipal* swimming pool in the world."

"Even so," I said, "that's still pretty impressive. How come you to move off and leave an attraction like that?"

"The main reason, I could get a job teaching school in Boise City," Marguerite said.

"You're a schoolteacher?"

"That and waiting tables here at the café, summers, when school's not in session," she said.

"Teacher's the best experience, they say," I said.

She cringed slightly and drew back from my limp try at humor, and I was afraid for a moment that she might walk away. But she must have been as lonely as I was. She stayed.

"Fresh remark," she said.

I was a little embarrassed, but I wasn't ready to give up. "You live near here?" I asked her. "Let me make it up to you by us walking you home when you get off work."

"Northwest part of town," she said. "But I don't even know you."

"I'm Buddy Hart from Oklahoma City," I said.

Never use your real name.

She hesitated, then nodded toward Sailor, who still hadn't said anything besides his one brief earlier comment. "What about him?" she asked, then turned from me to Sailor. "I don't know *you*," she said.

Sailor spoke up at once. "I'm Will Haley from Vernon, Oklahoma," he said, immediately canceling out my use of a fake name and hometown.

I must have looked as surprised by this as I felt.

"What's going on?" she asked, annoyed. "You two making up names?"

I was instantly ashamed of what I'd done, after she'd been so nice and friendly to us. I apologized. "That was real silly of me, Marguerite," I said. "I'm sorry. I don't know why I did that. It's *my* name that's Will Haley, actually. And I'm the one who's from Vernon, too." I nodded toward Sailor. "This is my cousin, Emmett Torley," I said. "He's from Mississippi."

Marguerite looked like she was considering what her reaction to all this should be. Then, apparently resolving things in our favor, she smiled again and stuck out her hand, first shaking mine, then Sailor's. "I'll just call you two 'Harvest' and 'Trash,'" she said.

"And what about us walking you home?" I asked. "What time you get off?"

"How old are you anyway, Harvest?" she asked me.

"Nineteen," I said.

She looked at Sailor. "Trash, is he lying?"

"Mature enough, Will is, that he oughta be able to draw the old age pension," Sailor said.

Marguerite studied the two of us, especially me. "I'm off an hour from now—9:30," she said finally. "You guys'll already be asleep by then."

"We'll be right outside when you come out," I said. "Wait and see." I hoped I didn't sound too eager.

A man in one of the booths called out for a coffee refill. Marguerite turned and went to carry the pot over to him.

156

Sailor and I laid our money on the counter with the check, then got up and left.

"Hey, pretty interesting, huh?" I said to Sailor when we were outside by ourselves and headed back toward camp. I was a little worked up.

"For you, maybe," he said, matter of factly. "I'm going to bed myself, but not with her. And, Will, she ain't the type of girl that's gonna go to bed with you anyway. Too nice for a quick pick-up."

"I'm not trying to go to bed with her," I said.

Sailor turned his head and glanced at me for a second, to check on whether I was joking, I figured. I wasn't.

At the fairgrounds camp, he said he'd see me in the morning, then disappeared into our tin-roofed shed of a dormitory. I went over and climbed into the cab of my dad's truck and sat there for what I thought from watching the moon was close to an hour. Then I got out and walked back to the Cimarron Café by myself. I was waiting there, near the front door, when Marguerite finally emerged, carrying her purse and with her white apron off.

She saw me, then glanced around a little, maybe disappointed. "Where's your cousin?"

"He had to go to sleep," I said. "We're getting up early in the morning for work."

"You're not sleepy?"

"Yeah, but I'd rather see you home," I said.

"You're a cute kid, Will," she said. "You can walk me home this one time, since you're here, but you're not getting past my front door."

"Fine with me," I said. I knew I was probably lying.

We started walking west on the sidewalk. And I don't know how it happened, but almost right away, she and I launched into what soon became a pretty serious conversation. Marguerite—Marguerite Littlefield, it was—wanted to know more about my favorite subject: me. So I told her a little about my life and about how I wanted to be a lawyer. She, in turn, explained more about why she was in Boise City. A boy she'd met in teachers college grew up in Boise City, she said, and persuaded her to move to his hometown to join him in teaching school. She and the boy—Earl Dean was his name—planned to get married. But at the last minute, he got cold feet and ran off to join the marines. Marguerite stayed on in Boise City because of her job at the local school. She was twenty-two.

Her house, when we came to it, was a small white frame bungalow. A streetlight at the curb lit our way as I walked her up the narrow sidewalk to the little front porch. We stopped and shook hands. "Good-bye," I said, accepting her earlier statement that I wouldn't be seeing her home again. "I'm really glad to know you," I added. And I felt that I *had* gotten to know her quite a bit in a very short time.

She must have felt the same way because she surprised me by saying, "Will, I've changed my mind. I'm wide awake. Why don't you come in? I'll make you some hot tea and put on an opera record. You like opera?" She opened the door.

I told the truth. "Never heard any opera, but this seems like a perfect time to do it," I said and followed her into the little house. Actually, I wasn't totally sure what an opera was. "Never had any *hot* tea, either," I went on, "but I always wanted to."

We went through a tight little living room and on into her tiny kitchen. Marguerite motioned for me to sit down at a small, two-chair oak breakfast table. She struck a match and lit the gas stove, then put on a teakettle of water to boil. "I teach eleventh and twelfth grade history and English literature," she said. "I once read that people in England drink hot tea. So, I decided to try it—and the same way they drink it, with milk and sugar. I turned out to like it."

"And opera?" I asked.

"I've never actually seen one performed, Will, but I was introduced to opera records—all the classics and classic arias—in a wonderful college music appreciation class," Marguerite said. She brought over two cups, a tin box of loose tea, and a china teapot and set them all on the table next to a sugar bowl, then got a small pitcher of milk from the Norge icebox and put that on the table, too. "Opera turned out to be as much a learned addiction for me as hot tea," she said.

"I absolutely love it. I'll put on a record of the great arias, or solos, from my favorite for you. It's called *La Traviata*."

She stepped just barely through the door between the kitchen and her small living room to an old-fashioned floor model, walnut-veneered Victrola record player. She picked out a record from a stack beside the Victrola and placed it on the turntable. She wound the machine with the attached hand crank, flipped the start switch, then carefully took the arm and set the needle down at the beginning edge of the spinning record. The opera's swelling overture began. It filled the little house with as dramatic a music as I'd ever heard.

Back in the kitchen, Marguerite brought over the steaming teakettle, put some loose tea in the teapot, and poured the hot water over it. "Have to let it steep," she said. "That's what the English people say—'steep.'" She sat down with me at the little table.

When the tea was ready and she had poured it through a strainer, I found the taste really strange, even with a lot of milk and sugar. But I wound up drinking three cups of it before I was through. And I would have had to admit that by that third cup, I was definitely beginning to get used to hot tea, to like it, even. And that was the way it was with *La Traviata*, too. At first, the music and singing were even stranger to me than my first cup of hot tea. But, before long, the wonderfully thrilling voices of the soprano who sang the part of Violetta and the tenor who sang Alfredo began to get to me, began to move me emotionally, began even to give me goose bumps. I'd never experienced anything like that from music. And the heartbreaking story of the opera, as quietly explained to me by Marguerite, simultaneously with the dramatic arias, got to me even more.

From time to time, she had to jump up from the table to change the record and wind the Victrola again, before it ran down, or to pour us more tea. But *La Traviata* swept me right along with it anyway, despite these small distractions, driving increasingly sadly toward a seemingly inevitable and tragic end. Alfredo returned at last, and he and Violetta were movingly reconciled. But it was much too late. Violetta died in the arms of her grief-stricken lover.

I saw that my schoolteacher interpreter wiped big tears from her eyes as the last sad notes of the music faded and she finished her hushed explanations of the opera for me. "I'm sorry," she said.

I was embarrassed that my own eyes seemed a little wet, too. I turned away for a moment.

Next morning at camp, Sailor had his work cut out for him as he tried repeatedly to get me up. I don't know how many times he must have had to shake me. On the dirt floor of the shed at the fairgrounds, I was wrapped up in my quilt, my head covered.

When I finally did get up and, still half asleep, started eating breakfast at the little card table next to the house trailer, I took some razzing from Spider. Sailor'd told everybody about my walking the Cimarron Café waitress home.

"Playing hide the bone with her, was you, Willie?" Spider asked, then threw his yellow-haired head back and laughed like crazy. I found him and his question really gross and offensive, especially because I was afraid that Bonnie, inside the house trailer at the time, might hear what he said. But Spider kept it up. "Get a little tallow on your pole, did you?" He laughed again.

"It's not like that," I said, disgusted. "And she's not that kind of girl."

"They all that kind of gal, Willie, if you know how to handle 'em," Spider said.

I busied myself with finishing off the bacon and scrambled eggs on my tin pie plate. I decided not to say anything else in response to Spider. And I especially knew better than to mention to anybody the subjects of opera and hot tea.

I walked Marguerite home from the Cimarron Café every evening after that while our combine crew was cutting wheat around Boise City. A couple of the last nights were in the face of thunderstorm threats that never materialized. She and

I listened to arias from a second opera—this one, *Carmen*. I liked it almost as much as *La Traviata*, although I couldn't help but be a little put out with Don José for not soon realizing just how poisoned he was becoming by Carmen and for not deciding to give the woman up.

One night on the way to Marguerite's house, telling her about my friend Junior, I recounted how he called the wheat harvest "an odyssey on the Great Plains." That caused her to ask me if I'd read Homer's *Odyssey*. I'd heard of it, of course, I told her, but I hadn't actually read it myself. So that night at her house, she got out a schoolbook translation of it, told me the story, and read me excerpts.

"Will, here's hoping that *you* make it back home in a lot quicker time than it took Odysseus," Marguerite said when she'd finished. "And that you find things there in a lot better shape than he did upon his return. You have a girlfriend waiting for you?"

The funny thing was that, the instant Marguerite said "girlfriend," *two* images, not just one, snapped into my mind—Rebecca Milton *and* Marcy Redelk.

"Not really," I said. I was well aware that Becca certainly wouldn't have agreed that she was my girlfriend. And it'd never occurred to me before to think of Marcy in that way.

"Me, Will, I don't have a boyfriend, either," Marguerite said. "Not now. Mine ran off and left me, as I told you."

"His loss," I said.

"He didn't think so," she said. "He had turned away from me and—I hate to say this—got involved with the football coach."

"How do you mean, Marguerite–'got involved'?" I asked.

"You know."

"Oh," I said.

"I haven't mentioned this to a soul," she said. "The coach left town. Hardly anyone but Earl Dean and I knew why. That's when Earl Dean enlisted in the marines. He'd been growing colder with me for some time before that. It just seemed that there was something wrong with me. That's the way it felt, still does."

161

I wanted to reassure her. "There's nothing wrong with you," I said. "You couldn't *be* more attractive."

"What I want is a husband and family, Will," Marguerite said. "But nobody around here's available. I'm stuck here, destined to be an old maid teacher."

"Go back to school, why don't you?" I said. "Study to be a school principal, or a college teacher. And while you're at it, you'll meet some guy good enough to deserve you."

"I wish *you* were older, Will," she said.

"So do I."

Friday, the ninth of July, was our last day cutting wheat around Boise City. Walking Marguerite home on our final evening together, I told her that my harvest bunch and I would be taking off north early the next morning, headed toward Limon, Colorado. I said that I was sad to be leaving her, that I wouldn't forget her. She and I promised we'd write each other, although I had the feeling that we both knew we probably wouldn't, that whatever the nature of our relationship was—and I wasn't sure about that—there was no future in it for us.

For the two nights before that final night, Boise City radio announcers had warned about possible tornados in the area. Each evening, huge black clouds had built up in the west, and there'd been a lot of fairly distant thunder and lightning. But both nights, the gathering storms had ending up blowing on around Boise City to the south, not even dropping much more than a sprinkle or two of rain each time.

Then on that last evening, as Marguerite and I stood on her front porch, saying good-bye before I left her house for the fairgrounds camp, the weather threat rapidly became an ominous reality. The big black cloud and the thunder and lightning in the west grew and spread, quickly came closer and closer, until Boise City—and Marguerite and I—were at last completely enveloped by an angry and increasingly dangerous storm. Almost continuous lightning flashed all around us, the blinding, jagged white, yellow, and red sky-veins lingering on afterwards in the blackness and in our eyes. Quick thunderclaps exploded in our ears like cannon roar. The air turned deathly still and hot.

Marguerite and I knew what these signs meant. We'd both grown up in different parts of tornado country. She leaned a little way out from the porch and surveyed the night. "Will, this sure feels like tornado weather to me," she said. "You'd better watch out on the way back to the fairgrounds."

"You take care, too, Marguerite."

We said another quick good-bye. I hugged her, then kissed her on the lips. She turned and went back into her house. I walked extra fast as I headed east on the sidewalk, but I didn't run at first. Each crack and flash of menacing lightning seemed close enough to strike me, and the almost instantly following boom of engulfing and deafening thunder shook my body and hurt my ears.

Then, just as I came to Boise City's downtown north-south street, the full storm hit with unbelievable violence and rage. Great tubs of rain began to fall on me, like a cow pissing on a flat rock, as Grandpa Haley would have put it. And a hard and punishing shower of marble-sized hail fell with the rain. I turned and started to run north along the west side of the street, my hands over my head for protection. An irresistibly powerful and vicious wind struck me with truck-wreck force at the same instant that I heard the alarming honk of Boise City's tornado warning signal, coming, it sounded like, from the courthouse yard. My expensive bulldogger straw hat was ripped off my head and was instantly gone for good.

I was roughly blown to the ground, and I knew at once that I wouldn't be able to get up again and stay on my feet. I rapidly crawled the yard or so necessary to get my body down into the weedy and grassy ditch at the side of the street. I pressed myself as flat as I could, face down, and grabbed onto the thick stalks of big sunflowers growing there, to keep from being sucked away by the screaming wind. Rushing water started to course down the ditch under me. I clawed my way up the ditch side a little, sunflower stalk by sunflower stalk, to keep from drowning or being swept away by the water.

163

People at home had always said that the yowl and roar of a rampaging tornado passing by sounded as loud as a freight train. They were wrong. This tornado was as loud as *two* freight trains, with all the boxcars blowing up at the same time. Behind the general roar, you could also hear the frightening crashes and crunches of the tornado chewing up and mulching the houses in its path and setting busted electric lines to crackling and fizzing in explosive short-outs. Great ragged pieces of wood, tin, and other debris began to fall from the sky, mostly somewhat north of where I lay.

All of these horrible happenings occurred in a mercifully short time, though it seemed much longer than it actually was. The tornado funnel—I never ventured to look up to see it, but I heard it well enough—soon passed by. It'd come from the southwest, and it receded toward the northeast, taking the ever lessening wind and roar, lightning and thunder, with it. The hail had stopped when the wind hit. Now the rain slowed to a drizzle. Then, all at once, everything was quiet.

I raised up, grateful to be whole and unhurt, though I was soaked and felt quite dazed. I began to hear scattered voices in the distance, people calling out for one another. I heard the sound of cars starting up and beginning to drive this way and that. I stood, a little shaky. Suddenly a fire truck, siren shrieking, gunned past me, headed west. And all of a sudden, I thought of Marguerite Littlefield.

I commenced running as fast as I could, then, in the same direction that the fire truck had just gone. Soon I came upon a swath of destruction that was, I thought, something like a North African city must have looked like after an all-out artillery and bombing assault had been rained down on it. Houses were reduced to twisted and jagged boards and timbers, strewn for blocks over now bare rock foundations and concrete storm cellars. Trees were shredded. Crumpled and upended cars were scattered about like gunned-down elephants. Light and telephone poles were broken over, snapped lines dangling from some of them and sparking like a welder's arc.

Just then, a white ambulance, its siren blaring, overtook me and zipped on past to the end of the block, then braked, turned

164

north into a driveway, and stopped. Two white-uniformed men jumped out of the emergency vehicle and ran forward with a canvas stretcher and a first-aid bag. They began to search in the debris of what had been a corner house.

It took me a couple of minutes more before I could locate the spot where the white bungalow I was looking for had stood. A nearby and familiar streetlight, oddly spared by the storm, still shone brightly. Keying off its location, I zeroed in on Marguerite's place, now almost unrecognizable rubble. But the roof of her little house, I saw, had been lifted off practically whole and deposited yards to the east. And it was under a widely overhanging eve of that roof that I found Marguerite. She was lying on her back, still wearing the purple dress I'd last seen her in, obviously not having had time to change for bed before the tornado struck. Both of her legs were clearly broken, one above, the other below, the knee. The top part of her left arm was broken, too, and its bloody and splintered bone showed through the flesh at the end of the short sleeve of her ripped and torn dress. She was conscious, her eyes open, but she wasn't crying or moaning any and seemed to be in shock.

"Marguerite, Marguerite, can you hear me?" I shouted, carefully lifting her head with my hands and looking into her blue eyes, now dulled.

She focused some with difficulty, then recognized me. "Will," she said weakly, "are you all right?"

"I'm okay," I said, "and you're going to be okay, too." I prayed I wasn't wrong about that.

I let her head back down gently, then jumped up and ran several yards to the west toward the ambulance men who were still combing through house wreckage over there. Closer, I yelled and waved my arms at them. "Help!" I shouted. "Woman here's badly hurt, needs to get to the hospital!"

The two men grabbed up their canvas stretcher and first aid bag and dashed toward me, then followed as I turned and ran back to where Marguerite lay.

They gave her a shot of morphine, quickly emergency-splinted her broken arm and legs, and got her onto the stretcher and into the ambulance. They wouldn't let me ride to the hospital with her, but I knew where it was, five or six blocks south and east. So I ran all the way there in my soggy shoes and clothes. I sat in the emergency room lounge for what must have been two hours or more, chaos all around me, as maybe two dozen other tornado victims with various kinds of injuries were brought in for treatment.

At last, Marguerite was wheeled out past me, now wearing a white cotton hospital robe and still unconscious from the ether. A nurse explained to me that they'd treated her for shock, fixed up and splinted her arm, then put the lower part of one leg, the upper part of the other, in plaster casts. I followed Marguerite's hospital gurney down the hall to a four-patient, shared room and watched as attendants slipped her over onto a vacant bed and covered her up to her neck with a white sheet. The nurse asked me if I was a member of Marguerite's family. I said I was.

No chair was available, so I stood anxiously at the foot of Marguerite's bed for another hour or so. Finally, she began to come to. I stepped to her side and waited until she seemed to be growing fairly conscious, then took her hand and spoke to her briefly to reassure her. After a moment, she went right back to sleep. I left to go and see about my own people. It was getting daylight outside.

I hadn't worried too much about my dad and the rest of our combine crew because I felt pretty sure that the tornado must have passed to the north of the fairgrounds. Turned out I was right about that. Nobody in our bunch had been hurt, none of our vehicles or machinery damaged. The whole crew was getting ready to eat breakfast when I got there. Everybody but my dad acted glad to see me, relieved that I'd made it okay.

Bonnie, already dressed and made up for the road trip, grabbed me and hugged me. "I was scared to death for you, Will," she said.

I thanked her, then sat down to eat. I related to the whole group what'd happened to Marguerite Littlefield and how I'd spent the night.

My dad seemed mad at me, though this may have been the only way he knew how to express the worry he'd felt. It was clear, too, that, early as it was, he'd already had a couple of shots of whiskey from his Echo Springs bottle. He objected when I said that I was going back to the hospital to check one last time on Marguerite.

"We heading out for Limon damned quick, Willie, if we're gonna make it all the way there before dark," Dad said. "And we sure'n hell ain't waiting around here for you, none."

Sailor helped me out. He said he'd come by the hospital in the Green Lizard to get me, then we'd catch up with the rest of the bunch, somewhere on the highway north.

Marguerite was awake when I got to her room at the hospital, but still a little dopey, at first, from pain medicine. One of her fellow teachers, an older woman, was at her bedside when I came in. The woman stepped out of the room, after I entered.

I stood next to the bed and took Marguerite's hand. We looked into each other's eyes. She grew a little more alert.

Finally, in a weak voice, she said, "You're a good man, Will."

"More of a man now, because of you," I said.

"And like a man, you're leaving," she said.

"No other way, Marguerite," I said. "You know that, yourself."

She cried a little. "I'll miss you," she said.

"I'll miss you, too."

Good-bye to Marguerite Littlefield. Good-bye to Boise City.

Chapter Nine

Sailor was waiting for me in the hospital parking lot. I climbed into the passenger side of the Lizard. He drove while I tuned his portable Admiral radio to the Boise City station to get some detailed news about the tornado. Three people had been killed, the announcer said, twenty-three seriously injured.

Just as Sailor and I were hearing the tornado report on the radio, the northbound street and highway that we were on took us directly across the terrible two-block wreckage swath that the tornado had made the night before. He and I saw for the first time how frighteningly close the storm path had come to the fairgrounds where our crew was camped. The tornado'd angled by, not more than a quarter of a mile north of the place.

When we were out of Boise City, Sailor pushed the Green Lizard above the thirty-five mile speed limit, trying to catch up with our harvest bunch who had left earlier. On the two-lane combined U.S. highways 287 and 385, we rolled through large and level fields of wheat stubble and plowed brown ground. The horizon was ten or twelve miles in the flat distance, with a few tree-shrouded farmhouses scattered here and there.

I switched off the Admiral radio to save the battery, then dozed, woke up, and dozed some more. The countryside we passed through turned for a time into a great green shortgrass prairie, isolated windmills stuck randomly around in it. Once, when I opened my eyes, I saw some rocky mesas to the east that would have been important landmarks for the people who'd traveled the old Santa Fe Trail, headed southwest. I woke up again, later, as we crossed the cottonwood-bordered Cimarron River, which coursed southeast along the bottom of a wide grassy valley. I knew that in the old days the river'd been hell for wagons to cross when it was flooded and out of its banks. Later on, hard to ford, too, for the great cattle herds and trail drivers that came this way.

Before Sailor and I'd gone much farther, I saw a sign that said "Welcome to Colorful Colorado." It was my first time in the Rocky Mountain State, though we were headed north along its monotonously smooth and less colorful eastern side, a long way from the Rockies. A highway sign announced "Springfield—30 miles. Lamar—78 miles." I went back to sleep.

A poor sparrow crashed into our windshield, and the bumplike noise woke me up. I looked out to see on every side a lot more spacious fields—some of cut-out wheat stubble, some of just-plowed ground, some green with rowed calf-high maize.

I roused up again when we came to the small town of Springfield, Colorado, home of the Longhorns, the local football team's name recalling the area's old cattle trail past. We drove through to the right of the little business district and the Baca County courthouse, passed a lumberyard and some implement dealerships on the outskirts, then continued on north.

"Lamar—45 miles. Limon—161 miles."

Trackless green prairie under a cloudless light blue sky, the hazy horizon maybe fifteen miles away. Soon, there was good interspersed farmland, too, most of it plowed after the wheat harvest. I dozed off again.

Sailor suddenly poked me awake. "Look off there to the right, Will," he said, motioning with his hand. "Rocky Mountains done calved."

It did seem like it. The Rockies were far to the west somewhere. We couldn't see them. But here in the southeast corner of Colorado, an odd little twin-topped peak, all by itself, stuck up maybe fifteen hundred feet out of the bald plains.

"Maverick calf wandered way off from its folks, looks like," I said.

We went gently down into a low, cottonwood-garnished draw and crossed over a stream. A sign said "Two Buttes Creek." I went back to sleep after thinking briefly that the sign should have said something like "Two-Point Peak Creek." They certainly weren't buttes.

I opened my eyes, later, just as we were passing about a dozen really strange, squatty, brown rock formations, seven or eight feet high, that were scattered along the left lip of the highway. I stayed awake long enough after that to watch us descend, some, down into rougher country with low rocky outcroppings here and there in an ocean of native green grass.

When I woke up again, we were passing through great upland farm fields, some in harvested wheat stubble, some plowed. We descended gradually then into a wooded, green, east-west valley and soon entered Lamar, Colorado, "A Historical Town on the Santa Fe Trail." It was a big town, too, thick with tree-shaded homes and a good-sized business district. Water-filled irrigation canals coursed through the town, then wandered off into the rich surrounding valley.

Going through Lamar, we passed the three-story limestone Prowers County courthouse, and on the east side of the highway, the Lamar Theater, blocks of businesses, a Madonna of the Plains statue, the red brick Lamar railroad depot, and more blocks of businesses. Then on the west side of the highway, we drove by a jagged-topped little rock structure identified by a large sign: "Ripley's Believe It or Not—Petrified Wood Building." Just across from this odd tourist attraction, alongside the highway, was our caravan of harvest bunch vehicles, which Sailor and I'd been trying since morning to catch up with, nobody in them.

We guessed that the crew had stopped for dinner in the adjacent Arkansas River Café. Sure enough, we soon found everybody inside the eating joint. Most of them were having plate lunches, but to hurry, Sailor and I sat down separately at the counter and ordered cheeseburgers. That was when I learned a second thing about states north of Oklahoma. The first thing I'd discovered earlier was that northerners put up thin, portable picket fences beside their highways to protect the roads from drifting snow during the winter. I'd started seeing these fences back down the road after we entered Colorado. Second, I found out that people up north didn't know much about how to make hamburgers. For one thing, they didn't grease and toast the buns. Too, they were chintzy with the onions and pickles. And a lot of times they used ketchup, instead of mustard.

You either ought to make a hamburger right, or you ought not to make one at all.

I noted with some worry that my dad didn't eat much food. He drank at least two beers, though, and that was on top of what I knew must have been a good load of whiskey. Spider had two beers, too, and he didn't eat much either, as far as I could tell. Both he and my dad were pretty wobbly when we left the café to go back to our vehicles. Dad's face was sweaty and flushed.

I decided that I had to do something. So, outside, I got next to my dad as we walked, and I said to him in a low voice, "Dad, you want me to drive your truck for you for a ways?"

But this made him mad. He glared at me. "Why would I want that?" he said, his tongue a little thick-sounding.

I stopped. From the passenger side of the Green Lizard, I watched helplessly as my dad walked unsteadily on to his black Chevy truck and climbed in under the wheel. Spider followed him and got in on the opposite side.

The Lizard was parked at the south end of our lined-up vehicles, but when we started to roll, Little Jim and Buford held back so that Sailor could pull out and pass them, then cut into our usual place just behind Dad's truck, combine, and header trailer train.

At the north edge of Lamar, we came to the Arkansas River, flowing southeast and full of water. I was glad that we could cross it on a bridge, unlike the old cattle drivers. We curved around to the west on U.S. 287 through rich, irrigated alfalfa fields. Then we turned back north after a little while, still on U.S. 287, a somewhat deteriorating asphalt road, and passed through more lush bottomland. "Eads—27 miles. Kit Carson—47 miles."

I slept some more, trying to catch up from the wide-awake night before. Now and then I roused a little and noticed that we'd entered an area of good dryland farming—some wheat cut, some not. After that we began to pass through green, gently rolling prairie, then wheat fields, again. Back to dozing.

"Jesus!" Sailor Torley suddenly said.

That woke me up. "What's wrong?"

He didn't have to answer. I could see. In front of us at that moment, my dad was driving halfway off the highway spraying loose gravel behind him. Then, as we watched, holding our breaths, he swerved back fully onto the blacktop, just in time to make it through a narrow concrete bridge.

"Too close a shave!" I said, relieved but still scared. "How long's he been driving like that?"

"Miles," Sailor said.

"What should we do?"

"What *can* we do, Will?" Sailor asked. "Ain't no way we can get him to stop."

Ahead of us, my dad kept veering on and off the highway, obviously unable to hold his lane. His combine and header trailer swung back and forth behind him like a swimming alligator's tail.

Just then, we came onto a series of white-on-red Burma-Shave signs.

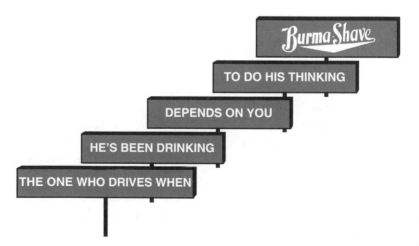

"We've got to do something, Sailor," I said.

"Agreed, son—but what?"

"Try to get up even with him, and I'll yell at him to pull over," I said.

But when Sailor started to move up, Dad swerved across the center line right then, a few feet into the left lane, and inadvertently cut us off.

Sailor dropped back, and we both watched my dad's alarming driving with a growing sense of impending doom. It wasn't much longer before things got worse. Dad once more began to drift a little off the road to the right. Then he suddenly veered left again, just as he approached another narrow concrete bridge, but this time he didn't get totally back onto the highway soon enough. The lower righthand side of his Chevy truckbed sideswiped hard along the bridge bannister, making a hell of a screeching noise. But he finally lurched completely enough to the left to keep the big wheel of the combine, trailing behind him, and the header trailer, behind the combine, from hitting the bannister, too.

Then suddenly, just after he cleared the bridge, he pulled completely off the highway to the right onto a grassy shoulder and gradually came to a rolling stop there.

"Thank God!" I said.

Sailor braked and drove off the highway, too, behind my dad. He waved for Buford and Bonnie to go on past us. They did.

I was worried to death. Sailor and I jumped out of the Green Lizard and hurried to the driver's side of my dad's truck. I yanked the door open. He slumped over against me. His cowboy straw hat fell off and hit the ground. I caught my dad's limp body and, with Sailor's help, managed to get him pushed back into the truck seat and close the door again. I was disgusted. He was dead drunk, totally passed out.

I picked up Dad's hat and put it on my own head. Sailor and I went around and opened the passenger side of the truck.

Sitting there, Spider wasn't in much better shape than my dad, though he was more or less awake. "What's a matter?" he asked us groggily.

"Go back and get in my car," Sailor said to Spider. It was a command.

Spider slowly understood, then slowly obeyed. He got out and staggered back toward the Green Lizard. Sailor and I reached into the truck together and dragged my dad over to the passenger side of the seat and propped him up there.

We closed the door, then both of us turned to inspect the righthand side of my dad's truckbed. It was a relief for us to see that the damage was much less than it might have been. A wide iron band that wrapped along the bottom of the bed, though it was scraped and boogered a lot, had apparently been thick and strong enough to take the whole force of the sideswipe, saving the truck from much more serious damage. Sailor and I walked back to the front of the black Chevy.

"Can you drive this thing, Will, loaded as it is and pulling all it's pulling?" he asked me.

"Yeah," I said. "It's a case of 'have to.'"

I crawled in, and we got underway again. My dad's truck labored pretty hard, dragging such a long load. It had a tendency to swerve back and forth, too, if you got up much speed. So I drove considerably under the limit, and after a while, I began to feel more and more in control. But I was still nervous every time I crossed a narrow bridge, and I was careful to hold back, if necessary, so I wouldn't have to meet any oncoming vehicle while I was on a bridge.

The highway we were on passed between two large lakes— I couldn't tell whether they were natural or man-made—then through great tableland fields with big tractors plowing in some of them. Next came vast green rolling prairies. And for some time before I actually got to the town, I began to see ahead the lone white grain elevator of Eads, Colorado.

The highway curved to the west toward the town. I didn't have to slow down much as I drove along the south side of this little "Home of the Eagles."

Dad was snoring loudly. His head, sandy hair blowing in the wind, was lolled back into the corner between the seat and the open passenger side window of the truck. At the west edge of Eads, the highway curved back north, and we passed the Kiowa County fairgrounds.

I drove for mile after boring mile through what was now somewhat rougher, slightly rolling grassland, dotted with scattered spiky yucca and gray sage. A few cattle. Some horses and windmills.

After a time, I was in farming country again, with big fields of wheat and wheat stubble, then more natural prairie grassland. I crossed over Big Sandy Creek, which was more sand than creek. Still following U.S. 287, I curved around to the left past a prairie dog town, went up over a viaduct above a railroad track, and began to approach the village of Kit Carson, Colorado. At an intersection, U.S. 287 was joined by U.S. 40, which came west from Oakley, Kansas. These combined highways would lead us on to Limon.

Junior Randall came to my mind. He and Martin, the guy he was working for, would probably be cutting wheat around Oakley by now, I thought. I wondered whether Junior'd be able to get off and come over from Oakley to see me in Limon, as we'd planned before we left home. I hoped so. I was homesick—and lonesome for Junior, my best buddy.

Driving into Kit Carson along its north side, I could take in most of the little town in one glance. On my left was the fairly impressive Kit Carson Motel and tourist cabins, with a natural rock, arched entryway. After that, there was a full block of businesses and stores. The water tower and a painted-white sheet metal grain elevator were the town's two tallest structures.

I was relieved to see our line of harvest vehicles stopped and waiting in the middle of Kit Carson, strung out by the side of the road. I pulled up behind Buford and Bonnie's house trailer. Sailor parked the Green Lizard right behind me. In the Chevy truck, Dad didn't move as I got out and walked around to the passenger side.

While I waited there for Jim Gruber, Little Jim, Buford, and Bonnie to walk back to join me and for Sailor to come up, I had time to read a Colorado historical marker that stood next to the truck: Kit Carson, the town, was named after "the famous trapper Kit Carson." No mention of the man as an "Indian fighter." A lot of old cattle trails passed here—in particular, the Texas-Montana, the Potter-Bacon, and the Chisum. And Kit Carson, Colorado, was an early-day coal and water station on the railroad that was now the Union Pacific.

The concerned harvest crew gathered with me around the open window of dad's truck. Wild-haired, his mouth open and eyes closed, my dad was slumped into the passenger side corner. I was embarrassed for him and for myself, embarrassed for our bunch to see Dad like that and for them to find out what'd happened.

Jim Gruber was the first one to say something. "I was afraid old Bob was hitting the bottle a little too hard. Don't know what we're gonna do with this guy."

Sailor showed everybody the badly scraped iron band along the bottom of the truckbed. "Sideswiped a bridge back yonder a ways," Sailor said. "Damned lucky Bob didn't wreck the cornbread hell out of his whole outfit. Scared the shit out of me and Will anyway. Then Bob just drove off the road and conked out. Will had to take over driving for him."

We all turned back to the open truck window to look at Dad.

"Will, can you keep on driving?" Big Jim asked me. "We need to move on."

I told him I could.

My dad began to groan and mumble a little, though his eyes remained closed.

"You think Bob's all right?" Bonnie asked me, worried. "Why don't you try to wake him up, Will? And I'll go get our thermos bottle of hot coffee for him."

She ran ahead toward Buford's truck. I opened the passenger door of the Chevy truck and took hold of my dad's shoulder and shook him a little.

"Dad!" I said. "Dad, you want to wake up now?"

He began to rouse. He opened his eyes, sat up, then turned and focused on the gathered crew. We were all staring at him like we'd been assigned to write a theme on the evils of strong drink. Dad's face first registered confusion, then surprise, and finally shame. I knew that he'd always prided himself on being able to hold his liquor, as people put it, and never, ever, letting whiskey keep him from doing his job. But it was clear he was beginning to realize that, this time, he'd gone over the line.

Bonnie came hurrying back with the thermos. She unscrewed the cap-cup and poured it full of steamy black coffee. "Here, Bob," she said. "Drink some of this, and you'll feel better."

Dad reached out his right hand, but it was shaking so badly that he had to use both hands to take the cup. He held it to his mouth, blew on it, then drank, first a little swallow, then a larger one. He paused a moment and, afterwards, took another couple of drinks. The coffee seemed to make him more alert.

"What's going on?" he finally asked, looking from one of us to another.

Sailor told him. "You sideswiped a bridge, Bob, then passed out."

"Tear up anything?" Dad asked.

"Naw," I said. "Only scraped the edge of the truckbed on the bridge bannister. Luckily, no bad damage."

He handed the empty thermos cup back to Bonnie, then took a package of Camels from the chest pocket of his gray work shirt. He shook out a cigarette, and Jim Gruber lit it for him, striking a kitchen match on the hip of his blue coveralls. Dad inhaled two quick and greedy lungfuls of smoke.

"Bob, why don't you let Will go on driving, 'tween here and Limon," Big Jim said to my dad. "It's not too far now, and he's been doing a pretty good job."

"You think I should, Jim?" Dad asked.

"Thing to do, Bob," the big guy said. "Give yourself a chance to sleep it off some more."

I never thought my dad would agree to such a thing, but he did. That was a strong indication of how ashamed, how embarrassed he himself must have felt about getting so drunk that for the first time in his life he couldn't take care of business.

"If you say so, Jim," Dad said. "You're the doctor."

"Here, Bob," Bonnie said and handed my dad the thermos bottle. "You may want the rest of this coffee after you get on the road again."

Everybody scattered to the various vehicles. I closed my dad's door, then went around and got back under the wheel

177

of his truck. Our caravan rolled out of town, northwest on U.S. 287.

"Limon—62 miles." Still a good way to go. Close to a couple of hours of hard driving.

The Union Pacific railroad paralleled us on the left and, past it, the cottonwood-decorated Big Sandy, as we angled on northwest through high plains wheat country.

Between my dad and me, there was an awkward silence. Neither one of us knew quite what to say.

Around a bend and on our left, I saw what remained of the old-time settlement of Wild Horse, now mostly dried up, but once probably about a four-store watering station on the railroad.

"Limon—48 miles."

My dad unscrewed the cap-cup of the thermos and poured coffee into it. I glanced over and saw that his hands were shaking less than they had been earlier. He was able to drink using only one hand. Taking his time, he emptied the cup, then screwed it back on the thermos bottle and set the thermos on the seat between us. He lit up a cigarette.

Finally, he spoke. "You doing a damn good job," he said. That was his first complimentary word to me in a long, long time.

"I'm doing the best I can," I said. "It's kind of hard to drive this thing."

"I don't mean your driving," my dad said. "You're doing good on that, too. I mean you're doing a good job all the way 'round. Ain't ever took the time to tell you, but I'm right proud of you, the way you're turning out."

"Appreciate that, Dad," I said. I did. But I was sort of shocked by this new departure in his treatment of me. He'd always been so critical. I liked it, though. "Good to know," I said.

"Well, it's the damn truth—the way I feel," Dad said. "I've rode you too hard. But I just didn't want you to turn out like me. Wanted you to make something of yourself."

"Wouldn't be so bad to turn out like you," I said.

"Yeah, it would, son," my dad said. "I got pulled in the opposite direction from the way you're headed."

"Who by?"

"Pa, really," Dad said. "He taken me plumb out of school before I ever even finished the fifth grade. Put me to working in the fields when I wadn't hardly big enough to keep a one-row walking lister plowing straight. Then whenever our own work got done, he farmed me out to other guys. Kept my wages hisself. I was just about a slave, like the children of Israel in Egypt."

Dad was talking a lot more than usual, but I was glad of it. He was telling me stuff about his personal history that I'd never known.

"Grandpa Haley didn't give you any of the money he got for your work?" I asked.

"Nary a nickel," my dad said. "I ever raised the question, Pa always said, 'You gittin' room and board, boy, and that's more'n you worth.' Them days, about all Pa wanted to do was hunt and fish. Same for Mr. Perkins." That was Mama's daddy, now dead—Mr. Perkins. "Pa always had me drive him and Mr. Perkins in Pa's Model T Ford. I drove 'em to the bootlegger, old Herb Stimpson. And I drove 'em to the woods to hunt squirrels. Drove 'em to the creek to fish for channel cat. The two of them just set up in the backseat and guzzled that old moonshine. Wadn't long before they begin to give me a sip of it now and then to keep me happy. That's how I got started drinking. Wadn't much bigger'n Millie and Mollie."

He took out another Camel and lit it from the still burning end of the one he'd been smoking, then dropped the discard to the floorboard and mashed it with the sole of his boot.

"You start smoking back then, too?" I asked.

"Naw, chewed Beechnut chewing tobacco, like Pa," Dad said. "Didn't start smoking 'til later. But the main thing is, living thataway, working and driving for Pa, I didn't get hardly no education at all. Weren't no way to do what I dreamed about doing."

"And what was that?"

"Be a doctor," Dad said.

"A medical doctor?" I asked. It was hard for me to picture my dad as a doctor, or wanting to be one.

"Yeah," he said. "I would have died to be a doctor. That's all I could think of, from when I was just a little kid. Like old

Doc Mason that looked after all of us. I wanted to be somebody, to help people."

"Same reasons I want to be a lawyer," I said.

"But the difference is, you *gonna* do it," my dad said. "You ain't gonna get trapped, like me, in no damn dead-end life."

"Life's a dead end for you, Dad?' I asked.

"Well, maybe not as bad as it could be," he said. "You mama's made me a good wife—a excellent wife, matter of fact. I got good kids. And I always been able to make a living." Dad took a drag on his cigarette and thought for a while. "But I shoulda made something of myself, and I never got half a chance," he said, finally. "I know as well as you that drinking much as I do has made things worse. And here lately, seems like the whiskey's done turned on me. Hits me a heap harder'n it used to."

Saying "drinking" right then apparently reminded him of his stash of Echo Springs. He opened the truck's glove compartment and pulled out an unopened half pint of the cheap whiskey that he kept there. He broke the seal on the bottle and started to unscrew the lid.

"Couldn't you cut down some?" I asked.

He stopped. "Could if I made up my mind to," he said. "Make up my mind to something, I stick with it." He sat there for a while, then slowly screwed the whiskey lid back on tight and returned the bottle to the glove compartment. He picked up the coffee thermos from the seat between us, poured a cupful from it, and quickly drank it down.

"I know you're tough like that," I said. "Do anything you decide on."

"Maybe I *could* cut down, Will," he said, the first time he'd called me by the shortened, more mature-sounding version of my name that I preferred. "We'll see. And Will?"

"Yessir?"

"Anything happens to me, I feel right good about you being able to take care of your mama and the family," he said. "You making a hand. You growed into a man, Will, and a dern good man at that."

"Nothing's going to happen to you," I said.

180

"Yeah, Will, something's gonna happen to all of us sooner or later," Dad said. He replaced the lid on the thermos bottle.

I suddenly remembered that I was still wearing my dad's nice cowboy straw hat. I took it off and handed it across the seat toward him.

He wouldn't take it. "Naw, it's yours, Will," he said. "I'll get me another'n."

I put the hat on again. It felt good. My dad leaned back in the truck seat and went to sleep.

U.S. highways 287 and 40 took us straight on northwest through rolling prairie. The Union Pacific tracks continued to run right beside us on our left, and Big Sandy Creek still coursed along, parallel, on the other side of the railroad tracks. After a while, we passed through the railroad town of Hugo, county seat of Lincoln County, and kept on going. "Limon— 14 miles."

Fourteen miles of high plains grassland. Then finally, coming up over a rise, I saw the white grain elevators of Limon outlined on the horizon of the clear, pale blue sky that I'd gotten used to seeing all the way from Vernon, back home. The sun was getting low in the west. At an intersection with east-west U.S. 24, our harvest caravan stopped, then turned left and drove into Limon, "Hub City of the High Plains. Elevation—4366'."

And you understood right away why Limon, which was at least twice as big as Vernon, was called a hub city. It was the crossroads for three U.S. highways and two railroad lines. U.S. 287, U.S. 40, and the Union Pacific railroad, all coming up from the southeast, the way we'd just traveled, went through Limon, then continued on northwest toward Denver, which was eighty-seven miles away. U.S. 24 and the Rock Island railroad, coming from the east, crossed the other highways and the Union Pacific at Limon, then veered off to the southwest toward Colorado Springs and Pikes Peak, seventy-four miles distant. I was hoping that I might somehow get to go down that way and see Pikes Peak while we were so close.

The town of Limon was laid out like a wide arrowhead that pointed straight south down E Avenue, a business street, to the yellow, red-roofed railroad depot that sat alongside the tracks, east of the main railyards and a roundhouse. Big Jim was at the front of our harvest parade, as usual, as we rolled into Limon on east-west Main Street, a few blocks north of the depot. We stopped momentarily at the downtown intersection of E Avenue and Main, right next to the white stucco Cozy Café and the Texaco Auto Service and near the Union Theater, then went on west. At the edge of town, Big Jim turned south at the Antelope Tourist Courts onto a gravel road. Barely past the Union Pacific tracks and just before Big Sandy Creek and the Rock Island tracks, on the other side of the creek, we cut to the right, off the gravel road and into a low grassy area, close to a stand of cottonwoods.

That was where we made our Limon camp, as, apparently, Big Jim had done the summer before. Buford parked his and Bonnie's house trailer. The rest of us made ourselves a kind of tent near them. We strung a rope between two trees and hung a tarp over it, then staked the sides of the tarp down. Big Jim and Dad went up and rented a cabin at the Antelope Tourist Courts, which was within walking distance, so we'd all have access to the common restrooms and showers there.

That first night, our whole bunch drove downtown and ate supper at the Cozy Café. Then back at camp, we bedded down. Lying in my quilt, I turned on Sailor's portable radio to get the news and heard that allied troops, led by the U.S. Seventh Army, had invaded southern Sicily. There was heavy fighting, the announcer said. He went on to mention something about the wedding of Betty Grable and Harry James out in Hollywood and the new world record for the mile of four minutes and two seconds, set by a Swede named Anderson. But my mind was still stuck on the Sicily invasion. Both my uncles, Clif and Wayne, were with the Seventh Army, I knew, though in different battalions. I turned the radio off and said a silent prayer for their safety.

Long trains came through all night on both sets of tracks—freight trains, troop trains, and regular passenger trains. At first, it was hard to go to sleep because of the frequent chugging, huffing, and puffing of the steam engines and the lonesome whine of their whistles. But I eventually got used to all this train noise and, that night and most nights afterwards, learned to snooze right on through it.

The next day was Sunday. We slept late. Then after breakfast at the Cozy Café, we came back to camp and unloaded our tractors from the trucks. We bolted the headers in place on the combines and hooked the combines to the tractors. We greased everything and filled up with gas. After that, there was time to kill. Most of the Limon stores were closed. Spider, hungover, went back to bed. Some of the rest of us found an open help-yourself laundry downtown and got our washing done. Bonnie bought groceries. Sailor and I drove around town and then out into the countryside. We scared up some pheasants in a field alongside one road and saw a small herd of antelopes in a big pasture along another. Then we came back to camp and "laid around the fort," as Sailor put it, listening to the radio and reading.

Monday morning, the twelfth of July, Jim Gruber and Dad went first thing to the Gleaner-Baldwin dealer's place in Limon to see if they could learn of anybody locally who was looking for custom combiners. Big Jim knew the dealer from the year before. The guy was about to go broke, Big Jim later told us, because he couldn't get any new equipment to sell. The man even offered to buy our combines and tractors, but Big Jim and Dad weren't interested. The Limon dealer was short on Gleaner-Baldwin replacement parts, too. Big Jim told our crew that if we broke something major on one of our combines, we'd probably have to drive all the way back to his own dealership in Vernon to get any new part we needed. But the Limon dealer *did* have a ready list of three local wheat farmers that we could go to work for right away. Dad and Big Jim hunted up the three men and made a deal with them.

That same morning, while Dad and Jim Gruber were at the Gleaner-Baldwin place, I drove the Green Lizard to the Limon post office to buy some penny postcards and to check on general delivery mail. It turned out that I was the only one who had any mail—two plain postcards, one from Marcy Redelk and one from Janie Marie. Again, nothing from Rebecca Milton. By now, I wasn't too surprised, and not even too disappointed.

July 6, 1943

Dear Will,

We had a great Fourth of July, with fireworks at the park. A friend of yours, Ronnie Dole, wanted to take me to the picture show last night, but I wouldn't let him. Saving myself for you, I guess. Ha Ha. The lady who's my boss at the library says you check out a lot of books. She thinks you're going places. So do I. Write back.

Marcy

July 5, 1943

Dear Will,

How are things with you? Fine, I hope. Grandma and Mama are doing all right. Millie and Mollie got sunburned at the swimming pool yesterday, but not too bad. Hope Daddy's doing okay. I don't hear anything from cousin Spider Deering. Could you please make him write me back or call me long distance, if he can. Please!

Love, Janie Marie

At camp, I handed Spider my sister's postcard and mentioned that maybe he should call her. But Spider just gave the card back to me after he read it and didn't say anything one way or the other.

Limon sat in a low east-west trough along Big Sandy Creek. The land rose up a couple hundred feet or more, both to the north and south of town, and it was on these high plateaus that the area's great dryland wheat fields spread out, almost forever. The lands of the farmers that we ourselves were going to cut for were located to the south of Limon. We roaded our combines out of town in that direction, and we were in the field and cutting wheat by eleven o'clock that Monday morning.

The grain was pretty good, too, making around twenty bushels to the acre, but the fields were hilly. Dad warned Spider again, in advance, about letting the clutch of his Farmall out too fast while he was on an incline, maybe causing the tractor to rear up and fall back over on him. But Spider was careful and had no problem with that.

My dad definitely reduced his drinking. He seemed nearly always to have a Coca-Cola in his hand, and he started eating so much ice cream that he just about busted out of his Levi's. Dad got the ice cream, evenings, at the downtown Limon Ice Cream Parlor on E Avenue. The whole bunch of us took to going there a lot of nights, after supper. I always ordered a dish of banana nut, my dad, chocolate.

But for me, the ice cream wasn't the whole draw of the ice cream parlor. There was a really cute blonde, about my age, who worked there, and she took an interest in me right away, it seemed like.

"You guys wheat combiners?" she asked me that first night, when she brought the ice cream orders over to our two tables. She was wearing a green cotton dress with a ruffled collar, and her hair was tied back with a green ribbon.

"How could you tell?" I said.

"Tanned up, and you talk like you're not from Limon," she said.

"You're right," I said. "Get many of us coming in here for ice cream?"

"A few," the girl said. "Not as many as come to the grain elevators, of course. My girlfriend likes to work at the Farmers Elevator every summer just so she can meet harvest guys."

"Looks like you're the one who lucked out, this time," I said.

She giggled, then went back behind the counter with her empty tray. But before we finished our ice cream, she came back again and stood by my chair for a while to talk some more. I was glad she did, though I was conscious that everybody in our crew was listening in on the girl's and my conversation.

She said she was going to be in the twelfth grade in September. Her name was Carol Anne. She played high school basketball and liked drama. Her dad was the county sheriff. I told her my name—my real name—and that I was from Vernon, Oklahoma. With a sweep of a hand, I introduced her to our crew—as a group, not one by one.

After we left the place, I took a lot of razzing in the car and back at camp, too.

Spider did most of it. "Sheriff gonna throw you in jail, Willie, you go to messing with his virgin daughter," he said.

But I didn't care about the kidding. I was pretty impressed with myself and my new girl appeal.

One evening at our between-the-tracks Limon camp, after we'd washed up but before Bonnie'd set our supper out, Sailor gave me my first lesson in what he said was an Asian way of hand-to-hand fighting. He'd learned it, he told me, from a shipmate who'd grown up in Hawaii.

He showed me how you could hack a man's hand to make him drop a gun or how you could knock him out by hitting his neck with the side of your hand. And Sailor could vise-grip one of my wrists with his right hand and make me go to my knees when he applied pressure and jerked down hard. He could get a grip on my two arms, then fall back and throw me over his head in a roll. He could lock a leg in one of mine and easily push me over backwards. He showed me how to whirl around and kick a man's head with a foot.

"I know you've boxed, Will," Sailor said, "but this stuff beats a boxer anytime. He sticks out a jab or throws a punch, you whack him or grab him, and it's all over before he knows it."

It seemed to me that Sailor was right, from what he showed me, and I decided to get him to give me some more lessons.

But it turned out, that evening, that something about Sailor's Asian fighting demonstration or about Sailor himself offended

Buford. He'd been sitting on one of the camp stools, idly watching Sailor and me and silently waiting with Jim Gruber, Dad, Spider, and Little Jim for Bonnie to finish laying out supper.

Maybe Buford didn't like it that Bonnie'd paused a couple of times between trips into and out of the house trailer to watch what Sailor and I were doing. Maybe Buford thought his wife was a little too admiring of Sailor, personally—darkly handsome with his middle-parted black hair slicked back neatly on the sides, his muscular chest and arms shown off to good advantage under a clean white T-shirt. Or maybe it was that Buford had become increasingly resentful of the fact that, evenings, after everybody else was in bed, Bonnie and Sailor often sat and talked by themselves for a little while at the lantern-lit card table at the side of the house trailer.

Whatever his problem, Buford, stocky and stout-looking, stood up and took a step toward Sailor and me. "Might beat a boxer, maybe, with that Jap way of fighting," he said to Sailor, his high voice challenging, "but a wrestler like me would throw you on your ass in a minute."

The rest of our bunch, including me, instantly focused our attention on Sailor, waiting for his reaction.

"Better watch out, Sailor," Big Jim said. "He might know what he's talking about." Big Jim, of course, had been a wrestler in college, as he'd told me when we were at Dimmitt.

Everything was quiet for a moment.

I had no doubt that Sailor could have put Buford down with one punch, or Asian whack, if he'd wanted to. But Sailor wouldn't be provoked. He was completely calm, and conciliatory, when he finally responded. "You might be right about that, Buford," he said.

Buford wasn't quite ready to let it go. "My name's Burford," he said, sounding the r.

"You might be right about that, Burford," Sailor said, repeating himself, and this time, carefully pronouncing the hostile Kansas trucker's first name correctly.

Bonnie came out of the house trailer with the last of the food and set it on the card table. Sailor put an arm around my shoulders, and we moved together toward our supper. Buford turned back, too.

We all filled our plates and cups and seated ourselves on the camp stools or on the ground, then started eating the supper Bonnie'd fixed. There was still some tension in the air and, fanning the flames, Spider decided to bother Buford a little.

"Buford," he said, "I mean, Burford, how come you ain't in the service, tough as *you* are?"

"I'll get some more tea," Bonnie said nervously. She got up and went toward the house trailer with the pitcher.

Buford glanced sideways toward Bonnie's back, as if he didn't want her to hear him. "I've got a . . . " He said the last word so low that we couldn't understand it.

"You got a what?" Spider said.

"I've got a hernia," Buford said.

"Doctors can fix a thing like that," Spider said.

"I've never been able to find time for it," Buford said. "Wear a truss."

Bonnie came back with the pitcher full of tea, and everybody went on with their supper.

About the third evening we were all at the Limon Ice Cream Parlor, I hit Carol Anne up for a date. She'd already told me that the ice cream place was closed on Sundays, so I asked her if she wanted to go to a picture show with me on the coming Sunday night.

"All right," she said, without hesitation.

Way to go, Will!

I said, "Tell me how to get to your house, and I'll come pick you up after I get back from the field and take a shower."

She gave me a nervous look. "No, I'll just meet you at the Union Theater."

"That's what you want," I said. We agreed on seven o'clock.

And she was already waiting in front of the theater that Sunday evening, when I parked the Green Lizard across the street and walked over—a Colorado cutie in a white peasant blouse, dark blue pleated skirt, and saddle oxfords, her curly blond hair brushed shiny and hanging to her shoulders.

After we said hello, I looked up at the Union Theater's marquee. "Oh, no!" I said.

Her face clouded. "What's the matter?"

"Robert Taylor's the matter," I said. What was showing was Robert Taylor in a war picture, *Stand By for Action*. "You think he's a mature good-looker?"

"Too girly," Carol Anne said.

"Bingo!" I said.

I bought the tickets, then the popcorn. There was a good cartoon. Next, Paramount News featured what was going on in the war in Sicily. I was glad that we seemed to be winning there, and I hoped my uncles were all right. I put my arm around Carol Anne once the main feature started. She didn't seem to mind. And I actually enjoyed old Robert Taylor for the first time ever.

Afterwards, Carol Anne wanted to walk home by herself, but I wouldn't let her. I loaded her into the Lizard, and she directed me north to her two-story white house, which sat on a corner in a nice residential neighborhood. I parked on the street in front. No lights were on in the house. Carol Anne didn't seem in a hurry to get out of the car, so I scooted over closer to her and put my arm around her. I decided to kiss her on the lips. She leaned as much toward me as I did toward her. But all of a sudden, the car door on her side was flung open, and there stood her beefy dad, the sheriff. He looked like a sheriff, holstered gun on his hip. He talked like a sheriff, too.

"Get in the house, Carol Anne!" he said and roughly grabbed her by the arm and pulled her out of the car.

"Sorry, Will," she said quietly. Then she turned and hurried away.

"It's *you* that's going to be sorry, young man," Carol Anne's dad said to me, bending over to look at me in the car. He was mad as a bull. "You're going to be *damned* sorry, if you ever come back around here or have anything to do with my daughter again. Harvest trash is not welcome."

That pissed me off. "How would Limon folks ever get their wheat cut if it wasn't for us?" I said.

But the sheriff was having none of it. "Don't back talk me, you little horse turd," he said. "I'm the law in Limon, and I don't need much reason to pistol-whip the shit out of you or drag your ass off to jail."

Right quick, I saw that there was no gain in arguing with him. "All right, Sheriff," I said. "Take it easy."

"Get on out of here then, and don't come back!" He slammed the passenger door.

I started the Green Lizard and drove off for camp. I never saw Carol Anne again. She was no longer at the Limon Ice Cream Parlor when we went there after that.

Early Tuesday morning, the next to last day our bunch cut wheat at Limon, my dad's old Gleaner-Baldwin broke down—just the kind of thing we'd dreaded. Some way, the elevator raddle chain that carried threshed wheat kernels up to the combine's grain bin got snarled up on a sprocket and, when it did, made such a racket that even I heard it above the roar of my Fordson's heavy motor. I slammed on the tractor's brakes, and Little Jim instantly jerked the clutch lever and shut the combine down. But when we went around back and opened the little hinged door of the elevator housing, we saw at once that the raddle chain was totally twisted and torn all to hell, past repair.

Of course, the Limon Gleaner-Baldwin dealer didn't have an elevator raddle chain in stock to replace ours, and it would have taken forever to try to get one shipped from the Gleaner-Baldwin factory in Independence, Missouri. Big Jim had the part we needed at his own dealership back in Vernon, so there was no choice but for him to take off home in his truck and get us a new raddle chain.

Little Jim and I had very little to do while he was gone, our combine being down, although my dad went ahead and paid both of us for two last Limon days. Little Jim stayed in the field with his gasoline-and-grease pick-up in case he was needed. I went on back to camp, read, and lay around. Both days, though, I helped pretty Bonnie Wynn load dinner in the

Green Lizard and then drove her to the field at noon. And I spelled Spider on his Farmall tractor each time while he ate.

The second day Bonnie and I were in the car together, going back to camp, I grew brave enough to quiz her about her relationship with Buford. But I started out indirectly. "How'd you like growing up in Meade, Kansas?" I asked her.

"Okay, I guess," she said. "Good little town. Home of the Dalton Gang hideout. Their house and barn hooked together with a tunnel."

"No lie?" I said. Then I got right to it. "How'd you meet your husband?" I asked.

She seemed a little embarrassed by the question. "I was out of high school, working in a grocery store," she said. "All the boys my age were off in the war. My brother, Dan, who's a lot older than me, was deferred from the draft, 4F, because he's so nearsighted. He'd been on the high school wrestling team with Burford and was the one who got us together. You know Burford was 4F, too, don't you, Will?"

"Yeah, he told us."

"So that's how Burford and I met," Bonnie said.

"Love at first sight?"

"Maybe not immediately," she said. "But it was good to have somebody to take me to dances and things. Burford's a great dancer. You wouldn't know it, he's so chunky, but he is. He grew on me. I'm comfortable with him. So I guess you could say that, yes, I do love him now."

"He's all right," I said.

Bonnie was quiet for a minute. "Will, tell me about Sailor Torley," she said, finally.

I told her as much as I knew.

"I like him," she said when I'd finished.

"I do myself," I said.

"He's probably not much for getting too attached to a girl, though," Bonnie said. "Going back to sea, he says, following the wheat harvest."

"That's what he tells me, too."

"Sailor's the kind of guy that a girl might run off with, though," she said.

We drove into our camp then. I helped her unload the dishes and dinner things from the Green Lizard. I walked down to the creek and carried her back a bucket of water, but she wouldn't let me help her with the washing. I went and lay down under the tarp to read.

After a while, I heard someone outside the makeshift tent knocking on the door of the house trailer. Before Bonnie could open her door, I scrambled up from my quilt to look out.

Standing there in his good Levi's, cowboy boots, and cowboy straw hat, a worn black leather suitcase satchel in his hand, was my skinny, redheaded best friend from Vernon, Junior Randall.

I was pretty happy. "Hey, buddy!" I called out to Junior. He turned, and I hurried over to shake his hand.

Chapter Ten

At the Limon Ice Cream Parlor that night, Junior Randall told his story again—for my dad and the rest of our crew. Martin Dugan, the man from Vernon that Junior'd been working for, had sold out in Oakley, Kansas, and gone on home.

"He was homesick for his wife, I reckon, and tired of the wheat harvest," Junior said. "His '41 Ford truck that I was driving threw a rod and tore the engine all to hell. We put the truck in the shop there in Oakley, but the mechanic said it'd take him several days before he could get to it and get it fixed. So old Martin, he just hunted up a guy that'd already been trying to buy his tractor and combine off of him and sold out on the spot for cash. Then him and Darrell, our tractor driver, up and left out in the pick-up for Vernon. Martin said for me to hang around Oakley until the truck got fixed, then drive it home. I took a notion to hitchhike over here in the meantime, see if I could find y'all."

Little Jim spoke up. "My experience, Martin Dugan's a odd duck," he said.

"That's the damn truth," my dad said. "I could tell y'all a funny tale or two about him."

"Go ahead," I said.

Dad grinned, then began. "Well, Martin Dugan is a guy that Pa Haley, my daddy, couldn't hardly stand," Dad said. "Little after I got married, me and Pa and my brothers was baling some cane hay for old Martin on that place he had up north of Vernon. Middle of the morning, he comes down to the field all dressed up in sissy-looking cowboy clothes and riding a paint horse that he's overly proud of. He commences to griping at Pa about our baling. For one thing, he gets down and hefts a bale and says we making 'em too light, then climbs back up in his fancy saddle. We was gittin' paid by the bale. Pa's chewin' Beechnut tobacco as always, and he all of a sudden lets fly with a big spit of it and, acting like it's a complete accident, splats the juice all over the side of one of old Martin's shiny cowboy boots.

"That damned near tears it! Old Martin jumps down off his horse, madder'n hell, and offers to fight Pa right there. But Pa won't take him up on it, says, 'Hell, Martin, I got a sixteen year-old girl that can whup *your* ass!' Which was probably true. Sarah probably could've whupped old Martin's ass. Pa says, 'I tell you what I *will* do, though, Martin. You seem pretty proud of that paint gelding you ridin', and I imagine you think he can run.'

"Old Martin takes the bait. 'This horse can outrun anything in Cash County,' he says. 'Wellsir, then,' Pa says, 'I bet you that, if we unhook old Jude, that little sorrel jenny yonder, from the buckrake, and we run her against your paint horse, here, down to around that tree at the far end of the field, Jude'll beat you back to the finish by at least a length.'

"Old Martin thinks that's the best deal he's ever heard of. What he don't know is that old Jude, even though she's got a hellacious knot on her left side, just right for a stirrup, is faster'n air *horse* we ever owned. 'What's the stakes?' Martin says. 'Old Jude wins,' Pa says, 'you give me fifty bales of this here cane hay, free. Your paint wins, we bale this whole field for you for nothing.'

"Old Martin says, 'That's a bet.' Me and my brother, Wayne, unhooks old Jude from the buckrake and takes the harness off of her. Pa makes some reins out of baling wire. He draws a finish line in the dirt with his foot, then climbs on old Jude, bareback. The two of 'em line up side by side. I start 'em by dropping my hat, and they're off. Hell, it ain't even a contest! Pa rounds the tree a length and a half ahead of old Martin and crosses the finish line nearly three lengths in front.

"Old Martin's as sour as a green apple, but he says, 'A bet's a bet.' And Pa says, 'You know, Martin, what I'm sorriest about is that I didn't just leave the harness on old Jude when I run her!'"

My dad was in a good mood after telling that Martin Dugan story. I was glad of that because it was time for me to put the proposition to him that Junior and I'd come up with.

"How much longer's it going to be before Jim Gruber gets back from Vernon?" I asked Dad.

"Day, or day'n half."

"And after that you'll be moving on up to Nebraska, right?" I asked.

"Yeah," he said. "Kimball, or maybe Sidney, just east of it."

"You won't be needing me for a while," I said. "What would you think about me and Junior, here, taking off and thumbing it down to Colorado Springs to see Pikes Peak, and then from there on up to Cheyenne for the Frontier Days rodeo? It's a short jump, according to the map, from Cheyenne to Kimball, and I could come right on over there and hook up with y'all again after the rodeo. Junior'd catch a bus back to Oakley to get Martin's truck and drive it home."

"But how would you find out, Will, whether we was in Kimball or Sidney?" Dad asked.

I thought a minute and came up with an answer. "You could send me a telegram in Cheyenne that I could pick up at the Western Union office, there, like general delivery mail," I said.

I knew from the look on his face, before he said anything, that my dad was going to agree to Junior's and my plan. "Well, I don't know why the hell not, son," he said. "You sure oughta see Pikes Peak while we're this close. Me and Shorty McIntyre run away from home on motorcycles when I was sixteen, and we rode up Pikes Peak *on* them Harleys. And far as the Frontier Days rodeo goes, I wouldn't mind myself seeing *that* sucker. So, y'all have at it, Will!"

"All right!" I said.

"But, Will . . ."

"Yessir?"

"Don't go and get no tattoo like me and Shorty McIntyre done." Dad had a blue and red sketch of a turbaned woman tattooed on the inside of his left forearm. He called her "Rachel from the Bible."

"Not aiming to," I said.

Bonnie loaned Junior an extra quilt, and he stayed all night with our crew under the tarp. Next morning, Thursday, he and I got up before anybody else, showered and shaved at the Antelope Tourist Courts, and put on our best cowboy clothes. I borrowed a tan suitcase that Sailor Torley'd bought in Boise City and stuffed a few of my things in it. I counted myself out sixty dollars cash and left the rest of my money with my dad.

I sat down at the card table outside the house trailer, wrote a couple of hasty postcards, and gave them to Sailor to mail for me.

Thursday, July 22, 1943

Dear Marcy,

Pikes Peak or bust! My Vernon friend, Junior Randall, and I are taking off a few days to go to Colorado Springs and then up to Cheyenne. Watch old Ronnie Dole! He's a wolf. And I'm sure his ancestors fought against the Comanche Indians! Check out *La Traviata* opera records from the library. I love it! Write me back, General Delivery, at Kimball, Nebraska. We're cutting there next—or close.

Your hitchhiking friend, Will

July 22, 1943

Dear Janie Marie

A quick note before I leave our bunch for a few days and run off to see Pikes Peak and then the rodeo at Cheyenne.

I can't make Spider write you, and he won't talk about it.
I hope nothing's the matter. Let me know if you need help.
Dad's really doing good, tell Mama. Y'all can write us
where we're probably cutting wheat next—General Delivery
at Kimball, Nebraska. We'll get it one way or another.

Love, Will

Junior and I gobbled down a few bites of breakfast with
the others. We said our quick good-byes just as the sun was
fully up, then hoofed it north to the pavement. There we walked
west to where the highways split. Taking the one on the left,
we went a few more yards down U.S. 24 southwest toward
Colorado Springs.

It was early in the morning, but pretty soon we heard our
first car coming. Junior and I both turned toward it in antici-
pation and stuck out our thumbs. The car was a two-seater
black '36 Ford, and it went right on past us without slowing
down a bit. And just as it passed, I saw first that it had an
Oklahoma tag, then that the first two numbers on the tag were
a six and a four, meaning that the car was from Cash County!

He and I dashed down the highway after the black Ford,
waving and yelling, "Hey! Hey!" But the car just whizzed on
out of sight.

That was a bad way to start the day, a bad omen. I couldn't
keep count of how many cars passed us by after that, with the
drivers not even giving us so much as a glance. Junior and I
stood out there for an hour and a half with no success. Then
Junior got the idea of waving a five-dollar bill at the next car
that came by.

That worked. A talky fat guy in a blue '38 four-door Dodge
pulled over and stopped for us. He told me and Junior that
his name was McKinney, that he was moving from Brooklyn,
New York, to Pueblo, Colorado—he pronounced it "Pewblow"—
and that he could drop us off, all right, in Colorado Springs
on his way. The backseat of the fat guy's old car was piled high
with clothes and books, so Junior and I both had to crowd into
the front seat with McKinney.

Junior and I hoped when we got in the car that the man'd generously refuse Junior's five dollars, like a person back home would have done, and say that he'd be glad to give us a ride for nothing since he was heading our way anyway. But we discovered that guys from Brooklyn, New York, were different from guys from Vernon, Oklahoma. This one snatched the money right out of Junior's hand, like he was picking peaches, and didn't even say thank you. The man was a preacher, too, he later told us—a Holy Roller, sounded like. Probably more interested in silver than souls, I figured.

By about noon, Junior and I were in Colorado Springs. We located the Gray Line office and bought ourselves a couple of tickets, put our bags in a locker there, and soon were heading out of town, up the twisty Pikes Peak gravel road, in a kind of stretch touring car with five other people.

The woman behind the Gray Line desk had tried to sell us a tour of the Garden of the Gods, too. But Junior'd asked, after looking at a brochure about that attraction, "What is it? A lot of big red rocks, scattered around?" And when the attendant responded that that was more or less the case, Junior and I had declined.

But Pikes Peak was worth the trip by itself. When Janie Marie was in the ninth grade, she'd been invited to go with the Vernon High School superintendent and his wife on a Colorado Springs vacation, to look after their little girl. Back home afterwards, Janie Marie couldn't stop talking about all she'd seen—the Garden of the Gods, the Cave of the Winds, the Will Rogers Shrine of the Sun, and especially Pikes Peak. I'd been pretty skeptical back then when she tried to explain to me how high the famous mountain was—something like four-teen thousand feet, she said. Near home, I'd been several times to Mount Scott, north of Lawton. Climbed on foot up its rocky side to the top, even. Mount Scott was probably about two thousand feet high, and I couldn't imagine anything higher. "Pikes Peak can't be taller than Mount Scott," I'd said. This made my sister laugh.

And I found out that she was right to laugh. Flatlander, plains guy that I was, I'd never seen real mountains until Junior and I got to Colorado Springs and had never even seen pine trees, either. The size and scenery of the Rocky Mountains thrilled me to my liver from the very first view I caught of the front range as we were coming west out of the prairie. Our Gray Line ride up Pikes Peak was wonderful—green, heavily forested steep slopes, mountain summits that reached to the clouds and beyond. I was as excited as a kid on his first day at school when I saw the snow on the ground after we got to the top of Pikes Peak. Snow in the middle of summer! Junior and I threw snowballs at each other, then wandered around marveling at the unbelievable view, though we soon had to slow down a little because the altitude and thin air up there made it hard for us to breathe. We cussed ourselves for not bringing a camera to record the whole experience for our friends back home.

Returning down to Colorado Springs, Junior and I got our bags out of the Gray Line locker, then bought ourselves some ham sandwiches in a little hole-in-the wall place and talked about what to do next. We'd seen all we wanted to see around there. We were ready for Cheyenne and Frontier Days. And we'd had enough of trying to hitchhike in Colorado. People just wouldn't pick you up.

"Instead of wasting money on a hotel room and catching a bus in the morning," Junior said, "why don't we just grab the first bus we can right now and ride all night?"

That was what we decided to do. We found the Union Bus Station, which was on a kind of seedy street, and bought Greyhound tickets to Cheyenne, with stops along the way and a middle-of-the-night change of buses in Denver. We weren't scheduled to depart Colorado Springs for close to two hours, so I came up with an idea about what we could do in the meantime.

"You saw that tattoo parlor just before we got here to the bus station," I said to Junior. "Let's go get us one."

Junior wasn't crazy about the idea, but he said that if *I* was going to get a tattoo, then he would, too. So we both did.

We put our bags in a locker again, then went to the tattoo place next door. We had the tattoos put high on our left arms so that they wouldn't show if we didn't want them to. The buzzing needle hurt like hell, and the tattoo guy, as greasy-looking as his machine, had to keep wiping beads of blood off my arm—and Junior's, too, later—while he was working on us. I chose the head of an Indian woman in red and blue. I was thinking of Marcy Redelk, but the tattooed woman actually looked more like Pocahontas, with kind of fluffy and limp feathers on her head. Junior got the face of a cowboy wearing a ten-gallon hat. The tattoo guy wrapped each of our left arms with a gauze bandage. We paid him and went on back to the Union Bus Station.

Two boys, a little older than Junior and me, followed us into the station, and before we could get our suitcases and sit down to wait for the bus, they sidled up and propositioned us about going outside and pitching quarters. It was a game that Junior and I were good at, though we'd never up to then pitched anything but washers for a penny each. But I was kind of leery of these two guys. Their hair was too long and ratty looking. And one of them, a little more muscular than the other, was wearing a dingy white T-shirt that said "Kansas Boys State—1942."

"You been in the reformatory?" I asked that one, pointing at the lettering.

He looked down at his chest. "This?" he said, and laughed. "Boys State's not a reformatory. It's a mock state government. Honor to get chose to go there."

Reassured some, I told the two guys to wait a minute, then went to the cashier and got me and Junior two dollars apiece worth of quarters. Back, I motioned toward the bus station's front door. "Lead on, McDuff," I said.

The boys hesitated. "What makes you think my name's McDuff, or whatever you said?" the more muscled-up guy with the Boys State T-shirt asked, a little belligerently.

"Just a saying," I said, concluding that they hadn't studied *Macbeth* in that boy's school. "Go on."

Junior and I followed them outside, then around to an alley between the bus station and the tattoo parlor.

"Let's go all the way back so we can pitch toward that brick wall," the shorter of the two boys said, motioning with his hand.

The four of us walked around a big pile of dumped-out garbage and some overflowing trash cans. At the back wall, we stopped, and Junior and I started to go into our pockets to get out our quarters. But just then, both boys stepped right in front of us, blocking our exit up the alley, and the littler guy pulled out a big knife and punched a button on it that made the deadly blade snap straight.

The bigger guy, the Boys State guy, was in front of me. He did the talking. "Okay, you two little bastards," he said, sounding sort of like a picture show gangster, "hand over all your money—folding money, too—and you won't get hurt."

I couldn't believe this was happening to me and Junior. Right in broad daylight! And it pissed me off, too. I'd worked hard for my money.

Instantly, I thought of Sailor Torley's Asian way of fighting. In one motion, I kicked the bigger guy as hard as I could, right in the crotch, then turned and gave a vicious hack with the side of my hand to the knife-holding wrist of the littler guy. Both boys let out a yell at the same time. The bigger guy went down to his knees and started making a noise like he was choking. The other one dropped his knife and backed off a couple of steps, holding his wrist, and looked like he didn't know what to do next.

I took a fighting stance. "Get the hell out of here before we call the police!" I said in my meanest voice.

"Yeah!" Junior said. He had his fists doubled up. "Get going, both of y'all!"

The smaller guy took the Boys State guy by the arm and helped him to his feet. The two of them began slowly to back up.

The bigger one was holding his crotch, a look of pain on his face. "We'll be back," he groaned. "We'll make you sorry."

"Better bring a lunch when you come," I said. "Might take a while."

I moved a couple of menacing steps toward them. They turned then and ran, quickly disappearing around the corner of the bus station.

"Life in the big city!" Junior said. He picked up the dropped knife, looked at it a second, then threw it over into a pile of garbage. "We shoulda showed 'em our tattoos right off, Will, and they'd have seen how tough we were, been too scared to bring us around here."

"You think Boys State was a reformatory, really, Junior?" I asked.

"Oughta been, if *that* guy went to it," he said.

It was already dark when our Greyhound bus took off north on a mountain range-skirting highway toward Denver. Junior slept most of the way there, and I did, some. We roused up and got off with our suitcases, of course, when the driver eventually pulled in and parked at the bus station in the "Mile High City." Inside, Junior and I ate some cheese sandwiches and drank a couple of Grapettes, then bought ourselves a sack of doughnuts for the road. We went out, finally, to wait to get on the Cheyenne bus. Several rodeo cowboys were already in line. A couple of them didn't look a whole lot older than me and Junior, and all of us were dressed about the same. Three rodeo guys were carrying bareback surcingles on their shoulders. The others had the bus driver stow their saddles and rigs underneath with the bags.

One of the older rodeo cowboys, who was right in front of us, turned. "You boys riding up at Cheyenne, too?" he asked Junior, friendly. This man had a bad scar over his left eye and a flattened nose that looked like it'd been busted more than once. He was letting the younger cowboy just ahead of him, who seemed to have had a little too much to drink, lean back against him.

"You bet," Junior said.

"Dip snuff?" the older cowboy asked then and proffered an open can of Garrett's back toward Junior.

"No thanks," Junior said. "Getting ready to eat me some doughnuts." He held up the sack to prove it.

The cowboy next offered the snuff past Junior to me. "What about you, son?"

I shook my head. "Doughnuts, too."

He turned forward then and put a pinch of snuff for himself inside his lower lip, replaced the lid on the Garrett's can, and put it back in a pocket of the black vest he wore. The uniformed driver opened the bus door and stood by it, ready to take tickets. "Come on, Jackie," the older cowboy said to the younger one in front of him, nudging the boy ahead. "This old Greyhound's gonna be a lot easier to ride than them saddle broncs of yours."

Settled on board the bus and heading north toward Cheyenne, Junior and I got comfortable in the Greyhound's soft seats. The wind was cool, blowing in the open windows. And both of us were sound asleep before we ever got to our doughnuts. We never knew it when we crossed the line into Wyoming, another new state for me.

Cheyenne, in my mind, had always seemed to be about like Oz, a kind of cowboy myth. But it turned out to be a real place, and a good deal like any other western town, except that that Friday morning was the start of Frontier Days. As Junior and I walked north from the bus station, all the downtown store windows we passed were painted up with images of bucking broncs and calf roping scenes, and the fronts of the two- and three-story buildings were decorated with red, white, and blue bunting.

He and I'd shaved and washed up in the bus station toilet and stashed our two bags in a locker, and now we were looking for a place to eat some breakfast. Junior'd said why didn't we just buy a couple of cups of coffee in the bus station and eat the doughnuts we already had, but I wanted to get out into the famous cowboy capital right away and have a real cowboy's breakfast.

That proved to be a lot harder to do than I'd figured on. Lots of people were already on the streets—most of the men in cowboy clothes, many of the local women in checkered gingham dresses, or calico, for the occasion. Banners hung across nearly every street. One said "Welcome to Cheyenne, the Magic City of the Plains." Another said "Welcome to the Frontier Days Rodeo—The Daddy of 'Em All!"

Pretty exciting for a couple of guys from Vernon, Oklahoma.

203

The first café we saw was packed, with people spilling out onto the sidewalk in front. The next one was the same way. Junior said that all the cafés were going to be like that. He was right. We finally found a hot dog guy, just setting up his wheeled stand on a downtown corner, and that's where we bought our breakfast—two hot dogs each, with mustard and onions—when the guy was ready. We found a sidewalk bench a block east of there and took our time eating. We followed the hot dogs with the doughnuts that we'd carried all the way from Denver.

Junior and I spent the day, then, seeing the sights of Cheyenne. First we took a two-hour city tour on an open-air bus, where the driver pointed out historic buildings and houses to us and told a number of sort of entertaining stories about what he called Cheyenne's "wild and woolly past."

Afterwards, Junior and I walked to the sandstone state capitol building, north of downtown, and, inside, strolled around its marble-floored halls. We came to the state senate chamber. It was open to the public, and he and I went in. At once, I felt almost as much at home in that high-ceilinged room of speechifying and semicircular-rowed desks as I would have in Joe Lammer's Confectionary.

I felt almost reverent, too, like I was in a church. "Junior, this is the kind of place I'm meant for," I said, as we stopped beside one of the desks and looked up and all around.

"Lot better life, Will, raising cattle and doing a little farming than you're gonna find in politics," he said.

"Maybe, but this is what I want to do," I said.

"Why?"

"I don't know," I said. "It's just what interests me, draws me. I want to help people. And besides, I don't want to wind up as just a paragraph in the *Vernon Herald*."

"Would that be so bad?"

"Would for me," I said.

"Maybe you oughta start then, Will, by running for student president at school when we get back home," Junior said.

"You think?"

"You want it, I want you to have it," he said.

That was the way a best friend ought to talk, I thought.

We left the capitol building then and went over to the Wyoming State Museum. Junior and I both were impressed by all the great old cowboy and Indian stuff they had. Later we walked back south to the Union Pacific depot and took a look at Big Boy 4004, the world's largest steam locomotive, designed, it was said, for the hard run between Cheyenne and Ogden, Utah.

Then we started worrying about where we were going to spend the night, after we got out of the rodeo. Cheyenne wasn't that big a place, and Junior and I figured that its hotels—and there weren't very many of them—would be just as overrun with rodeo fans as its cafés. We remembered a visitors' information booth we'd seen earlier. It was downtown on Cheyenne's principal east-west street, U.S. 30, also called the Lincoln Highway, which I knew I'd later be going east on, toward Kimball, Nebraska.

The woman at the information booth—she was wearing an old-fashioned red gingham dress and matching bonnet—seemed pretty frazzled. "Gentlemen," she said, "I'm afraid I don't know of a single vacant hotel room in town. Down the block west, here, though, are a couple of places that'll rent you an army cot in a kind of third-floor dormitory loft for ten dollars a night."

We thanked the woman and turned away. "Hell, Will," Junior said to me before we'd walked very far, "why don't we just sleep in the bus station tonight for free?"

I agreed that that was a good idea. We started toward the station then, thinking to look the place over more closely for when we came back from the rodeo.

"You know, Will," Junior said after a while, "I'm gonna go ahead on and buy me a bus ticket to Oakley, Kansas, now so I can take off early in the morning. I gotta get Martin's truck and strike out for home. And you can leave out tomorrow, too, to meet up with your crew in Nebraska."

That was what he did—bought his ticket as soon as we got to the bus station. But I decided not to buy mine right then. I thought I'd wait until after I could go to the Western Union office the next morning and pick up the telegram that would tell me exactly where my dad and our bunch were newly located.

205

The benches in the bus station looked pretty good, and a lot of them, we saw, were vacant.

"It'll beat the hell out of paying ten dollars a night," Junior said.

Afterwards, back in the main part of town, we caught a city bus that angled northwest, up Carey Street, to the Frontier Days rodeo grounds. We went early because we figured that our chances of getting something to eat would be better at the rodeo than at a downtown café.

A huge crowd was already gathering there. Junior and I bought general admission grandstand tickets, the only kind we could get, then sat down at a little outdoor eating joint under one of several umbrellas, and each ordered a couple of hot dogs. This time, we said we'd take sauerkraut with them, something different. We tried to buy beer, too, but were turned down because of our age.

Junior took ahold of the arm of the wrinkled old waitress who'd refused us. "Honey," he said playfully, "would you sell us a couple of Budweisers if we both showed you that we've got tattoos?"

"Not unless the tattoos're on your dicks," she said.

Junior quickly let go the old woman's arm. He and I ordered Coca-Colas instead.

We finished our supper, such as it was, and were up in the big wooden grandstand before it was quite dark outside, although the floodlights were already turned on. The grandstand faced east across a dirt arena. A guy was busy smoothing the arena with a harrow, drawn by a couple of heavyset workhorses. The chutes were across from us, facing us. That would be where all the cowboy action would start from. Above the chutes was a roofed, bunting-draped platform for the rodeo announcer, the events judges, and a brass band.

Our general admission seats weren't worth a damn—too high and too far north—but Junior and I were thrilled to be at Frontier Days, *wherever* we had to sit. He and I would have taken seats in the toilet, if those were the only ones left and you could even halfway see the rodeo from them.

The grandstand filled fast. Night fell. The band played "Red River Valley" and, after that, a couple of other cowboy tunes. Then the announcer, in a deep auctioneer's voice, welcomed us to the "Daddy of 'Em All—the largest outdoor rodeo in the world!" He introduced a couple of "dignitaries," as he called them, who were sitting in separate boxes down front—actress Claudette Colbert and Wendell Wilkie, the 1940 Republican candidate against President Franklin Roosevelt. I myself was a Roosevelt man, and I wanted to boo when people applauded Wilkie, but I restrained myself.

With the grand entry, hundreds of mounted and colorful cowboys and cowgirls burst into the arena, riding two abreast, until the arena was totally packed. We stood with the audience, then, as a flag group rode in. They stopped in the middle of the massed cowboys, and the band struck up the national anthem.

Neither Junior nor I'd ever seen anything like the first three competitions that opened the rodeo action. There was a four-horse chuck wagon race, then a wild cow milking contest, and finally, a wild horse race. In this last event, really rank mustangs were turned loose out of the chutes and into the arena. Each three-man cowboy team—and all the teams worked at the same time—had to rope a bronc and saddle it. Then a team member had to climb on and try to stay on until he could get the bucking horse across a finish line.

When the roping competition started, never a very exciting event to watch, Junior got a crazy idea. "Will, what do you say we try to get ourselves around there, back of the chutes, where the cowboys are," he said.

I didn't think it'd work, but I was wrong. We got down from the grandstand and walked around the north side of the arena fence to an area where a lot of pick-ups and horse trailers were parked and where there was a white-haired guy at a gate that led south toward the back of the chutes. I followed Junior, and we got right in close behind three cowboys. They were dressed just like the two of *us*—Levi's and cowboy shirts, boots, and hats—except that the others had small white cloth sheets with entry numbers printed on them pinned to their shirts or vests. But the old gatekeeper didn't notice the difference. He passed me and Junior right on through with the rest. "Boys, hope you have good luck in tonight's go-round," the man said to us.

We thanked him, then proceeded to the area under the announcer's stand and behind the chutes where a lot of cowboys were waiting their rodeo turn, getting ready. Some were standing, talking. Some sat or squatted on the ground. Several were stretching or limbering up. A few were riding their saddles, splayed out in the gravel, feet kicking back and forth in the stirrups, apparently getting themselves mentally prepared for saddle bronc rides. Four different cowboys were being taped up, or were taping themselves up, shirts off or Levi's down— a shoulder, a knee, a wrist, ribs. One little group sat off to the side, playing gin, slapping down cards in the dirt. Junior and I went over and stood to watch them. Everywhere there was a lot of jostling, joking talk and, regularly from above us, the booming, loud-speakered voice of the announcer: "Joe Ray McCarthy's time is '*no* time,' folks, and all he gets tonight is your applause. So let's give this old hardworking cowboy a big hand!" Mike chatter like that was always followed by strong applause from the grandstand.

Junior and I soaked up the exciting, sort of backstage atmosphere. Nobody paid any attention to us. He and I knew we were impostors, but we began to feel about halfway like real rodeo cowboys. At least I did. We hardly noticed it at first when a new guy came from the pick-up and horse trailer area and started talking to some cowboys who were squatting on the ground near us, sharing a pint of whiskey.

"I'm afraid Jackie's not gonna make it tonight," the guy said. "He's out there by Slim's pick-up, puking his guts out, sick as a dog."

The name "Jackie" caught my attention, and so did the new guy's voice. Just then, he turned and saw Junior and me, and I recognized him as the older, flattened-nosed, eye-scarred cowboy who'd gotten on the Denver bus just ahead of Junior and me.

"How you boys doing?" he said and stuck out his hand. "Maury Murphy. Long time no see."

Junior and I shook hands with him and told him our names.

"Where you from, boys?"

We told him.

"What you ridin'?"

We decided to tell Murphy the truth about ourselves, and I had a feeling that the truth was no surprise for him. "We're not really cowboys, except at our FFA rodeo back home," I said. "We're just enjoying the show and being here, back of the chutes. We snuck in, actually."

"Don't worry about it, boys," Murphy said. "Make yourself at home."

Just then, Jackie came staggering in—the same young cowboy we'd seen with Maury Murphy in Denver. The young guy slumped to the ground, sat, and put his head in his hands.

"Jackie, you look like a stocker calf with shipping fever," one of the cowboys sitting nearby said to him.

Jackie raised his face. "I can't make it, boys. Never *been* this bad off. Got the flu, or something."

"Whiskey flu," another cowboy said. Several guys laughed. "But they gonna disqualify you, Jackie, you don't ride the first night."

"I can't help it." Jackie put his head back in his hands.

"What about slipping in a ringer for you—your hat and vest and entry number—like we done for Charley Good down in Amarillo last year?" the first cowboy asked.

Jackie raised his head again. He thought a moment. "Yeah, but who'd we get?"

That was when Murphy turned to me and Junior. "Either one of you boys ever ride saddle broncs?" he asked.

Junior spoke up. "Will, here, has," he said. "Better'n a green hand, too."

"Oh, no you don't!" I said.

"You can do it, Will," Junior said to me reassuringly. "Here's a chance, the only one you're ever gonna get before you die, to ride at Frontier Days." He turned then to Maury Murphy. "Will can do it."

Jackie looked up at me. His face was white, and he seemed like he was close to throwing up again. "God, buddy, you'd save my life!" he said to me. "Save my entry fee, keep me from getting disqualified. You're close enough to my size, and you don't have to stay on for the whole eight seconds, 'til the buzzer. Just go out there and try to make it look good, bail out soon's you want to. I'll give you ten bucks."

I was scared to death, not so much about the fraud as about having to ride a bronc at the Cheyenne rodeo! Still, I asked Jackie a basic question. "Won't the judges see through it, know it's not you?"

Murphy answered for Jackie. "They might, but they won't say anything unless somebody raises a fuss," he said. "It's not like this ain't never been done before."

And that was how I wound up riding in the "Daddy of 'Em All." When the time came, they put Jackie's saddle on Old Ranger, the bronc he'd drawn—a really rank old strawberry roan. I borrowed Jackie's leather gloves and spurs. I put on his gray vest with the entry number, ninety-seven, pinned on the back. Jackie handed me his black cowboy hat, and I pulled it so low down on my head that I was lop-eared. Murphy walked me over, but he held me back a little until the last minute, and then, with my head down so that the hat would shield my face, I climbed up the side of the narrow chute and crawled aboard Old Ranger, got my boots in the stirrups, and glued myself to the saddle seat the best I could.

The announcer's voice came over the loud speaker. "And now, folks, coming at you out of chute number nine, we've got a great young cowboy out of Waxahachie, Texas, making a name for himself. . . ." The announcer paused, like he'd maybe seen though our switch, but then he went on anyway. "Here he is, folks—Jackie Tyrell!"

I was ready to go, but my heart was pounding. I took a deep breath and nodded to the man on the gate. He swung it open, wide. Old Ranger exploded out of the chute with three of the spine-joltingest crow-hops in rodeo history, with me leaning way back, holding my left arm out and high and my spurs raking the bronc's shoulders with every jump, just like you're supposed to do. I thought for a second or two that I might have a chance to make it to the buzzer, but then Old Ranger decided to mix some wild spins in with his jumps, and on about the second spin, me and him "parted company," as cowboys used to say.

Hitting the dirt on my right side, with my elbow against my ribs, almost knocked the wind out of me. But I was instantly conscious of the need to get out of there before I was recognized as a ringer. I scrambled up, ran to the chutes, and quickly climbed over a gate. I was back with the cowboys behind the chutes and under the announcer's stand by the time the announcer was winding up with the words, ". . . so let's give him a big hand, folks."

"Way to go, Will!" Junior said, excited. "Proud of you!"

Maury Murphy slapped me on the back, and the other nearby cowboys looked on approvingly. "You done real good, son," he said. "Poor old Jackie's gone back to Slim's pick-up to lay down. But I'll give you the ten bucks myself, and he'll pay me back."

"Naw," I said. "Keep the money. It was a thrill for me to do it." I gave him Jackie's hat, vest, gloves, and spurs.

"Well, I'll trade belt buckles with you then," Murphy said.

"You mean it?"

"You bet, son," he said.

I undid my belt and took off my plain, shiny brass buckle. Murphy and I made the exchange. His buckle was oval-shaped and looked like gold. In the middle of it were the words "Champion, Bulldogging," and, top and bottom, "Denver—1942." I snapped the buckle on and re-cinched my belt.

Doing this, I was, for the first time, conscious of a sharp pain in my right side, worse when I took a deep breath. "I think I broke a rib," I said.

Murphy pulled my shirt out of my Levi's and rubbed his hand under it, around on my right side. "No bump," he said. "Not broke. Just cracked, my guess. The only thing you can do about it, son, is eat some aspireens and tough it out. Tape it up, you liable to get pneumonia, not breathing deep."

A cowboy beside Murphy fished a little tin of St. Joseph's aspirins out of his Levi's pocket, opened it, and held it out toward me. "Here, take a couple of these and keep the rest," he said.

"Much obliged," I said.

Another guy handed me a bottle of Schlitz beer. I swallowed two aspirins, then washed them down with a couple of slugs of the Schlitz.

Junior and I sat around with the cowboys for a while longer, then said our good-byes and went back to our seats in the grandstand. We watched the bulldogging—and Maury Murphy looked pretty good—then the bull riding, always the last event.

"Man, high point of your life, Will!" Junior said to me when we were getting up to leave. "Rode in the Daddy of 'Em All!"

"Yeah, but I kept thinking all the time of the Abraham Lincoln story about what the guy said who was getting ridden out of town on a rail."

"What?"

"Lincoln said the guy says, 'Boys, if it weren't for the honor of this, I'd just as soon walk!'"

I started to laugh when Junior did, but I had to catch myself because of the stab of pain in my right side.

It was after ten o'clock at night by the time Junior and I caught a city bus back down Carey Street to the center of town, then walked over to the Union Bus Station. We found a vacant waiting room bench near the back, long enough for both of us to stretch out on, and lay down. The bare wood of the bench was hard, and I had trouble at first getting comfortable, especially with my cracked rib. But I soon fell asleep, not too long after Junior did.

Then suddenly, about three o'clock in the morning, a cowboy-looking law officer with a badge poked me awake, his night stick stuck in my stomach, and Junior after me. "Get up, you two, and get out of here!" he said. "You can't sleep in the bus station."

Junior and I both sat up.

Rubbing the sleep from my eyes, I said, motioning toward Junior, "But this guy's got a ticket."

"Let me see it," the officer said to Junior.

Junior handed it over.

"Your bus don't leave 'til 7:30 in the morning," the man said. "I'm not gonna let either one of you stay here in the bus station. Get on out, and don't come back until thirty minutes beforehand."

That didn't sound fair—or legal—but Junior and I weren't in any position to argue. We found a park bench a couple of blocks away. It was cold outside, but we managed to sleep a little, sitting up.

Later I went with Junior back to the station. We got our bags out of the locker, bought a couple of cups of coffee, and then I walked him outside to his bus.

"Take it easy, Junior," I said.

"See you back home, Will," he said.

He stepped up into the bus. The door closed. The bus backed up, then pulled out. I stood there until it was out of sight.

Finally, walking away by myself, carrying my borrowed tan suitcase, I was the lonesomest I'd ever been in my life. Never had felt so alone before. Strange town. Didn't know anybody.

I went to the Western Union office. Sure enough, there was a telegram for me. Typed words pasted on the yellow sheet read "STAY THERE STOP COMING TO RODEO STOP WILL CALL STOP DAD."

Will call? How in the devil would my dad *call* me in Cheyenne? *Where* would he call? And how would he and the crew find me, or I them, among the crowds of rodeo fans and Frontier Days celebrators? Like Stanley trying to find Livingstone in Africa.

It was Saturday, and posters announced that the big downtown Frontier Days parade was to begin at ten o'clock that morning. I came up with two plans for getting reunited with my dad and the harvest bunch. I decided that the first thing I'd try would be to walk east to the edge of town on U.S. 30, the highway my dad and the crew would be coming into Cheyenne on. I'd wait there at the side of the road and try to catch them arriving. My fallback plan was to try to get a ride on some vehicle in the Frontier Days parade, with the hope that, watching the parade, my dad or some of our bunch would see me.

For breakfast, I bought a hot dog and a Coca-Cola on the street again. Afterwards, I checked at Western Union—the only place, I figured, that my dad could possibly call me—to see if there was any telephone message for me. None. I walked east on U.S. 30, to the edge of town. I waited and watched for what I figured was a little over an hour. Nobody came—at least, nobody I knew. Back to Western Union. Still no call for me, the agent said. He seemed put out to be asked again.

I found where the parade was forming, to the east of the state capitol. I saw that there were a couple of covered wagons and two stagecoaches in line. Even though I told them my story, that I needed to be seen in the parade, the drivers of both wagons and the first stagecoach turned me down. The driver of the second stagecoach, though, said, "Matter of fact, young man, the fellow who was supposed to ride shotgun up here with me still hasn't come. If he doesn't show up by the time the parade starts, you're the guy."

And the man didn't get there, at least not in time. *Hallelujah!*

His big white ten-gallon hat and red vest were on a seat inside the stagecoach. I pitched my straw hat in there and picked up and put on his hat and vest. I was changing hats here lately, I thought, faster than Hedda Hopper. I crawled up beside the stage driver. He handed me a Winchester rifle, then started the four-horse team forward. The parade began.

The fallback plan worked! Just as we came even with the First National Bank, on a downtown corner, I saw my dad, then Sailor, then Big Jim Gruber, back from Vernon and finally, the rest of them, at almost the same time they saw me on the stagecoach and decided to trust their eyes. We all yelled excitedly at each other and agreed to meet right on that very corner in thirty minutes. I felt I had to go on to the end of the parade to keep my end of the bargain with my stagecoach driver.

Reunited again!

The words "Will call" in my dad's telegram, he told me, hadn't been part of his message at all. They were just Western

Union's signal to the Cheyenne agent that *I* would call for the telegram, in person.

I saw the rodeo a second time, that Saturday afternoon, with Dad, Big Jim, and the others. Afterwards, when we got ready to divide up into three vehicles and leave Cheyenne, my dad asked me to ride with him in his black Chevy truck. I thought that was a little strange. Jim Gruber and Little Jim climbed into the pick-up together, Sailor, Spider, Buford, and Bonnie into Sailor's Green Lizard.

We headed out of town east on U.S. 30 in the direction of Kimball, Nebraska, undoubtedly toward more moveable adventures.

Chapter Eleven

Missing in action! Uncle Clif, my favorite, was missing after some heavy fighting in Sicily. Dad waited to tell me this bad news until he and I were out on the highway toward Kimball. He hadn't wanted to spoil my time at the rodeo, and he wanted me and him to be by ourselves when he told me. That was the reason he'd asked me to ride back to Nebraska with him.

Cowboys don't cry, people used to say. But that wasn't true. I cried. So did my dad, even though that was unusual for him, sober. All I could think of at first was that my laughing and teasing, sandy-haired Uncle Clif, close as an older brother to me, was lying hurt in a ditch somewhere, unfound. Then I got to hoping that maybe he was all right but was in a prisoner of war camp, and that that hadn't been reported yet. I wouldn't let myself even consider the possibility that he was dead. Not Uncle Clif.

The telegram from the War Department had been delivered to Grandma Haley on the day that Big Jim Gruber'd gotten back to Vernon to pick up the combine raddle chain we needed. He'd brought the message back to Dad in Limon.

"Clif likely laying out in the woods somewhere, Will, waiting 'til the Germans pass so he can get on back to his own unit," my dad said, as much to reassure himself, I thought, as to reassure me. "That boy's smart, always gonna make it somehow."

"I think so, too," I said. That was certainly what I *hoped*, what I was praying for.

Dad switched the subject then. "Will, you heard from your sister Janie Marie since we been on the road?"

"Nothing but postcards, Dad," I said. "Why?"

"Your mama sent word by Jim Gruber that Janie Marie ain't been feeling good," my dad said. "Been down in the dumps, seem like, too. She gonna take off work, told your mama, to go visit that Wofford girl from school, the one whose folks moved off to Edmond."

"That doesn't sound like Janie Marie—taking off work," I said.

"It don't," Dad said.

After about forty miles of grass and prairie on U.S. 30, east out of Cheyenne, the Union Pacific railroad running alongside us, we passed through Pine Bluffs, Wyoming, "Elevation— 5047'." A rocky bluff, the reason for the town's name, I figured, and a stand of short pines marked its south side. Dad didn't stop at a Wyoming historical marker that we passed, of course, but I read its heading anyway on the fly: "Old Texas Cattle Trail." Pine Bluffs was a long way from the Lone Star State, where the longhorns were rounded up in the old days and headed north.

A couple of miles more and we crossed the state line into Nebraska, another new state for me. A sign said "Nebraska— Home of Arbor Day." A few *more* trees wouldn't have hurt the state any, I thought.

"Bushnell—9 miles. Kimball—21 miles."

The Union Pacific railroad continued to parallel us on our left, with a green valley of rich fields on the other side of the tracks. To the right was rolling prairie and past it, up on top of a bluff, was what appeared to be pretty good farmland. Here and there were east-west shelter belts of planted trees, but there were no native trees at all on Lodgepole Creek, right there, as the highway crossed over to the creek's other side. We whizzed past Bushnell, not much of a town, with its gravel north-south main street, very few stores, and four metal grain elevators, "Kimball County Grain Co-op" painted in black on one of them. I was glad my dad and Big Jim hadn't decided to headquarter in Bushnell. There was a lot of wheat to cut around there but nothing else to do.

"Kimball—12 miles."

Rolling on east through the irrigated Lodgepole valley, we could see that on each side of the valley, up on the ridges, north and south, there were stretching acres upon acres of good dryland wheat fields. We soon passed Oliver Reservoir, apparently the source of the valley's irrigation water, which we'd noticed coursing in roadside canals.

A tourist court on the north side of the highway and an implement dealer's place on the south welcomed us into the outskirts of Kimball, Nebraska, which looked to be about twice the size of Vernon. U.S. 30 became Third Street. Dad drove right on into the middle of what was a solid grain town, with lots of tall cedar trees along Third and many big elm and other planted trees on the side streets. He braked the Chevy truck at the intersection of Third Street and U.S. 71, which was also Kimball's north-south Chestnut Street. A highway sign there said that Sidney was thirty-eight miles farther on, east on U.S. 30. Across the intersection in that direction, on the south side of the road, we could see the three-story limestone Kimball County Courthouse.

Dad turned left on Chestnut Street toward Scottsbluff, and we drove through a good two blocks of Kimball's stores and businesses, passing city hall, the Goodhand Theater, and a fraternal home. At the large sheet metal Kimball County Grain Co-op elevator, we went under a railroad trestle, then continued on north, and in a little while, saw a sign that said "Scottsbluff—44 miles."

Five miles out of Kimball, we passed through terraced farmland as we rose toward the crest of the east-west ridge. On top we saw rolling-hilled, tableland wheat fields extending out ahead and to the right and left all the way to the horizon. At the end of a long roadside shelter belt of locust and elm trees, Dad turned right onto graveled County Road 43. Two miles farther on, he slowed, then made a right turn into the wide yard of an old white frame farmhouse and a faded red barn that sat on a rocky hill, surrounded by long strip-fields of wheat interspersed with bare strips of plowed ground. A new-model black Buick car was drawn up close to the house.

Dad steered the truck over to the left toward the old barn, where our crew'd already arrived ahead of him and me. We pulled up by Buford and Bonnie's house trailer, which was parked next to a metal hand pump on a water well's square of concrete, and stopped near our other two trucks and the pick-up. The combines and tractors, I saw, sat in the grass on the east side of the barn, ready to go.

The old barn, no longer in use, was to be our sleeping quarters. I found my stuff piled to one side inside the big sliding door. I unpacked the tan suitcase I'd carried on my trip and gave it back to Sailor, with my thanks, then rolled out my bedding quilt. The physical activity gave me shooting pains in my right side. I winced, apparently noticeably.

"You hurt yourself some way, Will, while you was gone?" Sailor asked me.

I explained about the cracked rib and how I'd gotten it as a ringer riding a bucking saddle bronc. I showed him and the others my gold-colored belt buckle.

Spider, listening in, looked at me like he thought I was making up a story. "I *bet* that's what happened, Willie," he said, and laughed. He was jealous, I thought.

I decided not to say anything at all about my tattoo yet, although it was beginning to itch. I'd already stripped off the bandage discreetly and discarded it.

Big Jim made an announcement. "Soon's everybody's washed up, we going to the house. Old Man Stilwell's woman, Ruby, come out a while ago, when we first drove up, and said she was gonna make supper for us this evening."

"And what's the story on her?" Spider asked.

"Well, I cut wheat right here last year," Big Jim said. "And Ruby done all the dealings. Old Man Stilwell didn't come down but twice while I was here. He's a big shot up in Scottsbluff, which is a pretty good-sized town. Made a lot of money in insurance and real estate. About seventy years old now."

"And Ruby's his wife?" Spider asked. "She's a lot younger."

"Not his wife," Jim Gruber said. He grinned. "Kind of like, what I guess you might say, his mistress. Used to be a hooker, she'll tell you herself. Told me. Ain't ashamed of it. That's how she and Old Man Stilwell got acquainted, she says. Then he bought her a place to live in there in Scottsbluff, but, summers, she moves down here in this old house where Stilwell grew up as a boy. Ruby's a good gal. And she handles old Stilwell's money like it was her own."

As soon as I met her, Ruby reminded me of a really cheerful and funny aunt, the kind you like to tease and joke with and are always glad to see. She had frizzy, hennaed hair and was slightly built. Her face was plain except for a hawk nose, which, if her skin hadn't been so pink, would have made you think she was part Indian. But her lively, laughing green eyes were her best feature. And, man, could she cook!

Ruby'd made us a meatloaf that would have won a prize at the county fair. Served everything herself after she'd seated us at a long dining room table. Wouldn't hardly let Bonnie help her. Chattered all the time, carrying things back and forth from the kitchen. And she wasn't the least bit embarrassed about her past. Several times she openly referred to the fact that she'd originally come to Scottsbluff as a "working girl," as she put it. She referred to the man that kept her up as "Mr. Stilwell."

"Mr. Stilwell told me he wanted me to cook for your whole bunch, Mr. Haley, while you're cutting for us and the neighbors, too," she said to Dad, standing right next to him as he ate. "Mr. Stilwell's mother always cooked for the visiting thresher crews when he was little. So I cooked for Mr. Gruber, here, last summer. And I'm glad to do it again, this time, Mr. Haley, if you buy me the groceries."

"Call me Bob," my dad said. "But we wouldn't want to put you out."

"Putting out is what I do best," she said and winked at Dad.

He laughed with the rest of us, then reached over and patted her on the back, a little below the waist.

Uh-oh.

220

"You and Bonnie, here, can work together, Ruby," my dad said.

It came a big rain that night. It hailed some, too, but the hailstones were only about as big as English peas and, luckily, didn't come down thickly enough to damage the area's wheat. The worst thing about that night was the lightning. Ruby told us the next day that she thought there was something about the rocky hill where the barn and house sat that someway *drew* the lightning. It sure seemed like it. The crack and boom of the strikes, constant for maybe thirty minutes that night, were sudden explosions that seemed like they were going to blow apart the old barn where we were bedded down. Sailor said he'd noticed that the barn had lightning rods on it. That was a comfort. Even if the barn got hit, I thought, it wouldn't burn down around us. And before the lightning started, Sailor's portable Admiral radio was so staticky that we couldn't get any reception worth listening to—no music and no news.

Next morning, Sunday morning, the twenty-fifth of July, it was too wet to cut wheat, so Sailor and I decided to go hunt rabbits. I got my pump-action .22-caliber rifle out of the trunk of the Green Lizard, where it'd been stored ever since we'd left home, and cleaned it up a little. Big Jim said Sailor could borrow his bolt-action .22. Spider wanted to go with us, too, and Sailor said it was all right. So after breakfast, Spider asked Ruby if he could borrow a semiautomatic .22 rifle we'd seen in the house, above the fireplace, the night before.

She said, "Sure! But be careful, darling. The safety on that thing's off after each shot, and it's ready to fire. Kind of dangerous."

It was a beautiful clear day—warm and getting warmer. Everything smelled fresh after the rain. Sailor, Spider, and I drove east in the Lizard for about five miles until we came to a large patch of natural grassland on the north side of the road. Sailor parked, partly in the ditch, and we got out, crossed over, and climbed through a barbed-wire fence and into the pasture.

We started walking, looking to scare up a rabbit or two. Right away Spider annoyed me and Sailor. He fired his gun even before we ever saw a rabbit. Said he wanted to get used to the borrowed rifle. Shoving his yellow hair back from his eyes, he twice sighted and shot at a field lark on the ground and, luckily, missed both times. Later, for no apparent reason, he shot into the grass about fifty yards in front of us. You could tell by how awkward he looked that he'd never had much experience with guns—maybe not even in the army, since he'd been in the tank corps. Spider's dad apparently hadn't been like mine. My dad had had me out in the woods, hunting squirrels, from the time I was in grade school.

About a quarter of a mile north of the road, we suddenly jumped up a couple of jackrabbits. They took off in a mad, zig-zagging, flop-eared sprint straight ahead of us, maybe a quarter of a football field away. Sailor, Spider, and I, side by side, cut down on the rabbits at the same time. And somebody hit one of them—I thought it was me. The shot rabbit dropped and tumbled to a dead halt in the short grass. The other one kept going and escaped.

Sailor and I walked forward to find the jackrabbit we'd hit. We didn't notice that Spider hung back, messing with his gun. Suddenly, a shot rang out behind us, and dirt kicked up from the bullet not five yards in front of me.

"Good Lord, Spider!" I said, mad. "You could have hit one of us!" Then I looked down and saw that the legs of my Levi's were tattered, inside and close to the knees. The .22 bullet had apparently gone right between my legs as I was walking. Seeing that, I was even madder at Spider. "You came close enough to rip my pants!" I said.

Spider hurried up to Sailor and me. "I'm sorry," he said. "This gun just went off, on its own."

"Look here at where the bullet came through," I said. To show him, I put my hand down to touch the tattered denim near my right knee. When I did, my fingers came back covered with bright red blood. "Shit for breakfast, Spider!" I said. "You shot me!"

"No, I didn't," he said, as if he was trying to argue me out of it.

He and Sailor dropped to their knees in the grass in front of me. I leaned down. All three of us examined the damage. The bullet had gone cleanly through the thigh of my left leg, not hitting a bone, then gouged out a four-inch ditch in the muscle just above my right knee. There was hardly any bleeding.

The oddest thing was that I hadn't felt anything at all when the bullet hit me, at first didn't even know I was shot. And I still wasn't feeling any real pain from either leg wound.

"Will, let's get you back to the car," Sailor said. "We gotta run you to a hospital."

He and Spider each got in under my arms, and we started toward the road, them trying to carry me. But that didn't work. It hurt my cracked rib too much. "Let me go," I said. "I can walk all right by myself."

It was true. They put me down. We hustled to the Green Lizard.

Just as we expected, nobody was at the Stilwell place. Everybody'd obviously gone into Kimball, for supplies and things. Sailor rapidly drove us, too, into town. There we lucked out and right away found Ruby, Bonnie, and Buford, just as they were coming out of a Chestnut Street grocery store. Sailor pulled up in front and called them over to the curb.

I thought Bonnie was going to faint when Sailor told her what'd happened, though I spoke up right away to try to reassure her. "I'm not in too bad a shape," I said. "It doesn't even hurt. No bone got hit, and I'm not hardly bleeding."

But Bonnie continued alternating between ringing her hands and patting me on the shoulder through the open back window of the Lizard. "You poor thing, Will!" she said. "Poor thing!"

Then Ruby took charge. She told Buford and Bonnie to carry the groceries on home in her black Buick. She ordered Spider to get out of the Green Lizard and go with them, then replaced him in the Lizard's passenger seat, the gangly Spider alibiing and explaining all the time, the best he could, about how my getting shot wasn't really his fault.

She pulled her door to and turned to Sailor. "Let's go to Sidney!" she said. "That's the closest hospital. Kimball hasn't got one."

We sped off east, leaving Bonnie, Buford, and Spider on the sidewalk, gazing worriedly after us.

A concrete ribbon of highway carried us along the floor of a long shallow valley that continued all the way to Sidney. We sailed past the little one-elevator town of Dix. Tall cottonwoods lined our road. Irrigated alfalfa. Bluffs to the north and south, with short pines growing on some of them. We didn't even slow down for the small three-elevator town of Potter. Five miles from Sidney, we passed by a U.S. Army installation on the north side of both the highway and the Union Pacific track. It was an army depot, a big sign said, for war ammunition and equipment.

Then "Welcome to Sidney—One of America's favorite stopping places since 1867."

The three-story brick hospital was on our right, just as we got into town. Sailor almost skidded the Lizard's back tires as he rapidly cut into the circular driveway in front and braked to a stop at the emergency entrance. He let Ruby and me out, then drove off to park. With her beside me, I walked in under my own power. My legs had begun to ache a little, but still not as much as my fractured rib.

A young nurse in a white uniform put me in a wheelchair and rolled me along a hallway, then in behind a curtained-off area, leaving Ruby outside it. The nurse quickly helped me get undressed—totally—and then into one of those awkward, open-in-the-back hospital gowns. A short baby-faced doctor in glasses came and examined my wounds. He told me that he was going to have to clean both of them, stitch up the scooped-out place above my right knee, and put a drainage tube through the left leg along the route the bullet had traveled.

"Not terribly serious damage," he said. "You're lucky—soon going to be as good as before."

The next thing I knew, I was in the operating room, and a woman was putting an ether mask over my face. That was the *last* thing I knew, too, until I later woke up, groggy and a little nauseous, in one of the hospital's wards, with Sailor and Ruby standing on each side of my bed.

I stayed there overnight. The hospital people then loaned me a set of crutches, told me to come back in three days to check the drainage and change the dressings, and let me go.

We started cutting wheat the morning I got back to Kimball—not me, but our crew. Bonnie filled in for me on the Fordson tractor. I hung around the Stilwell place, helping Ruby a little.

On the second evening after that, I went to the water pump with our whole crew, except for Bonnie, who was helping Ruby in the house, as everybody washed up before supper. A dull brown U.S. Army sedan drove into the yard. Everybody stopped and looked as two husky, white-helmeted Military Police sergeants, wearing well-pressed khaki uniforms and with side arms on, got out of the car. The two of them started over toward us, and as they did, I noticed that Spider moved back behind our little group, like he was trying to get out of sight.

"Good evening, gentlemen," the slightly older of the two MPs said, when they'd come up to us.

"How are you?" my dad said. "Anything we can do for you?"

"Sir, yes, there is," the man said. "Is one of you Corporal Troy Deering? That's who we're looking for."

Everybody was silent for a moment, then Spider, obviously realizing that he had no alternative, stepped forward. "You found me," he said. He tried to sound jaunty, but he looked scared.

"You're under arrest for desertion," the older MP said to Spider. He took a pair of handcuffs off his belt. "Turn around," he ordered.

We were all stunned. Spider pivoted and put his long arms behind his back. The MP clicked the handcuffs on him.

The younger MP addressed the rest of us. "He have a bag or something?"

"I'll get it," Little Jim said and headed toward the open barn door.

Then my dad spoke up. "Spider," he said, "what've you done, son?"

"Well, I back talked a shitty little lieutenant that I couldn't stand, over yonder in Kentucky," Spider said. "Him and me went to fist city, and he put me up on charges. That's when I run."

"You didn't realize that the army'd find you?" Dad asked.

"All I knowed, Bob, was that I weren't about to let nobody lock me up in no stockade if I could help it." Spider said.

He began to cry.

That just about made *me* cry. "Where are y'all taking him?" I asked the MPs.

The older one answered. "The army's been looking all over for Corporal Deering. They checked with the wife of one of you, a Mrs. Haley, in Vernon, Oklahoma, where he was supposed to be working, then traced him from there up this way to the Kimball area. Me and Sergeant Jenkins, here, are stationed over toward Sidney at the U.S. Army Depot. We got orders to come and find Deering and arrest him. We'll take him back to the depot, then transport him from there by train to Fort Campbell, Kentucky—for court martial."

The MPs walked Spider to the army car. We followed. Little Jim came with Spider's beat-up tan pasteboard suitcase. The younger MP took it and pitched it into the back seat of the car, then he and the other one helped Spider get in beside it.

Before the MPs closed the door, I stepped over and touched Spider on the shoulder. "We'll wire your mother some money," I said, "so she can get you a lawyer for the trial."

He wasn't crying any more but was still noticeably upset. "Much obliged, old buddy," he said to me. Then he brightened a little and, nodding back toward the handcuffs, said, "I'd shake hands with you good-bye, Willie, if I could."

"That's all right," I said and moved a step away from the car.

Spider looked over our whole bunch for a moment. "Thanks for the work, Bob," he said. "And thanks to *all* y'all for everything. Sorry I had to leave out like this."

"Let's go," the younger MP said and closed the rear door on Spider.

The two sergeants got into the front seat then. The motor started, and they drove off. All we could see was the back of poor Spider's head through the rear glass as the brown army sedan reached the road, turned left, then quickly disappeared over a hill.

I'd never liked Spider a whole lot, but I hated to see anybody in as much trouble as he was. Besides, Spider was kinfolks, and he'd been a part of our combine crew. I felt bad for him.

With Spider gone, Dad started driving the red Farmall tractor in the absent cousin's place. I drove Dad's grain truck because he thought that'd be easier on my legs. It was—and easier on my rib, too. Bonnie, of course, continued to drive the Fordson. We were lucky to have her.

On my first trip to town with a load of wheat, I emptied up at the Kimball County Grain Co-op elevator, then detoured by the post office before going back to the field so I could ask for general delivery mail. There was a letter for Spider. The familiar handwriting and peach-colored envelope told me that the letter was from my sister Janie Marie. I folded it over and stuck it in my hip pocket, thinking maybe I'd send it back to her later—and tell her about Spider being arrested by the MPs. There was also a postcard for me. It was from Marcy Redelk.

July 27, 1943

Dear Will,

I loved the records of *La Traviata*! And I remember seeing a picture show one time with the same story. Robert Taylor was in it, but he wasn't very good—too much of a pretty boy. I think you're right about Ronnie Dole. By the way, he's taken up with Rebecca Milton. I saw your friend Junior Randall, who's back here and telling about Cheyenne—and your tattoo! He says Ronnie Dole is going to run for student body president, but you can beat him, even though Ronnie's a senior and you're a junior. I'm for you.

Your friend,
Marcy

Robert Taylor was not very good, a pretty boy? *All right!* It made me feel good to hear that. And Marcy's postcard also set me to thinking more about the student body presidency back home in Vernon. I was disappointed in Rebecca Milton.

Our wheat cutting north of Kimball went well. Dad drove the Farmall tractor without complaining. But one morning when I woke up early in the barn, I found that my dad's bedroll hadn't been slept in the night before, and I didn't see him at all that morning until the rest of us went into the house for breakfast. Dad was already there, sitting at the dining room table, shaved and ready to go to the field as soon as we'd eaten. Ruby smiled at him a lot while serving the food—and he at her. It seemed pretty clear that Dad'd made new sleeping arrangements, but he was still holding down his drinking pretty well. *Can't have everything.*

And something was going on with Sailor and Bonnie, too. It got to be a habit for Sailor to get up during the night, after he thought all the rest of us in the barn were asleep, and slip outside to meet Bonnie. I followed him quietly the first night and saw what was up. The two of them got together in the dark at the corner of the barn and walked around behind it. They were holding hands.

But that didn't keep Sailor from working out with me every morning after we'd greased up and before we started cutting. I did upper body calisthenics with him, and he jogged around the field if there was time. His knee had healed enough so that he no longer had to wrap it. I kept up the arm and chest part of the Charles Atlas dynamic tension exercises that Sailor'd taught me. I felt like I was putting on some weight—bigger muscles, I hoped. My Levi's and shirts were getting tighter.

One day, after taking a truckload of grain into Kimball, I raced in dad's Chevrolet truck over to the hospital at Sidney and got the tube removed from my left leg and the stitches taken out of the gash above my right knee. The doctor said that I was healing all right. I returned the crutches that the hospital had loaned me, then stopped at a drugstore on the way out of town and bought myself a cane, which I thought I'd better use for awhile.

Janie Marie, my tiny older sister, for God's sake!

She saw me and stepped out from around a corner of the Kimball County Grain Co-op elevator building and stood wearily beside the scales, brown leather suitcase in hand. It was my first grain-hauling trip of the day, a little over a week after we'd started cutting wheat near Kimball.

Janie Marie'd been waiting at the elevator since early morning, she later told me, hoping to spot one of our harvest crew and connect up with us. I asked her what she would have done if Dad had been the one who'd shown up at the elevator instead of me. She said that she would've stayed out of sight and waited until some other member of our crew finally came.

I jumped out of the truck and hugged her, then got her into the cab with me. We stayed in the truck after I drove into the elevator. We talked while they lifted up the front end to let the wheat slide out the back. Then we talked some more afterwards out in the elevator parking lot.

Janie Marie was pregnant!

She blurted that out, right off. Nobody knew—especially not Mama—and, of course, Janie Marie didn't want Dad to know. She hadn't heard a word from Spider, and the only thing she'd been able to think of was to come up to Kimball to talk with him personally about getting married. She started crying while she told me all this. I hugged her up and tried to console her.

She cried some more when I told her what'd happened to Spider—that he was likely by then to be in a military stockade in Kentucky, awaiting a court martial for desertion, and that she had to reconcile herself to the fact that he was now totally out of the picture.

"I love the idea, Will, of having a baby, of being a mother, but I was so stupid about Spider!" Janie Marie said. "I should have known better. I doubted that he would marry me anyway—and now he can't."

I held her tightly, then pulled back to look her in the face. "How pregnant are you?"

"Enough," she said, "but just barely." She paused. Her face wrinkled up, like she might cry again. Then she got control of herself and went on. "What am I going to do, Will? Mama would rather see me dead in a casket than pregnant. You know that. And, oh my God, the way people in Vernon talk! I'd never be able to live there."

She was right, I knew. And there was only one thing for me to say. "You don't want to have the baby, Janie Marie. You can't. You'd be ruined."

She nodded her head in agreement. "But I can't bring myself to focus on the alternative, Will. Is that what you're thinking about—the alternative? What?"

"Yeah," I said. Neither one of us could bring ourselves to say the word.

"But I have no idea how you go about a thing like that, Will," Janie Marie said.

"Neither do I," I said. "But there's someone who I bet does know, though."

I told Janie Marie about Ruby. She didn't say anything. We sat there in silence for a full minute. I knew then that we'd reached some kind of unspoken agreement on what to do next.

I started the truck and headed for the Stilwell place as fast as I could. I'd be late getting back to the field, but I'd let my dad think that I'd had to go to the house for something.

That night, my dad was put out with Ruby. "What I still cain't understand," he said, "is why in the hell she'd just take off like that without saying something, without making arrangements for what we'd do without her." Our crew was all gathered in the house for supper. Dad and I were in the kitchen helping Bonnie get the food ready.

"Like I told you," I said, "I came by here this morning because I forgot my cane. And Ruby told me to apologize to you, but that she had to make a rush trip back to Scottsbluff for something. Probably have to stay the night, too. She gave me the noon dinner she'd fixed for us, and I took it to the field, in her place."

"Never said why she had to take out in such a hurry, Will?" my dad asked.

I didn't answer that question. Instead, I said, "More than likely, we'll have to make our own breakfast in the morning and fix tomorrow's dinner for the field, too."

"No big deal," Bonnie said. "I used to do that all the time by myself before we lucked onto Ruby."

Dad was still puzzled by Ruby's unexplained absence, though, and he didn't like it. He grew even more puzzled and more upset when Ruby came back a day later and kicked him out of the Stilwell house so that he again had to sleep out in the barn with the rest of us. But I was thankful that he never figured out what was behind everything.

Ruby brought Janie Marie back to the Stilwell house a little after noon on that next day after she'd left. The place had two bedrooms. Ruby put Janie Marie in the back one and kept the room's door closed all the time. I zipped by to see my sister that first afternoon after one of my trips to the elevator with a truckload of wheat.

Lying in bed, covered with a sheet, she looked wan, and sad. "Was it just awful?" I asked her about the abortion.

She raised up on an elbow. "It wasn't too bad—the actual procedure," she said. Ruby'd told me that the doctor she planned to take Janie Marie to was totally competent and a man she trusted. I'd given Ruby the man's fifty dollar fee in cash.

I sat down now on the side of the bed and took Janie Marie's hand. "You made the right decision," I said.

"I know I did, Will," she said. "But it's such a shame that I *had* to make it."

I knew how she felt. I wasn't proud of my part in the whole business, but it couldn't be helped. I leaned down and kissed Janie Marie on the forehead. "You're a wonderful person, big sister," I said. "I love you."

"I love you, too, Will. Grateful for all you've done for me."

Janie Marie kept out of sight when any of our crew was around. Nobody besides me and Ruby ever knew that she was in the house during the three days and nights she stayed there. I thought one time that Bonnie might have suspected that something unusual was going on, but she never let on or asked any questions of Ruby.

I swung by the Stilwell house in dad's truck on the morning of the day that Ruby planned to take my sister to the Kimball bus station so she could go back home to Vernon. Janie Marie was, by then, in pretty good shape physically, and she was getting better emotionally, too, though I figured that it would take some time for her to become her old self again, if she ever did. She and I hugged, and I tried to reassure her the best I could.

Poor old dad, though! On the very evening that Ruby would have probably invited him back into the house for the night, Mr. Stilwell himself showed up. And the man, a little bitty dried-up guy who always wore a suit and tie, stayed on for our two remaining nights there. Long enough to see our crew off, when we all pulled out for Rapid City early Saturday morning, the seventh of August.

I wrote a quick postcard to Marcy Redelk and mailed it as we passed through Kimball, toward Sidney.

August 7, 1943

Dear Marcy,

Finished here in Nebraska. Rushing to leave for Rhame, N. Dak. But we're going to stop a while in Rapid City, S. Dak., in Sioux Indian country, to see Mt. Rushmore and the Black Hills. Glad Junior made it home. Tell him hello. Too much has been happening here to put in a postcard, but maybe I'll tell you some of it when I see you. I'd appreciate it if you would go and meet my sister, Janie Marie, and try to be a friend to her. Write me—General Delivery, Rhame, N. Dak.

Your friend,
Will

Chapter Twelve

Sailor got behind the wheel of his old Plymouth, the Green Lizard. I rode shotgun. We took our customary place in line as the harvest parade hit the road again—right behind my dad's truck and combine, right in front of Little Jim's gray GMC pick-up. Buford and Bonnie rode at the tail end, in the drag, as usual, pulling our chuck wagon, the house trailer. Big Jim Gruber rode in the van, at the point. It didn't take us long on the familiar highway east of Kimball to get to Sidney. There we soon passed by the hospital where my legs had been repaired after I was shot.

Led by Big Jim, our caravan turned north in Sidney onto U.S. 385. But, from our position behind Dad, Sailor almost immediately pulled off the highway and stopped at a Nebraska historical marker without my asking, letting Little Jim and Buford go on past us. The marker said that after General George Armstrong Custer reported finding gold in the Black Hills of South Dakota, sacred to the Sioux and protected by treaty, miners began slipping into those mountains illegally. Then, in 1874, the army suddenly quit enforcing the treaty with the Sioux and allowed a massive gold rush to begin. Sidney, 265 miles south of Deadwood, was the closest railhead. Overnight, it became the jumping off place for great quantities of freight and people heading north across the North Platte River at Bridgeport to the Black Hills, and it was the return point for the big shipments of gold that came back south.

Sailor fired up the Lizard again, and we took off. The railroad paralleled us on the left.

"Bridgeport—40 miles."

We drove through much the same kind of rolling high plains country that we'd just been combining in, north of Kimball. Big fields of cut-out wheat stubble, some plowed under. Houses widely scattered. Shelter belt strips of planted elms and evergreens. We sped past the one-elevator town of Gurley. Then there was more mostly flat and fairly good farmland. We wheeled past Dalton, hardly big enough to have its own water tower.

Sailor passed Buford and Little Jim and deftly inserted the Green Lizard back into our place in line, just as the harvest caravan rolled into Morrill County. Soon we began to drop down toward the valley of the North Platte River. Rolling shortgrass prairie surrounded us. No natural trees. Down we dropped, then down farther, and into the miles-wide and well farmed valley floor. Off to our left about six or seven miles, we began to see two peaks, one of them sort of like a human-made, stepped pyramid.

U.S. 385 dead-ended near the south bank of the North Platte, and we turned northwest there, upriver through occasional houses, shelter belts, and irrigated farms. The day was mostly sunny, with a line of high clouds suspended over the riverbed.

When the two whitish peaks we'd been seeing were immediately on our left, U.S. 385 cut back to the north and into green and wooded Bridgeport—"Trail City USA." Sailor and I kept with our usual practice and stopped at a Nebraska historical marker on the edge of town. The names of the two peaks were Courthouse Rock and Jail Rock. They'd been important landmarks on the Oregon Trail, which passed through there in 1850, the Pony Express route, 1860 to 1861, the Deadwood Trail, 1874 to 1886, and the Mormon Trail, 1847 to 1864. The telegraph line reached Bridgeport in 1861, as did the Burlington Railroad, in 1899.

Driving north through town, we crossed over the North Platte River. There were cottonwoods and lots of sand, with a winding stream of fairly clear water. "Alliance—40 miles."

On the narrow blacktopped U.S. 385, we followed the river northwest for a short way, then veered to the right and began the long climb out of the valley, through grassy bluffs, then rolling prairie. No native trees. Finally, up on top, we saw great, cut-out wheat fields in all directions.

We whizzed by the one-store town of Angora. On the other side of it, we began to roll through miles and miles of grassy sandhill mounds, interspersed here and there with some irregularly shaped, already harvested wheat fields.

"Get a big bulldozer in here for a few days, and you could flatten this country out to pretty tolerable farmland," Sailor said.

Evergreen shelter belts. Wheat land a little more level. We entered Box Butte Canyon. Dark-soiled plowed farmland. Flat valley, east and west. Then back up on the high plains and more wheat land.

Before long, we came to the large and sturdy, brick-street town of Alliance, Nebraska, with its impressive five or six blocks of two- and three-story brick business buildings. We passed by the Alliance Theater, the BPOE lodge, and the Drake Hotel, and then, on the far side of the downtown section, Sailor and I finally saw the harvest vehicles we'd been trying for miles to catch up with again. Buford's orange Dodge truck and house trailer were parked in front of the combination Conoco filling station and Box Butte Auto Repair. The rest of our vehicles were stopped alongside the highway, just beyond Buford's. Sailor cruised past the whole caravan, then pulled off the highway and stopped in front of Big Jim's blue Ford truck.

He and I got out of the Green Lizard and walked back to the auto repair place. We found our people, bunched up, talking, just inside the front door. Buford's truck was out of commission, they told us. The motor'd nearly burned out from running with low, or no, oil. It was going to take a couple of days to get the motor fixed.

Dad spoke to the burly, and worried, Buford Wynn. "I reckon the rest of us'll just go on to Rapid City, Buford, because I want time for us to see Mount Rushmore and the presidents' heads—and the Black Hills," my dad said. I knew that we didn't plan on cutting any wheat in South Dakota, because there wasn't much wheat on the west side of that state. We'd leapfrog it and jump to North Dakota, where the grain probably wouldn't be totally ripe yet. There were at least a couple of days to kill now. "Our bunch'll stay all night tonight in Chadron State Park, like Jim Gruber, here, says." Dad went on. "Then two or three nights in Rapid City, where we'll wait for you, and pull out for North Dakota the minute you and Bonnie get to Rapid. How about that?"

Buford said in his high voice that he guessed that'd be all right.

But his young and pretty blonde wife had a different idea. "Honey," she said, "I'd love to see Mount Rushmore and the Black Hills myself. I've seen the presidents' heads in newsreels, and I want to see them in person."

Buford sounded a little whiny when he responded. "There may not be time to do that, baby," he said to Bonnie, "if it takes long to get this motor fixed."

But Bonnie already had a plan. "Here's what I'm thinking," she said to Buford. "What if I go on with the rest—and wait for you with them in Rapid City?"

From the way Buford pursed his lips, it was obvious that he didn't like that idea. "But where would you sleep?" he asked.

"We could take the house trailer with *us*," Bonnie said. She turned to Little Jim. "Trailer hitch on your Jimmy pick-up, isn't there?" she asked him.

"Sure is," Little Jim said.

Buford hated to give up. "But I would be here all by myself," he said to Bonnie, his voice even more high-pitched than usual.

"It won't be for long, honey," Bonnie said reassuringly.

Buford seemed to slump then, resigned. He didn't say anything more. I felt sorry for him again, as I had before, and I figured everybody else did, too.

But Bonnie's decision stood.

Sailor and I unhooked the house trailer and backed it away by hand from Buford's Dodge truck, then hitched it onto Little Jim's pick-up as soon as he got into place. Bonnie stepped inside the trailer for a moment and brought out a bunch of sandwiches she'd made earlier, then handed them around to all of us to take with us for the road. She kissed Buford on the cheek. We all scattered to the vehicles, leaving Buford standing by the side of his truck with his sandwich in his hand, looking pretty glum.

Just as I knew she would, Bonnie walked with me and Sailor all the way up to the Green Lizard. I gave her the passenger side of the car and, myself, climbed into the backseat.

Our line of vehicles, each one in its usual place, except for Buford's orange Dodge, pulled out north. "Chadron—58 miles." The state park where we'd spend the night showed on the map to be a few miles south of the town of that same name.

Good wheat fields in mile-long strips, mostly already harvested, alternated with dark plowed ground. All along the highway there were lots of blue flax, in flower. Wild or planted on purpose? I had no idea. But either way, the effect was what you'd call lovely.

We ate our sandwiches in the car. Bonnie switched on Sailor's portable radio, and as long as we were close to Alliance, back behind us, the reception was pretty good. We got some music. A new song, "Don't Get Around Much Anymore," started with the words "Missed the Saturday dance . . ." It made me feel really homesick for Joe Lammer's place and my Vernon friends. But the little radio soon got too staticky, and Bonnie had to turn it off. Then she talked Sailor into playing his French harp while he drove. She asked for "Pretty Redwing" first and sweetly sang the words with him as he blew the melody—the same as she'd done before when we were at Dimmitt.

After a couple more songs, Sailor quit and put the French harp back into his shirt pocket. Bonnie scooted over close to him and lay her head on his shoulder, then closed her eyes and dozed off. We crossed over the fairly scanty Niobrara River.

Sailor and Bonnie's relationship worried me. I knew it wasn't right, what was going on. Bonnie was a married woman, and I was disappointed in Sailor for taking up with her, as he'd obviously done. But I still liked him—a lot. I still liked Bonnie, too. But what about her? Was she turning out to be the kind of wicked woman that Mama had all along said she was? I couldn't make myself think so. And the more I considered the whole situation, the less I could really blame either Sailor or

237

Bonnie. They were good people. They'd just happened to be thrown together when both of them were lonesome, for different reasons. Couldn't really help themselves. Still, I worried.

We drove on through a mostly featureless Great Plains landscape. Like Bonnie, I dozed off for a while. When I looked up again, we were still in the midst of a rolling high prairie. Then we descended some and crossed a cottonwood-laced draw. We came back up in a long climb to the top of some grassy bluffs with white, gravelly soil showing through the vegetation. Up there, we were again in stretching native grasslands as far as I could see, with some rougher country off to the west and a few shelter belts of elms and evergreens scattered closer, here and there.

Finally, and all of a sudden, large and spreading, green-knobbed islands of tall and thick pine forests rose abruptly up in front of us. Chadron State Park—a welcome relief from the bare sameness of the plains, an isolated foretaste, I figured, of the Black Hills, which lay farther on north.

Our caravan pulled in and parked on the west bank of winding Chadron Creek, then made camp in the trees, next to an outdoor grill and a concrete picnic table with the name of President Roosevelt's Civilian Conservation Corps—the CCCs—stamped into it. Bonnie brought some round steaks from the little icebox in the house trailer. Dad said he'd grill them. Little Jim and Big Jim gathered kindling. Bonnie asked me and Sailor to climb a high wooded hill to the west with her, to watch the sun go down.

I used my cane as the three of us made our way up a gravelly wash, but my legs felt good, seemed to be healing. My rib wasn't giving me much trouble either. We soon reached some thick clumps of pine trees at the crest. We stopped among them to gaze at the big setting sun, red-orange behind a wide and wispy cloud-veil that glowed pale crimson. It was a stunning scene that, as the cowboy song put it, "no artist e'er could paint."

Sailor tried for a little humor—and maybe a prediction. "Red clouds in the evenin', Sailor be leavin'," he said.

But this light comment didn't change the magic of the moment. The three of us were quiet.

Finally, Bonnie spoke up, her voice hushed. "This is the most beautiful place I've ever been!" she said.

That statement might have sounded exaggerated to some people, I thought, but maybe Bonnie hadn't been to too many beautiful places up to then. Flat western Kansas, where she came from, was like my home country in western Oklahoma—fairly uninspiring. Not the kind of landscape that gave you cold chills, though it did have its own type of spare beauty. For prairie people like Bonnie and me, there was something awesome and exhilarating about being among pine trees. The fresh green scent. The sound-deadening rug of pine needles underfoot. The mysterious message of the wind up above. And that was exactly the kind of place where we were standing, right there, witnessing, it seemed to me, maybe the most dazzling red sunset in western history.

Bonnie, between Sailor and me, reached out to the left and took Sailor's hand. The three of us stood in silence again. Then she turned to look at Sailor. "I wish you and I could build our own little log cabin, right here, and stay forever," she said, wistful.

"What about me?" I asked. It was kind of a joke, and an intrusion on the moment, too.

"You could live with us, also, Will," Bonnie said. With her right hand, she took mine. The three of us were joined together. The sun was nearly down.

We stood there some more, part of a sort of fairy tale—and I loved it. But I soon spoke up with another practical, and light, question. "How would we make a living?"

"We'd manage somehow, Will," Bonnie said. "I don't know—maybe weave baskets out of pine needles and sell them to tourists. Or tan deer hides and sew jackets and vests. We'd make it, though. No doubt about that."

But I'd broken the spell with my prosaic question. We all could feel that. Then Sailor brought us back even closer to reality. "Long way from here to the sea," he said.

He slowly let go Bonnie's hand.

And just then, from down below, came my dad's penetrating whistle for us—the undulating two-syllable call that horsemen used to get their animals to come in from the pasture.

"'Bout to get dark," Sailor said. There was a sadness in his voice.

I felt sad, too. Bonnie dropped my hand. The three of us turned and walked single file, back down to camp—and supper.

Next morning, early, I woke up in my quilt on the ground to the inviting smell of the camp coffee that Dad'd made and the low sound of his and Sailor's conversation as they squatted near a crackling fire in the grill. Little Jim and Big Jim were washing up at the nearby park pump. Bonnie was still in the house trailer. Sailor's quilt, not far from mine, clearly hadn't been slept in.

I'd worn my clothes to bed for warmth. I got up and went over to the grill, picked up the blue porcelain pot, and poured myself a tin cup of hot coffee.

"Sleep good, Will?" Sailor asked.

"Fine," I said. "You?"

He knew what I meant by that question but didn't answer. Just grinned a little, then looked away.

"Java's pretty stout this morning, Will," Dad said. "Put hair on your chest."

"I could use some," I said standing next to the fire, sipping the coffee.

"Liable to turn your tattoo, there, brown," Dad said and pointed toward the top of my left arm, where my T-shirt sleeve had bunched up a little.

"Hadn't aimed for you to see that yet."

My dad didn't make a fuss. "Reckon you got a right, Will, to do as silly a things as the rest of us."

He went back, then, to the earlier talk between him and our Mississippi cousin. "Like I told you, Sailor, you decide to come on back to Vernon with us, we'd treat you right and you wouldn't want for work."

"Much obliged, Bob," Sailor said. "Oklahoma's got a heap of sandy beach, but you ain't got no ocean to go with it. When we wind up the wheat harvest in North Dakota, think I'll crank up the old Green Lizard and drive on west to Seattle, catch me another ship. Least I can do for the war effort. And going to sea's my life, Bob."

Dad didn't try to argue. "I've flat admired getting to know you, Sailor, and you've sure as hell made us a hand. Gonna hate to lose you."

I felt the same way about Sailor that my dad did. I liked the way he looked—his muscular build, his dark features, and his middle-parted black hair. I liked his offhand comments. He was fun to be around. He had a good slant on life. He'd made me build myself up, get in shape. He'd encouraged me in my ambitions, and he'd practically broken me of my old "can't" way of thinking about things.

But what about him and Bonnie? What would become of them?

Not a question I could answer right then.

We ate breakfast. The morning was partly sunny, with some high scattered clouds. Breezy and coolish. The Chadron, Nebraska, announcer on Sailor's portable radio said that the day's temperature would stay in the low seventies, then added, "But the last time we said that, it got up to eighty-five."

When our caravan took off for Rapid City, I decided to ride in the pick-up with Little Jim, rather than in the Green Lizard. I didn't want to put myself back into the middle of whatever was going on between Sailor and Bonnie—or be an active party to it.

We trailed north on U.S. 385–to the town of Chadron. More than a month too late for "Fur Trade Days—July 2." We dead-ended at the edge of Chadron, then turned straight west. "Hot Springs—57 miles." Soon, at a major highway intersection, we turned north again, and right there, I made Little Jim pull off the highway for a Nebraska historical marker. He didn't want to stop, but after we had, he asked me to read the historical marker aloud. I wasn't sure whether the problem was that Little Jim couldn't see the marker well without glasses, or that he couldn't read well.

Anyway, I recited the marker's words for him: The east-west Fort Pierre-Fort Laramie Trail passed through here, 1837 to 1850. This point was approximately the migration center of the vast northern buffalo herd. Two hundred fifty thousand buffalo robes were bought from the Indians of the area by the American Fur Company. White traders with the Indians worked this region until the 1880s, the ruts made by their wagons still visible nearby.

Rolling hills. Some pretty good farming. Nice prairie grass. We crossed the White River—not much of a river. Yellow mustard plants in the highway ditches. Fifteen miles of visibility. Beautifully green hills in every direction. Vast buffalo and Indian country.

We passed a series of white-on-red Burma-Shave signs:

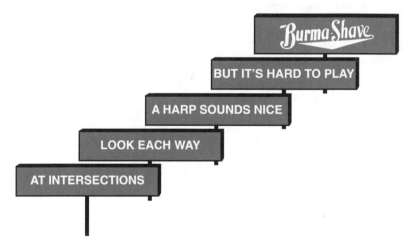

We entered another new state for me, South Dakota. Grasslands. Gently rolling landscape. Long lines of trees in the draws. A little scattered strip farming of pretty nice wheat land.

Then, some twenty miles north in the distance, we began to see wooded, very dark-to-black mountains on the horizon, under high fluffy clouds. So *that* was why they were called the Black Hills. The trees looked black from a distance.

At a little town with the strange German-looking name of Oelrichs, a sign told us that the Pine Ridge Sioux Indian Reservation was due east, but we ourselves continued north on U.S. 385. We crossed the Angostura River on a tight concrete bridge with arching metal supports overhead. Some alfalfa fields were along the highway.

Ahead and to the left, the pine and spruce trees of the Black Hills, now closer up, appeared bright green, of course, not black. We came to a Y in the highway. U.S. 385 went on northwest toward nearby Hot Springs and into the Black Hills. We turned northeast, instead, to skirt along the east edge of the mountains toward Rapid City on narrow blacktopped State 79.

"Buffalo Gap—8 miles. Rapid City—48 miles." More and more pine and spruce trees of the Black Hills on our left. Grassy-pastured hills and bluffs to the right.

I made Little Jim stop for a South Dakota historical marker on State 79, just past a cutoff on the right toward the little town of Buffalo Gap. I read aloud for Little Jim. Just west of here was a break in the mountains. Jebediah Smith, "a courageous and brawny trapper," with twelve other men and a Bible, "his constant companion," followed an old buffalo trail through this break and became the first white man to enter the Black Hills, in 1823. Smith's three goals were to "serve God, provide for his family, and explore the untapped American West," and he "was successful in all three goals." He was later killed by a "Comanche lance" on the Cimarron, his body never found.

The Sioux Indians of Jebediah Smith's time, I figured, probably didn't think of their sacred Black Hills and the American West of those days as being "untapped." And it was strange, I thought, that the old trapper's last wanderings took him way down to Comanche country, near present-day Oklahoma. But I imagined that the Sioux were probably grateful to Marcy Redelk's people for putting an end to Smith's explorations and incursions into Indian country.

Twenty-eight more miles toward Rapid City—grass and bluffs on the right, Black Hills on the left. The clouds over the mountains became a little thicker and darker, the clear sky to the right a little deeper blue than we'd seen it before.

Arriving in Rapid, a pretty big town, maybe about the size of Cheyenne, we followed State 79 as it turned west on St. Joseph Street, which passed by a seven-story, dark brick hotel and carried us on through the main downtown business district. Ahead on a high grassy hill on our right, we noticed that white rocks had been laid out to spell "SMD," which somebody later told us stood for the South Dakota School of Mines. And curiously, across the highway south on an equally high hill, we could see a life-sized statue of a green, long-tailed and long-necked brontosaurus, and there seemed to be other dinosaur statues up there, too.

Just after we passed between the two hills, Little Jim pulled off the highway to the right, behind the other vehicles, and we all circled up for the night in a vacant grassy roadside area. As soon as we got settled, Big Jim surprised us by announcing that he was going to climb up the north side of the dinosaur hill. He'd noticed the statues on top the year before, he said, but hadn't gone to see them up close. Now he wanted to.

So the whole bunch of us, my dad and Little Jim included, decided to go with him. We crossed the highway and started up a sandy and rocky path that was worn in the grass among the low bushes that grew on the slopes of the hill. The climb was fairly hard, and we learned when we got to the windy crest that we could have actually *driven* up to what was called "Dinosaur Park" on a road that came in from the south and east. But we made it to the top on foot. We walked around and looked closely at five giant concrete statues of various types of dinosaurs, their bodies painted green, their underbellies, white. A sign said that the statues had been constructed by the WPA in 1936—certainly an interesting government-financed project, I thought.

The sun dropped low in the west toward the darkening Black Hills. We picked our way back down the path to camp, washed up, then walked together a block or so east and ate supper at the Custer Café. Another place, it turned out, that didn't know how to make hamburgers right.

We passed around among us a tourist brochure that we found in the café. It said that sculptor Gutzon Borglum's heroic carvings of the giant Mount Rushmore heads of the presidents—Washington, Jefferson, Theodore Roosevelt, and Lincoln—had been finished just the year before, 1942. Dad wasn't alone among us in wanting to go and see this famous sight, as well as the buffaloes and other wildlife in the nearby Custer State Park. But was I the only one of our harvest bunch who wondered what the Sioux Indians must have thought about white people butchering up one of their sacred mountains the way they'd butchered the buffalo? And what about a park being named after General Custer, the man who'd caused the gold rush into the Black Hills and, in that and his warlike ways, had helped bring on what for the Indians was the end of the world?

Next morning, we rolled out of our bedding—Sailor and Bonnie came out of the house trailer—a little later than usual. We walked over and ate breakfast at the Custer Café again. Then we divided up—Little Jim and Big Jim in the GMC pick-up, unhooked from the house trailer, Dad, me, Bonnie, and Sailor in the Green Lizard—and all headed southeast on State Highway 16 to see Mount Rushmore. We were soon deep in the Black Hills. We came to the small mountain town of Keystone, whose main street featured a number of tourist attraction signs. One in particular caught my eye: "Reptile Gardens— See Live Alligators and Rattlesnakes!"

"Bet them gators're tired from hiking up here, all the way from home," Sailor said.

Out of Keystone, we continued south on the narrow, winding asphalt road and, before too long, entered the grounds of the Mount Rushmore National Memorial. All of a sudden we got our first clear view of the presidents' heads. The sight made me catch my breath. The monument looked just like it did in the pictures, but the scale of it was more massive and towering than I'd imagined possible, and the whole thing was much grander, more patriotically inspiring, more emotionally stunning, too.

We drove into the gravel parking area, just below the giant heads, after passing three Indian tipis that we saw pitched in the grass near the entrance. A hand-lettered cardboard poster was stuck in the ground in front of one of the tipis, but we went by so quickly that I wasn't able to read what it said. We parked, and while the rest of our bunch were still slowly getting out of the vehicles and stretching their legs, I jogged back down a way to read the poster. It said "Black Hills belong to the Lakotas." I knew from a book that "Lakota" was the name that the western Sioux called themselves.

A bareheaded old Indian man with long braids and dressed in khakis and a wool red and white plaid shirt came, bending over, out of the nearest tipi, then straightened up to confront me. He had a big nose, sloping forehead, and the most wrinkled skin I'd ever seen up to then on a human face. Why did he look familiar? It was only later that I realized his profile was almost exactly the same as the Indian's on the U.S. nickel.

The old man held up a hand to stop me. "No pictures," he said.

"Don't have a camera," I said.

"You're about the first *wasichu* who don't," he said. He pronounced the word "the" like it started with a *d*, and there was a slight whistle when he said an *s*. The old man dropped his hand and stood relaxed. "The *wasichu* man always wants to take a picture. *Wasichu* ladies want to get in the tipi with me." He laughed then—sort of a "heh heh heh."

My dad yelled at me from the cars. "Will, you coming?"

"Coming," I hollered. To the old man, I said, "Can I come back and talk to you?"

He grinned. "I'm not leaving any time soon."

I ran to catch up with my bunch. Together, we trudged up to the base of the presidents' heads, blocked finally from going farther by huge piles of gray rocks and scree, scraps from the carvings above. We all stood, looking up, moved.

"That's the most beautiful sight I've ever seen!" Bonnie said earnestly.

She should have said the *second* most beautiful sight, I thought—right after the sunset at Chadron State Park that she'd similarly remarked on two evenings before.

A slim park ranger in a greenish uniform walked over to us. "Any questions, folks?" he asked.

Nobody had a question except me. "What's that old Indian doing down there by the parking lot?"

The ranger seemed a little embarrassed. "Charley Crow Bull," he said. "They call him a Sioux 'holy man.' But, ask me, he's

246

a nuisance—him and his squaws, too. They've now been camped there about three months. Protesting Mount Rushmore, he says. Demanding the Black Hills back. Says they're like a church to the Sioux Indians. Says General Custer was a criminal, got what he deserved at Little Bighorn. The old man's a bother for tourists, but we haven't tried to run him off. Not yet. But winter's coming. It's already pretty cold at night, and we expect that the old man'll freeze out soon enough and return to his tar paper shack at Pine Ridge."

Back at the cars, I thought Sailor understood, but nobody else did, when I said that I was going to stick around there and talk to the old Indian guy some more and that they could pick me up on their way back from making the Custer State Park loop and seeing the buffaloes and other wildlife.

The Green Lizard and the pick-up left as I walked down to the tipis. The old man was sitting on one of two pine logs that were pulled up toward a small fire. Some kind of stew, it looked like, was cooking in a blackened pot hanging from a tripod over the low flames.

"Still no camera," I said to the old man as I came near, holding my hands out to show that they were empty.

"Have a seat," he said and motioned me to the other log.

I did. "What's wrong with cameras?" I asked.

"You heard of Crazy Horse?"

I said I had.

"My grandmother's brother," the old man said. "Nobody today knows what he looked like. Never allowed pictures. Steals some of your spirit, he said. Me and him got the same what you call 'medicine.'"

We both sat without talking for a while.

I was the one who started the conversation back up. "Park ranger says your name is Charley Crow Bull."

"That's my *wasichu* name."

I went on. "Says you're a Sioux—Lakota—holy man."

"We don't say 'holy man,'" he said. "We say *wichasha wakan*. It's like what you call 'medicine man.' That's me. I run *inipi*, sweat, lodges. I'm a *yuwipi* man, too. I can see things—visions, you say. I got some powers. Healing. But I can't do anything with some of these *wasichu* diseases. My poor sick wife's back home at Pine Ridge. Got TB. I can't help her. I feel bad. She needs to go to a *wasichu* doctor, but she don't want to." The old man shook his head, then changed the subject. "What's your own name?" he asked me.

"Will Haley."

He startled me with his next comment. "You smell like Indian to me."

"What do you mean, 'smell like Indian'?" I asked. "I don't have any Indian blood."

"I don't mean you *smell* like Indian. I mean there's something Indian about you, or a spirit in you that likes Indians."

"I come from Comanche country down in Oklahoma," I said. Then, I added a kind of lame statement. "Some of my best friends are Indians."

"That's what I figured, looking at you when you was coming this way, little while ago," old Crow Bull said. "I got the feeling that you are going to be a *wasichu* leader one of these days. You can help us get back our *Paha Sapa*—Black Hills—that they took away from us, crazy for gold."

"I'm still in high school," I said.

The old man ignored that. "*Paha Sapa* to us is like a church is to you *wasichu*," he continued. "Maybe us Indians ought to chisel your church buildings all up until they look like Sitting Bull or Gall or Spotted Tail. And then we could put alligators on show in front of them, too." Crow Bull punctuated this last statement with his "heh heh heh" laugh. In a little while, he went on. "But us Lakotas, we don't carve faces like you *wasichu*. We know that *Wakan Tanka*, what you call the Great Spirit, is everywhere and in everything—the rocks, the trees, the animals, the two-leggeds, the four-leggeds, even the little ant people we call *tajuska oyate*. And everything in this world is in a circle, all connected together. All dependent on each other. Hurt one, you hurt the rest.

"The *wasichu* killed us Indians. They poison us with all their diseases that we never had. They kill off *tatanka*, our buffalo brothers. Then they take natural things and remake them the way they want to. They can't help it. They take our sacred mountain and then carve their leaders' big faces in it. They say: 'Look at us white people. We can make Nature better. We're bigger than Nature. We are more powerful than *Wakan Tanka*.'"

We sat. Then old Crow Bull suddenly turned and yelled toward the tipis. "Hey, somebody! Stew needs some more water. It's getting dry."

Three Sioux females emerged at once, one from each tipi. The nearest two were good-looking young women, probably not yet twenty and wearing Levi's and sweaters. The farthest was a really old woman in a traditionally cut, calf-length, flowered cotton dress. Her face was even more wrinkled than Crow Bull's.

Pointing with his lips toward the two younger women, the old man said to me, "This is Anna and Margie, my nieces."

I said "hi" to them. They smiled but didn't offer to sit down.

The old woman brought over a bucket of water and added a couple of dipperfuls to the bubbling pot. She didn't look directly at me or Crow Bull.

"This is my mother-in-law, Charlotte Feather," the old man told me. "We're not supposed to talk to each other. She's helping out, since my wife's sick."

The old woman went back to her tipi.

"These girls are helping me out, too," old Crow Bull said. He pronounced the word, "girls" like it was "guzz."

The two young women giggled behind hands lifted to their mouths, then turned back, too, and reentered their separate tipis.

"I got that *hehaka* power, that elk power, from the time I was young," the old man said. "Counting coup on the women."

Was that intended as an explanation for something? Were the young Sioux women he'd introduced me to really his nieces?

We talked some more then, but on other subjects. Old Crow Bull asked me about myself and my life, and he told me more about his own and about the Lakotas. He told me that he supervised Sun Dances that the Lakota still held, privately, and about other piercings he sometimes did for people who wanted them for religious reasons.

Finally, my harvest crew returned. Sailor drove the Green Lizard up close, the pick-up stopping behind him. "Let's go, Will," Sailor called through the open window. "We all headed for Deadwood, see where old Wild Bill Hickok got killed. You'd like that, wouldn't you?"

Old Crow Bull spoke up before I could answer. "Will wants to stay and eat stew with us Indians," he said.

The old man was right. "I *would* like to see Deadwood," I said to Sailor, "but I think I'll stay here a little bit longer. You think y'all could come by and get me on the way back from Deadwood? Would that be too much trouble?"

In the car, Sailor consulted Bonnie and Dad, then turned back to me. "Might be late, Will," he said. "Might have to carry these guys back to camp in Rapid City, first."

"That'd be all right," I said. "I'd sure appreciate it."

"See you then, Will," Sailor said.

The two vehicles took off.

We ate the stew that the old woman, Charlotte Feather, served up for us in mismatched bowls. It was good. The two young women, Anna and Margie, sat on the log next to Crow Bull. Charlotte Feather went back to her tipi.

Crow Bull pointed toward my bowl with his lips and said, "*Shunka*—dog. You know us Lakotas eat dog."

I almost gagged. The two young women giggled. The old man laughed his "heh heh heh."

"Just kidding," old Crow Bull said. "Us Lakotas eat dog, all right, but we save it for special times, ceremonies. This is cow-beef stew."

Thank God!

Afterwards, with the two young women looking on, but not saying anything, the old man and I talked some more. Or *he* talked. I listened, mostly.

In the late afternoon, the air grew cooler. Crow Bull and I both got a little of the sniffles. He sneezed once, then put a finger to a nostril and blew his nose on the ground. Some-time later, I felt the need to blow my nose, too, and took out

250

a blue bandanna and did so, then folded the cotton cloth and put it back in my pocket.

Old Crow Bull noted what I'd done. "You *wasichu* try to keep everything!" he said.

I must have looked like I'd been scolded. "That's a joke," the old man said. Heh heh heh.

After a while, Crow Bull started on another subject. "The other morning, something came to me, a vision, like," he said. "I don't know how it's going to happen or when it's going to happen, but I see that the white man's lights and electricity's, sometime, all going to go off. Maybe it's a long time from now. I don't know. I didn't get that part. But the juice is going to quit, some way. The white man's going to have a lot of trouble because of this."

He stopped talking for a moment, then continued. "And, Will Haley, I can see you as a leader. Maybe not right now. But one of these days. Maybe you'll be the one to help when the lights go off. Or maybe you might even prevent this thing from happening. I wish you could come to a Sun Dance or I could put on a sweat for you, give you some special power, to get ready."

"I wouldn't mind that myself," I said.

Crow Bull spoke up again. "Maybe there's something else we can do," he said. "How would you feel about getting pierced?"

"Pierced where?" I asked.

"Right here where you are," Crow Bull said. Heh heh heh.

"No, I mean where on my *body*?"

"Ear."

I didn't say anything, and the old man took my silence for consent. He turned to one of the two young women. "Anna, go get me my medicine box."

She got up and went into the nearest tipi and was soon back with a rectangular little homemade pine box. Lightning-like symbols and what looked like steps were painted on it in red and black. Old Crow Bull opened the box, fished around, and came up with a very small homemade earring stud with the tiniest circular flake of glassy black obsidian glued onto a short and thin silver spike with a cap on its point.

251

"This *inyan*, this little black rock, has special, sacred power," the old man said to me. "I picked it up myself from the home of some ant people." Then he looked into the pine box again and took out a sharp-pointed awl. "You right-handed or left-handed?" he asked me.

"Right-handed."

"Your power's on the right," he said. "We'll use that ear. Take off your hat."

I took it off. The old man got up and held the point of the awl in the fire for a minute, wiped it off on his shirt, then waited for the point to cool. He stood over me and put a hand on the top of my head and began to sing a chant. I didn't understand the words, of course, but I felt a tingle, like electricity, that started at the top of my head, then went all the way to my feet, until I was warm all over. I felt some kind of power pass from the old man to me, though I certainly couldn't have explained this to anybody.

His song ended, and Crow Bull quickly put a small piece of wood behind the lobe of my right ear and punched a hole all the way through to the wood with the awl. Then he inserted the stud's silver spike in the new hole and capped it, leaving the little round piece of shiny black obsidian showing in front.

"I'm going to smoke you now," old Crow Bull said. He had me stand up.

From his pine box, he took out a small tied bunch of cedar branches and an eagle feather fan. He put the cedar to the flames of the cooking fire until it was glowing, smoking. He "smoked" me, then, up and down my whole body, using the eagle fan to brush the smoke all around me and from my head down to my boots.

"Breathe in," he said, "and wash yourself in this medicine smoke."

I inhaled the wonderful smell from the smoldering cedar, and I moved my hands back and forth to bring the smoke to me and around my body, almost like I was lathering up in the shower.

Then Crow Bull said a few words of obvious prayer in Lakota, ending with the phrase "*Mitakuye Oyasin*," which he afterwards explained meant something like "All my relatives." "It's the way we wind up our prayers and ceremonies," he said. "We pray for everybody and everything."

Dark settled around us as we sat by the fire that the old man kept built up and burning. Then Sailor finally returned to get me.

I shook hands with Crow Bull and wished him good luck. "I'm glad you came to see me, Will Haley," he said. "You'll do good."

I climbed into the Green Lizard with Sailor, and we headed toward Rapid City and our camp.

"Will, you look like you just saw Jesus," Sailor said.

We rode on a while before I responded. Finally I said, "I wouldn't go that far."

At the Custer Café the next morning, I told our harvest bunch a little about old Crow Bull and how I'd gotten my small obsidian ear-stud, which they all wanted to take a closer look at.

The whole group, including Dad, seemed impressed, but he said, "Wear that thing, Will, you liable to get called a sissy."

"Not if I tell how I got it, and why," I said.

"Maybe," Dad said.

We all ate heavy breakfasts. Afterwards, dad pushed back from the table and, patting his stomach, which was pooching out a little, said, "My clothes are getting too tight."

Too much ice cream, too many Coca-Colas, I knew. But that was a lot better than too much liquor.

Then Dad turned to me. "Will," he said, "your *own* clothes a mite too tight."

It was true. The cowboy shirt I was wearing was too snug across the shoulders, the Levi's, too tight around the waist. A bit short, too. I'd put on some muscle and apparently had continued to grow a little.

"Come go with me, Will, and I'll buy you a new suit of clothes," my dad said.

That was certainly something different. Nearly all my life, I'd bought my own clothes and school supplies with my own money, money I made working in the fields and at various town jobs.

"You got a deal," I said.

It was still pretty early that morning when he and I, and Sailor, who'd driven us, got back to camp after buying our stuff at Rushmore Drygoods downtown. We saw as we pulled into the vacant lot that Buford's orange Dodge truck was there, his and Bonnie's house trailer already hooked up to it, ready to go. Little Jim and Big Jim were finishing gassing up the last of the other vehicles, my dad's truck.

Sailor parked the Green Lizard and shut off the motor just as Buford and Bonnie came out of the house trailer. Bonnie looked like she'd been crying. Sailor, Dad, and I got out of the Lizard and walked over toward her and Buford.

"Drove all night," Buford said to the three of us. Then he faced my dad. "Bob, me and Bonnie are turning back. This is as far north as we go with you."

Was I the only one who noticed that Buford was holding a little snub-nosed pistol down along his right leg?

"Suit yourself, Buford," Dad said. "You and I all square?"

"All square," Buford said.

"Well, I hope you a lot of good luck," my dad said to him.

Bonnie spoke up. "But I don't want to turn back." She moved a half step toward Sailor.

Dad took my arm. "Come on, Will, let's get ready to head out of here for Rhame," he said.

I reluctantly walked away with him toward Big Jim and Little Jim. When we'd covered two or three yards, I said in a low voice, "Dad, Buford's got a pistol."

"Know that, Will," he said, "but he ain't gonna shoot nobody. It's the same as a barking dog don't bite."

I hoped he was right about that. "You think Bonnie's going to stay with Sailor or go with Buford?" I asked Dad.

"Will, that ain't something me and you can decide," he said. "Ain't nair one of them three that ain't full grown. They'll figure it all out for theirselves without no help from us."

He and I came up to Little Jim and Big Jim.

"Ready to hightail it out of here, Bob." Big Jim said.

"Can we get to Rhame tonight?" Dad asked.

"Start now and run hard, we can," Big Jim said.

Dad turned to me. "Will, you ride in the pick-up with Little Jim." Then, to the other two, he said, "Let's line up and drive to the street. We'll set there and wait on Sailor."

But I couldn't stand the suspense. As Dad, Little Jim, and Big Jim got in and started their vehicles, then began to ease toward the street, I turned and quickly walked back to where Sailor, Bonnie, and Buford were still standing by the house trailer.

Everything looked about the same as it had earlier. Bonnie was still standing a little closer to Sailor than to her husband. Buford still held the pistol along his leg. It didn't even seem to me that the three of them had said much to each other since I'd left them.

"What're y'all going to do?" I asked, glancing from one to the other.

Buford said nothing. Bonnie searched Sailor's face with teary eyes. He'd made no move toward her.

"Sailor, what do you want me to do?" Bonnie asked.

"Sweet Bonnie girl," he said, "I want you to do whatever *you* want to do. You know how I feel about you."

Why didn't Sailor give her more encouragement? I wondered. That was my first thought. My second thought was that maybe Sailor knew that Bonnie's coming with him, when he was soon going to be shipping out to sea again, might not be the best thing for her.

Bonnie's expression as she faced Sailor changed then, from a questioning one to something like an apology. She took a step back from Sailor toward her husband.

When Bonnie spoke it was to Sailor, again. "Buford's been good to me," she said. "I love him."

"I know that," Sailor said.

The decision was made.

Buford looked at me. "See you, Will."

"See you," I said.

He turned, walked forward, and got into his old orange Dodge truck.

Bonnie seemed to want to kiss Sailor good-bye, but instead, the two of them just shook hands.

Sailor said to her, with a soft tenderness in his voice, "Be happy, Sweet Bonnie."

"I'll try," she said. "You, too."

Then she looked at me, and that made her start crying pretty hard. She reached out and hugged me to her. "I won't ever forget you, Will," she said between sobs.

I don't know why I wasn't crying, too. I was about as sad as she was—sad about the whole thing. Sad I wouldn't see Bonnie again. Sad that Sailor and Bonnie were breaking up without ever having had much of a chance to be together. Sad that the only possible decision they could have made was such an unhappy one for them. Sad that life suddenly seemed to me to be so confusing and unfair.

"I won't forget you either, Bonnie," I said.

She pulled away from me and, without looking back, ran to get into the truck with her husband.

Chapter Thirteen

I crawled into the Green Lizard with Sailor. The old Plymouth was last in line that Tuesday morning, the tenth of August, as our harvest caravan lit out on the last leg of the trail toward Rhame, North Dakota, our final northern destination. We were, of course, minus three of the original crew that had left out of Vernon with us. We'd lost Spider in Nebraska. Now Buford and Bonnie were gone, too.

Losing Bonnie hurt me the most, of course. Hurt Sailor, too, I could tell, though he didn't say anything about it.

We started northwest out of Rapid City on State Highway 79. The Black Hills were on our left for a while, great rolling prairie on our right. We soon ginned past the small town of Sturgis, which looked like it'd once been what people called a "wild and woolly" mining and frontier town. I'd have liked to have looked around there a little, the same as I wished I could have seen Deadwood, but we had to head on north without stopping. We soon left the Black Hills behind us.

We glided by Bear Butte State Park, which was laid out around an imposing and longtime natural high-point landmark for white travelers, a holy place for the Sioux. Sailor read the sign as we passed, then roused himself enough from his melancholy to sort of mutter, mostly to himself, "Park your bare butt here."

We wheeled straight on north along the western edge of the state of South Dakota, just like we were on the last section of the old Western cattle trail that'd come up from Texas and passed through here.

Lord! What treeless, rolling-forever grassland stretched out ahead of us and around us in every direction! And I could see from the practically blank area on the South Dakota map I'd unfolded in my lap that we weren't going to pass through any other kind of terrain for a long, long time. The town of Buffalo, which didn't look like much on the map, was going to be about the only town we'd find between where we were and the North Dakota border.

I tried Sailor's portable radio, but I couldn't get anything out there in what really were the "wide open spaces," as people said. Neither Sailor nor I was in any mood to talk, so I kind of put myself in something like a waking trance and let the uneventful miles, and telephone poles, slide on by. At one point we cut over to U.S. 85, a little better and not so narrow a highway, and kept on going north.

After a long while, Sailor brought me back to reality when he suddenly began singing: "Buffalo gals, ain't you comin' out tonight, comin' out tonight?" I was glad that he seemed a little more cheerful than when we'd left Rapid City. Our caravan pulled into Buffalo, a tiny town in the middle of a great expanse of treeless grasslands, and stopped to eat. In the Custer Café— I swear to God that was the name—I knew by now not to order a hamburger this far north. I'd learned my lesson. Instead, I got a little steak and some German-style sour potatoes.

From Buffalo, it was something over thirty prairie-land miles more before we crossed the North Dakota line—and entered another new state for me.

Just there, Sailor and I whizzed past our final series of Burma-Shave signs.

Sixteen miles farther on, with the grasslands becoming rolling wheat fields, we came to the town of Bowman, North Dakota. It looked to be about the same size as Vernon. Our U.S. 85 dead-ended at Bowman's football field on the southwest edge of town. We turned generally west there on U.S. 12 toward a North Dakota wheat-land sun that was hanging low on the horizon.

Burlington Northern railroad tracks ran alongside us on the right. Fifteen or so miles with rolling wheat fields stretching out north and south on both sides of the highway, and we finally arrived at the end of the trail we'd been pointing toward since we'd left home.

Our caravan slowed as we approached the roadside Farmers Union Oil filling station at the south end of town near the railroad depot and three metal grain elevators. We turned right, there, off State Highway 12. We crossed a double set of tracks and drove north on a graveled main street into the block-and-a-half, four-streetlight business district of the little village of Rhame, North Dakota, about a third the size of Vernon.

In the town's second block, we saw on our left a wide grassy vacant gap between two buildings. To the south was the awninged, two-story frame building that housed the Rhame Bar and Grill on its lower floor, and to the north was the long, one-story old frame IOOF hall—the Odd Fellows' Hall—which sat on the corner of the next cross street. Big Jim turned and led us into the open space, and that was where we made our last harvest trail camp of the year.

Toward the back of the vacant area, there was the remnant of an old wooden building. We stretched our tarp from its east wall and laid out our sleeping stuff underneath. It was a good thing we did, too, because it drizzled rain that night, and our makeshift tent kept us reasonably dry.

The next morning had a wet feeling to it, though the rain had stopped for the time being. Rhame was to feel wet to us nearly all the time we were there. It would rain often that time of year, slowing our combine work. Old unpainted Rhame buildings and area farmhouses and barns seemed always to be dark with undried moisture. The thirties, we learned, had brought terrible dust storms to the Rhame area, the same as nearly everywhere else up and down the Great Plains, but you wouldn't have known it from the rainy days and nights we experienced in Rhame that August of 1943.

The people, though, proved to be really friendly to us transients—welcoming. Maybe because so many of them were immigrants themselves or the children and grandchildren of immigrants—Norwegians, mostly, with some Germans, Swedes, and others—who'd homesteaded the land in the early 1900s.

Too, we were to learn from old-timers that winters were harsh there in the southwest corner of North Dakota, and because of the heavy snows and many days of below-zero weather, people were shut up indoors a lot during the long cold months. So they seemed especially glad to be able to get out and about during the summer and wheat harvest season, glad for human contact.

Wheat combiners—and combines, tractors, and trucks—were in short supply locally, as in so many other places we'd been. And that was another reason, apparently, why people were happy to see us.

That first morning in Rhame, we'd just barely finished shaving and getting dressed and were still in the process of cooking breakfast on Dad's coal-oil camp stove, when a middle-aged guy named Lars Anderson, thinner than Big Jim, but just as tall, drove up in a fairly new Ford pick-up and got out to introduce himself. He took a tin cup of coffee that Dad offered, then told us that he ran the Farmers Union Oil filling station at the south end of town and would like to have our gasoline and oil business.

"You'll sure get it," Big Jim said. "I traded with you last year, and you treated me right."

"I remember you," Anderson then said to Big Jim as the two of them shook hands. "Welcome back! Three days from now, we hear, the OPA is coming out with new regulations, cutting the value of gas ration stamps from four gallons to three gallons, but that won't bother you folks much, with your 'C' books and stickers."

Dad began to dish out the bacon and eggs onto our crew's plates. "Have some breakfast with us, Mr. Anderson?" he asked.

"Ate before I came," Anderson said. "But thank you." Then he got down to probably the main reason he'd shown up so early. "You folks be interested in selling your equipment?"

"Nawsir, believe not," Dad said. "Main way we got to make a living."

"Okay," Anderson said. "No harm in asking. But even after you get through harvesting, here, I'd still be interested in buying any equipment you want to sell—combines, tractors, trucks, the whole thing."

"Much obliged," Big Jim said. "We'll let you know if we change our minds. But you could maybe help us with something else, though."

"And that'd be?" Anderson asked.

"We looking for a tractor driver and for a guy with a wheat truck," Big Jim said.

Anderson responded immediately. "The oldest Betz boy is looking for work. Farm raised, he'd make you a tractor driver. And Oscar Egeland's got a truck with grain sideboards, and he wants some hauling. I'll have them come by here to see you, a little after noon."

Dad and Big Jim both thanked him.

Anderson then made us another offer of help. "You folks won't have any trouble finding wheat to cut," he said. "I know several farmers, mostly southwest of here, between here and Sunset Butte, who need custom combining. I'll put you in touch with them. The Bersagel boys, for one, will be in my place this morning."

"I cut for them two boys last year," Big Jim said. "Bachelor brothers. Be good to see 'em again. Good old guys."

Sure enough, the Bersagel brothers—Dad was to call them the "Bicycle Boys"—would turn out to be our first customers. They were in their mid-fifties and, I was to find, lived alone in an old unpainted two-story farmhouse southwest of Rhame. And Dad and Big Jim would hire young Rud Betz, too, blond-headed and red-faced, to drive the Fordson tractor and would make a deal with chunky Oscar Egeland to be our third trucker.

What a help to us Lars Anderson proved to be! And before he left that morning, he told us that he'd lately bought the old IOOF hall, just to the north of our camp. Said he ran it as a skating rink on lots of weekdays and as a dance hall on Saturday nights. There was always a fine, top-notch orchestra, the way he put it, for the harvest dances, and he said that our crew'd all be more than welcome to come. Then he added, finally, that he'd keep the door near the back of the IOOF hall, on our side, unlocked and that he'd be happy for us to go in any time we wanted to to use the toilet and the shower there.

We all thanked him again. He left, and we sat around and ate our breakfast.

Dad, Big Jim, and Little Jim went off after a while to the Farmers Union gas station. I walked to the Rhame post office on Main Street. Sailor went with me. There was no mail for any of us. Nothing from Marcy Redelk. It was too soon after I'd last written her from Nebraska.

Sailor and I then walked on around and looked at the town. It was so small that we didn't have to drive. At a wood-floored drugstore and soda fountain, I bought and thumbed through a booklet on Rhame's history that was put out by the local community club. I read aloud to Sailor a funny item I found in the booklet:

HOW SMALL IS SMALL?
You know you are in a small town when . . .
Third Street is on the edge of town,
Every sport is played on dirt,
You are born on June 13, and your family receives gifts
    from local merchants because you are the first baby of
    the year,
You are run off Main Street by a combine,
The biggest business in town sells farm machinery,
You miss a Sunday at church and receive a get-well card.

I thought that pretty much described Rhame. The town had two churches. St. Mel's Catholic Church was on the west, post-office-butte side of town. The Lutheran Church was on the east edge, just before the hills with the water tank. It was also just slightly south of the Rhame Public Schools complex, which consisted of an older three-story brick building with a little bell tower, and an art deco kind of two-story structure, built by the WPA.

More of the town's block and a half of business buildings, nearly all wood frame with high facades, were on the west side of Main Street than on the east side. There was the drugstore, of course, the post office building, a little bank, a wood-floored hardware store with a glass-globed gasoline pump out front on the street, a telephone office, a rooming house and hotel, two grocery stores, a drygoods store, a barber shop, two bars, three eating places, a J. I. Case implement dealership, which was oddly housed in a quaint little log cabin, a funeral parlor, and, farther out, a blacksmith shop and a lumberyard. There was no picture show in town. It looked to me like the Saturday night harvest dances at the IOOF hall would be the only entertainment available in Rhame.

Walking by the Hanson Funeral Parlor, Sailor and I stopped to look at an antique hearse there. It sat under the establishment's adjoining open-air porch. Maybe a Studebaker, the hearse was a model from the 1920s. Behind its cab, the lamp-topped and windowed van part was beautifully constructed of wood, with almost real-looking funeral drapes and cords expertly carved into it. The whole thing had once probably been painted a rich blue, but that color was now faded into an attractively graying lavender.

"Be almost worth kicking the bucket if you could count on getting carried off in that rig," I said.

"You ought to try to buy that old thing, Will," Sailor said. "Take it back home and drive it to school. Be great to pick up girls in."

I said I *would* try to buy the old hearse, except that I didn't figure it could make it all the way back to Vernon in one piece. Intriguing idea, though, I thought. So was another one I was soon to hear from Lars Anderson's plump and good-natured wife, Hattie. She asked if I'd be interested in staying on in Rhame after the harvest to take a teaching job in a little school

263

near Sunset Butte. She said that in North Dakota, you could teach in a country school with only an eighth-grade education. There was something sort of appealing about that prospect, but I declined anyway and told Mrs. Anderson that I was making other career plans.

Dad made a deal with the next-door Rhame Bar and Grill—where a cute fresh-faced, yellow-haired girl named Katie worked—to fix us all a daily sack lunch to take to the field. And on the second morning following our arrival in Rhame, which was Friday, the thirteenth of August, despite my dad's misgivings about this being bad luck, we pulled our combines out to the Bicycle Boys' place southwest of town. There, and nearby, we found a great number of good, but often really hilly, wheat fields, interspersed with rough breaks of untilled, wild grassland overgrown with the low bushes of chokecherries, buffalo berries, and sage.

The boy Dad'd hired, Rud Betz, who turned out to be a nice kid, drove the Fordson tractor for Little Jim's combine. My dad volunteered to keep on driving the Farmall tractor that pulled Sailor's Gleaner-Baldwin, even though my legs were healing up very well and not giving me any trouble. Dad did that because he knew that I liked being a trucker better than being a tractor driver. It was not as boring a job, and you didn't have to work in as much dust and chaff either.

It soon turned out that there was one Rhame resident I was never going to feel friendly toward. He was a tough-looking, rawboned Norwegian guy named Helmut, apparently just out of high school, who delivered freight from the Rhame railroad depot with a team of horses and a wagon. A show-off, he always whipped his horses into a dead run from the depot to downtown and fancied making fast, tight turns, skidding the back wheels of his wagon around gravel street corners like a race-car driver on the Pikes Peak run. The guy'd swagger into the Rhame Bar and Grill and, ignoring me if I was talking to Katie, start monopolizing her time, hardly letting her wait on anybody else.

But one evening when I was in the place, Helmut did say something to me. Being sure that Katie was watching him and listening, he turned in my direction all of a sudden—I was sitting on a bar stool right next to him—and said, "That an earring you're wearing?"

"Sort of," I said. "It's an Indian thing."

"Indian *squaw* thing, I guess," he said, and laughed.

Katie took up for me. "Leave him alone, Helmut," she said.

"You're right," he said. "The squaw's not worth messing with." Then he went back to ignoring me again.

So I ignored him, too, until he left.

Dark-skinned, humpbacked Little Jim Swyden found romance! It made you think that there was, indeed, somebody in the world for everybody, like the poets said.

After our bunch finished cutting for the Bicycle Boys, we pulled onto a neighbor woman's place and started combining her wheat. She was a widow with no children—a solidly built, large, round-faced German woman, Bertha Graaf, that my dad, of course, soon called "Big Bertha." Her husband had been killed in a tractor accident the year before, and she'd continued living, alone, in their two-story frame house, milking a half dozen cows and doing the plowing and wheat sowing on the place by herself. "Farms as good as a man," Lars Anderson said of her. It was true.

At the end of the very first day that we cut for Big Bertha, she had gathered her cows up in the old faded red barn. Wearing big blue overalls and a farmer's straw hat and carrying a couple of buckets, she was getting ready to go in and milk, when our harvest bunch stopped at the adjacent windmill and metal water tank to wash up before heading on into town.

Out of his pick-up before the rest of us, Little Jim called to the woman just as she was about to enter the barn door. "Use a little help with the milking, ma'am?"

She turned. "I wouldn't refuse you, little fellow," Big Bertha said. She laughed.

Little Jim hurriedly joined her, and they soon disappeared inside the barn.

265

The rest of our harvest bunch laughed, too, but not so loud that Little Jim or Big Bertha could hear us.

Helping out Bertha with her milking and other chores got to be a habit with Little Jim. Sometimes he was late getting back to town after work. So it was no surprise to any of us that on the second Saturday night we were in Rhame, the two of them met by apparent agreement at the front door of the IOOF hall and went into the harvest dance together. Big Bertha had fixed herself up nicely. She wore a pretty red dress, and her brown hair was done up in braids, which were wrapped tightly around her head. Little Jim wore his newest pair of blue overalls and a white shirt. They made a very interesting couple on the dance floor, wholly mismatched in both height and weight, but they didn't seem to care the least bit about what onlookers thought of them. Big Bertha smiled her cheeriest and proudly introduced Little Jim to anybody who came near, and when she was talking to him directly, she called him "Liebchen." He beamed each time she said that.

I got into trouble that first harvest dance. I looked for Katie as soon as Sailor and I went inside the hall, and I found her right away, drinking a Coca-Cola with a girlfriend, next to the stand where Lars Anderson's wife, Hattie, sold hotdogs and cold drinks. Hattie didn't sell liquor, but a number of seemingly good-humored men around the hall were now and then, I saw, sipping from their own little bottles of schnapps or whiskey, and nobody minded.

Katie acted glad to see me. And before long, she and I started dancing to the lively music, played by the Dakota Five—drums, a fiddle, a guitar, and two accordions. Not a great dancer to begin with, I needed considerable instruction from Katie— and she was glad to give it—especially because, in addition to the polka, which I could do like a regular two-step, but with more exaggeration, there were two other dances that were strange to me. One was called the "schottische," I learned, the other, the "butterfly." Both were sort of put-your-little-foot kinds of dances. I did the best I could with them. I managed not to disgrace myself with clumsiness, and Katie seemed to have a good time.

Until Helmut showed up.

He stopped just inside the front door to the hall and stood, sullen-looking, watching me and Katie dance. When the Dakota Five finally took a break and she and I walked over to talk with her girlfriend again, Helmut was right in front of us in a flash. And this time, he didn't ignore me. I wished he had. He stepped up close to me, his face red, his eyes mean. I could smell the schnapps on his breath. Then, very offensively, he reached a hand out and brushed the black obsidian stud on my ear- lobe. "How's the squaw doing tonight?" he asked, and sneered.

I swatted his hand away. I was hot. "Don't give me any shit!" I said.

My quick and angry response seemed to stop Helmut for a moment, like it was something he'd not expected.

Katie tried to intervene. "Here, you guys!" she said. "There's no use to get mad. Let's just all have fun."

People around us turned to look. Sailor quickly stepped over to my side. "You all right, Will?" he asked quietly.

"I'm all right," I said.

Helmut found his voice again. "You're *not* right, either," he said to me, his face reddening more. "But I'm going to make you right. Let's go outside."

We headed to the back door, people crowding after us. We soon squared off, facing each other in the grass between the hall and our harvest camp and under a ring of dim light that was put out by the hall's back-steps bulb.

I let Helmut come at me first. I figured he'd be awkward, and he was. He lunged and threw a big roundhouse right that a blind man could have gotten out of the way of. I ducked under it, stepped to my left, and hit him straight on the jaw with my hardest right, all my new muscle power behind it. Helmut went to his knees. I waited until he was up, expecting him to swing wildly a second time. But he surprised me by suddenly lurching at me again, and instead of hitting at me, he grabbed me in a tight bear hug. He tripped me, and we fell in a grunting heap in the grass. He jerked forward and got himself quickly into a sitting position on my stomach, his knees pinning my arms, and started to choke me with both hands. I finally worked my right arm free and hit him a sharp blow on the neck with the hard edge of my open hand—Sailor's Asian fighting teaching coming out. Helmut instantly stiffened, then let go my throat and rolled off me long enough for me to jump to my feet. Again I waited. He was quickly up from the ground, too. He roared and came at me. I popped him with two straight lefts to the nose, followed by a right to the pit of his stomach. He bent over and coughed. I straightened him up with a right uppercut, then finished him off with a quick left hook to his ear and a right to the jaw. He sat down. I stood waiting, but the fight had gone out of Helmut. I left him there with a couple of guys who appeared to be his buddies and, joined by the crowd, went on back to the dance.

I wasn't proud of what I'd done, but I wasn't too ashamed of it either.

After that, our time in Rhame went well, until the awfullest possible thing happened on what was a cold, wet-feeling, overcast day—the final day of our North Dakota cutting. It'd rained the night before, and we weren't able to get into the field again–a particularly hilly wheat field we were finishing up for a farmer named Carlson—until well after noon. My truck was the first to begin loading once the combines got under way. Before long, Dad stopped his Farmall on a steep hill near where I was parked, so Sailor could dump their combine's full wheat bin. I pulled the Chevy in under the spout as Sailor let it down. The grain poured out. The bin emptied. The spout went back up. Sailor engaged the Gleaner-Baldwin's clutch again, and the machine's innards began to purr loudly, ready to go, and its big twelve-foot reel began to turn. I stood up in the wheat in the back of my truck, leaning on my scoop handle, waiting for Dad to get the Farmall in gear and moving, pulling the combine on ahead, so I could jump down.

Then, to my horror, Dad did something that you would have thought that he, of all people, would never have done, as many times as he'd warned against it. I never knew if he was distracted in some way, or thinking about something else, or what. He certainly wasn't drinking, or at least wasn't drinking much. I knew that. But Dad suddenly let the Farmall's clutch out too fast. The tractor's front end reared straight up, right off the ground, then swung all the way back over. With a terrible crash, the whole machine fell upside down, squarely on top of Dad before he could get out of the way, and crushed him with killing weight between the tractor above him and the combine's metal front frame, below.

Dad never cried out, but Sailor and I sure did, and we were both immediately down on our knees at Dad's side in the wheat stubble. But there was no way! There was no way we could get Dad out. He was impossibly pinned under the big tractor. No way we could get the tractor off of him soon enough. No way—and I hated to think this— that he could live.

His face and hands were free and clear, but his body was terribly broken up. It was obviously just a matter of time for him.

"Hold on Dad!" I said. "We'll get some help."

Little Jim's combine was on the other side of the field, behind a hill. He and Rud Betz couldn't see the wreck. But nearer Big Jim Gruber and Oscar Egeland had jumped out of their trucks at once and were running toward us.

"No need to hurry, Will," Dad said. His voice was a groan. He spoke to me, but his eyes were staring straight up, past the upside-down Farmall, at the cloudy sky. "Ain't no way I'm gonna make it alive out of this. I'm too messed up."

"We'll get you out, Bob," Sailor said.

Big Jim joined us, kneeling down next to me, his normally red face now white with alarm. "You're gonna make it, Bob!" he said. It was a kind of plea. "Don't give up!"

"Naw, boys," Dad said, forcing out the words and still seemingly looking at the clouds, as a trickle of blood began to come out of the side of his mouth. "This is the end of your old friend, Bob Haley."

"No it's not, Dad," I said. But I knew that he was right. I could hardly breathe.

"I'm dead, boys," my dad said. I let out an involuntary moan when he said that, and he turned his head a little and focused his eyes on me for the first time. "Will, tell you mama that I love her. Always have. She may not believe it, but it's true. I'm sorry for the way I treated her, tell her."

I took one of his hands in both mine. "Don't talk like that, Dad," I said. "You've been a good man, all in all." I had to work at not crying.

"I love all y'all—your mama and you kids," Dad said. Then he reached out his other hand to Big Jim, who quickly took it. "Jim," Dad said, "you been a good friend to me. Much obliged."

"Naw, much obliged to you, Bob," Big Jim said. Tears began to run down his face.

Dad focused on me again and gathered his strength for a moment for some more words. "Will, I want you to carry me home. Bury me next to Pa, down there at Vernon."

"I'll do it, Dad," I said. Now, *my* tears had started, too.

"And, son."

"Yes, Dad."

"You the man of the house now, Will. Look after you mama and the girls and you grandma. I know you can do it. You *are* a man. And promise me one thing."

"Whatever you say."

"Promise that this won't keep you from going on ahead and being a lawyer."

"I promise," I said.

And then he was dead. My dad took a deep, rattling last breath, and the life went out of him when that breath did. It hit me hard that he was gone for good. He wouldn't be back.

I'd never seen anybody die, let alone someone so close to me. The shock was awful. And the sense of loss made me ache all over. Kneeling there on the ground, I suddenly felt alone and empty, too. I was on my own.

Then, gradually, I started thinking about how Mama would act in a crisis-time like this. "Life goes on, son," she would say. "We can't help the dead. We've got to think about the living."

I wiped away my tears, stood up, and pulled myself together. I began to make a plan, because I had to.

Chapter Fourteen

I went up to Carlson's house and telephoned the Hanson Funeral Parlor to get a hearse sent out for Dad's body. With a truck and log chain, the others and I toppled the Farmall tractor off of him and set it back upon its wheels. Little Jim and Rud finished cutting the last of Carlson's wheat.

We left the Farmall in the field. It wouldn't run. Carlson used his own John Deere tractor to road Big Jim's Gleaner-Baldwin into Rhame. Rud, on the Fordson, pulled my dad's combine in.

I drove the Chevy truck to town and made arrangements to have Dad's body embalmed and sealed in a good metal casket, so it could be shipped home by rail. My plan was to sell the truck, our combine, and our tractor—the whole thing—if I still could, and go back to Vernon on the train myself, with the casket.

At the Rhame telephone office, I asked the woman to place a call for me to Mama, at home. Mama answered the phone right away and immediately guessed the reason for the call.

"It's your dad, isn't it, Will?" she asked, as soon as we'd barely said hello. "What's happened to him?"

I didn't try to drag out the message. I didn't know how. "Mama," I said, "he got killed today in a tractor accident."

I heard her draw in her breath. "Drinking heavy?" she asked.

"Not at all," I said quickly. "Dad'd pretty much sworn off, or cut way down, ever since before Nebraska. It was just a dumb accident, Mama. Tractor turned over on him. I'm sorry."

Mama was still Mama—solid, calm in a time of trouble, and thinking of others. "How are *you* holding up, Will?" she asked.

"Best I can," I said. "I'm going to try to sell all our equipment here in Rhame and bring Dad's body home on the train. I'll send you a telegram from the Rhame depot to let you know when to meet us in Duncan."

Then Mama suddenly changed the subject to some great news that she knew would cheer me up. "Will, your uncle Clif's not missing in action anymore. They found him—alive!" she said.

"Oh, man!" I said. "Is he all right? Where is he?"

"He lost an arm, son, the War Department notified Grandma Haley, but it's his left one, thank goodness," Mama said. "They say he's otherwise okay."

I'd soon be seeing again the man who, all my life, had been like my older brother, maybe closer. "He's coming home then?" I asked.

"In about a month, they say, as soon as they get him patched up."

"Hallelujah!" I said this so loud that it probably hurt Mama's ear.

She gave me more of the facts. "When the American soldiers in Sicily took over a town called Messina, which just happened not long ago, they wound up liberating Clif and a bunch of others from a temporary prisoner-of-war camp there."

"All right!" I said. I couldn't have been happier. But then I quickly remembered the sad reason for my call. And I remembered, too, something that I was supposed to say to Mama. "Dad's last words were to tell you he loved you, Mama," I said. A big old sob caught in my throat.

"I never doubted that he did, son," she said. "I loved him, too."

I knew where Lars Anderson lived, in Rhame. I drove to his house and, after he and Hattie invited me in and offered me a cup of coffee, which I turned down, I told them the bad news about my dad. Both of them were shocked and sorry to hear it. Hattie hugged me, and I thought she was going to cry.

"Yeah, sure, Will," Lars said in answer to my question. "I'll buy your stuff. Jim Gruber's, too, if he wants."

We came to a quick agreement on price. Lars would pay me three hundred dollars for the Fordson, twelve hundred for the Gleaner-Baldwin, and thirteen for the truck. There'd be money left over after paying off what Dad owed the First State Bank in Vernon.

Lars Anderson and I agreed to meet downtown at Rhame's bank the next morning, the same place I was supposed to get together with Carlson, the farmer. They'd both pay me off in cash.

Back at our camp, after I told him what I'd done, Big Jim Gruber decided he'd sell out, too—his damaged Farmall tractor, if Lars would buy it, his combine, and his Ford truck. He'd keep his GMC pick-up to drive home in.

And Big Jim had already been thinking about the future. "Will, I know a guy back home, over by Grandfield," he said, "that I think you and me can buy a couple of late-model Gleaner-Baldwin combines off of. I'd sure like to partner up with you next summer, Will, the same as I done with your dad."

"It's a deal," I said. "No question I'm going to *have* to keep following the harvest, to make some money. Going to have to farm bigger, too. Got Mama, Grandma, and the girls, now, to look after. And I've got to lay up something to get me through law school later on."

It turned out that Little Jim had decided not to return to Vernon. He was holding hands with Big Bertha when he told me that. The three of us were standing by her old Chevrolet car on the dark street in front of our harvest camp.

"Will," he said, "I found me a home, the first'n I ever had. Found Bertha, here—first'n that ever loved me. And she's gonna marry me. Think of that!"

"Proud for you, Little Jim," I said. "Looks like you hit the jackpot."

"You helped me, Will," he said. "You acted a real friend to me. I won't forget it."

273

Bertha bent over a little, put a big arm around Little Jim, and squeezed. "Liebchen," she said, looking into his eyes. Then she turned back to me. "And the little fellow's giving up that kinder's teething medicine, too."

"Don't seem to need it as much," Little Jim said.

I put the two of them in Big Bertha's Chevrolet car, Little Jim doing the driving, and saw them off, toward Big Bertha's farm.

That night, I woke up under the tarp at about two in the morning. I got up out of my quilts to go pee. It was a clear night and, once outside, I saw the most amazing sight of my life— the northern lights that everybody'd talked so much about. High in the night sky to the north, above the IOOF hall, weird and wispy veils of pastel reds, purples, greens, and yellows surged and waved, dancing, rolling, constantly changing and rearranging themselves. It was a better show than the Fourth of July fireworks at Vernon. And an almost magic feeling.

My dad had promised from the start that we'd "see them northern lights" before our harvest summer was finished in Rhame in late August. He was right about that except that now he wouldn't see the marvelous sight himself. It made me sad to think about that. I finally went back to bed.

Early next morning, another of Dad's predictions came true. "Snow be flying" before we would come home from the harvest, he'd said. He was right again. Frost covered the grass when we woke up, and later that morning, the North Dakota sky having clouded over, light snow flurries began to blow around Big Jim, Sailor, and me, as we huddled next to Dad's camp stove and cooked up our last harvest breakfast.

After we ate, we took down our tarp and folded our bed clothes. Sailor loaded his stuff into the trunk of the Green Lizard. Big Jim and I put most of ours, and Dad's, in the back of the GMC pick-up and covered it with the tarp. I packed my own shaving things and a change of clothes in a little leather handbag I'd bought.

Then came the hardest part for me, saying good-bye to my cousin Sailor Torley, before he was to head off west toward

Seattle. Neither one of us much knew what to say to each other, but we both knew what we were feeling.

We hugged. A kind of unmanly thing to do, but it seemed right.

We quickly stepped back. "Will, you got what it takes!" Sailor said. "You gonna amount to something."

"I learned a lot from you," I said. I meant it. "Thanks a million!"

But Sailor couldn't be serious for long. "Go on out there, now, son," he said, "grab the old bull by the tail, and look him square in the eye!"

"Good luck getting a ship, Sailor," I said.

"I'll get one," he said. "And I hope you a lot of luck, too, Will. I'll sail up the old Potomac River and come see you in the White House one of these days."

We shook hands. He crawled into the Lizard, and was gone.

Big Jim Gruber, keeping his GMC pick-up, sold his truck and equipment to Lars Anderson just like I had, including his bunged-up Farmall tractor. He drove me in the pick-up to the Rhame railroad depot that last morning. There, with the steam engine huffing and puffing in front, we both watched as Dad's casket was carried off of Hanson's black hearse and loaded into a baggage car of the passenger train, just before I was to climb aboard the train myself. Then Big Jim and I shook hands.

"Your dad was the best friend I ever had, Will," he said. "And I'm looking for you to be another one."

It would take me three days and most of three nights to get home, with layovers and changing trains in packed stations that were swarming with travelers, mostly servicemen in uniform, first at Minneapolis-Saint Paul, then Des Moines, and, finally, Kansas City.

On the first day of the trip, after a black porter came through my chair car, banging a chime and announcing "Dinner on the diner, diner in the rear!", I decided to try a sit-down meal. I had a lot of cash on me and in my leather handbag—too much, really, for comfort. I picked up the handbag and went back. I stepped into the swaying diner. A black waiter in a white coat surveyed me and my cowboy clothes with a look of skepticism, like he could tell that this was a new experience for a country boy like me, which it was. Then he seated me at one of the several rose-decorated, tableclothed tables with a dressed-up old guy, who turned out to be a traveling salesman. The waiter shook out my napkin with a flourish and laid it in my lap, then handed me a heavy leather-backed menu.

The cheapest thing I saw when I opened it was chicken pot pie for two dollars and a half. That was what I ordered.

"Anything else, or anything to drink?" the waiter questioned.

"No that's all," I said. "And water's just fine."

The waiter sighed noticeably, poured me a glassful of water, then went away to the kitchen with my order.

The traveling salesman at my table didn't want to talk, and neither did I. So after we'd briefly introduced ourselves and said hello, he went on eating in silence, and I waited for my food.

It came before long—a single cup, no bigger than a coffee cup, with a crusty biscuit on top of it. I must have looked sort of disappointed when the waiter set it on the table in front of me, because he quickly announced, as if to reassure me, "Your chicken pot pie, sir."

Surely, I thought, that cup wasn't all I was going to get! "No vegetables?" I asked the waiter. "No soup or salad first?"

"Exactly what did you order, sir?" he asked, seeming a little offended.

"Chicken pot pie," I said.

"What does that look like in front of you, sir?" the waiter said.

I ate it, but that was my last visit back to the diner during the journey home. I lived on sandwiches and Coca-Colas that a passing porter sold in the chair car.

My train pulled into the Duncan depot late at night, but the Stigler-Martin Funeral Home hearse was there from Vernon, waiting. And so was Mama and my sweet older sister, Janie Marie. They'd received my telegram. We hugged, and all three of us had a hard cry. Then we straightened up and silently watched as Dad's casket was unloaded from the train's baggage car, carried out, and carefully slid into the back end of the hearse.

On the way to Vernon in Mama's car, me driving, I brought her and Janie Marie up to date on what I'd gotten for our combine, tractor, and truck and about my plan for following the harvest again with Big Jim Gruber and farming on a bigger scale.

"We'll make it," Janie Marie said. "I don't need to go to college myself, but we're going to make sure that you get to go to law school, Will."

"Don't be crazy, Janie Marie!" I said. "You're definitely going to college, no two ways about it. And I'm going to law school, too, when the time comes. You and I and Mama, we'll all have to work hard, but we're used to that."

Before we got home, Mama reported to me about Spider Deering. She'd talked with his mother on the telephone. The money that Dad and I'd sent got Spider a Kentucky lawyer, and the chances were good, Mama said, that Spider might get leniency in return for agreeing to be shipped overseas and into combat right away.

The following Saturday night, my slim, redheaded best friend, Junior Randall, came by the house to get me in his old pick-up. I'd seen him briefly at my dad's funeral, but we'd had no chance to talk much.

"Sure sorry about your dad, Will," he told me again when I climbed in with him. We headed toward Joe Lammer's.

"My dad died working," I said. "And he died more or less sober. Pretty good combination."

Junior changed the subject. "What're you gonna do now, Will?" he asked. "How y'all gonna make a living?"

I told him about my farming plans and about going to the harvest again.

"Still set on law and politics for a career?" Junior asked.

"Still am," I said.

"Then that's what I *want* you to do," he said. "But in the meantime, I'll partner up with you, Will, and me and you'll farm the shit out of this old country."

Downtown, Joe Lammer's was packed, as usual. A lot of people said hello to me in the lobby. Some mentioned that they were sorry about my dad. Mine and Junior's high school friend, Don Milford, when he joined us, wasn't the first to notice my little black ear-stud, but he was the first one to get up enough nerve to ask me about it.

"It's an Indian thing," I said. "Got it put on me up in the Black Hills."

He didn't seem totally satisfied with that brief explanation, but he didn't say anything else on the subject. Neither did Junior.

Joe Lammer's front screen door opened behind us, and who should come in together, holding hands? My old grade school sweetheart, Rebecca Milton, looking as stunning and wholesome as ever, and Ronnie Dole, tanned up from working, I knew, as a lifeguard at the Kraker Park swimming pool all summer.

"Oh, Will, you're home!" Becca said.

We hugged. Then I shook hands with Ronnie. He didn't look so tough to me. If I do run for student president, I thought, I can beat this guy—big old lazy town boy!

Then I noticed that Becca was surveying me pretty carefully. I saw her eyes settle on my black ear-stud for a second. Then she glanced at the bottom part of my tattoo, which was showing beneath the partly rolled-up left sleeve of my white T-shirt. She saw, too, I figured, that my chest and arms were more muscled than they were when I'd left home. And I thought she could tell that I was a little taller than I had been.

Our eyes met. "You look so different, Will," she said.

"How?" I asked. "More mature, would you say?" I couldn't help it.

Becca answered at once. "That's it!" she said. "That's exactly it."

Ronnie shifted impatiently from one foot to the other. "Come on, Becca," he said, taking her arm. "Let's go see if we can find a booth in the back somewhere."

"Wait a minute, Ronnie," Becca said to him. Then, to me, she said, "I was sorry to hear about your dad, Will."

"Thanks," I said. "How come you didn't write me while I was gone?"

"I meant to," she said, "but things were so busy here."

Ronnie pulled on her arm. "Come on, Becca."

"Call me, Will," Becca said.

"Okay." But as soon as I said that, I realized I didn't mean it.

The two of them started through the crowd. Just then, I saw Marcy Redelk passing Becca and Ronnie and coming from the opposite direction toward me. She looked great in a gray sweater set and pleated navy blue skirt, her dark hair fixed in back with a barrette.

"Will!" she said, green eyes sparkling. "I heard you were back, and I hoped I'd see you tonight."

I smiled and said hello. We shook hands. I thought about hugging her, but the right moment for doing that passed too quickly.

Marcy said hello to Junior and Don. "Kent and I've got a booth all by ourselves," she said. "Why don't the three of y'all come on back and join us?"

"Good plan," I said. And then, while she was still right in front of me, and before she turned to lead the way, I suddenly reached out, pulled her to me, and hugged her. The whole thing was a little awkward, I knew, my getting around to the hug so late. But Marcy didn't seem to mind. She hugged me back and, before we stepped apart, kissed me lightly on the cheek. *All right!*

The four of us then pushed our way through the people to the booth where Marcy's cousin and my high school buddy, Kent Coffee, sat. I was glad to see Kent. Marcy Redelk and I scooted in beside him. Don and Junior took the opposite side of the booth. Thin Walt Mason soon came and asked for our drink orders.

After that, we all sat strangely quiet for a while, nobody knowing what to say. It was like we almost needed to get acquainted with each other again. Then Don Milford made an attempt at conversation. "So, how'd it go, Will—on the harvest, I mean?" he asked me. "Much happen to you?"

"Not a whole lot, Don," I said. "About the usual—cut out the wheat in one place, move on to the next."

Right then, that great new song, "Missed the Saturday Dance," started up on the jukebox in back. But now the words didn't sound so sad to me, or make me feel so lonesome, as they had the first time I'd heard them, up north.

"You want to dance, Will?" Marcy quietly asked.

"I don't see why the hell not," I said.

She and I got up and, holding hands, walked back to the dark little dance floor. There, I gathered her in my arms. We paused a moment, then began to glide—float, really—as the music took us over.

And that was the way it was for me after I got home at the end of the summer of 1943.

Following the harvest.

The End

Acknowledgments

The people and events in *Following the Harvest* are fictional, but writing the story was an especially enjoyable exercise for me because it brought back a lot of personal memories. Beginning when I was twelve, I followed the wheat harvest myself for nine summers in a row, all the way from my southwest Oklahoma hometown of Walters to Rhame, North Dakota.

Growing up in Walters (suspiciously like the town of Vernon, in this book) was good. I liked, and like, the people there, including my old pal Ernest F. Hoodenpyle, Jr. I liked the people I met in Rhame, too, and in the other harvest towns.

My sister, Sue Stauffer, still living in Walters, refreshed my own harvest-days recollections with reports of the conversations she had with several old-time Oklahoma custom combiners at my request. I appreciate that.

I'm grateful to my remarkable wife, Margaret Elliston, for her help and inspiration and for reading the manuscript and making frank and kind-hearted suggestions. My smart daughters and son, Kathryn Harris Tijerina, Laura Harris, and Byron Harris, also gave me loyal and diplomatic advice about the manuscript. I'm grateful to them, too.

I want to express my thanks to the author of the little piece "How Small Is Small?" which I fairly recently ran onto in Rhame, North Dakota, in a locally produced booklet: Jane Fischer, editor, *The First 75 Years: Rhame, North Dakota* (Bowman, N.D.: Bowman County Pioneer, 1983). I used a portion of the "How Small Is Small?" piece in chapter 13, but set it back in 1943.

I especially want to acknowledge old John Fire Lame Deer, a Lakota holy man whom I got to know much later, of course, than the time of this story and whom I admired greatly. He was a wise and witty man who, unfortunately, has long since "gone south," as he would put it.

Finally, many thanks for the excellent efforts of my splendid agent, Elaine Markson, and for the terrific encouragement and assistance of the folks at the University of Oklahoma Press, especially Karen C. Wieder, Acquisitions Editor, Literature, and Jennifer Cunningham, Associate Editor.